Doors In The Air

Doors In The Air

Marshall Pickens

Corvid Publishing

This is a work of fiction. All characters, organizations, and events portrayed in this novel are either products of the author's imagination or are used fictitiously.

Doors in the Air

Copyright 2022 by Marshall Pickens

All rights reserved.

To my wife Stacy for putting up with all of everything that goes into this.
You're the best. I love you.

Chapter One

The darkness moved. It slipped from shadow to shadow using the smallest as shelter from the ever-watchful sun. Twitching where the unblinking sun touched, each move came slower and slower. The eye of the great flame, covered by soot and smoke in his world, burned brightly here with its painful, unblinking stare. Hiding in the darkness between rocks, it watched the soldiers move away. One looked back and saw only the thin shadow of the rock.

A tickle of cool air ran through his shadowed form. It was like a highway leading him toward the partially open door. He had been born in the dark chaos of the first war so many worlds away from this desert, and after passing through so many doors connecting so many worlds he had learned to feel that breeze. Too much effort had been used to escape during the heat of the day. He would need to rest and wait for night before he could try for the door. The memory of the sun burning him was reflected by the heat waves dancing on the orange brown rocks. He'd made the crossing into this world joyfully with the smell of so much in front of him only to find it too difficult alone. Now his only hope was that the next world would be more hospitable.

Watching as the soldiers swept back and forth, and as the sun slowly gave way to the relentless push of night, he scanned his surroundings hoping for an obvious sign of salvation. Finally, he saw it. The sun was setting behind him, and a sliver of light to his left drew his attention.

As the shadows from the rocks stretched away, he slid along them reaching out toward that light. Touching the frame of the door he grinned to himself. If he had flesh goose pimples would have stood out because of the temperature drop as he slid through. Looking back onto the heat-blasted world he had just left hope rose in him again.

The last days of fall dropped golden from the aspens around him as he slid from shadow to shadow looking for anything that could nourish him after his long flight from the soldiers. He had believed anyplace would be better than the world he had lived in. It had been all but emptied long ago, and he existed on scraps. When he had seen the first door finally open all rational thought had left him and all he could do was jump though in hope of finding something better. The hot sunbaked world he had found himself in was not what he had wanted. He had been through many worlds, but this was the first time he had gone ahead alone.

An unfamiliar noise interrupted his thoughts, and his eyes searched the strange landscape. Finally, he saw movement and leaped toward it. Easily able to move from one tree formed shadow to the next he followed along and watched a young man picking up dead sticks. His chance came when the young man sat down to rest in the shade of a thin evergreen. Sliding into that shadow he touched the young man's mind and found there what he had been most hoping for, doubt, confusion, and more than a little anger. He nursed it, whispered to it. His strength wasn't what it had once been, but it was enough for this one impressionable young man. The boy knew that while he was out here another was flirting with his girlfriend. His fear was stoked into a flame by whispers from the shadows until he jumped up and stalked back to camp.

The darkness laughed to himself as he flowed from shadow to shadow. He watched gleefully as the sun dipped behind a range of mountains. Twice in less than a few hours he had seen the sun set. It was a good omen.

They reached the camp just in time to catch exactly what he had wanted. The girlfriend was kissing another boy. It was too good to be true. He jumped through the new fallen darkness as the first boy began to yell at the girl and boy. He whispered into the ears of the new lovers that they didn't have to put up with his ranting. They were adults and could do as they liked.

The shouting drew others and soon he had them taking sides. If he had known anything about candy and babies, he would have used a very worn-out cliché. Out of it all, and because of it all a sickly-sweet aroma drifted to him. He breathed it in and felt his strength returning. If the campers had been looking, they would have seen eyes opening around them peering out of the shadows. Now rather than jumping from one to the next he whispered simultaneously to all. Whispers of strength being challenged into the ears of one, and whispers of pain experienced long ago to the other. All the while egging on the spectators to choose sides and defend or attack.

Soon a word was met by a shove, and the shove met by a thrown fist. He reveled in it all. Drinking it all in and becoming stronger with each moment. Finally in the chaos of it all he pointed out a stick was stronger than a fist. The boy reached out grabbing the axe leaning against the woodpile and swung it with all his might. More eyes opened in the shadows as the delicious taste of chaotic pain flowed to the shadows.

This would be his world. No others had come here. He had crossed the barren desert to get to this land flowing with milk and honey. Soon he would drink in the chaos of an entire world gone mad.

Chapter Two

The tubby balding man wheezed as he ran down the sidewalk and passed the boys and girls club. He looked back over his shoulder to see if they were still following him and watched as they flitted between the strange multi-colored statues dotting the lawn. His mind paused for a moment because of the strangeness of seeing the wonderfully colored flags and happy family settings of the statues being overrun by men with guns intent on killing him.

His moment of reflection was broken by the sharp report followed by the sound of a bullet passing altogether too close to his head. His one saving grace was the fact that they were terrible shots and needed to be much closer to do any real damage. Of course, he thought, that wouldn't take too long since he wasn't exactly in any kind of shape but round these days. As he struggled to breathe and run at the same time he wondered if they would kill him or if his heart would explode on its own before they could shoot him.

Ahead of him he saw a slight chance for escape. A chain link fence surrounded what looked like a junkyard of broken-down snowmobiles, four-wheelers, and motorcycles. If he could just get over the fence, he could hide well enough that they might never find him. He hoped that they weren't the kind that would be smart enough, or patient enough to look for very long before deciding that they lost him. The only problem was that the fence was a good six feet high and even if he jumped, he would only be just able to reach the top of it, not to mention the barbed wire that he would have to go over.

Mentally reaching inside himself, concentrating to get past the overwhelming beat of his heart and burn of his lungs, he tapped the nameless power and believed. He pictured one of the links in the fence expanding and stretching until it was big enough for him to run through, and his belief that it truly would work became a conduit for the power. Grinning and panting as he ran through the fence, he let his concentration go a little too early and tripped as the closing fence caught his foot. After rolling a few times he pulled himself up on a broken-down machine with the words Arctic Cat painted in neon green on the side. Spitting dust and a little blood from a newly split lip he decided it was as good a spot to hide as any. He tried his best to slow down his labored breathing so they wouldn't hear him so easily, but it was no use he just wasn't used to running and his breathing had never come easy. When he had been sent on this mission, they told him it would be one of diplomatic relations and times of negotiation. He was supposed to make contact with whoever was most suited to warn about the darkness. They never told him there would be running involved.

Across the street in the deeper darkness of a shadow cast by the streetlight, eyes watched patiently as the men searched for a way over the fence. A voice whispered in their ears pointing them to a loose gate they could squeeze through. The whispers were irritated at the slow progress and hinted at pain to come if this were not taken care of quickly.

Then they were there. He had greatly overestimated his ability to hide and underestimated their willingness to look for him. One of them gave a shout and, pulling their guns, the rest came for him as he backed himself farther into the darkness behind the broken-down machinery. Eyes opened in the darkness around him and he felt a pressure on his mind. With a mental wave of his hand, he brushed it away like a gnat. His belief and the power that came with it was too much for the still weak darkness and the eyes blinked out. Then he saw the smiles on the faces of his human pursuers and knew their intent was to kill him, and he believed. To the very core of his being he knew he could do what needed to be done, so he raised his hand and pictured in his mind a mighty fist of air. They tumbled like broken dolls. Some of them came to a very abrupt stop on broken down machinery while others simply tumbled to a stop in the dirt and came up shooting.

In his mind he saw the air thickening and catching the bullets. Once they were suspended in midair, he brushed them aside with a wave of his hand. He hesitated then undecided on what to do next. He had an aversion to killing. It wasn't that they didn't deserve it, but he had never done anything like that before. So he closed his eyes. Around him two snowmobiles and three ATVs rose into the air, hung there for a second, then hurled themselves at his attackers. When he opened his eyes, he started coughing uncontrollably because of the dust his attack had kicked up. Then he heard them calling, and the rough slap of shoes on pavement told him of more coming. Turning he ran to the gate in the fence. A length of chain secured the gate, but the bars had been stretched out where they had squeezed through. Sucking in his stomach he realized that he still wasn't small enough to make it. After all that running, he thought, I should be thinner. Pushing hard against the gate he managed to open it wide enough for his roundness to fit through.

He stopped and bent over trying to catch his breath. How many of them could there really be he wondered as, again, he started running. But he just wasn't a running sort of man and within a few seconds they tackled him from behind. His palms scraped on the pavement and started to bleed, his breath was knocked from him, and he thought for a second that he was going to pass out, but when they rolled him over he was able to see their grins all too well.

He was trying to bring to mind a way to knock them off him, but every time he started to get it formed, they hit him and he lost his concentration. The lights that hit his eyes at first seemed to be left over from the last punch on the side of his head, but the light didn't fade this time.

"Hey," a voice called from over his head, "I called the police!" The voice paused, "Scott is that you?"

Feeling a knee press onto his chest, he heard one of his attackers yell back, "James, this is none of your business."

"Look," the voice came closer, "I don't want any trouble but why are you beating up some old guy? I mean, is this some kind of skulls initiation thing?"

"Look, idiot," another voice spoke, and they all moved toward his savior, "I'm giving you one chance to get out. I suggest you take it." He couldn't see his savior, but he knew that whoever it was didn't stand a chance against all these thugs.

"How bout if I pay you to let the old guy go, and we all pretend this never happened?" The voice was even closer now.

"Can't do that James. You wouldn't understand, but we have to do this."

"You don't have to do anything, man. Now how bout you just let the guy go before the police show up and everything will be forgotten."

"We gave you a chance, you should have taken it. You two," he could hear movement, "grab him."

A whooshing sound almost covered up, "I don't think so," then all the thugs around him started screaming and falling down. Hands grabbed him and dragged him to his feet. When he took his first breath his lungs burned, and he started to cough. The air burned with spices and his eyes felt like they were melting. In front of him he heard a door open, and he smiled. The hands thrust him forcefully into a car then slammed the door. He couldn't see much through his blurred vision, but he was almost sure that he saw the shadows reaching out for them as they drove away.

Everything was silent for a few moments as they drove. He watched through blurry eyes as streetlights flickered by. Sucking in a rasping breath he said, "Thank you for saving me." He looked over at the young man sitting beside him in the driver's seat, "You risked your life for me. I don't know if I can repay you."

The driver looked over, "You could buy me a new can of bear spray."

"Bear spray?" He was confused. He knew what a bear was but why would you have spray for one?

"You know, bear spray. It's like pepper spray but a whole lot stronger. I carry a can with me because I like to go hiking on my lunch breaks, and around here you never know when you might run into a bear." The driver's hands tightened their grip on the steering wheel in an effort to keep them from shaking. "My name's James, and I seem to be unable to control the fact that I'm still talking."

"Rupert."

James' fingers tried tapping out Mozart on the steering wheel as his brain tried to process what had just been said, "What?"

"Sorry, my name's Rupert. Rupert Mundovi."

James chuckled, and realized that it sounded slightly insane, "I can't seem to stop talking and you," he paused to check traffic then merged into the right lane, "well," he shook his head and glanced at his passenger and all he could think of was, "uhm…"

Rupert tried to smile reassuringly while wiping his still stinging eyes, "It's your nerves."

"Yep." James nodded. His mind skipping to his friend who always said things like yeppers and he chuckled to himself again and thought, again, that he was sounding a little crazy. All things considered, however, he figured he had every right to sound crazy right now. "So, uhm," turning his blinker on he pulled into the left turn lane and stopped at the red light, "what was that all about back there?"

Rupert sighed, "They were trying to kill me."

Thinking that would win the obvious statement of the year award James just looked at Rupert until the light turned green and he took another left before realizing he had no idea where he should be going. Deciding on the hospital he maneuvered into the right lane, "So why were they trying to kill you?"

Rupert looked at him through blurry red eyes and James realized that the wheezing he had been hearing for the last few minutes was actually Rupert breathing. It sounded to him like a tiny little Darth Vader had gotten stuck in a paper bag and he wanted to chuckle again but stopped himself. Finally, Rupert said, "I suppose it won't change anything if I tell you, but first do you mind telling me why you helped me, and where you're taking me?"

Holding the steering wheel with his left-hand James rummaged through the center console with his right until he found a package of travel Kleenex. He handed it to Rupert and gestured to his head, "We're headed to the hospital."

Rupert took one of the tissues and touched it to a wet spot on his forehead, pulled it away, and looked at the blood on it, "Ah." He paused for a moment then took a clean tissue and touched it to his head again. Nodding to himself when it came away free of blood he said, "I'm actually all right. There's really no reason to go to a hospital."

James looked at him skeptically, "Really? You just got beat up in the middle of the street and you're fine?"

"Actually, yes."

Shrugging and thinking that no hospital meant less work for him, "Okay, then where to?"

"The Catholic church in Eagle River would be fine."

They drove in silence for a minute before James finally said, "Look if you really don't want to tell me why a group of college students was trying to kill you in the middle of the street, I guess that's your prerogative."

Rupert shook his head, "No, that's not it. I'm just a little shaken up still and trying to figure out what to say." He stared at James for a moment then said, "I am amazingly grateful, if I hadn't already said that." He watched James nod and then continued, "So, why did you help me?"

James stared at a red light waiting for it to change and finally said, "It was the right thing to do."

Rupert nodded slowly, "I suppose that's as good of an answer as I could ask for." He took a deep breath and let it out slowly then continued, "They were trying to kill me because," he paused and looked over at James again and making up his mind he continued, "because there's a monster I'm trying to kill that they don't want me to kill."

James laughed. Rupert looked shocked for a moment then started laughing. Finally James said, "Right. Look if you don't want to tell me I understand."

Rupert sighed for what seemed to him the millionth time, "No, it's not that. I just phrased it wrong I guess." He paused and thought for a moment before continuing, "There's someone here that's trying to cause problems. I'm supposed to convince the authorities to help me stop him, but none of them believe me. Those guys who tackled me work for him."

James looked a little confused, "Why wont the police believe you?"

"Because," Rupert watched the street lights fly by out the car window, "He's not entirely real."

"He's," James paused and looked over at Rupert, "I'm sorry but did you say he's not entirely real?"

Still looking out the window Rupert asked, "Do you believe there are things out there in the darkness that we don't quite understand or even know about?"

James thought for a moment while he accelerated past the stoplight and watched the streetlights flash by. It was one of the few times of the year in Alaska that the streetlights would be on but there was no snow. Usually when it was dark at this time of night the snow would be at least a foot thick, but they were having a warm fall and the snow that usually came around Halloween was about a month late. It gave the landscape a sad, almost dead, quality. The aspens that dominated the landscape had all lost their leaves and stood with their bare white trunks, cracked and peeling like skin from a decomposing skeleton. He liked it much better when they were covered with a good thick layer of snow, or when the green and gold of the aspen leaves reflected back the midnight sun of the summer. This time of year between the green of the summer and the softness of the winter was depressing. It seemed like the land was dead and waiting for a magic spell to bring it back from its cold grave. It was the perfect setting to worry about those things that go bump in the night. It was the time when smart people huddled around a bright fire and talked about brighter days.

Pulling his mind back James said, "Sure, I guess, there's lots of things we don't understand yet."

"Well," Rupert turned from looking out the window, "this is one of those things."

"Right," James wasn't quite sure what to say to that so just nodded a little.

Rupert's shoulders slumped and he seemed to shrink in his seat, "This is exactly what's happened every time. Do you know you're the first person here to help me with anything?"

"Well," James continued to just watch the road, "you have to admit you sound a little crazy."

Rupert nodded, then sat up a little bit straighter, "But isn't it a little bit crazy to help a complete stranger in a very hazardous situation?"

A crooked smile played across James' face, "Yes, I suppose it is."

"So since you're already headed down the crazy road why not go one step farther with me?"

A laugh escaped James' mouth before he could stop it, "Sure," he said, "Why not."

Rupert grinned, "All right, let's pretend for a second that those guys weren't trying to kill me out of sheer randomness. I mean look at me," he gestured at himself, "I'm not exactly what you'd call a threat to humanity."

James nodded and smiled, "Sure, but they could have been doing some crazy gang thing."

"Sure," Rupert said and nodded, "but it sounded like you knew them. Am I right?"

It was James' turn to frown, "Yes, and that's one of the things that's really bothering me right now."

Rupert nodded again, "Do they seem like the kind to do some crazy kill the tubby old guy gang thing?"

James shook his head, "No."

"Then there must be a different explanation. Such as I know something they don't want me to tell anyone, or I'm trying to stop them from doing something."

James realized Rupert was starting to sound less crazy and nodded for him to continue.

Rupert nodded back, "Do you believe in God?"

James was nodding before he realized what Rupert had said, "What?"

Rupert grinned at him, "Do you believe in God?"

"I," James finally took his eyes off the highway in front of him and raised his left eyebrow at Rupert, "what does that have to do with anything?"

"Everything," Rupert said, "Tell me again why you helped me."

James looked from the road to Rupert and back again then answered slowly, "It was the right thing to do."

"Exactly," Rupert nodded vigorously, "and that means you believe there is such a thing as right, which means that you believe that something set up some standards."

"Look, just because I believe in doing the right thing doesn't mean anything about me believing in God, and what does me believing have to do with anything?"

Rupert waved his hand at the world, "Believing has to do with everything." He turned to look back at James, "So you don't believe anything is out there watching over us?"

"When you put it that way it sounds like my dad teaching me how to use a chainsaw."

"Um, are you joking?"

He laughed, "No. We would go out every Christmas to cut down a tree for the house and finally my dad decided to let me do it. He stood right behind me and coached me through the whole thing."

"Well, I have no idea what Christmas is, or what a chainsaw is, but the idea seems to be the same, yes."

"Then the answer to your question would be no. I could see my dad, and I knew that if something went wrong, he would step right in to help. I've seen lots of things go wrong in this world and nothing stepped in to help."

"So do you believe in anything?"

James looked a little irritated with the turn of conversation, "Look, religion isn't something that I discuss very often. What a person believes is their own business not mine. All the belief in the world can't change whether a person gets hit by a car the next day. You could believe the purple flowers in front of your house talk to you and it seems to have the same effect as believing God talks to you. And, anyway, what does this have to do with those guys beating you up in the middle of a street?"

"Everything. Your beliefs led you to know you were doing the right thing. You stood in front of numerous enemies that were not yours and saved someone you didn't know. Your beliefs had everything to do with this." He gestured out the window at the passing trees, "You're right in the fact there might be no difference between believing that a plant talks to you or God talks to you. Where the difference comes in is what you do with that belief."

"Okay," James was getting tired of the weird conversation and was glad to turn on his blinker for the Eagle River exit, "but, seriously, what's your point?"

Rupert sighed, "What would you say if I told you an evil darkness had come into your world from a different world and convinced those guys to believe in him?"

"Those guys beat you up because an evil entity sent them to kill you." James stopped at a red light at the end of the exit ramp and waited for it to change. He was thankful the Catholic Church was right across the street. He just wanted to be rid of this guy, get to his uncle's house here in Eagle River, and call Katie to tell her about his crazy night. She was going to get on him about stepping into a situation like this, but no matter how crazy a guy was they didn't deserve to be beat up in the middle of a street by a bunch of hopped up college students.

"In short, yes. I," he realized that they were about to pull into the parking lot of the church, "well, I guess it really doesn't matter now." The light turned green, they crossed the intersection, and turned into the parking lot of the Catholic Church. The balding little man sighed and opened the car door, "I do thank you again for your help, and I am sorry I got you involved in this. I hope they don't come after you because of me." He extended his hand, "May the Flames light guard you and warn you if they approach." He got out of the car and closed the door. He stopped halfway to the door of the church, turned, smiled, and waved good-bye.

Looking at him in the glow of the parking lot lights he wondered how anyone could feel threatened by him. He had a ring of hair circling his balding head, and at about five foot four he was almost as wide as he was tall. He gave the impression that if you put a brown robe on him he could beat out Friar Tuck for the part of Friar Tuck in a Robin Hood play. James chuckled to himself; I guess that would make me Robin Hood, or Will Scarlet. Yeah, he thought, I would rather be Will Scarlet. Less pressure to be in charge.

The odd thing was when the Friar had held out his hand and said his little blessing he could feel the strangest tingle run down his spine. It was most likely because it had been a long day and the aftereffects of the adrenaline rush were wearing off. He still couldn't believe he had faced down all those guys at the same time with only a can of bear spray. This was one story he was not going to include in his email to mom.

Chapter Three

The sky was a wine dark purple. Those that had been traveling the Glenn Highway a few hours earlier would have been distracted by the dancing green and red lights over mount Susitna to the northwest. It was almost eight thirty in the morning and the sun wouldn't be making an appearance for at least another two hours. When the sun finally came up it would be a lazy late arrival. The worship of the sun that had covered a multitude of ancient lands had never really caught on here. It was hard to worship something that took its sweet time getting up in the morning, looked around for a few hours, decided it was too much effort, and went back to bed for nineteen or twenty hours. On the other hand, people had worshipped cats and they did basically the same thing.

When he popped open the door to his white four door Geo Metro he was still wondering if the night before with the crazy little balding guy had really happened. Fighting off a bunch of crazed college guys with a can of bear spray? Being lectured about what he believed on some spiritual level by a man that seemed to have a bad case of asthma? He shook his head and bent over to look in the driver's side mirror. It was annoying having to put in contacts every day, and every year he told his family that for Christmas he would love to get laser eye surgery, but instead he always got boxer shorts. Actually, last year he got a putting mat for his living room. He didn't think anything short of a miracle could save his golf game, but it was all for fun anyway.

He blinked his blue eyes to straighten out the contacts and ran his hand through his short-cropped brown hair. He thought he was handsome, but not so much that he was going to be vain about it. As long as he was good enough looking for Katie to say yes and go out with him today that was good enough. He had asked her in passing conversation what she thought her perfect man would be like, and her answer was close to what he looked like. It was a little manipulative of him, and he was fairly sure she answered the way she did because she was being nice, but he would take anything he could get. He stepped back from the mirror a little to get a better look at himself and thought what he saw wasn't bad. Six foot two inches tall, about one hundred eighty-five pounds depending on when he weighed himself, and fairly athletic. He wished he had the energy after classes every night to go and work out so that he could look like one of those guys on the cover of <u>Men's Health</u> but that might never happen.

He had dressed in a hurry and hoped he would be warm enough going for a walk with Katie. His choice in clothes had always tended toward earth tones and was rather rumpled. He wore denim jeans that were wearing out at the edges of the pockets, a hunter green Carhartt sweatshirt, and to top it all off a bright red down jacket that he had gotten for free. He would never have chosen it for himself but when someone tells you that their three-hundred-dollar jacket doesn't fit them and would you like it, you don't tell them the color is wrong. Realizing it was way too cold to stand and look at himself in his car mirror he jumped into his Geo, which he had begun calling his getaway car. He chuckled to himself and realized he had made a getaway in a car that was most likely run by two squirrels fighting with each other in the engine compartment. Now, at least he could say his car had earned the green racing stripes running down the sides. He had originally wondered, when he bought the car, why anyone in their right mind would think it was a good idea to put racing stripes on a car that struggled to make it to sixty miles per hour. It was a good thing those goons last night hadn't had any cars or he would have been toast. He was still slightly worried by the fact that he had known some of the guys. There might be some trouble at school, but most likely he could avoid them until things blew over. On the other hand if someone had shot a can of pepper spray in his face it might take him a while to get over it.

  He watched as the streetlights flipped by and wondered what time the sun would decide to show itself today. At this time of the year it most likely wouldn't make it above the mountains until after ten. A group of guys caught his attention standing on the bike trail along the road. He found it odd that they would just be standing in a group watching traffic go by at this time of the morning. Granted it wasn't too early, but guys that looked like that didn't have a reputation for getting up at the crack of dawn. He was used to seeing the Army guys out on the trail at this time. They would be in all their gear with a rucksack on that looked like it held a dead body. Each one would be sporting two or three reflective stripes so that if a car decided to swerve twenty feet off the road they would know to miss the Army guys on the trail.

  At first glance he thought they were moose. They liked to strip the bark off the underbrush that grew at the roadside. Also, someone had told him once that they like to just stand on the road because the pavement radiated back the heat it took in during the day. He wondered if the moose believed in some way that the pavement created the heat. He chuckled. Maybe the moose believed in a higher power that had gifted them with this great black heater, and as a test of their faith every once in a while something would come along and randomly hit one of them. As sarcastic as he was being, that sounded a lot like life to him. You thought you had been blessed by whatever event it was but if you didn't keep your eyes out eventually a truck would come and side swipe you on the road of life. He could probably write a self-help book around that theme and make millions. We are just moose standing on the road of life.

It was all because of a moose that he met Katie in the first place. One wandered onto campus and was getting agitated by all the people leaving their ten o'clock classes. He very distinctly remembered the clock tower sounding eleven and his stomach growling. The world seemed normal that day. A heavy frost was on the ground, and it made the grass sparkle like rhinestones, not those cheap ones that you see on hello kitty bags for pre-teens but the good rhinestones like you saw on Elvis. A slight breeze made him pull his collar up around his cheeks. Shouts rang across the grass but seeing as how it was a college campus shouts weren't that big of a deal. On any given day you could hear everything from shouts about someone's mother to arguing over the meaning of a poem by e.e. comings, but the tone of them made him look up this time to see a moose standing on the path about twenty feet away.

He looked at it. It looked at him. He thought vaguely how big a moose really is. Its line of sight was over his head. He didn't have time to think of much else because it started coming toward him, and it was looking distinctly irritated. Putting up his hands he started backing away, "Good moose." His mind skipped wildly over why one was called a moose and lots were also called a moose. Why not meese? Most likely because they distinctly did not look like meese. They were much bigger than meese, and it looked much angrier than you would think a meese could be.

He glanced over his shoulder to see how close he was to the nearest door and was a little distraught to see it was a good ways away. He glanced back at the moose in time to see that it was picking up speed. Should he run or hold his ground? His body said run. It was more emphatic than that really. It more screamed at him to run, but his mind said that if he ran it would just run after him and then stomp on him. People died from being stomped by moose. You would think in the winter without antlers they wouldn't be much of a threat but when you see the fact that their hoof can reach your face without even stretching you begin to think otherwise. So his brain said to stand. He asked his brain, if it was so smart, stand and do what when the moose gets here? His brain said that the moose was just as scared of him as he was of it. He doubted his brain actually knew what it was talking about, and he was starting to think his body had the right idea when a snowball hit the moose in the side of the head. Now his brain, which had realized it was out of the decision making process for the foreseeable future, found this very funny and actually giggled a little. Normally giggling was something that a college brain would never be caught doing, but it was a little off because of the whole situation.

Realizing that he had stopped backing away and was looking around to see who had the audacity to throw a snowball at a ticked off moose, he decided to make a break for it. He ran. Later he would be told that the moose had been distracted enough that it didn't notice he was gone until he was almost at the door. He had wondered what a distracted, ticked off moose looked like, but decided it was better not to know first hand.

Panting he asked, "Who threw the snowball?"

A random onlooker answered, "It was some chick from over toward the food court."

"Anybody know who it was?" He held up his hands to the guy that had answered, "Other than saying it was some chick."

"Ya." He turned to the girl that had spoken up and she said, "Her name's Katie. She lives in my dorm."

He hadn't cared if she was the poster child for the company that sold ugly sticks, he was going to take her out to the best dinner he could afford. Which, by the way, had been a subway sandwich and soup at the local Safeway. It had confused him why the locals called it Carrs, but you get used to things. It had been total good luck on his part that she was, to put it nicely, beautiful.

Thinking of that first date made him smile. You had to hold onto those good things in life. There were too many times that people clung to bad memories and wouldn't let them go. He had made a conscious decision that he would rather think about her smiling over a sub sandwich than think about his class he was skipping to see her smile again today. He and a friend of his had once taken the time to figure out how much they were paying per hour to go to classes. Most likely this was something every college student had done at some time or other. What it came down to was he was paying around a hundred dollars to take Katie on a picnic in below freezing weather today.

Passing the people on the trail his Geo started to shake. The steering wheel pulled hard to the right into the other traffic lanes, but because of the small size of the car he was able to get it under control and pulling hard he guided it into the grassy median. Jumping out he realized his hands were shaking and his heart felt like it was going to explode through his eyeballs. This is too much adrenaline, he thought. Along with last night, and now almost going into traffic in a car that's built out of secondhand plastic, he hadn't felt this wired since going on the roller coasters at six flags.

He looked down as he went around the front of his car and saw what he expected to see, a blown front tire. Growing up his dad held competitions between himself and his brother and sister to see who could change all the tires on the car the fastest. Back then he thought it was fun but a little silly. Now, standing in thirty-degree weather at the side of the road he realized he could change this one tire on his car in less than five minutes. Making a mental note to call his dad and thank him for his foresight he popped the trunk and got started.

He pulled into a parking space on the University of Alaska campus between a Ford truck and some type of gargantuan SUV. He never understood Alaskans affinity for backing into parking spots. It was, he had discovered, almost a rule that if you had a truck or an SUV in Alaska you had to back into your parking space. No one knew why exactly, and beyond that no one really knew why they owned a truck they never hauled anything in, or an SUV with four wheel drive they drove alone in and never went off road. After he got out he looked back and felt like his poor little metro must be feeling a bit intimidated. Especially with its sad little spare tire making it tilt a little to the side. He shook his head. If some spare tires could be called doughnuts then his was one of those miniatures you bought at a gas station.

"You're late."

He turned away from his car and grinned at seeing Katie walking across the parking lot. "I almost died." He wiped the smile off and tried to look as pitiful as possible.

"Right." She walked right up to him and stopped so that he would have to look down at her. Looking up at him she realized that she liked the fact that he was taller than she was. It made her feel good. Like he was somehow more solid. "Is there anything that I need to save you from this time? A rabid chipmunk perhaps?"

"Most definitely." He turned and pointed to his car, "You need to save me from that death trap. Or at least kick it for me." Her laughter was intoxicating. He wished he could be poetic and tell her how it lifted his spirit. How it brightened his day like sunshine from a clear blue sky reflecting off fresh snow, but instead he decided to keep it simple, "You look beautiful today."

She smiled at him and curtsied, "Why thank you, James. I'm wearing my best Levis and hiking boots."

"So," as he turned he slipped his arm around her waist, "do you mind if we take your car?"

"Are you kidding?" She looked up at him in mock surprise, "There was no way you were going to get me in that little thing you call a car anyway." She snuggled up to his side and then pulled him toward the left side of the parking lot, "I parked down here."

She let him drive. In her mind it was a conscious decision. It was her way of saying she trusted him. That she was willing to let him take the lead. A long time ago her mother had told her relationships were like dancing. If both people tried to lead then both people would end up hurt, and it was more fun if she let him lead anyway. He seemed to have a way about him. As she looked at him she tried to place it. It wasn't that he was bossy, or that he tried to take control. It wasn't that he was overtly strong either. He just had something about him. He was laid back, but not lazy. He let things slide off him, but he still cared. She thought if she really had to call it something she would call it quietly confident.

"Are you a religious person Katie?"

The question caught her off guard for a second, and it took a bit to pull herself out of her thoughts and respond to the question. She tended to overanalyze things he said lately just because it was only the beginning of the dance and she wasn't quite sure what kind of dance he was trying to lead her in. She responded in the only way she could think of, "Lemon tart?"

He blinked. Slowly he took his eyes from the road and looked at her and blinked again. "I'm sorry, but what?"

"Exactly." She nodded at him.

"Ahh." He looked back at the road. "Let me see if I can be less random about my questions in order to facilitate better interpersonal communication."

"Are you taking a psychology class this semester?"

He smiled toward the road, "Why yes. Yes I am. However, I don't think I need psych classes to pick up on the fact that I tossed you a question out of left field."

She took the opportunity to rub his leg. She liked his legs. They looked nice in denim. Was it weird to say that a guy had nice legs? She shook herself out of the moment of distraction, "Honey, you know I don't play baseball. Now what were you asking?"

"Well," He sighed and tried to pull his thoughts together, "I had a strange conversation with that guy I told you about on the phone about last night. He asked me what I believed about God, or even if I did believe in God." He glanced over at her to see what her reaction was so far. This was a little bit of a touchy subject to be starting out with on your first real date. He didn't know how she would react. Maybe her parents were pastors, or maybe she would think he was stupid for bringing it up. "Anyway, it just got me thinking, and I was wondering if you were religious at all."

She kept her hand on his leg and started tracing little circles in the denim, "I went to some church as a little girl, I can't really remember anything about it. I think my parents believed that it would help me grow up better. I really couldn't tell you where I stand with the whole thing right now."

He nodded and glanced over at her, "You know I'm doing a history major right?" When she nodded back at him he continued, "I've studied everything from Buddhism to the local Methodist church, and it strikes me every time that they all seem to have some things right and some things wrong." He took the Thunderbird Falls exit and looked for a parking spot at the head of the trail.

They got out and started pulling out the makings for their picnic. As he watched her carry the bag of utensils over to the stretch of ground they would be using he couldn't help but smile to himself. Today he was happy. Last night seemed a world away. When he told her about it she had gotten a kick out of the whole thing. He hoped that maybe she looked at him differently now that she knew he had single-handedly taken on a group of thugs with nothing more than a can of bear spray. It felt wrong to bring it up now for some reason, however. Like he would be bragging, and besides he would rather focus on her right now and put the memory of that strange man and his questions out of his head.

The picnic took on that romantic quality every person dreams about. He found himself saying things just to get her to smile, and she found herself smiling no matter what he said because she couldn't help herself. Eventually she found herself holding his hand as they walked up the trail toward the falls, which they could hear in the distance. She couldn't feel his hand very well through the purple and green knit mittens, but that really didn't matter.   Everything was so quiet. The aspens were bare and gray and seemed to go on forever. Bones of the dead summer waiting to sleep beneath a blanket of snow that would come soon enough, but for now all was quiet. It was an in-between time. That gray time that is not summer or fall, but not yet winter either.

She looked over at him as he walked quietly along and realized the land around them seemed to fit perfectly. "James," he looked over at her, "maybe it doesn't matter if there is a God." She stopped walking and reached for his other hand. "Maybe what matters is what we do right now." She looked up at the cloudy Alaskan sky, "If there is a God he would want us to do the right thing now, and if there isn't a God we should still do what we think is right. Just look around us." She let go of his hands, "I was thinking about this, and I think I can't control a lot of things that happen around me. I wish it was warmer today." She heard him sigh his agreement, "I wish the aspens were golden with autumn leaves instead of dead, but I can't control that. What I can control is myself, and I can see the beauty in the day as it is. Even if it's not how I would like it to be. So I guess what I'm saying is that if you ever see the guy who asked you that again you can tell him it really doesn't matter. What matters is what we do because even if there is a God, we can't do anything about what he's going to do." She looked over at him to see if she had embarrassed herself.

He nodded, "Seize the moment and do what is right in that moment because it's all you can do." He touched her cheek, slid his fingers down her jaw line, tilted her chin up a little and kissed her. His heart was beating so hard he was sure she would be able to feel it through his lips. The first kiss is the most frightening and most wonderful moment in life. It's a rush of adrenaline and emotion like none other. It's like stepping off a cliff and finding yourself caught in the arms of angels. He broke the kiss with multiple thoughts at the same time. Depending on her reaction he would either have to make a joke, apologize, or ask if he could try one more time just in case he had gotten it wrong the first time. As he leaned back, she melted into his arms.

"I was hoping you would do that." She whispered into his chest.

The sound of footfalls slowly pulled them back to reality. James took her hand and pulled her onto a river overlook that was off the path. It was built of sturdy redwood with a railing that was high enough to keep small children from falling the seventy-five feet down to the river below, but also low enough for people to lean on and admire the view. Leaning his back against it he pulled her close and breathed in the scent of her hair.

When his body stiffened in her arms she looked up at him to see what was wrong. His eyes were following something down the trail and her first reaction was that there was an animal on the trail. She tensed up and turned abruptly so she could get an idea of what they would need to do to get away. If it was a bear it would be hungry and looking for its last meal before it went down for its long winter nap, and if it was a moose it might just ignore them and move on. A group of men were disappearing around a bend in the trail to the left and to the right was nothing. Not a single thing. No bear, no moose, not even a squirrel. "What was that all about?" She looked back at him. He shook his head and stared at the area where the group of men had just disappeared.

"Nothing." He said. "Just one of those weird déjà vu moments." He looked back at her and smiled his best smile. Hoping that he hadn't completely ruined the moment he tried to salvage something by winking at her and saying, "Has anyone ever told you that you're prettier than a waterfall?"

"Well," she leaned out from the railing and looked upriver to where the sound of water falling hundreds of feet roared at them, "since you can't actually see the falls from here I'm not sure how to take that." There are moments when time moves slower than normal, and there are times when it seems to fly by. Both of these are of course just perceptions because time is time and a second is a second, but sometimes, just sometimes, it might just be true that a second isn't a second. When a loud crack jolted James out of his slow progress of looking Katie up and down while she leaned out over the railing, time seemed to do everything but what he wanted it to do. She tipped forward so fast as the railing cracked that even his automatic reaction to reach out and grab her wasn't fast enough. His fingers grazed her pants leg as her weight pulled her over the edge. The second crack seemed to slow time to a crawl as he realized that the entire deck was sliding away from the trail. Katie's scream cut through the thick molasses of time surrounding him and he slid onto his stomach reaching over the edge hoping she would still be there.

The deck tilted at an absurd angle, but it was just enough to grab her wrist with his right hand as she held onto some bushes growing from the side of the gorge. "Hang on!" At his scream she looked up, her eyes wide. He had never seen her scared. Nothing could scare her. She had faced down a seven-foot tall angry animal in the middle of campus. Sliding toward the edge he grabbed onto the decking with his left hand. Half of his mind screamed at him that they were going to die, the other half started talking to him.

James, now is not the time to panic.

Right, he thought. If ever there was a time to panic, now was it.

If you panic you can't think, if you can't think you can't save her, if you can't save her you'll never know what the next date will be like.

Huh, good point.

Now, look at her. Let her know that you have it under control.

I don't have it under control if you haven't noticed.

Oh, believe me, I noticed. That doesn't mean she needs to know that.

Right.

He was scared, and he wasn't sure what he could do. He took a deep breath to settle his nerves and looked down at her. A door seemed to open in his mind and a calmness came through it. He could do this.

She looked up at him. She could feel the nothingness beneath her feet. Could feel her hands slipping off the brush. She knew there was no way he could pull her up with one hand. Then he smiled. She was sure they were going to die. Every fiber of her being screamed that they were going to fall and that would be the end, and he smiled at her. Not like a crazy grinning in the face of death kind of smile, but more like a, isn't this an interesting situation kind of a smile.

"Are you hurt?" His voice was soft. Almost like they were sitting back at the picnic just having a conversation. "Are you hurt?" He repeated.

"I," she blinked, "I don't think so."

"Good." He smiled again and she was almost sure now that they were going to be fine. "Now," she had to strain to hear him over the pounding of her heart, "this is what I want you to do." He looked back up at the tilting deck then back at her, "hang on just a sec." He chuckled to himself, "As if you can do anything else right now." He shifted his body to his right then looped his right leg around the post of one of the railings that was still in place. He locked his ankles together then let go with his left hand. He dangled, holding on with his legs. Grabbing her left arm below his own hand he said, "I've got you so I want you to let go with your right arm. Grab my arm and pull up." When she reached up for him he pulled up with his legs and arms enough so that he was able to let go with his right arm and grab under her arm. "Quick, reach over me and grab the deck."

Pulling on him like a human ladder she grabbed the deck. He grabbed her belt and pulled up. He would have to apologize later for giving her a wedgie on their first official date, but for now it was the best he could do. She struggled up and finally he saw her feet disappear from his line of sight. Swinging his body to his left he pulled himself up the deck. Katie grabbed his arms and helped him onto solid ground.

They collapsed against the nearest tree and just sat. It seemed like ages passed. Empires could have risen and collapsed in the time they simply sat. Finally after an eternal three minutes James put his left arm around her and pulled her close. "Are you all right?"

"I don' know." Looking over at him she smiled slightly, "How bout you check to see if I've broken anything."

He chuckled, and then laughed, "I didn't think I would get to play doctor until at least the third date."

"Well, saving a girl's life tends to speed up the normal process."

He shook his head, "It wasn't anything really. I'm sure you would have been fine."

Her smile disappeared, "I would have died James. I'm not even joking." Letting out a deep sigh she leaned against him again. After what had just happened, she needed to feel his solid presence against her, "I was sure we were dead. Then you smiled at me." Lifting her eyes, she met his, "Are you insane?"

"What?" He half smiled, not sure what she was getting at.

"We were hanging a million feet off the ground on the brink of death, and you smiled."

"Well," he shrugged, "It wasn't that big of a deal. Once I knew you weren't hurt, I knew everything was going to be fine."

She wrapped her arms around his waist and squeezed, "You're my hero."

The rest of the day was a strange mixture of giddiness and a sense of relieved anxiety. Everything seemed to be waiting for something else. They didn't want to admit how close they had come to seeing what was on the other side of that one-way door, but at the same time all they had to do was look at each other the right way and they both knew what the other was thinking about. The day ended where it had begun, in the parking lot. It seemed appropriate. A parking lot isn't really any place at all. It's an in-between place. No one goes to the parking lot just to go to the parking lot. They go there to get somewhere else. And so there they were, in that in between place. "Where do we go from here?"

Katie rose up on her toes and kissed him, "We have time to find out don't we."

He smiled, "Yes, we do." He returned her kiss, "I'll see you tomorrow."

"Breakfast?"

"Captain Crunch at eight thirty."

His mind wandered and he drove through town on autopilot. He was halfway out of his car in the parking lot of Barnes and Noble when he realized that he couldn't remember actually stopping at any lights. Looking around he didn't see any cops chasing him so he assumed that he must have. He locked his car and looked around. The sun was already setting even though it was early yet. It was around five thirty in the afternoon and dusk had turned the world purple. From here until around Christmas it would just keep getting darker. As he walked toward the bookstore, he was certain that he wouldn't have a problem with depression this year. It never hit him hard like some people, but when it was dark so much of the time it was hard to keep your spirits up. They had a technical term for it. It was called SAD: Seasonal Affective Disorder. Basically, he thought to himself as he looked up at the darkening sky before heading inside, if you didn't get enough sunlight you got depressed. For himself it wasn't too bad. He just felt less like doing things, and more like sitting around on the couch in the lobby of the dorms. He felt slower and wasn't as apt to put up with people. That's why he went to the bookstore. It was his way of being around people but not having to talk to them. You could grab a coffee, a magazine, and sit next to the fire and no one would bother you unless they knew you really well. It was lovely.

His friend Richard was what you would call an extrovert. He loved to be around people. He was the energizer bunny of humans. He just kept going, and if he wasn't around people, he became depressed. He thought James was strange for wanting to be alone. In fact, most people did. They treated it like it was a disease that could be cured if they just tried hard enough. They all figured he didn't want to be around people because he just hadn't been to the right kind of party yet, or he just hadn't met the right kind of people yet. So, what did they do? They forced him to go to parties, or they would hook him up on blind dates. When he flat out refused, they would trick him into being at what they referred to as the right place at the right time. Most of the time he could put up with it. He had to admit that most of the time he did have fun at the parties. It was just that he couldn't take it for as long as Richard and the others could. They could, James thought, be at the same party around people for days on end. For himself however, after a few hours he was done. Then he would slip off, find a good book, and read.

Somewhere in our culture an amazing thing had happened. People had been trained to see books as the same as a wall. You didn't disturb someone who was reading. It was bad manners. It was downright rude in some cases. Now it really depended on what they were reading, and what kind of person they were, but no matter what there had to be a special case to interrupt someone who was reading. Take for instance a man reading a newspaper. If it's your dad, then it really depended on the relationship you had with him as to whether you could interrupt. If it's some guy in a bookstore, then culture demanded the only way you could interrupt was if the building was on fire. So James decided for the thousandth time he would take advantage of this cultural oddity and would retreat into a book. Tonight he was in a strange mood so maybe he would dig into some Robert Burns poetry and think about how her skin felt under his fingertips. He smiled to himself, yes, that is exactly what he would do.

Normally it would sound like a contradiction to want to be around people but not want to interact with them, and on a few occasions his friends had pointed this out to him. He liked to observe the world. To put it in a different way, he liked to people watch. People were just so interesting. A friend had once told him a story about this very café and how he had watched a gentleman in a fuzzy pink tube top feeding coffee to an oversized white teddy bear. Personally he had never seen something like that, and James half thought his friend had been making it up, but you never knew with people.

As he stood in line waiting to get his tall raspberry mocha he looked around the tables. By the door a man sat with his head behind an open laptop. Speaking of strange cultural oddities, that was one of the newest ones. Going out into public for the specific purpose of cutting yourself off from the public. But, James thought, who was he to say anything. After all, what was the difference between a book and a laptop? They both achieved the same goal. By the window on his left sat a young man and a young lady. Facing each other across their coffee cups they were engaged in some sort of deep conversation. His mind started asking questions. Were they dating? Were they related? He had learned from years of being by himself and watching people you could tell a lot from body language. The main key was physical contact. He watched as the young man reached out and covered her hand with his own. She didn't pull away or find some polite way of getting out of it, like reaching for her coffee cup. She simply started tracing circles on his hand with her thumb. Definitely dating, or else that was one strange family.

He heard the door open and glanced to see who it was. There was a fairly good chance he would recognize the person. It was close to the campus and for all of the three hundred thousand people that called Anchorage home it still had a small town feel. He was struck by a feeling that he recognized the man that came through the door but he couldn't quite place where he knew him from. Then it all came rushing back. The dark night. The streetlights cutting small yellow holes in the pavement. Bear spray cutting a hole in a mob. The man waved at him. What am I supposed to do James thought to himself but found himself waving back. That's where good manners will get you, he thought. If I wasn't raised to be polite, I could have just pretended I didn't recognize him and gone on about my business. Well, either way he would have to wait. He turned to the counter and received the standard greeting that sounded something like hello, what would you like. James was sure you could build a robot that could say the same thing then pour your coffee. That way he wouldn't have to endure casual conversation with the people behind the counter asking him how he liked the weather. As it was, though, he smiled politely and asked for his raspberry mocha. He really didn't like coffee, but a mocha tasted more like hot chocolate, and when you added the raspberry flavoring it tasted nothing like coffee. The only reason he didn't ask for raspberry flavored hot chocolate was because the caffeine helped sometimes.

 His drink was warm in his cold hands as he turned to face the tables again. He decided that he should at least go and see how the man was doing. He could hear his father in his head telling him that it was the right thing to do. His father would talk to anyone. He had been constantly amazed by his father's capacity to hold a conversation with absolute strangers. On the one hand sometimes he found it irritating to find out that a person he had never met knew his entire life's story because they had talked with his dad in the grocery store checkout line. On the other hand, he was beyond positive that they had lived a better life because of all the friends his dad had made.

 As he walked toward him Rupert indicated with a smile that he should sit down. "You look like you're doing well." James said as he pulled out the chair across from him.

 "Yes, yes, quite well. Nothing else has happened since we met." He let out a wheezing sigh. "I don't know why I was picked for this job." He took a deep but visibly difficult breath in. James could hear him breathe. It was an odd thing. Everyone breathes but you never really notice it. He was sure everyone made a sound when they breathed, but again, you never really noticed it. With this guy, however, it was like a tiny steam engine was running inside of him and you could hear it puffing. "Yes." The man said, "As you have noticed my lungs are not quite what they should be. You would think with all our knowledge on healing that a person could be allowed to take a breath without struggling."

"Is there something I can get you?" James worried for a moment that he had saved him just to watch him die here in a coffee shop.

"No, no, I'll survive. I have for the last forty years. I thought I was going to die last night when those thugs were chasing me. I assumed that I would stop breathing and just drop dead before they could even reach me." He paused for a moment, looked at James, then said, "I don't believe that I properly introduced myself last night." He straightened up in his seat, smoothed his clothes and said, "I am Rupert Mundovi cleric of the fourth order of Saris and third-class negotiator."

"Oh." James sat and stared. It took his mind a second to register what had been said. It was odd. Not odd like a person all of a sudden peeling their skin off and you realize that they're actually a giant cockroach underneath, but just odd enough to give you pause. "Well, um, I'm perty sure I told you my name last night. I'm a student at the local university here and" James paused as his one part of his mind caught up with the rest of the conversation, "did you say you were a cleric?"

"Yes. I suppose that might not mean anything to you." He took in a slow noisy breath, "I also suppose I should have just told you my name. My title means nothing here. There are no orders here, and the records and negotiations that I oversee have nothing to even do with this place." He looked around and lowered his voice as if someone might be eavesdropping and leaned forward in his seat "In fact the records make no mention of this place at all. We were all certain that it, or anything like it, did not exist. Actually," he let himself settle back in his chair, "there were a few that were certain that something like this was out there, but we all took them for loonies." He shook his head, "We never called them that, but it was just sort of understood that it was a crazy idea to think that there were other worlds. I mean what would be the point of creating other worlds..."

"Hold on," James waved his coffee cup in front of Rupert trying somehow to get his attention and force him to stop talking, "did you just say other worlds?" If someone was eavesdropping this was most likely the point in the conversation where they would realize that they either needed to pull out their cell phone and tell their friend about how they always run into weird people in the coffee shop or check to make sure no one slipped something in their non-fat soy latte.

"Oh, there I've done it again." Rupert looked disgusted and shook his head almost as if he were yelling at himself, "It's so disorienting being in this place. I can't talk about normal things because they aren't normal here."

"Go back a little. What did you mean by," parts of James' mind argued with other parts about what to argue about and the first thing that came out was, "um that whole other worlds thing?" James was sure that he was going to regret asking the question. He knew that the man was, as he had said moments ago, a loony, but before he could take it back and extract himself from the conversation he was answered.

"I know it seems like crazy talk." James mentally agreed with him and wondered if he knew the appropriate phone number to get a crazy person picked up, "Me sitting here telling you that other worlds exist. That they are connected by doorways that open only one way, but you have to think to yourself and answer this question: why would those men be trying to kill me if I was just some crazy out on the street?"

"For money?"

"If I had money, do you think I would be staying at a church?"

"Well, maybe you said something they didn't like."

"That," he paused, "is entirely possible. They did seem like the sort to get angry over a few words. Especially after what I saw at that rally." They sat in silence for a few moments. James drank his mocha. Rupert bit at his right thumbnail then said, "Has anything strange happened to you today?"

James' shoulders rose in a noncommittal gesture, "Why do you ask?"

Rupert took two deep breaths. James could hardly stop himself from trying to breathe for the man, "I need you to believe me," Rupert finally said. He gave James a half smile, "You are the first person to sit and talk with me. The first person to help me. You are my first real chance to do what I came here to do, and I can't let it slip away. So, please, did anything strange or out of the ordinary happen to you today?"

"Not really. Unless you count finally going out with a girl that I really like."

"No, that doesn't count, but good for you." He tried to force a smile, "Every person deserves to be happy." Rupert looked out the window then back, "No one tried to harm you?"

"No." James paused and wondered if he should tell the crazy man about Katie and himself almost falling to their deaths. Why not, it wasn't as if he was sitting here having a crazy conversation with a person talking about other worlds, "Actually, there was one strange thing today."

"Really? What?"

"When Katie and I were out walking, a platform that we were standing on collapsed and we almost fell over a cliff."

Rupert leaned forward excitedly, "Really? Would you have been hurt?"

"Well, thanks for the sympathy." James decided that he couldn't fault the guy for reacting inappropriately. After all, maybe on his world people were happy when someone got hurt, and maybe chocolate milk really came from brown cows.

"I'm sorry." Rupert leaned back and the sounds of his quick, shallow breathing started to creep James out. "I didn't mean to sound happy that you could've gotten hurt. I hope all that happened was someone got a scratch."

"Actually, if we hadn't been lucky and grabbed onto something we might have died." James immediately regretted saying that.

"That proves it!" Rupert smiled like he had won an argument.

James took a deep breath, thought for a moment about the best course of action, pushed himself back from the table, smiled politely, "Accidents happen. I'm sorry, but I really need to be going. I'm glad that you're alright."

"Please wait." Rupert stood and looked around, "I," he paused and looked around again, "I know that I seem strange, maybe even crazy, but I really need you to believe me."

His wheezing breath was almost hypnotic to James, "I just," he shook his head and thought to himself that there were limits to a person's requirement to be polite in society, "I really do need to be going." He turned to leave and realized that he wasn't turning. There was a moment of panic, but it passed swiftly as he thought he must be a little on edge about the whole day and now this. He turned to go again and again nothing happened. Slowly he licked his lips, breathed in through his nose, and looked down at his feet. He was wearing his tan and forest green hiking boots. One end of the laces on his left foot was broken off and he remembered that he needed to replace it before it got too bad. The solid rubber soles, that were such great traction on walks like he had gone on today with Katie, were a good two inches off the ground. "Well." He wiggled his toes and thought about screaming. "Well." He would have continued on with his mind stuck in a loop looking at something that he couldn't comprehend except from across the table Rupert cleared his throat. James looked up.

"Please," Rupert looked to the left and back, "Please," then he looked out the window, "Just let me explain."

"Well." James rubbed his jaw and looked from Rupert to his shoes and back then said, "May I sit down?"

"Oh," Rupert nodded, "of course. I normally would never do something like this. Actually it's almost forbidden where I'm from, but what was I to do? You're in danger, and on top of that I have no one else who will even say hello to me." He waited for James to sit back down then lowered himself into his chair. "I really am quite sorry about all that. You seemed to take it quite well. The only other time I have done something like that here the poor girl screamed until I thought the authorities were going to come so I stopped and she ran as fast as I think I've ever seen anyone run. That's why I decided to lift you so that you wouldn't be able to run." He took two deep breaths, "I hope you aren't angry."

"I," James tried to slow his whirling thoughts and make some sense out of what had just happened, "I'm not angry, just," again he tried to collect his thoughts into some sort of coherent pattern, "just not quite sure what happened."

"I think it would be best if I showed you something to prove what I've been saying. Also it would be better to talk about these things somewhere not so public."

James knew that some measure of safety could be had with the public around, but at the same time he really was starting to wonder what had just happened. He sighed as again his father's voice reminded him that doing the right thing wasn't always convenient, "All right." He paused, "Can I stand up?" And in this case doing the right thing might actually be insane.

Rupert grinned, "Yes, of course."

James stood and looked down to see his feet firmly planted on the tile floor of the coffee shop. So much for a quiet night reading alone, "Is what we're going to see close or what?"

Rupert shook his head, "No, unfortunately. The door is maybe an hour from here."

James nodded, "Of course it is. We could take my car, but the spare tire isn't good for more than a few miles."

Rupert looked confused, "Spare tire?"

"Ya, I got a flat on the Glenn Highway this morning. Huh," he paused and thought back on the incident, "I almost died there too."

Maybe all this wasn't crazy talk. After all, he had been floating a few inches off the ground.

"You see? You are in danger." Again, for more times than James could keep track of, Rupert looked around as if he was making sure no one was following them. As they walked out into the parking lot Rupert asked, "What exactly is the problem with this spare tire?"

From across the parking lot James pointed to his little car and said, "You see my car? The white one there?" He glanced over to see if Rupert knew which one he was talking about. "All the tires are supposed to look the same, and that one is too small."

"Oh, and that causes problems?"

"I take it that you haven't been around too many cars?"

"No, not really. We have different means of getting around where I'm from." They reached the car and Rupert looked down at the tire, "So should it look like that?" He pointed to one of the good tires.

"Ya, but I really don't have the money right now to go and buy a new tire."

"It should be fine now."

"What do you mean?" James glanced down at the spare tire and found it to be not a spare tire. All he could do was to blink a few times. His mind was even out of things to say at this point. The tire was exactly like all the others. It didn't look brand new. It looked like the others. Exactly like the others. He looked over at Rupert and took a few seconds to really stare at him. He didn't look exceptional in any way. He looked out of shape, slightly older, and tired. For someone that had just changed his spare tire into a normal one in the space of a few seconds, and had before that levitated him off the ground, he looked especially non-wizardly.

"I assume," said Rupert, "that it will work now?

Chapter Four

The sun had set, and it was cold. Not the bitter scared for your life cold that it would be in December and January, but still cold. As the students shuffled in and shook themselves, trying to remove the cold like so much dust, you could tell who was new and who had been through an Alaskan winter before.

Those who had spent a few winters in Alaska had become acclimated to the weather. Some would argue that a person doesn't get used to being cold or hot, but humans are amazingly adaptable creatures. The new ones all wore marshmallow puffed down jackets with wool mittens, scarves, and stocking caps. The others came in with just a heavy sweater or sweatshirt with the hood on poking fun at the marshmallows. Asking them how they were ever going to survive when it actually was cold. You could hear the statements of, "This isn't cold. It's only a degree below freezing." As they filled the seats in the classroom others who were much more knowledgeable about Alaskan weather chimed in with, "Just wait till you get a week where the high is negative ten." Others would chuckle and add, "Then the wind starts blowing." The days found the temperature rise above freezing and the nights would see it dip below. The Alaskans didn't consider it winter until it stayed below freezing all day.

Katie pulled off her red and black striped stretch gloves and settled into her night class. She wasn't fond of taking classes at night. They tended to be once a week and lasted for three hours. Not only was that a really long time to sit through any class but it put a real crimp on your social life when you couldn't go out with your friends. Other classes you could miss one in a week and not feel too bad, as long as you didn't do it often. A night class, however, if you missed one it was like missing an entire week of class.

She had really thought about skipping this class because she didn't want her date to end. James had been wonderful. Not only had he saved her life, but he was funny and to top it off he was good looking. If it had been any other class, even any other night class she would be at Barnes and Noble right now snuggled up in front of the fire teasing him about the fact that his choice of reading material was a comic book. Tonight was different. She had to take either philosophy or understanding music or something fluffy like that to round out her liberal arts education, so she chose philosophy because it sounded the most interesting. After the first night she was hooked.

All her friends would tell you she liked to argue. Sometimes it was just for the sake of arguing. She tried to see the other person's point of view and then find a flaw with that point of view. She had considered going into politics but realized there were so many holes in their arguments it would drive her crazy. Philosophy intrigued her. It revolved around the real questions and the real arguments. When she was here, she felt like she was finally finding the answers.

The professor was interesting, and that was actually more of a bonus than she would have thought. Last semester she had taken a required sociology class. At the end of the semester, she believed firmly that the professor should have taken himself out of the social experiment called humanity. He was so boring. He was obviously very smart, and he obviously knew sociology very well, but strangely enough he didn't know how to interact with people. She had thought about the irony of that way too many times during that semester. A person who studies people for a living and doesn't know how to interact with people was, in its own way, amusing.

Professor Merrill, on the other hand, knew how to talk to a person. Maybe it came from the course of study itself. Socrates was a professional at interacting with people and he was said to be the father of philosophy. Professor Merrill was well spoken and funny in a sarcastic sort of way. He knew how to put completely strange and foreign ideas into words that made sense. After her first class with him, introduction to philosophy, she had decided that he was one of her favorite teachers. This was now the third class she had taken from him. The first two had been out of her control, but this one she had chosen to take.

A clear voice rose above the class noise, "All right, lets get started." He stood behind a plain wooden podium. It was what would be called fake wood and was starting to peel in places. He rarely stayed behind the podium preferring instead to pace, point, and interact with the students. He would occasionally find his way back to the podium to remind himself of some point or the other that he wished to cover. Three hours was a long time with one class and staying on track was important, and yet he had a tendency to allow himself to get off on tangents. Some were completely useless but interesting. For instance, he liked to compare things to movies, or the Simpsons. Other tangents were important, and he allowed the students and himself to go down those bunny trails because he felt that allowing a bit of leeway to the discussions could bring better clarity to a subject.

Standing behind the podium he reached into his shirt pocket and pulled out a pair of reading glasses, "Now then, you were all to have read the section of the Leviathan by Thomas Hobbes that I assigned last week and finished a write up on it. Please make sure that it gets handed to my TA by the end of the class. Let's see," he ran his finger down a piece of paper on the podium then looked up, "I suppose the best thing to do is just get started with this long dark night of the soul." He removed his glasses and set them down on the podium beside the paper.

"Essi est percipi. Does anyone in class know what that means?" He looked around the room for a raised hand and seeing a few he pointed to a young man in the back.

"To be is to be perceived." The young man stated confidently and looked quite pleased with himself. Everyone knew that the first few questions of the night would be easy and if you got those you had a good chance of not being called on for the real hard ones. Like why do we exist, or something like that.

"Very good Tom." He stepped out from behind his podium and began to pace in front of the class. Coming to a student's desk in the front row he paused, "Do you mind if I borrow your pencil?"

She smiled, "Not at all professor. As long as it comes back the same as it is now."

He laughed, "Nothing is ever the same as it is right now my dear, but that is a discussion for another night." Picking up the pencil he held it out in front of him. "Can you all see the pencil?" He waited for most of them to nod, "Good." He then bent his arm and held it behind his back away from the class. "What about now? Can you see the pencil?" Again he waited for most of them to shake their heads. "Now for the big question." He paused and looked around the room for a good target, "Mark," Mark's shoulders slumped as if he had been hit, "Mark, can you see the pencil?"

"No sir."

"See that wasn't so hard now was it?" Some students in the class smiled because they knew that the hard question was still to come, "Now, Mark, does the pencil still exist?"

"Yes." Mark shifted in his chair knowing that something was going to happen.

"How do you know that it still exists?"

Mark frowned slightly, "Well, because, things don't just cease to exist because they're behind your back."

"Prove it."

Mark stood up, walked down the three rows of desks in front of him, and looked behind the professor's back, "There it is. It still exists."

"Ahh," the professor smiled, "but can you prove that it exists without looking behind my back? Can you prove that it exists from your desk?"

Mark walked back to his desk, looked for a few seconds at the professor with his hand behind his back, and said, "I can see that you are holding something, and I know from previous experience that you were holding the pencil so the only logical explanation is that you are still holding the pencil behind your back."

The professor positively grinned, "flawless western logic, and as a side note who was it that invented that form of logic?" He didn't wait for anyone to raise their hand, he simply pointed to a young lady in the middle of the class, "Amy?"

"It was Aristotle, sir."

"Very good Amy, now back onto the amazing topic of pencils and existence." He looked back at Mark, "Now let me get this straight. You say that because I was holding a pencil in my right hand and am now holding something in my right hand behind my back that it must be the same pencil. Is that generally what you were saying?"

Mark looked a little suspicious but nodded anyway, "Yes, that is the basic idea."

The professor took his hand from behind his back, and where a pencil had previously been there was now a golf ball. He smiled and waited a few seconds for the idea that he was trying to get across to sink in. "To be is to be perceived." He placed his hand with the golf ball in it behind his back and this time when he brought it out he held a black plastic comb. How do you know that something continues to exist when you can not directly perceive it?"

One of the older students spoke up from one of the middle rows, "If I left this class room y'all wouldn't simply blink out of existence." You could tell when they had become comfortable with the classroom setting because they weren't afraid to speak their mind.

"Of course it wouldn't blink out of existence because we would all be perceiving it while you were gone."

Another student from his left chimed in, "So the only person who could prove that the pencil still existed would be you because you still perceived that it existed."

"Correct."

"So," Mark jumped back in, "Its existence depends on your perception of the event." The professor smiled at him, and Mark continued, "To our perception the pencil seemed to magically change into a golf ball, but to your perception something totally different happened."

"Exactly." Said the professor. He reached into his back pocket and pulled out the pencil and handed it back to the student in the front. He then walked back to his podium, glanced at his notes and smiled. When he looked up he said, "Today's lesson is on perception of reality." He began to pace across the classroom once again, his hands folded behind him, "Your assignment for last week was to read a section out of The Leviathan by Thomas Hobbes." He turned, "Katie, what did you think the central theme of the reading was?"

There was silence as she took a few moments to get her thoughts in order. She had found that the professor responded better to your answers when you took the time to think them out before you spoke. If the answer was wrong he still would treat you better because at least you had taken the time to think it through rather than just spouting off the first thing that came to your mind. Katie smiled, "I think I see what you are getting at sir. Thomas Hobbes is saying that we need a government because we all perceive things differently and that can lead to disputes so there needs to be a centralized authority to say what is the," Katie paused to make quote marks in the air with her fingers, "correct perception. He says that in a state of nature every man will go against every man because he doesn't trust your perception of things and so he had better get you out of the way first before you do something to injure him."

This time the professor grinned, "Exactly." He turned to a young lady in the second row, "Yuko," She smiled suspiciously back at him, "How are you doing tonight?"

"I'm fine." She answered slowly, waiting for something else.

Professor Merrill turned to the rest of the class and gestured to Yuko, "Now wouldn't you all agree that Yuko here is the nicest person in this class." There was a general murmur in the room of sure and I guess so then one voice from the back said, "You haven't seen her at six thirty am for her math class." Then the room broke into laughter. Even the professor laughed, "Now, now, I didn't say she was the nicest person in the world, just the nicest person in this room." He turned back to Yuko, "Now, Yuko, let's set up a scenario here. Remember it's just a hypothetical situation and there are a lot of holes in it so just go with it." She nodded for him to continue, "Let's say that something terrible has happened and our government has collapsed. We are living in a state of anarchy. No rules, no police, no fire department, no electricity, all of it is gone. Food is hard to come by because trade has been cut off and people haven't quite learned how to grow their own food yet. Do you have any siblings Yuko?"

Yuko nodded, "Yes, I have an older brother and two younger sisters."

"Wow," the Professor gave an exaggerated sigh, "three girls. I feel for your brother." The class chuckled. "Now let's say you found out where you can get a loaf of bread for your family. It could possibly be the last one in the whole city. On your way out of your house your older brother convinces you to take a gun with you for protection. Do you own a gun, Yuko?"

"No, but my father and brother have rifles that they use to hunt with."

The professor smiled, "Of course they do. This is Alaska after all. Anyway, you have a gun. You get to where the bread is hidden; you tuck it under your jacket and start home. On the way home you see a man walking toward you. You move to the side of the street to avoid talking to him, and he moves to that side also and is still coming straight at you. If you don't get this loaf of bread home your little sisters will starve. There are no police because the government has collapsed. The man walking toward you reaches into his coat and starts to pull something out while looking directly at where you have the bread tucked into your jacket. What do you do?"

"I would run."

"All right, and in this world that we live in now that would be the best option because you could find someone to help you, but in my hypothetical world there is nowhere to run. Also, in my hypothetical world, you can't outrun the man and you know it before you even try. So you know you can't outrun him, and you know that if you don't get the bread home your sisters will starve, and finally you know that everyone in town is starving and desperate for food. What do you do?"

"I would pull out my gun and tell him to leave me alone."

"Okay, good, and then he pulls out a gun and points it at you. What now?"

"I..." she hesitated to answer, "Well, I would..."

"You would what? Remember, your family's lives are on the line."

"Fine," she looked irritated, "I would shoot him before he could shoot me."

"Very good." He turned back to the class as a whole, "We have to make decisions based on our own perceptions. No one would fault Yuko, the nicest girl in class, for shooting the man. She can't read his mind. She doesn't know if his gun is actually out of bullets, and he is just hoping to intimidate her into giving him the food. All we can rely on, like Thomas Hobbes said in your reading, is our own perception of reality. There is no right or wrong. Sometimes it's right to lie, and sometimes it's right to kill."

Chapter Five

"Chaos."

"What?" James looked over at his, up till now, silent passenger.

"Chaos is what they're after." Rupert looked sheepishly at James. "I should start over again. I was thinking and didn't really mean to say that out loud."

James took a deep breath and let it out slowly. "Look, I think I have been very patient, and, honestly, the only reason I'm wasting my four dollar a gallon gas is because you did some things back there that shouldn't be possible. So, yes, I think you should start over again."

Rupert nodded, "There are those of my order back home that would swear the best approach to this would be only to tell you what you need to know, and possibly lie to you about the rest simply to get you to do things in the quickest way possible." Rupert looked at James for a second, "I must say that I honestly considered doing that because I was sure you wouldn't help me if I simply told you the truth."

James shrugged, "My mother always said honesty was the best policy."

"Well, you had a wise mother. On the other hand, I'm sure you noticed times in your life when omitting a few facts sure made things go smoother. If I told you everything right now I worry you wouldn't agree to help me. Not so much because it's horrible and frightening, which it is, but because you would think I'm some raving lunatic."

James looked over at Rupert, "Isn't that why we are going to see this door of yours? So you can prove you're not a raving lunatic."

"Yes, yes, but the other reason I'm hesitant to tell you the truth is because it is horrible and frightening. Since I've been here, I've heard stories about monsters and frightening things, but they're just that, stories. These monsters are never really seen, they just lurk at the edge of imagination. Even religious monsters," He pointed out the window to a large new church on a hill just before the exit to Eagle River, "like your demons are not so much seen as felt every once in a while. Even then it could just be passed off to being afraid of the dark, or mental illness. You never truly encounter monsters, and neither had we until our door opened. My point is that I worry about telling you everything for fear that what needs to be done will not get done because you will freeze at the wrong moment if you truly know what you're facing. Whereas if I told you only limited amounts of information then you could move on with the belief that you could conquer whatever you face."

James' left eyebrow lifted slightly, "So you're implying I can't beat these unimaginably horrible things."

"Don't you see?" Rupert slumped lower in his chair, "This is exactly the problem I'm talking about. I haven't actually said anything. In fact I was just being hypothetical, but you took it to mean the obstacles in front of you might be overwhelming. What if you take something else the wrong way? Does it mean I should just tell you everything and hope it all works out for the good or should I accidentally leave some of the scarier things out so you don't freak out and run?"

"Are you asking me? Because if you are, I'm going to say I need to know it all up front."

"Of course you would. So would I if I was in your place. But what's the better course of action; to try and explain the workings of a hurricane to a bird so it will understand the situation fully and make an informed decision about whether to fly to someplace it has never been before, or to just yell at it and get it to fly away from the hurricane?"

"So now I'm a bird?"

"No," Rupert looked over at him, "you can't even fly."

"See, I know I can't fly so…" James looked over at Rupert, "Ha, ha, very funny."

"Sorry, when I start to get too stressed I make bad jokes, but the point's still the same. A lot of what I could tell you, you wouldn't be able to understand because it comes from a lifetime of living in a different world. It would take me months to explain why we believe what we do, then I would have to convince you of those beliefs, and then I could get you to understand the urgency of this mission." He looked out the window at the aspens speeding by, "I don't have time for that."

"Well," James looked out the window at the Peters Creek exit, "from where we are now, I estimate we have between forty five minutes and an hour, depending on traffic, until we get to where you said this door is. So how about you tell me the most important parts. I would also appreciate it if you told me how you changed my tire like that."

"That part will have to come last because you'll need to understand a lot before you can understand that." He paused and stared out the window for a few seconds. Finally, he looked back over at James, "In my world we have a picture that represents chaos. It is a circle made up of multiple snakes. Each snake is biting onto the tail of the one in front of it trying to eat it, and in the middle of the circle is a single snake biting its own tail. Each snake grows stronger for a time by eating the snake in front of it, but after a while it all dissolves into death.

"What we're dealing with here is one of those snakes. A being that gets its strength from devouring other things. The hard thing to understand is that it doesn't physically devour them. This is why I said to truly understand this it would take months. It feeds off of an individuals, or societies, emotions. The more chaotic things get the stronger it becomes until it truly can devour them physically. They start out small and insignificant. They whisper in your ear. At first they can't affect things directly, but when they get strong enough they can. They convince you that what you're doing is either good and right, or they just convince you that it's good for you. Either way the chaos begins. They feed on it and grow stronger. The end result being that they feed on life itself and the world dies." He looked out the window and remembered reading a summary of the report given by Winston to the council.

After the discovery of the door by Winston and students from the local university the decision had been made to send someone through it and assess the situation. Theologians wanted to know if this fit with their religious beliefs, scientists wanted to know if this was truly another world, and the military wanted to know if this was truly a threat or just a heat crazed dream of some local university kids.

Different plans were put together, different teams were suggested, and different strategies were argued over. The religious sect believed that they should be the ones in charge since it seemed to be exactly what the sacred books said would be there. The military, of course, wanted to send in a team of some kind. Most likely heavily armed and ready to shoot anything that moved. Eventually they settled on a mix. It would be a small team, out of necessity for stealth. It would include a highly trained monk. Winston was chosen because of his knowledge of the area and his proficiency in the healing arts. There would be a four man military detachment, and one scientist along to record and analyze anything the others couldn't figure out.

At the same time scouts had been sent out to find the other door. If the scrolls were correct each world had two doors: one coming in, and one going out. Each door connected to a different world. The scrolls weren't clear on why this was, or even how this worked, but if there was a threat from one direction there might be a threat from the other. Then there was the question of what came through the door in the desert. It had been at night and none of the witnesses were able to describe it well at all, but from the few descriptions it couldn't be good.

They had posted guards at the door they knew about and watched as the small group of six disappeared through a hole in the air that a few months ago they all would have sworn couldn't exist. Then they waited. A week went by, then a month, then two. Finally during a random check they opened the door and saw Winston running toward them. Behind him a living darkness seemed to flow and ripple. In Winston's hand he held a staff that none of them had seen before and at random intervals he would point the staff back at the darkness and a shaft of light would push it back for a moment.

All this Rupert had read in the written summary. None of the others had survived. When asked what had happened all he would do was shake his head and say they all deserved to be remembered.

He told of a world devoid of life. Sucked dry by the evil that now inhabited it. Small pockets of resistance held out, some stronger than others. He had seen beings of great power and light, but they were vastly outnumbered by the darkness. Finally, he told them the darkness had started fighting among itself and devouring those too small to fight back. He believed it was one of these little ones that had been able to sneak its way through the door and was now loose in their world. Rupert had read through the report as the record keeper for his order. He had read tales of monsters big and small.

"So," James looked over at him, "I still have no idea what's going on."

Rupert sighed and brought himself back from thoughts of home, "To put it simply there are doors that lead from one world to the next. My people only know of three worlds so far. The one before mine, mine, and yours are the only ones we have actually had any contact with."

"Doors? Now I know you said you were taking me to a door to prove your point, but I thought you really meant there would be a house attached to it." James looked down and saw that they were going to need to stop for gas when they reached Wasilla, "What exactly do you mean by doors?"

"Well," Rupert thought for a moment, "picture an old wooden door about six and a half feet tall and about three feet wide. It has a knob on the left side and opens toward you."

"Right," James looked at him to see if he was making a bad joke again, "I know what a door is, but what do you mean by doors between worlds? Is it in some kind of temple?"

"Wouldn't that solve a lot of problems?" Rupert shook his head, "There was literally only one person on our world that actually believed in the existence of the doors. We all thought he was a little eccentric, or a little crazy depending on how worked up about the subject he got."

"Really," James said slowly, "I guess I don't see what's so hard to believe about doors connecting other worlds together."

Rupert chuckled, "Well, I see your sense of humor is still intact. That's a good sign."

"I would call it more a cynical sense of sarcasm." James looked out the window at the Knik River wondering for a second if he would see a moose today. "It's my defense mechanism. When I get into a conversation that I can't quite handle I start getting sarcastic."

"I totally understand. I unfortunately deal with stress in a much more physical way and can't breathe well. Anyway, the fact that the doors lead to other worlds isn't the real kicker. What would make your keen sense of cynical sarcasm kick in even more?"

"Let me think," James paused long enough to make sure that he was taking the left side of the split that led to either Palmer or Wasilla, "I guess the only thing that could make it an even better story was if it was invisible."

"Exactly."

James chuckled, "You mean to tell me that these doors are invisible?"

"Exactly, but not only that, they are connected to nothing. They are free standing, and can be anywhere in the world. So far the only ones we have found seem to show that they are in remote locations that once had large civilizations around them."

James looked out the window, "A large civilization huh. Before we got here the largest civilization was a group of Native Alaskans that, in this area, didn't number more than a few thousand."

"Yes, and our door was found in the middle of a desert that hasn't seen more than half an inch of rain a year for the past ten thousand years. The fact is there are some things that suggest the doors were put there by someone, and at the time they were the centerpiece to a large civilization."

"Okay, so let me get this straight," James changed lanes so that he could stop at the gas station that was just past the Welcome to the Home of the Iditarod sign, "there are invisible doors that lead between worlds." He nodded to himself, "Sure, I guess I can handle that. It's not so bad. That's what you're taking me to see, or not see since they're invisible."

"Right, but you can touch it and even poke your head through and see my world."

"Okay. So why don't the crazy, what did you call them, agents of chaos just open the door and come on through. Oh, and just so you know the term agents of chaos sounds a little like an old Edger Rice Burroughs story."

"Who?"

"He wrote story's back in the, well back about fifty years ago and they all sounded like the daring tale of James versus the agents of chaos."

Rupert nodded with a half smile, "It does sound a bit melodramatic, but I really didn't know how else to put it. It is what it is. I guess if you wanted me to water it down a little bit I could call them the maladjusted workers union for less order." James turned on his blinker and pulled into the gas station. Rupert looked around and asked, "Why are we stopping?"

"Well, the car can't get us there on crazy stories alone. I need to put some gas in it."

"No you don't." Rupert said, "We need to get there as fast as possible."

"Well, you see," James looked down at the fuel gauge and was only slightly surprised to see that it read full.

"I see what?"

James pulled through the line of gas pumps and back out onto the road through Wasilla and on to Big Lake, "Nothing your little magic tricks can't handle I guess."

Shrugging, Rupert said, "Normally things like that aren't allowed but under the circumstances I think I should be given a little leeway."

"Sure, sure, I won't tell anybody that you filled up my car without even a blink if you don't."

"Some might say this is not a situation for sarcasm, but I understand where you're coming from James."

James raised one eyebrow but continued to look straight ahead, "Do you really?"

Rupert sighed, "Think about it. If you find this all hard to believe, then just think of my position. If what I'm telling you is true, then I'm in a completely foreign world trying to convince people there are invisible doors leading to their world and evil black wispy things might come through and tell you to do bad stuff. Oh, and if you listen to them, they'll eat your soul."

Glancing over at him James wondered why they sent Rupert. Even the name Rupert wasn't exactly one to instill a sense of either fear in enemies or confidence in allies. The man was on the short side, decidedly pudgy, his mom would call him roly-poly, or maybe husky to be polite. He was mostly bald and then there was the breathing thing. You could honestly hear him breathe. It reminded James of a chubby little Darth Vader. The only thing that was missing was a pair of thick glasses. "Why did they send you?"

"I've been thinking the same thing myself for the past thirty four days."

"You've been keeping track?"

"Oh, yes." Looking out the window at little shops Rupert asked, "How much longer do we have?"

"Maybe twenty minutes."

"Hm. Anyway, back to your original question about why the bad things didn't just open the door and come on through. There is only a knob on one side of the door. That fact wasn't known before we sent an expedition through the door we found in the desert. We waited for them to come back and never realized they couldn't come back without us opening the door from our side. Because of that almost the entire team died on the other side of the door. Only a monk named Winston survived to tell of it. A lot of speculation went on after that fact was realized. Why would there only be one way through? Some thought it was designed that way to keep whatever was on the other side trapped there. Others asked why build the doors in the first place if you wanted to keep something trapped why not just seal them up, or not build them at all. The short of it is each world has two doors. One you can open, we call that going down, and one you can't open, we call that going up. The terms I've heard people use here are heaven and hell. You can get yourself to hell all you have to do is open the wrong door, but to get to heaven someone from the other side has to open the door for you."

"So how did you get here? If what I am hearing is correct, the door in your world with a knob opened into that place where your team all got killed, so that means the door from your world to mine didn't have a knob on your side."

"Correct. How we found the door is what led us to decide to send someone here to warn you. Something slipped through the hell door when we opened it. We were able to catch up to it just as it slipped through the door into your world."

"That still doesn't answer the question of how it got opened."

"We don't know. It was open when we found it. The thing we followed most likely tried to close the door behind itself but was too weak to do so. Once we realized your world was very populated we left someone there to keep the door open and called a council meeting to decide what to do about it." James took a left turn at a large fireworks stand that had an inflated gorilla outside of it. "The council decided the best course of action would be to start by sending a negotiator to try and convince the people of your world they were being threatened. I volunteered."

James looked sideways at his passenger, "Why would you do that?"

Shrugging Rupert answered, "It sounded exciting at the time. I thought all I would have to do was announce I was from another world and I had grave tidings about a common enemy." He looked out the window and realized he was starting to recognize the area he had wandered around in thirty days earlier looking for someone to talk with. "I didn't count on a few things however."

"Oh really," James arched one eyebrow in what he thought was a good imitation of Spock from Star Trek until he realized Rupert would have no idea who that was or what Star Trek was.

"Yes, really. I didn't count on the thing getting help so quickly from the local population, and I didn't count on the rest of your world being so skeptical." He put his elbows on the dashboard and rested his chin in his hands. "If I had thought about it a little more I would have realized at least the skeptical part before I came through, and I would have rehearsed my story a little better. The first five people I came into contact with thought I was a loon. The next two offered me spare money they had in their pockets and said they were sorry for what happened to me in a place called Viet Nam." James laughed in spite of himself, and Rupert looked over. "Where is this Viet Nam?"

"It's a country that my country went to war with about thirty years ago."

"Why would they think I was in a war thirty years ago?"

James shook his head and thought that if Rupert were making this all up he was really good at it, "It's a long story, and you would have to understand a lot about our culture and our nation to get why they asked and to get why I think it's funny."

"This is exactly my point." Said Rupert sitting back in his chair, "For me to understand one thing would take more explaining than you would want to do, and yet you want me to explain the nature of all kinds of crazy things in the space of one car ride."

"All right. Point taken." James swerved slightly into the oncoming lane to see if he could pass the minivan that was going thirty-four miles per hour in a fifty zone. He needed a lot of empty space to get his metro up to passing speed. He worried sometimes about killing the hamsters that must be running so hard in the engine compartment. He turned his blinker on and floored his gas pedal. The RPMs jumped and his car did what James referred to as a slightly fast saunter. As he was slowly gaining ground on fifty miles per hour he said, "So, for now I'll take your word on the invisible door thing. At least until we can get there and you can show it to me, or whatever, since it's invisible."

"Thank you very much." Rupert took as deep of a breath as it seemed he was able, "You have no idea how happy that makes me."

"Now, on the other hand," James pulled back into the right hand lane, "What is the big deal with the bad guys? At first you said that if you explained the whole thing to me I would freak out and not want to help you at all. Now you are talking about them like they are wisps of smoke that just tell you to do bad things every once in a while. So which is it?"

"Again, it is hard to explain."

"Well, before you start, could you tell me where to go from here?" James looked over at Rupert, "This is as far as you explained it to me."

"Give me just a moment." Rupert closed his eyes, took a few breaths, and then asked, "Do you see anything?"

"If you would tell me what I'm looking for I might be able to tell you."

"It should be glowing red."

James slowed down a little and started looking for a red neon sign or something like that then with a small jump in his stomach realized that there was a glowing red line on the road that hadn't been there before. "Well," he blinked a few times, "that is definitely weird."

"So you do see something?"

"Ya, you could say that." In the now pitch black of the Alaskan night the red line glowed like a road sign to hell.

Rupert opened his eyes and looked down the road. He smiled and looked back over at James, "That's great. I'd never done that before, but as my teacher said 'all you need is to believe and it will be granted to you'."

"Right." James wondered how much more if this he could take. He was fairly proud of himself for being able to take things in stride and let a lot just roll off his back. Most things you couldn't do anything about anyway and he decided not to let those bother him. He'd come to a realization a while back that the only thing you could really deal with was yourself. You might not be able to change the circumstances, but you can change how you react to them or deal with them. On the other hand, he had never had someone pulling glowing red lines out of thin air before. How was he supposed to deal with that? So he just sighed and thought, well it can't get much stranger. "So I should just follow the glowing red line then?"

"Yes. My memory of the area around here is not that great, but the line will show you where to turn." At those words James noticed the line taking a right hand turn at an old gas station, so he turned on his blinker and made a right.

James shook his head, "Well, back to what we were talking about before the, uh, glowing line appeared. By the way, can anyone else see it?"

"Well," Rupert looked confused for a second, and then looked out the back window, "no, no one else can see it."

"Okay." James wondered if the very non-wizardly looking wizard beside him really had any idea what he was doing. "Have you ever done this before? I don't mean the red line thing. I mean fighting the bad guys thing?"

"No. That's why I needed help."

"Well, why didn't you just go back through the door and get some of your buddies to come and help you?"

"I kept thinking I could get the job done and it really wasn't all that dangerous, it was just frustrating because no one would listen to me much less believe in me. Not even the priest that took me in would believe me. He was nice, but any time I tried to talk about invisible doors he just would smile and say he had some work to do, then he would ask me if I needed a ride to the bus station to look for a job." Rupert looked out the window at the glowing red line stretching out in front of them for a second. "Then the attacks started." He looked down at himself and thought with a sigh just how unprepared he had been to face any kind of confrontation. "At first they were little things I thought were just accidents or a coincidence. Things falling and almost killing me. A car blew a tire and almost ran me over while I was standing at the bus stop.

"When those didn't work it started getting more confrontational. Random people would suddenly turn and attack me." He shook his head and stared for a moment at the red line stretching out in front of them. It reminded him of what he had done that day to inadvertently start the worst confrontation. It had started with a red marker as well.

He had been walking across what the people in this world called a university. It was nothing like the stone halls and silence of his university back home, but this was a different world after all. He was just glad that enough things had been the same for him to even communicate. The language had been the hardest part but again all it took was a little belief. He was wondering why so many students were gathering out on the grass in an open space when his thoughts had been interrupted by something hitting him in the back. He had to admit that he didn't exactly have animal-like reflexes so he was a little slow to turn around, but when he did all he found was a red marker lying on the ground at his feet. When he looked up, a young lady with flaming red hair was running up to him, "I am so sorry sir." She knelt down and picked up the marker, "I was trying to throw it to my friend over there and I guess I just don't have a good aim."

He smiled his best smile, "It's all right." He didn't get many chances to make good impressions on people here, "No harm done." He extended his hand, "My name's Rupert Mundovi."

She smiled back and shook his hand, "Mine's Katie."

"Well Katie I was wondering why all these students were out here in this decidedly cold weather?" He was slipping back into what his friends called his negotiator voice, "and why you would be throwing red markers across the lawn at your friends."

She smiled and said, "I'm glad it didn't hurt you." Then she pointed around the stretch of grass at students on their knees writing on poster board, "We're making signs for a march that we are going to have tomorrow. If you would like to stay, the professor that organized the march will be giving a lecture out here on the grass in a few minutes."

"Wonderful." He looked around at all the young adults taking a hand in their community and it gave him hope for this world, "What is the march going to be about, if you don't mind me asking?"

"Well," she stepped back and held up her poster for him to see. It was a rainbow with flowers in the corner of the poster. In the center drawn in large puffy letters was the word tolerance.

"Ah." Rupert had to stop and think for a second. That word could mean many things to many people. As a negotiator it could stand for how much latitude you had with the person you were dealing with. As a parent it could mean how much you were willing to put up with from your children before they got into trouble. He assumed though that since they were going to be marching with this idea through the middle of town that she was talking about tolerance on a societal level, about how people in general interacted with each other, the idea of not killing someone simply because they bumped into you by accident. "That is a very noble and worthy cause to be marching for." He almost cringed because he was starting to sound old.

"Well thank you." She gave him another smile, "I hope you can stay for the lecture."

"I believe I will." He smiled back at her then turned to see where he could get a good vantage point for this lecture on tolerance. It made him wonder again what they would be talking about. The word tolerance itself immediately begged the question of tolerance to what? He wondered how this professor would answer that question.

He asked around a little about where the speech would be given from until he found a good spot that was out of the way and yet close enough to hear what would be said. After a few minutes he noticed a few what he assumed were students running some black cords out from a building then hooking them up to various boxes and poles. He really didn't understand what they were doing but it seemed that everyone around him took it as a sign that the lecture was about to begin. Eventually a young man with shaggy brown hair stood up and walked to the pole thing that Rupert had watched them set up. He tapped the end of it and Rupert was surprised to hear the sound amplified and coming from the black boxes around the area. So that was what they were for, he thought. It was a different world indeed. The young man adjusted the height of the pole then covered the end of it to say something to another person close by him. There was a few seconds pause until a dark green heavy shirt was thrown to the young man. He caught it, leaned toward the pole, and said, "I hope you all brought something warm to put on because if you hadn't noticed it is Alaska and it tends to get a little chilly when the sun goes down." He pulled it on over his head and Rupert noticed that in the middle of it was a blue circle with the words Alaska Grown in the middle. This must mean something important Rupert thought, or it was just regional pride of some sort. Like kids from his hometown insisting that he wore that floppy red hat every time he came home.

Once the young man had gotten himself straightened out he pulled the end of the pole off and spoke into it, "I would like to thank everyone that came out today to help prepare for the march tomorrow." He paused for some scattered applause, "I would especially like to thank Don Chon and Katie Lynn for organizing tonight and for getting all the paperwork done so the march can legally happen." He paused to look out over the crowd, "I know they were both here. Anybody know where they are?" There was some yelling that came from the far left of the grassy area and Rupert saw the redheaded young lady who hit him with the marker was being pushed up to the front along with a dark haired young man. Once they reached the front the young man that had been speaking said, "Let's give them all a big round of applause." He turned to the two of them, "We were going to get you two a present but to be truthful none of us has any money." Everyone seemed to find that amusing and while they were laughing the two disappeared back into the crowd.

"Now for the main event." The young man paused and waited for people to settle in and for the general noise to die down. "We were going to have the head of the philosophy department wrestle the head of the science department here tonight but we couldn't keep the mud from freezing so we decided to have professor Merrill come and talk for a while." He paused for a second then added, "It should be just as exciting as watching frozen mud." Everyone erupted into laughter again and the young man handed the device off to an older gentleman.

He was not imposing in any way. He stood about five foot seven and looked like he was somewhere between in shape and out of shape. He had a thick head of gray hair parted over his left eye and deep age lines around his eyes and the corners of his mouth. Tonight he was wearing a dark green sweatshirt with UAA in yellow lettering on the front and a pair of khaki colored Dockers. "I'm glad you set up a microphone because that frozen mud can really interfere with your voice after a while." He waited for the mild laughter to die down then continued, "Tonight I'm going to be talking about magic." He raised his left hand and a blue light seemed to hover directly above it. There were some ohhs and ahhs from the crowd of university students, and some comments from around the grassy area. He closed his hand and the light disappeared to be replace by a green light when he opened his hand again. It too vanished and was replaced by a red light when he closed and opened his hand once again.

"Magic, as we know it today, is the art of perception. What you see is what you believe, and the more you believe it the more likely you are to see it. Children see magic everywhere because they are the most likely to believe that magic exists. Adults shake their heads and try to find a," he made quote marks in the air with his fingers, "reasonable explanation for it all." He walked up to a student sitting on the grass about ten feet from Rupert, reached out to the student, and pulled a coin from his ear. "Now to the observer, with a little suspension of disbelief, it looks like there must have been a quarter inside Danny's head, but to the magician the quarter was never in his head it was in his hand the whole time. Perception of the event leads to a person's view of the truth. To a young child," he walked over to another student, reached out and pinched her nose, "when you do that you can run around and say you just stole their nose. They believe it." He paused and looked around the audience, "Just like some of you believe getting a diet Pepsi with your Big Mac means you're eating health food.

"Tolerance goes hand in hand with perception. Should you call the child an idiot and ground him for a week because he believes you stole his nose? Should you make fun of someone because they truly believe something is true when you think it is not? The answer to both of these is no. Why? Because their perception is different than yours. What they saw and what you saw could be two completely different things. Maybe you saw the reflection of something and they saw the shadow of it. One of you thinks it was a horse, the other thinks it was a moose. Should you degrade that person and ostracize them because of their perception of the truth?"

Rupert could feel a pressure building in the air and stopped watching the speaker for a moment. Looking around he was almost sure he could see the shadows moving contrary to the light. Squinting his eyes and focusing he realized that he couldn't see through the shadows.

The Professor started pacing in front of the seated students, "Our world today is full of people drawing arbitrary lines in the sand only to watch the waves of time come in and wash those lines away. We have religious and political groups saying there is black and white and if you don't see it like they do then you are ostracized and you are the enemy." He pointed randomly into the crowd, "Will you make it into their version of heaven? Only if you see the world the way they do. If you see it differently then off to burning hell you go."

The pressure in the air continued to build and Rupert could feel more than hear whispers at the edge of his senses. He shook his head and felt the whispers slide over him like oil. His training allowed him to acknowledge them yet ignore them at the same time.

The professor pointed behind himself as if there was another audience behind him, "Tolerance begs them," he emphasized the word them as if it was a swear word, "to open their minds and admit they could be wrong. Admit they don't know everything, and they don't have all the answers. Admit there is no black and white, no right and wrong. We must be willing to tolerate all people's perceptions of the truth."

When he paused to take a breath a student stood up and raised his hand. Professor Merrill smiled, "Well, thank you for raising your hand, but before you ask a question you must introduce yourself to the crowd."

The student smiled, turned to the majority of the crowd seated on the grass, "First, I just have to say doing anything to promote peace in our world is a wonderful cause and I think you're all doing a great thing by giving up your free time tomorrow to do that." A round of applause broke out through the group. He waved at the group and said, "Hello everyone, my name is Sam."

With almost one voice the mass of students answered back with, "Hello, Sam."

Sam waited for the general nose to die down after that then turned back to the professor, "Now that I feel like I've introduced myself at an AA meeting my question is this." Sam paused to collect his thoughts then continued, "Actually I would like to start with a statement and then follow up with a question if you don't mind?"

The professor smiled indulgently and Rupert thought he saw the shadows of pointed teeth in his smile as the professor said, "No, I don't mind at all."

"Thank you." Sam paused again, "You started off by talking about magic, and perception of the event. My statement is that no matter what your perception there is still a single true thing that happened. Danny didn't really have a quarter in his head, and I would feel confident telling someone that believed he did they were wrong." He shook his head, "That was a very convoluted statement. Let me see if I can put it a little better." He paused to think again, "The magician knows what he is actually doing. Just because the crowd sees it differently doesn't mean the crowd is right. It just means they haven't learned the truth yet." He took a deep breath, "So using your metaphor of magic there really is a true and a false. My question then is do you really think there is no such thing as right or wrong?"

The professor smiled and this time the shadows around him seemed to slide out into the audience. Rupert looked around to see if the students noticed but they were transfixed by the encounter. Through his oily shadow filled smile the professor said, "I would like you to know you actually did very well in stating your question." Sam smiled back at him, not seeing the blackness stretch towards him. It was good for him to hear he had done well. The professor continued, "As to the case of right and wrong I think each person's situation determines what can be construed as right or wrong. Also those ideas can be fostered by different societies. We could go into hours of talking about how the early settlers in America saw some things as wrong which we think are perfectly fine today. Your point about the magician is a good one. There is a reality, but whether it matters or not is where you're wrong."

"But that's my point sir," Sam interrupted, "I apologize for interrupting but what you just said really is important." Sam bit his lower lip and absentmindedly waved his hand in front of his face. The darkness reaching out toward him from the professor seemed to dissipate for a moment then he said, "You just said I was wrong. How could I be wrong if there was no such thing as right?" He turned to the students, "Tolerance means putting up with something or someone you believe to be wrong. If they were right and you were wrong they would be tolerating you not the other way around. Should we be tolerant of people that are wrong? Yes. Should a math teacher be tolerant of a student that says two plus two is twenty-two? Yes. But that math teacher should also correct the student and say the answer was wrong, not just pat the student on the head and say nice try now go and play." Sam took a deep breath and continued talking before anyone could interrupt him, "I know I was raised differently than some of you, and I'm not going to talk about religion, but I do think some things are always right and some things are always wrong."

When he had finally stopped he turned back to professor Merrill who was shaking his head. "This is what we have to be vigilant about. I'm sorry Sam but some of what you said," professor Merrill shook his head and pushed his hands out toward Sam and the seated students. Rupert watched the darkness flow from his hands. The pressure was almost unbearable now with the whispers pressing in painfully. Shaking his head he heard the professor continue, "Your brand of tolerance simply tells people they're wrong. How is that being tolerant? Why not just tell them they're wrong and you're right and get it over with. So tell me Sam, what do you think is wrong and what is right since you know."

Sam looked flustered and again tried to brush away the darkness that he could feel around him but this time the darkness stayed. He answered anyway, "I don't claim to know all the things that are right and wrong, but I do know that I do things that are wrong sometimes. Like lying to my parents, or stealing candy from the store when I was little, and I know, before you say anything, that any of you could think of a time in the world when both of those things were right and not wrong. But tell me a time when rape is right. Tell me a time when helping a friend up who has fallen down is wrong."

"But don't you see Sam?" Professor Merrill said, "If you let those things go to their logical conclusion then all you get is intolerance. If you start by saying these things are always wrong and you condemn the people that do them without even knowing why they did it the only end result is intolerance." Now the professor turned to the crowd of students, "It starts with his ideas of right and wrong and his tolerating those people that are wrong by correcting them so that they are right."

A voice from the back of the crowd yelled, "My brother's gay! Do you hate him because he's wrong?"

Sam tried to see where the statement had come from but the sun had gone down long ago and the building lights didn't shine in that area, "Look. I never said I hated anyone."

Another voice called out, "That is where it leads Sam. As soon as they refuse to see things your way you stop tolerating them and they become the enemy."

Sam felt something hit him on his right shoulder and turned to see an empty water bottle on the ground. "You need to leave, Sam." Another empty water bottle hit him on the leg, and then another one hit him in the back. Finally when one missed his head by a few inches he reached down and grabbed his backpack, "Fine," he looked at them all, "I see how tolerant you all are of different points of view." Sam walked into the darkness of the cold Alaska night.

Everything was silent. Then someone started clapping. When the students looked around to see who it was they found themselves looking back up at Professor Merrill. "Very good." He clapped some more, "This is the attitude that we need to go into tomorrow's march with. We need to be ready to fight off intolerance by whatever means necessary."

Rupert heard some cheer, some clap, and others just started talking amongst each other, but throughout all of it he couldn't shake the feeling he had gotten when he had seen the look on the professor's face when the first bottle was thrown. Professor Merrill had been smiling but the smile had sent shivers up and down Rupert's spine.

He hadn't been present when the door had been opened the first time and the creature had gotten through, but from what those present had told him, that was the feeling. Along with panic and a sense of abject terror, but that was beside the point. He walked around the ring of students watching as they broke off into groups of twos and threes to disappear into the lights of school buildings or the darkness of the Alaskan night. He was looking for Sam. The boy's last statement as he had left the gathering had struck him and he wanted desperately to speak with him about it.

When he had come on this assignment he thought it would be obvious what he was facing. The reports by Winston from the other world were tales of stark differences and destruction. Rupert had come into this world expecting to find the people here fighting for their lives against some monster, and he would negotiate a treaty between his world and theirs to fight the monster together. What he had found was far different. He found that chaos can be patient, and everyone overlooks the small things until they've become so used to it that when it becomes dangerously large they're still willing to overlook it.

He was scanning the crowd when he felt a hand on his shoulder. "Excuse me, but you seem to be lost. Can I help you?"

Rupert had been looking into the lights of one of the nearby buildings and it took him a moment to focus on the figure in the darkness behind him. "I'm not lost." He smiled at the man, "I was actually looking for someone." He looked around to emphasize his point, "With all these students milling around here I completely lost him."

"Oh really? What's his name? I work here and maybe I can help you find him?"

"Well, that would be very helpful of you." Rupert extended his hand, "My name is Rupert Mundovi."

The man took his hand in a strong grip, "Well, Mr. Mundovi I am glad you came out for our gathering tonight. My name is Merrill, Oren Merrill, and I'm a professor here at the University of Alaska. Now who did you say you were looking for?"

Rupert inadvertently took a step back at the realization of whom it was that he was speaking to. He had a sudden sense of fear for the young man that had been brave enough to confront this very man in front of all his friends. He felt strangely protective of him and didn't want to give professor Merrill another reason to look him up tonight. "Oh, I didn't recognize you in the darkness. That was a very good speech you gave tonight."

"Well thank you."

Rupert continued speaking before Merrill could continue, "I was wondering if I could ask you a question?"

The professor smiled and nodded amiably, "Certainly."

"What is the end result of tolerance?"

The professor looked a little taken back by the simple question, "Why, peace of course."

"Of course." Rupert nodded, "But just imagine for a second the world you're postulating."

"I imagine that world everyday, and wish it would get here sooner."

This time it was Rupert's turn to smile and nod, "Don't we all, but think about it. A world in which there is no idea of right or wrong means we would have no reason or ability to punish anyone for committing a crime. In fact there would be no such thing as crime because you couldn't say what a person did was wrong."

Professor Merrill squinted at Rupert who was now standing half in the light of a building window and half in darkness, "I'm sorry but you didn't say who you were looking for?"

Rupert pressed on because he knew as a negotiator that a good way to get a person to tip their hand was to press them until they slipped, "In a world like that a person would kill his neighbor for a pair of shoes simply because he knew no one would be able to do anything about it."

Shaking his head Professor Merrill said, "If you are going to get belligerent I'm going to have to ask you to leave the campus."

Rupert snorted in disgust, "You wish for a world without accountability so that you can do what you wish when you wish." He decided to take the confrontation to the next level so he stepped forward, reached out, and pushed him, "I know who you are, and I know that all you are aiming for is…"

Before he could finish his sentence Merrill reached out and grabbed his shirt and pulled him into the darkness away from the protective light of the windows, "I don't know what you're trying to pull but I will call security and they will arrest you."

With nothing more than a thought Rupert Mundovi, trained monk of the order of Saris, reached into the mind of Oren Merrill. Rupert's order of monks had been founded by a visionary centuries before in order to learn to look into people and find the truth. Rupert's ability to do this is what made him such an exceptionally good negotiator. He had found that it was much easier to do this and get a true answer when the person was caught off guard or was upset and not able to hide their feelings as well as they normally would. In that moment when he saw behind the brown eyes of the professor all he saw was darkness. An explosive force struck him in the chest. Flying backward he landed hard on the grass.

For all that reaching into someone's mind was an amazing ability it pales in the light of being able to take a breath at the right time. Rupert's wind was knocked out of him and all he could do was lay on the ground and gasp for air as he watched Merrill walk toward him.

The professor knelt down next to him and Rupert felt a weight press down on his chest threatening to crush him. "Who are you, and where did you come from?" Rupert gasped for air and thought to himself that even if he was willing to talk he couldn't right now anyway. Merrill shook his head, "We knew someone would be coming, but I personally thought it would be a more," he shrugged his shoulders, "imposing person than you." He looked Rupert up and down then looked over his left shoulder into the darkness, "Maybe you're a decoy."

Rupert felt the weight on his chest lighten and for the first time in what seemed like an eternity he was able to take a breath. He steeled himself with the thought that he had been trained since he was five years old on how to lift objects. All he needed to do was believe. Professor Merrill rose ten feet into the air and was flung like a ragdoll into a grove of aspens. Rupert got up as quickly as possible and with short little gasps of air ran toward the lights.

James pulled the Geo to the left of the road to avoid a huge pothole in the now dirt road that the red line was leading them down. "Professor Merrill?" He looked over at Rupert and had a mix of thoughts zip through his mind, "Are you sure? I know Sam and he wouldn't hurt a fly, but I also don't think the professor is some evil monster hell bent on ravaging the planet and eating our souls."

Rupert frowned and looked out the window. He had had a sinking feeling James wouldn't believe him when he started telling the story, "How do you know?"

"Well first," they bounced hard over a rock James hadn't seen and cringed hoping this wouldn't kill has fragile little car, "first off Merrill has been teaching at that school since before I got there three years ago, so how could he be a monster that came through this door of yours a month ago?"

"He isn't the monster. It isn't strong enough yet to take physical form like that." At least he hoped it wasn't, "All I know is what I saw, and what he did." He stopped to take a deep breath, "Look if you want some kind of proof how's this?"

"How's what?" James said, looking over at him.

Rupert smiled and pointed back out the front window, "Look out the window."

James swung his head around quickly and felt his stomach sink thinking that they were about to hit a tree or something. What he saw was a far sight more troubling. The Geo was still going forward at the same rate of speed, but it was currently about ten feet off the ground. James clinched his teeth, took his foot slowly off the gas, and said, "Okay, well, I uh." He looked back over at Rupert and saw that he was grinning from ear to ear. "I see you're having fun with all this."

"Why yes, I am." Rupert pointed out the window, "I know to some people seeing is believing, and it seemed you were that way so I thought I would show you something to help you believe what I've been saying."

James nodded, "Sure, sure." He squeezed the steering wheel a few times just to make sure things were still real, "Now, uh, do you think you could put us back down?" Having a second thought he added quickly, "Softly, please? I don't want to find out if you can heal broken legs as easily as fixing flat tires."

They fell into silence as James drove past an old wooden sign with the words Camp Maranatha painted on it in white letters. James sighed and wondered if this was the church camp his friend had tried to talk him into helping at the year before. That memory made him chuckle to himself, not because it was funny or even all that pleasant, it was just that in contrast to what was happening right now it was down right hilarious.

How did he get here, he wondered. His car had just been floating ten feet off the ground. On the positive side it had saved him some gas money, and the road was a lot smoother if you weren't actually on it, but on the negative side his car had been floating ten feet off the ground. He silently nodded to himself, yep, things were getting perty weird. Old fashioned twilight zone kinda weird. His father had always told him to do the right thing no matter what. Up till now that had included things like opening the door for strangers. James knew helping Rupert had been the right thing, but what had he opened a door to this time?

How was he supposed to handle all this? I mean on the one hand he had a passenger in his car that could do crazy amazing things. That was real. That led him to believe the stories Rupert had been telling him. On the other hand, who would accuse a college philosophy professor of trying to destroy the world by having a tolerance march through downtown Anchorage Alaska? If you wanted people to fight with each other go to New York, or if you went to Iraq all you would have to do was throw a rock and the country would explode. I mean really, what the heck kinda stupid monster would try and start a war in Alaska?

Chapter Six

There was always a little bit of chitchat as people filed out of the long night class. Some of it invariably was about the lesson but most of it involved personal life. What were you going to do with so and so, or did you make call backs for the play? Of course like every college and university around the world one of the main past times, and conversation topics was on relationships. Before she had even made it to the lecture hall door Katie had fielded at least a dozen questions on her date with James. With most people she just stuck to generalities like yes we had a good time, and we went to Thunderbird falls for a picnic. Then she would have to say that they were right. He was thoughtful and romantic to set up a first date like that. With closer friends she went into a little more detail about how they had almost died in that freak accident and that he had saved her life. She even told one of her girlfriends that she was fairly sure she could fall in love with someone like him, and maybe even him. After that conversation she found herself standing alone for a second and thinking back, not so much on the date itself, but on James.

It wasn't his looks that grabbed her; there were guys that were better looking than he was. Not to say that he was bad looking because he was very cute. What grabbed her was his self-assurance. So many people around her were still trying to figure out who they were or what they were supposed to do with themselves, and James just didn't seem to worry about that. She really had no idea, now that she thought about it, if he knew what he wanted to do with himself, or even if he was comfortable with who he was, but it seemed that way. He projected this sense of calm. Like when they were hanging from that breaking deck and about to slip off to their death he still just smiled at her and she knew that it was all under control. She realized now that it most likely wasn't all under control at the time but that isn't what really mattered because he had made her think that it was all under control. That is what she liked about him.

True they had only gone on one date, but here on campus that really was only a formality. They had actually spent dozens of hours together. That had classes together, and that had led to study sessions with groups and alone. There were parties on the weekends that they had both gone to and he had walked her home from. So it wasn't like that was the first time they had ever spent any time together, but it was the first time he had kissed her. She smiled, that was another thing about him that she liked. He was old-fashioned romantic. Somewhere along the line his father had taught him how to actually be a gentleman rather than what guys seemed to think would pass for one these days.

When he had been walking her home from a party she was sure that he was going to kiss her. They were, after all, alone in the dark and flirting like crazy. It looked suspiciously like he was going to go for the kiss when they had stopped to talk under one of the lights along the path, but he stopped. When she had asked him about that night he said that he had made it a policy to focus on getting to know a girl's personality first rather than just getting to know if she was a good kisser or not. He had hastily thrown in that that she was a great kisser by the way. Then he had thrown in that she also had a great personality, in the actual personality sense of the word not in the guys talking about girl's body type of a way. Then, again, he had said that she had a good one of those too. After that he had sighed and asked if he was in trouble or should he just kiss her and make up for anything that he had said wrong. That had made her laugh so hard, but she had been looking for an excuse to kiss him again so she took it.

Thinking back on it, their first date had been a good one. Other than the whole almost dying a horrible death thing it had gone very well. She was really looking forward to breakfast with him the next morning. She wanted him to kiss her good morning, but she would wait and see what happened over their captain crunch.

She had just started to open the door to the lecture hall when a voice from behind her said, "Katie?" She turned to see who was trying to get her attention, and noticed the professor at the front of the class waving at her. She pointed at herself and he nodded. Wondering what he could want she started the long walk across the hall to the front of the room.

By the smile on his face she was hoping that it didn't have to do with her grades. She was one of the heads of the tolerance committee that he worked with, maybe it was about that. She smiled at him as she walked up and thought that as far as professors go he was a good one, and then because she had just been thinking about her relationship with James she wondered if the professor had anyone in his life. She glanced at his hands which were resting on the podium and didn't see a ring on any fingers, but in this day and age that really didn't mean much. She giggled to herself and thought that with his stance on tolerance of everything he might just be dating one of his students, but she was fairly sure that it was either illegal to do that or at least would get him fired. When he looked up at her and smiled right at the time she was thinking of him dating one of his students it made her throat tighten up and she had to force a smile. She looked around and realized that she was the only one in the room with him, and she really hoped that he wanted to talk about her grades now. Tolerance is one thing, she thought to herself, but you can take anything too far and that would be too far.

"I'm glad I caught you." He moved around from behind the podium, and Katie thought that was about the worst choice of words right now. "I wanted to talk with you about two things." He leaned over, picked up his briefcase, and started digging through it, "First was about the paper you turned in last week."

"Did I do something wrong?" She had hoped to talk about grades, but now she was worried that the talk might not be so good. She wasn't all that great at writing papers. She had asked Laura to edit it for her, but there hadn't been any time in their respective schedules to go over it so she had just had to turn it in.

"No, no." He looked up at her and smiled again. She noticed that he was smiling a lot lately. "There are just some grammatical mistakes that I think you could fix." He finally pulled out her paper and handed it to her. "You are close to getting an A in the class and I think that if you took some more time and went back over the paper that you would be able to get over that edge and into the A range. Now," he set his briefcase back down, "you don't need to go adjusting any of your ideas or your thesis; those were all great, it was really just your grammar. In fact your thesis on action was a refreshingly useful one. Usually in these papers all I get are hypothetical situations that no one can ever figure out, and that don't actually help the world do anything." He stopped and his brow wrinkled in thought, "Come to think of it that is the definition of most of philosophy, so it was good to hear your hands on what we can actually do with philosophy to make the world a better place paper."

This time she smiled, "Well, thank you. And thank you for giving me the chance to repair some of the damage that I'm sure I did to the English language."

They both laughed a little in the it wasn't funny but it was supposed to be, and the professor said, "There was one other thing that I was hoping you could help me with."

She nodded in what she hoped was a serious fashion, "What is it?"

"Well," he moved back around to the other side of the podium and looked down at what appeared to be a planner, "In light of your paper, and your commitment to the tolerance committee I was hoping you would be willing to put some action into another project along the same lines as the march that you helped to organize."

"Sure," then she thought about how much time she had put into organizing that march and added, "If I have time." Then she also thought about some of the people along the march route holding signs saying they were all going to hell.

"I know that there were some hard times with the march, and things got a little rough, but that's what I wanted to talk with you about. There's what can only be called a hate group that will be doing a march to counter ours in a few days and we need to do something to derail it." He looked from her to the window and out at the world, "If we can get the word out and make sure that as few people as possible show up for that march then, hopefully, they'll see their message of hate is not accepted here." He flipped through his day planner and continued, "What I was thinking was," just then the double doors at the other end of the room opened with a bang and three young men came striding into the room.

They walked directly up to the professor and the one in the lead said, "There's been a problem sir, and we thought you needed to know."

"Well," Professor Merrill looked flustered. He turned to her, "Katie, I'm sorry but I really need to talk with these guys." He glanced from them to her and said to her, "Do you have time to stop by my office tomorrow around noon?"

She thought about it, "I don't have a class then," she said, "so, sure, I can come by."

"Thank you so much." He smiled and escorted her a little ways toward the door. Just as she was about to leave he said, "Oh, and your paper is due back to me by our next class."

She smiled and nodded, "Right, it'll be spotless."

"Good, good," he said as she walked out the door. "Now, Scott," he turned to the three standing around his podium, "What seems to be such a problem? Since his girlfriend wasn't in tears tonight I assume you missed James again."

"He just gets lucky." Scott was not much different from the two others that stood with him. He was a little broader in the shoulders, a little taller, but other than that he was your typical university student. Shaggy brown hair topped his six foot frame and average brown eyes looked out at you from what could only be described as an average face. Truth to tell this was exactly why Merrill had chosen these three. No one would notice them in a crowd. If asked to describe them they would match the description of ninety percent of the student population. Scott had risen to the top because of better response time. While the others were still thinking about things, Scott was acting. So far he hadn't made any irreparable mistakes because of acting too hastily.

In fact the only mistake that had been made really hadn't been his fault. In other circumstances Scott would have been made an example of and dealt with harshly, but because of the delicacy of the current situation he needed to keep Scott around. Those thugs Scott had picked to help deal with the stranger who had shown up at the rally a few nights ago had been perfect for the job. They would have made it look like a mugging in a bad part of town. Three people had died in that part of town in the past few months anyway, and Merrill was fairly sure the stranger didn't have any normal forms of ID. Then James had to show up. University students were all a bunch of do-gooders wanting to change the world. Why couldn't they just be like their parents and sit back and not get involved? Now he had to kill him, and that would be tragic because he could really use Katie for his plans, but with James dead she would be of no use to anyone for a while.

Scott took one hand out of the pocket of his Levis, "That guy you had us go after in Mountain View was picked up by James about forty minutes ago. I just talked to someone that saw them leaving Barnes and Noble together."

Merrill sighed, "Do you have any idea where they were headed?"

Scott nodded, "Tommy took off after them figuring they would be headed down the Glenn highway. He caught up to them around the first Eagle River exit and phoned me to say that they blew right past it. He called again a second ago but the call was breaking up perty bad. It sounded like they were headed toward Wasilla."

Looking out the window Merrill wondered why these things always had to happen at night. He really did prefer doing things in the light of day. It really was one of the things he didn't like about Alaska. Here in Anchorage it wasn't so bad. This time of year he wouldn't see the sun until after his third class of the day. He could totally understand ancient cultures having crazy festivals at this time of the year. You needed something to break the darkness up. The only good thing about it right now was the darkness really would help him get some things done without a lot of prying eyes. The cold would help with that as well.

"So they're headed toward Wasilla." And most likely the door Merrill thought. He looked over at the three of them, "I'll take care of James from here. You all need to get to work on that anti-immigrant march you're supposed to be leading in a few days."

"Why are we wasting our time with this stuff?" The other two with Scott nodded agreement, "I mean what do competing marches have to do with anything? I think it would serve us better to just start shooting some people, or even better we could use this new stuff that we learned to crush some peoples windpipes."

"Oh yes," the professor nodded and took a few steps toward them, "I can see it now. Which one of you would like to dress up like Darth Vader?" He looked around at them, "Would it be you Scott?" Shaking his head he walked back over to his podium and started straightening the papers on it, "If only physical violence is used then the reaction will be the exact opposite of what we want." He looked up at them, "Just think back to September eleventh and the reaction people had to that. Did they fracture and start to fight with each other?" He waited until they shook their heads no, "Exactly, and what we want are riots in the streets. We want mass pandemonium. If we just cause some random violence, even if it is Darth Vader style violence they'll just pull together and become an even stronger group. What we need is to divide them first along lines that they think are uncrossable then start the violence."

"And us marching through the middle of Anchorage pretending that we hate immigrants is supposed to do that?"

One of the others with Scott raised his hand slightly, "I actually do hate immigrants."

"Oh," the professor shook his head, "Well, thank you for that Ryan." His voice fairly dripped with sarcasm. Turning back to Scott he said, "This is why I have a philosophy degree and you're majoring in forestry. We use tolerance, Scott, because it can be the ultimate in hypocrisy if used correctly. We say that there are no moral absolutes and people shouldn't get angry just because someone disagrees with you then we get angry with people who don't agree with that very moral statement. We teach people not to have a moral compass, and yet we write newspaper articles lambasting anyone who disagrees with our stance on tolerance. When a society has no moral compass except their own flawed sense of personal judgment and justice all that is left is exactly what we want, chaos. They will continue to get angrier and angrier because it seems that no one is listening to them, and why should they listen since they have their own idea of what is right and wrong. Everyone thinks that their idea should be tolerated, and they stand firm for that, while at the same time they get angry at the person who stands firm for their own moral ideal.

"The meeting the other night was a perfect example. Sam stood for his ideals and was shot down for it. That crowd showed no tolerance for his ideas while at the same time making posters that said to tolerate all people. That is exactly what we want because eventually those empty water bottles will turn to baseball bats, then to guns, and firebombs. So you see," he looked each of them directly in the eye, "they need to feel like they are being open minded, but to do that they need something to point at as being wrong." He chuckled to himself, "It is so circular sometimes that it makes me smile. They preach tolerance, and yet they won't tolerate you marching against immigrants. They preach the absence of a right and a wrong but their actions say that they think they are right and you are wrong. The absolute hypocrisy of it is what will cause them to collapse like a house of cards. When things really get bad they'll have no foundation, and they'll have alienated each other so that no one will want to help."

"Won't that take a long time?" Being twenty-one had made Scott a little impatient, plus the fact that he really couldn't handle any TV show that was longer than thirty minutes.

Merrill sighed, "Not as long as you might think." He dropped his papers into his briefcase, "Now, I have work to do, and so do you. Good night. Oh, and Scott, keep your cell phone on I might need you later tonight." He turned and walked out of the lecture hall. Flipping open his cell phone he knew he needed to make a very important call.

Chapter Seven

The Geo bumped to a stop on the dirt road. The red line they had been following turned right down a path into the woods about twenty yards back. They passed a church camp and turned right into the outskirts of nowhere. On one side of the dirt road there was a small lake, and on the other side was what Alaskans referred to as muskeg. It was a treeless landscape that was mostly plant matter about a foot thick. In the winter time the muskeg would freeze solid. Even in the summer the ground was still partially frozen beneath it. Engineers in the northern latitudes had needed to learn whole new ways of building because of the muskeg. If you dug it up the ground would thaw and it would all become a huge bog that could swallow tractors.

Back during World War Two the Alaskan Canadian highway had been built to get military supplies to Alaska. Alaska was under attack by Japan at the time. The road engineers had lost entire vehicles into the muskeg as it thawed. If you looked closely there were dozens of types of plants in a single square foot of it. In the summer it would bloom with all types of flowers and berries. Kids loved to play on it because it had a springy feel to it. In some places the muskeg would give up to six inches before bouncing back. In other parts of the United States a person would have to worry about poisonous snakes hiding in the thick plant growth, but here in Alaska there were no snakes. James always figured the lack of poisonous snakes was just God's way of balancing things out. That way when you were running from the largest bear in North America intent on turning you into a late summer snack you didn't have to worry as much about what hole you jumped into. On the other hand you did have to worry about moose trying to stomp you to death, and at least three different kinds of bears either trying to eat you or just trying to defend their babies. But all in all the lack of snakes was nice.

The headlights of the Geo struck a metal bar blocking the road ahead, but with the red line heading off into the woods by the lake it was just as well. James pulled the car up toward the bar and saw that beyond it the road ended at what people called a VFR station. He wasn't quite sure what that meant, but he knew the building with the weird cone thing coming out the top of it was definitely for airplanes. As he swung the car to the right to try and get enough room to back up and turn it around he thought he saw the door to the station standing open, but when he looked over his shoulder there wasn't enough light to see, and it didn't really matter right now anyway.

This was about the only time, he thought to himself, that having a car that could almost fit in your pocket was a good thing. There was no way a pickup truck could have turned around in this tight space. He would've hated to back the Geo up all the way to the church camp half a mile away just to turn around. The fact there were no lights out here, and the road was almost the same color as the muskeg, would have made for a very interesting ride.

Once the car was turned around he pulled it back up to the spot where the glowing red line now disappeared to the left into what he could only call a tunnel of death. Every Alaskan having lived here for a while had a certain sense of where was okay to go and where was not okay to go. Quite a few Alaskans, James had noticed, ignored this sense. Oh, they knew it was there, but this was Alaska they thought you were supposed to go charging into tunnels to see if a bear was sleeping there. This trail was giving him the creeps. Mainly because it was the exact kind of place moose mamas with their little babies like to bed down for the night and wait for stupid tourists to come by. The moose mama would of course use the situation as a teaching moment for the little ones and point out the best places to stomp on a tourist so they stayed alive the longest and felt the most pain.

James wished there was enough room to angle the car so the headlights would point down the path, but he couldn't without sinking his back tires into the muskeg. So instead he dug around under his seat and when he didn't find what he was feeling for he turned and leaned into the back seat.

"Uhm, excuse me."

James looked over his left shoulder at Rupert still sitting in the passenger seat, "What?"

"What exactly are you doing?"

Still digging around in them under the back seat James said, "You have noticed it's dark outside right?"

"Yes, what's your point?"

"Well, I don't know about you, but I can't see in the dark."

"Neither can I. That still doesn't answer my question as to what you are doing back there."

"I'm looking for my flashlight."

"Oh, right." There was a slight pause. "Your what?"

"Flashlight. You know."

"No, actually, I don't." James heard the car door open and a few seconds later a blue light flooded the back seat. "Does that help?"

James blinked in the now brightly lit back seat of his Geo and saw sticking out from under his emergency blanket the black handle of his flashlight. Whoever's idea it was to make something black that you would need to find in the dark should be shot James thought to himself. He shook his head because he hadn't thought it was strange when he looked up to see the light coming from Rupert's left hand. That's not so bad compared to having your Geo fly through the air with you in it. Maybe if it had been during the day it wouldn't have been so bad, but it had been really dark. James wondered if he could tell any of this to Katie without sounding like a complete loon.

He got out of the car and took a few moments to stretch because anyone with a Geo Metro knows that any trip longer than thirty minutes is going to require a trip to the chiropractor. Turning on his flashlight he aimed it at Rupert, "This is a flashlight."

"Oh," Rupert actually sounded impressed, "How does it work?"

James thought for a second about how to explain batteries, incandescent light bulbs, and possibly electricity to someone who could make his hands glow and decided it could wait for a better time, "I'll tell you on the way back."

"So I guess we don't need this," Rupert's hand went dark or, as James thought, back to normal.

"Actually," He looked at the red line leading off into the woods, "The more light the better." A moose wouldn't know the difference between a flashlight and someone's hand glowing an eerie blue color, but the more he could see the more comfortable he would be with the whole situation.

"Sure," Rupert raised his right hand this time and once again a blue light illuminated the Alaskan darkness. Rupert looked over at James and wondered at the young man. He was glad James had something of his own to illuminate this darkness. He knew it must be hard to be in such a strange situation. What was normal to him was not necessarily normal to James. He had learned over the last few weeks here that these people, and this world, did a lot more with machines than his world. He wasn't sure if it was from a lack of belief or if things had just taken a different path here. Either way he thought James was handling the situation very well considering everything that had happened over the last few hours.

Rupert started walking down the trail, and was glad he recognized the area. He had, after all, spent about a week just circling the door too nervous to go much farther than half an hour away.

He'd felt so confident stepping through the door into a new world until he remembered there wasn't a single city within a hundred miles of either of the doors on his planet. That had plucked a string on his nervous system for a few minutes after he crossed the threshold of the door, but once he had pulled his lunch out of the sack, and had a good drink of water he was fine.

"Slow down." Rupert was startled out of his thoughts. James put his hand on his left arm, "I don't know how you do," he gestured to Rupert's glowing right hand, "what you do, but I know there are animals out here that can hurt me so let's slow down a bit."

"Oh, right." Rupert didn't realize that he had been striding down the path like it was a sidewalk back home.

"So is it magic?"

"What?" Rupert stopped and looked over at James.

"You know," James looked warily into the dark beyond the reach of either his flashlight or Rupert's hand, "Making your hand glow, lifting my car off the ground, filling my gas tank, changing my tire."

"Oh, that." Rupert looked puzzled, "What's magic?"

James looked him in the eye to see if he was joking, "Well," he thought for a second, "maybe you have a different word for it."

"I doubt it," Rupert shrugged, "I'm not actually speaking your language, so I doubt there would be a mistranslation between us."

"You're not actually… what?"

Rupert sighed. In order to reach the level he had within his order he had to teach classes on different things to prove he knew them well enough. "Well," he paused and realized when he had been teaching the students there had shared a certain set of understandings they had all gained by growing up in the same world. What did James know to begin with? Where should he start? "Well," he paused again.

"Look, if you don't want to tell me that's fine."

"No, no, it's not that. I'm just trying to decide where to begin."

"Do you say certain words and things happen? Do you wave your hands around?" James pantomimed by waving his flashlight in a star pattern.

"Oh, no," Rupert smiled, "It's nothing like that." Rupert reached up and rubbed his balding head with his right hand. James just blinked and shook his head at the scene of a middle aged balding man rubbing his head thoughtfully with a hand that was glowing like it was about to go nuclear. Finally Rupert pointed to the sky, his hand glowing like some otherworldly beacon, "Do you believe the sun will come up tomorrow?"

James had no idea where this was going, "Ya." He said slowly.

"It's like that. Kind of." Rupert blinked a few times, "To put it in short form try to imagine a pool of power out there," and he waved his hand around in the air, "When the world was first created it was made available to people." He held up his hands, "Now don't ask why it was made available, or why it was put there in the first place because that conversation could take weeks."

James had to smile to himself because watching Rupert talk was like watching a child run around with a sparkler on the fourth of July. His glowing hand made patterns in the sky, and James was sure Rupert wasn't even aware of it. "All right, there's a pool of power, right next to the invisible door."

"Yes," Rupert smiled, then frowned, "No," He shook his head, "Now your just being sarcastic. Anyway, if you can focus on something and truly believe it will happen you can tap into that pool of power and make it happen."

"Right," James frowned, "I could stand here all night believing I could fly and nothing would happen."

"But you don't really believe it, do you? Not in the same way you believe the sun's going to come up tomorrow. You need true belief to make it happen." Rupert stepped toward him, "If you stood here all night you would still have a doubt in the back of your mind that you could really fly, because you've never done it before, and you've never seen anyone do it before. You might make yourself believe that theoretically it's true and theoretically it's possible but you wouldn't believe it," he reached out with his glowing hand and touched James on the chest, "in here. For it to work, and to be able to tap into the reservoir of power that's available you must believe it like you believe the sun is going to come up in the morning." He took two steps back, bent his knees, and jumped into the air. James watched, a little stunned, even after everything that had happened as Rupert floated in the air. With his hand glowing and his feet slightly tucked up under him James imagined Rupert as the slightly balding angel that always gets left out of the stories because everyone wants to picture angels as strong beautiful Abercrombie and Fitch models.

Rupert slowly came down and when his feet were firmly on the ground he pointed in the direction of the red line. "We should get going. It's getting late." He started walking again.

Jumping to catch up James said, "So you can do anything?"

"Well," Rupert looked over at him, "Within reason, and within the limits of your own mind."

"What does that mean?"

"If it's too complex for you to figure out in your own mind then you can't do it."

James thought about it for a second, "Like creating the universe."

Rupert laughed, "I most definitely can not create the universe. Actually, I don't think I can create anything." Rupert stopped walking, "James?"

James looked back at him over his left shoulder, "Wha…" his right shoulder struck something hard enough to knock him back two full steps, and drop his flashlight. "Ow," he rubbed his arm, "Why didn't you warn me?"

"Sorry."

"Right, that smile on your face tells me you're not."

Rupert continued smiling, "Well, if seeing is believing then running into it should help even more don't you think?"

"Running into it?" He looked around and saw nothing. The stars twinkled overhead. The aspens leafless arms made white skeletal patterns against the blue glow of Rupert's hand. He bent down and picked up his flashlight. Shining it in a circle he still didn't see anything.

Rupert walked past him with his hands extended in front of him. When he stopped he left his glowing right hand in the air and pointed with his left hand. "James I would like to introduce you to the invisible door that is not supposed to exist."

Tentatively extending his hand James felt his fingers touch a solid object. His palm flattened out on the surface of the door and he thought it felt wooden. He started to slide his hand toward where he thought the edge would be when something hit him. Pain blossomed up his left side and new stars appeared in his vision.

A cracking sound made him look up and he realized that he was lying on the ground watching a tree fall straight toward him. His first reaction was to roll and as his side pressed into the ground he felt one of his ribs move. Letting out a yelp of pain he felt the tree hit the ground where he used to be.

A blue white light appeared cutting off the stars and he heard a voice say, "Can you get up?" He raised his head and looked over to see Rupert kneeling, his hands raised in front of him palms out. Around them a wall of bluish white light glowed. It cut them off from the rest of the forest. Rupert looked at him, "Can you get up? Are you injured?"

"I," James sat up and clutched his hand to his side. It felt like a fire was spreading up the left side of his body and into his face. Breathing came hard, "I," he gasped, "I think I can."

As he pushed himself up off the ground he watched as in slow motion fingers came up through the ground. It was a hand made of dirt and rocks. Nothing like this had ever happened to James before and when he took a deep breath to yell at Rupert it caught in his throat as pain filled his body. Gasping for air he watched the hand grab Rupert's leg and yank.

Already kneeling, Rupert found himself falling forward. Something had grabbed him from behind. Rupert rolled to see a hand pulling him toward the lake. James watched as the fingers on the dirt hand started to open, but in that instant Rupert must have stopped thinking about the protective field and it vanished. The darkness that filled the void left by the glowing wall was almost absolute.

James was all but blind as he waited for his eyes to adjust. He had managed to get himself to a standing position and was looking around to see if Rupert was all right when he saw something out of the corner of his eye. When he turned he realized the red line that had guided them to the door was still glowing on the ground and there was someone standing over it. He watched as the person raised his hands. James didn't think he could dive out of the way of whatever was coming without killing himself so he started looking around for something to hide behind. He saw Rupert lift his right hand and wave it like he was trying to brush away a mosquito, and when James looked back his attacker was gone.

He stumbled over to Rupert and extended a hand to help him up. Behind him he heard a noise like a backhoe starting up and turned. A very large man was pulling a tree out of the ground. "Seriously?" James mumbled. When he was younger he had seen a show where a man had ripped a phonebook in half, but this was craziness. He looked over at Rupert expecting him to do something and to his horror saw the same look on Rupert's face he was sure was on his own.

Rupert looked at him then back at their attacker, "Duck!"

James looked back in time to see the tree swinging toward them like a baseball bat. Popping instantly through his mind was the thought that sometimes you're the bat and sometimes you're the ball. As he ducked he could only laugh at the stupidity of a cliché like that right before he died. He heard the tree hit and crack. Branches splintered and flew around him. When he didn't feel any pain his first thought was he might be dead, but when he took a breath and his side decided it was time to lay railroad spikes into his nervous system he knew he couldn't be dead.

"The door." Rupert mumbled.

James looked over and realized the tree had hit the door. Mr. big and ugly with the tree hadn't known where it was and they had been lucky enough to crouch behind it. He looked back over at Rupert and saw him close his eyes. Great, James thought, just the time for him to have a nervous breakdown. Or maybe his lungs had finally completely closed up on him. He glanced back wondering when another tree would come flying at them only to see the big guy being pushed sideways into the woods.

"Run for the car."

"What?" James gasped out the word.

Rupert looked over at him and James could see even in the darkness he was struggling for breath, "I'll hold him." He gulped down more air, "You run for the car."

"I'm not," the pain in his side stopped him for a moment, "not leaving you," again the pain shot up his side and caused his jaw to lock.

They both looked at each other unable to speak, and breathing like the world was going to run out of air. After what seemed like minutes James reached out and grabbed Rupert by the arm. Pulling him to his feet he reached out with his other hand to find where the door was. Too bad he wasn't going to get a chance to look through it, he thought. Even as he pulled him around the fallen tree James noticed Rupert never took his eyes off the spot in the woods where their assailant had been pushed.

They ran and stumbled their way back down the trail. James didn't remember it being this long. In the light of half a moon his white Geo Metro stood out like a glowing beacon of hope. As he struggled to get into the driver's seat he could only laugh at himself in the realization that he had just mentally referred to a Geo Metro as a glowing beacon of hope. He managed to get the key in the ignition and start the car. He waited until Rupert was in the passenger seat but decided that he didn't really need to wait for him to close his door. It was the only time in his life that he could remember spinning the tires on his little Metro.

The only thought in his mind as he slid the little car around the gravel corner and pointed the headlights at the church camp ahead was, come on baby you can go faster than this. He had just made a hard left turn with the lights of the camp glowing on his right when his headlights illuminated a huge pothole. He yanked the wheel hard to the left to avoid it but his right tire caught the edge and dropped into it. As the car jolted in and out of the hole James' side exploded in pain, then he watched the world in front of him shrink into a tiny gray dot and disappear.

In the darkness James felt himself floating. A warm breeze drifted over him with the smell of flowers. He found it amusing that he didn't know what the flowers were. Shouldn't a person at least know what flowers they were smelling in their own dream? He also wondered if he could imagine up some cute girls to take care of him. He looked around and still only saw darkness. Well this isn't a very interesting dream. He tried to move and found quite quickly that his side still hurt. Now that, he thought quite angrily, was just not fair. If you're going to pass out from pain the least your body could do was to let you have a dream without the pain in it. The breeze he'd first felt got stronger and in a weird horror movie kind of way it felt like it was going into his side. He tried to pull away from it but again realized that he couldn't go anywhere. He started to panic when he felt the breeze start to move things around inside of him. Now, he could find humor in most things but this was really starting to freak him out.

With a final tug in his side James flinched and sat up. With his breath coming in short gasps he opened his eyes and found himself looking directly at the trunk of a pine tree. "What," he felt around on his side with his hands, "just happened?"

"You passed out from your injuries." The voice came from behind him and to his left. Turning he saw Rupert kneeling and staring at him, "Are you all right now?"

"What?" James was still trying to process the change from total blackness to this.

"I have some training in healing, but not a lot. Do you feel all right?"

James realized two things simultaneously, first his side didn't hurt anymore, and second he was fairly sure he hadn't blinked since he had woken up. He took a deep breath to check his side and blinked a few times, "Ya," he looked over at Rupert, "I think it's fine now."

"Good, because I don't know how to operate the vehicle, and" he looked over his shoulder, "I think I hear them coming."

At that moment James realized he could hear crashing in the trees bordering the small lake. He jumped up and ran toward the car. Reaching for the handle he heard Rupert yell, "Get down!" Now, in his life James had been in a lot of situations where people would yell get down for various reasons. Playing hide and seek as a child. Out in the woods doing paintball games with his friends. Even playing video games online with the other guys in his dorm. However, in none of those situations did a real basketball sized ball of fire fly over his head and strike a tree, which then splintered in half and burst into flames.

"What the hell?!" James had been raised by his parents to think cursing was the sign of an uneducated mind, but right at that moment he was sure his father would forgive him. He looked through the windows of the car at Rupert and felt the need to say again, "What the hell?" With that he opened the door and realized he could start a stick shift while he was still getting into the car. A feat which he was sure had never been accomplished before, and he was sure he could never do again because later thinking back on it he had no idea how he had done it. He slammed the door shut and instantly felt a wave of heat and the car rock on its wheels.

Looking over, expecting to see Rupert climb into the car, he saw the portly man stand and walk around the rear of the car. With a determined look on his face and every breath wheezing like the little engine that could he raised both his hands. James felt the hair on his arms stand up and watched as most likely the coolest thing he had ever seen happened right before his eyes.

Blue light gathered around Rupert's hands and then with a crack two blinding bolts of lightning shot into the darkness of the woods. Since James had been looking directly at Rupert his vision now consisted of nothing but bright white streaks and blue spots. From the direction of the door he could hear trees cracking and smelled smoke. A banging sound next to his head caused him to flinch, and after blinking a few dozen times he could just make out the shape of Rupert through his driver's side window.

Running his left hand along his door until he found the crank for the window he tried rolling it down. After two revolutions it stuck. Rupert yelled through the window over the sound of crackling flames, "Go!"

"But what about..."

Rupert slapped the window with his palms, "Just go!" He looked over his shoulder into the woods, "I have to take care of these."

Finally able to see well enough to look past Rupert into the red glow of the woods, "What are they?"

Rupert looked back at him, his eyes wide, "I don't know." He turned and took a step toward the burning woods. James heard him say again, "I don't know." He said something else but it was lost in the appearance of another fireball.

Not knowing what else to do James shifted the car into gear and pressed the accelerator as far as it would go. After a few minutes and numerous turns he realized only one headlight was working. What happened to the other one? What if he got pulled over for only having one headlight working? Looking out the window at the single beam of light he started laughing out loud. He had just seen most likely the strangest thing in the history of man and he was worried about his headlights. But seriously, he thought to himself, what would he tell the police officer? Well, you see officer there was this fireball. No, sir, it wasn't the first fireball that knocked out my headlight. The first one missed me by a few feet and took out a tree. It was the second fireball that hit my car. Yes sir, that's right, a fireball. Oh, and then there was this guy throwing lightning. No sir, I haven't been drinking.

He turned left off Horseshoe Lake road and onto Big Lake road and wondered where he should go. He thought about going back to the campus, but possibly Rupert had been right about professor Mundovi. Even if he was behind all this there was a certain safety in numbers. What could he do to him with all those students around? Then he thought back to flying cars and balls of flame over his head. What couldn't he do? Could he just make his heart stop in the middle of class? Everyone would think he had a heart attack and never know what really happened.

He couldn't go and stay with anybody because other than his uncle all the people he knew up here lived in the dorms, and he definitely didn't want to get family involved in this. He got to the Parks highway that ran through Wasilla and turned right. He thought maybe he could get a hotel room in Wasilla and wait for a few days then head back to the door. If Rupert wasn't still there maybe he could go through to find help.

Driving through town he couldn't believe this was happening to him. He decided he needed to think for a second so he pulled off the road into the parking lot of a strip mall. He pulled the handle on his door and couldn't get it open the first try, so he pulled it again and pushed with his shoulder. The door popped open and he almost fell onto the pavement.

Once he had climbed out he looked back to assess the damage. The driver side door was dented and scorched, but with a little pushing or pulling it still worked. His driver side mirror was missing in action. The black plastic housing for it was slightly melted but still there, and for whatever reason his driver side headlight was busted out. Staring at his little car he realized he should apologize to it. He had constantly referred to it as a death trap on wheels figuring if he ever was in an accident it would just crumple like an old soda can. Looking at it now, however, he was almost stunned to think of all it had been through in such a short time. On the other hand there had been some magic involved. He had gotten a free tire change and tank of gas out of the whole thing.

It was hard to look on the bright side of a situation that he really knew nothing about. For all Rupert had told him he still didn't understand what was happening. He got the fact that someone was trying to kill him. James sat down on the pavement and marveled at the charred spot on the side of his car. Why people, or whatever they were, were trying to kill him was a different matter.

He wished he had someone to talk this out with, and he didn't mean Rupert. That guy just seemed to get him more confused than anything. What he wished for was that his brother was there. They hadn't talked in a while, but that didn't mean they weren't close. It was just that guys, especially guys from his family, weren't all that great at communicating. The nice thing about it was they all understood that fact. After three months of not talking to each other one could call and it would be like they had talked only yesterday. If a birthday card was a few days late, or in some cases a few months late that was no big deal because it was sure the other person would do the same thing someday, not on purpose mind you, it was just the way they were.

Since no one was there to talk to James fell back on the only thing he could do, he talked to himself. He figured he was smarter than your average bear, so figuring out why fire throwing philosophy spouting demons from another world were trying to kill him shouldn't be too hard.

So, self, why are people trying to kill me?

I got nothing.

Well, this is starting just great.

Hey, don't blame me. I was in the same places you were and I got nothing.

I guess for starters the question is should I take Rupert at his word?

The man just shot lightning out of his hands. I would lean toward believing him.

Good point, and as a side note that was really cool.

Yes, yes, now back on topic. If we take him at his word then what does that mean about why people are trying to kill us?

I know something I shouldn't?

Or, you know someone you shouldn't.

Right. All this started after I saved Rupert from being stomped into road pizza on Mountain View.

So maybe they think you saved him because you know him.

And if I know him then I know what they're trying to do.

Now we both know that in reality you know nothing.

Well, I do know Rupert, and I guess now I know some things.

But by and large you have no idea what's going on, you are ignorant, you are for all intents and purposes brain dead in this situation.

Hey now, let's not get rude here. You're my brain remember so if anyone is at fault here it's not me.

Oh sure, you were just along for the ride. Did you even consult me before you decided to play hero and rush into the middle of a gang with nothing but a can of bear spray?

Now be reasonable. It was the right thing to do, and if I had taken the time to think it all through he would have been dead before I could help him.

Yes, and then where would we be? Back at the dorm talking with Katie on the phone and looking forward to kissing her over a bowl of Captain Crunch. That would just be terrible wouldn't it?

Hey, again, I did the right thing. Someone needed help and I helped.

Fine, I'll concede this round to you. So what have we figured out so far?

I think it's all a big misunderstanding. They're trying to kill me because I saved Rupert which they think means I know something.

Which you don't.

Exactly.

At this point in the game not knowing something could be bad.

Yes. Like not knowing how to shoot lightning out of my hands.

That could come in handy.

So now that Rupert's gone, or at least not with me, do you think they'll leave me alone.

Oh please, be reasonable about this. Now that he's gone they'll focus on you thinking you're the only thing they have left stopping them.

Stopping them from doing what is the question.

Why, world domination of course.

Headlights swept over his eyes blinding him for a second as the sound of maniacal laughter died down in his head. Sometimes he wondered about his brain. He was fairly sure that if left to its own devices it would try to devour New York, but that was for a different mental breakdown. Right now he had a car pulling up to him to worry about.

Please don't be the police he thought as he stood up. All joking aside, he really didn't want to explain what had happened to his car, and why he was just sitting here in this parking lot.

The car stopped, and in the orange glow of the streetlights he knew it wasn't a police cruiser. Maybe it was just a nice person who lived around here wanting to know if he was okay, and if there was anything they could do to help. That would be nice. It would be a real change of pace to have someone offer to help him.

Three guys got out of the car and started walking toward him. He walked around the car to meet them so they wouldn't see the driver's side of his Geo. There would be fewer questions if they didn't see the burn marks. As they walked up to him he realized he recognized them from school, and from the gang on Mountain View that was going after Rupert.

One of them stepped to the front and said, "It's him." Then he turned to the other two, "See I told you I recognized that car, and you guys said I was crazy for stopping."

James tried harder to think of their names but could only remember Scott so instead he just said, "Hey, fancy meeting you all out here."

Scott said, "No kidding." He stuck out his hand, "I don't think I ever had a chance to explain to you what was going on the other night. I'm sure it looked worse than it actually was."

James shook his hand without thinking about it, "Right," he figured if he just played along things would go smoother, "I'm sure it wasn't what it seemed at all." He winced as he heard the sarcasm in his own voice.

"Look, James, it's all a little complicated." Scott smiled and looked around James at his car, "You having some problems?"

James involuntarily took a step back, "Um, ya, I was just having some car trouble, but I think it's fine now."

Scott smiled again and in the odd orange glow of the parking lot lights he looked like he had another face made of shadow layered over his own, "So, you fix cars by sitting on the ground next to them. That's a very Zen way to work on a car." His buddies laughed at his attempt at humor. "If you need a lift back to campus we would be glad to take you. We were heading back that way."

"No, no, it's fine now I'm sure. I was just thinking about some things is all."

The two guys behind Scott fanned out to each side of him, "It's really no trouble at all. In fact I think it would be in the best interest of everyone if you just came with us."

James turned to move around the car and was confronted by one of the other guys. He slowly turned the other direction and came to the slow realization that he was surrounded. He thought about fighting them. If he acted first he knew he could take one of them down fast, but the other two would beat the tar out of him before he could get into his car. "Sure," he smiled at them, "a ride would be nice."

They escorted him over to the car and let him into the back seat. As the car pulled out onto the road James looked out the back window and felt a little sad at leaving his brave little Geo Metro out there all alone. It had done a good job, and, he thought to himself as he leaned back in the seat, it got great gas mileage.

He looked down at his watch. Seeing the hands point to nine thirty he decided he would close his eyes for a while. He wasn't about to try and jump out of a moving car, and who knows, maybe he could clear up all this misconception and still make it to his breakfast date on time.

Chapter Eight

Rupert Mundovi had loved to hear tales of the great heroes of history when he was growing up. He and his cousins would get together and whack at each other with sticks, one group first being the evil Antillians and the other group being the noble Empire of the Sacred Flame. They would recreate great battles and hit each other with sticks. The Empire would always win of course.

That was the last time Rupert could remember fighting anyone, and as he tried his best to sneak through the woods surrounding the door he wished all they were throwing at him were sticks.

His cousins would always end up making fun of him because of how many times he would have to stop and rest. Sometimes he would run and tell his mom or an aunt, actually he wouldn't run and tell them it was more of a panting walk. He had never been good at physical activities, and that was one of the deciding factors in why he chose to enter the order.

He knew he was smart, and he also knew he had a knack for seeing peoples thoughts and intentions. He wondered now if that was the result of being teased so much. It was a type of defense mechanism to protect himself from the worst attacks. He'd never dreamed he'd be using that skill while trying to kill an unknown number of people on a strange world.

Thinking about it that way was almost too much. He had to narrow it down so he could focus. If they got close enough he could read their intentions. This gave him a slight edge in knowing where to turn, and when they were going to attack.

Looking right he strained to peer into the darkness. Faint orange light flickered through the wispy aspens from the fire that had started earlier. This was joined by what little light was filtering through the clouds from the half moon. Once your eyes adjusted there was enough light to see quite well. The only problem was in the fact that the light was inconsistent. In some places it was bright enough to blind your night vision, and in others there was no light at all.

Light, however, was not necessary to feel the malicious intentions of whoever was to his right. He knew he was not hard to track through these trees. Doing anything in the wilderness was another thing he'd done very little of before now, and it meant he really had no idea how to move through this without sounding like a bowling ball trying to quietly roll over a case of eggs.

He had learned quickly in the last half hour that if he waited for them to act it was too late, so rather than wait to see some new monstrosity come charging through the fire lit woods he thrust his palms toward his adversary. A hard ball of air the size of a dog ripped through the trees and smashed into the person about twenty yards away. When he didn't get back up Rupert realized he was smiling and mentally patting himself on the back. On the one hand he was proud of himself for holding his own against at least three opponents, but on the other hand he did feel a little bad about killing someone. Again, however, on yet another hand they were trying to kill him, and they had started it.

He was fairly sure there were only three of them, and with the one he'd just knocked down he thought that left only one. The first one had been cocky. Just standing in the open hurling fireballs at Rupert and James made him easy to kill. Thinking back on the stories he'd been told as a child he couldn't remember an overly cautious villain. It was the first time he'd ever summoned lightning. It was the first time he'd ever killed a man. This was a night of firsts. The lightning came almost without thinking. The fire had been flying by in great rippling lumps. Having only enough time to decide between defense and offense for once in his life he opted for offense. There was no mother to run to and tattle. There was no safe monastery where he could hide away from the evil in the world. He had gotten James involved in this and he would make sure that James was safe.

It was easy to believe that he could do it. He needed to do it. The lightning had felt warm on his fingertips, and he could remember the sound as if the world was breaking as it leapt from his hands. The brightness of it had seared onto his eyes and into his mind the image of a man flying backward with a hole burnt through him.

He was in shock when he realized James was still there. Sending James away hoping he would be safer as far from this madness as possible meant he was now alone. Fire had started to climb the trees around him, and for a time he had wandered through the woods without thought. Then he felt them.

Just like now. At the very edge of his senses he felt a presence. It was the last of the three. With all the noise he was making the person was headed right for him. They were too far away to do anything yet so he waited. He held his hands out as if he were holding a large pitcher. Focusing on the space between them he started gathering air and compressing it into a tight ball.

He could still hear his instructor telling the class to empty their minds. For a ten year old that was the most difficult part. His mind was always full of things. What had helped him most was a simple statement that sometimes it helped to focus on your breathing. For him that was all it took. He could feel his breath rattle around inside of him like it was a separate thing, some beast living inside of him. He focused on it, and in that breath rattling silence he formed a picture in his mind. The air was made of strings. He pulled them together and rolled them into a ball. There was no doubt in his ten-year-old mind that he could do this. There was only belief.

Opening his eyes he could feel the ball in his hands. It was solid as a rock. He pulled it back toward himself with his hands and with a shove threw it at the target the instructor had set up. A bush about three feet to the left of it exploded into a hail of fragments. The moth that had caught his eye at the last second had vanished in the destruction.

His instructor came over to him, smiled, and patted him on the back. He still remembered the lesson he had learned that day. Belief could make it real, but you had to focus to make it happen.

Among the flickering light of this other world he pulled the strings of air together. He faced his target and waited. The air grew hard in his hands. It was hot from the fire around him. In his mind he knew the next step would bring his attacker close enough. He focused on his breathing to calm his nerves and settle his shaking hands. He saw movement through the trees and with a breath he threw the hardened ball of air at his target. Branches snapped as it flew. At the last moment the light from the fire illuminated his target. Rupert saw a young man. Surprise and fear filled his eyes as he was lifted from his feet and thrown backward. Slamming into a tree Rupert could hear something break.

Not knowing quite what to do, Rupert stood frozen. Watching the firelight dance across the body of the young man. He realized then how much he wanted to go home. This was not right. He was not supposed to be killing people. He came here to help them, talk to them. The only person he'd really talked with was now in danger, and Rupert realized he didn't know what to do. The more he thought about it the harder it was to get a breath of air. Smoke was billowing around him, filling his lungs. His eyes burned. His mouth tasted like ash.

He stumbled forward following the edge of the lake. Hoping it would take him away from the destruction and the smoke, and hoping he could find the door again. In a clearing ahead he saw a tree leaning against nothing. He started to run to it and after a few faltering steps realized running was not in his best interest. His lungs already burned, and he was getting only enough air to live much less run.

As he walked up to it he pictured in his mind the same strings of air wrapping around the trunk of the tree. They lifted it and carried it away from the door. He let the tree drop with a thud and extended his hands to touch the door. Sliding them along the surface he found the knob and turned it. Pulling he could feel it scrape along the dirt below.

Light flooded through. He put his hand up to shield his eyes. Voices were coming from everywhere and all he could think to say was, "Help." He wasn't even sure he had gotten it out so he said it again and again until finally someone put their arm around him and guided him to a seat. Looking up he saw a uniformed guard. When the guard handed him a canteen of water he almost started crying.

After two long drinks he felt revived enough to actually say something coherent. "You need to prop the door open so it doesn't close behind me." His words came out as a half rasp half croak. He would have laughed at himself if he had enough air in his lungs. As it was, he needed to take another breath just to say one more sentence, "I need to see the high council."

People started talking around him. Things were being moved. Calls were being made. He felt fine just sitting there. It was nice to just sit there knowing he was back in his world where there were no monsters trying to kill him. No young men that reminded him of his cousins dying because he had broken them against a tree.

He wasn't quite sure how long he sat there, but eventually another guard wearing a very clean uniform helped him up and took him to a waiting vehicle. The guard said it would take him to the capitol. He asked how long the ride would be but didn't really listen to the answer. Laying his head back against the seat he closed his eyes.

Chapter Nine

"Hey." Someone pushed him, "Wake up princess."

James sighed. He had been awake for a few minutes already. Lying there with his eyes closed he hoped they would say something that would help him figure out his situation. No one had said anything. The silence had actually been worse than if they had been talking about how to kill him. At least then he would've known what was coming. James thought about talking with them. Student to student kind of conversation to get them to help him, or at least tell him what was happening. While he was thinking about that the car came to a stop.

He opened the door and stepped out into the parking lot where just a few hours ago he and Katie had parted ways with a kiss. Some days just go down hill don't they, he thought. It was only about ten fifteen, maybe he could explain that he really didn't know anything and still have time to get a decent night's sleep before meeting Katie for breakfast. He shook his head and thought about pigs flying.

The three students led by Scott escorted him to one of the faculty office buildings. James was glad they were back inside because the temperature had really started to dip. It wasn't the time of year where it was constantly below freezing yet, but it was darn close.

Only a few lights were on inside the building as they led him up a flight of stairs and down a hall. The lack of conversation made James feel like he was being escorted to the electric chair. "So," he looked over at Scott, "I didn't realize that being a T.A. was so much work." Scott said nothing so James added, "Just out of curiosity does he call you Igor when no one's looking?"

Scott grabbed him by the arm and spun him around, "Look, you little..." The door opened behind them and Scott stopped mid sentence.

"Thank you Scott. I'll take care of it from here." James turned to see a familiar face looking out from the light of the room. "Now, James, if you would just come in and have a seat maybe we can get this all worked out."

For a second as James watched the three henchmen walk away he felt a glimmer of hope. Maybe they could work it out. He turned and walked into the room. He wasn't surprised to see that it was fairly small. The walls were white and mainly covered with shelves, which in turn were covered with books. James wondered if the professor had really read all of these or if some of them were just for show. James had a beautiful copy of Moby Dick on his shelf but he refused to actually read it. He had gotten through two chapters one time and realized it was the most boring book of all time, but it looked darn good on his shelf.

There was one window in the back wall of the office. It framed the professor as he sat down behind his glass and metal desk. It was the one thing that really stood out to James as he came in and sat down. He had always pictured professors as having large wooden desks that looked like they came from the eighteen hundreds. His advisor had one, and all the professors he had gone to see had sat behind just such a desk. James figured it came with the office. In here, however, it was glass and metal. It was a strange contrast to the white walls and brown of the books on the shelves.

"So," the professor sat down in his black, fake leather, office chair, "Scott tells me you got mixed up with the wrong people."

James immediately felt irritated. Scott hadn't talked with the professor before he left, and after almost being turned into very burnt toast he was going to disagree on who exactly the wrong people were. He was tired and could feel the irritation turning to sarcasm in his mouth, "Well, sir, I'm not sure I would take Scott's word for anything right now."

"Now James," the professor leaned forward resting his forearms on the glass top of his desk, "things aren't always what they seem."

"But sometimes," James interrupted him, "they're exactly what they seem. Scott and his buddies were beating Rupert in the middle of a street. How can that be misinterpreted?"

The professor's eyes got a little wider, "James you have to understand the big picture, and you know how certain people can get a little too overzealous with certain tasks."

James realized this conversation wasn't going how he hoped. "Overzealous? Is that what we're calling it now?" James paused, took a deep breath, and thought for a moment trying to decide how to approach this. He decided to play dumb, at least a little, "Why'd those guys bring me back here to talk to you in the middle of the night?"

"I was worried about you and put the word out that if anyone saw you they should bring you to see me."

"Why would you do that?"

"Well," he leaned back in his chair, "The other night a man tried to fake his way onto campus during our tolerance rally. I confronted him and he became violent. Earlier today Scott," he gestured toward the door, "told me he saw you with the same man in Barnes and Noble."

James raised an eyebrow quizzically, it was something that he had practiced doing when he was in Jr. High because he thought it made you look cool now he just did it out of habit, "You're talking about that balding, overweight guy with really bad asthma?"

Merrill chuckled good naturedly, "The man I confronted looked harmless enough to begin with, but believe me he is anything but."

"Well great, so you heard from your T.A. that I was in a bookstore with an overweight asthmatic and you sent out the cavalry to drag me into your office any time of day or night." He paused, "Even if the man was high on PCP, LSD, and a couple others that seems a little odd. Why didn't you just contact the police?"

"Oh, I did, but I feel a little responsible for the students here and I was just keeping an eye out for you."

"Well, when your boys picked me up I was not with the aforementioned person, and I was with my own car, which they forced me to leave in Wasilla. How does pulling me away from no one in the middle of the night help keep me safe?"

"I'll have to talk with them. It seems they were, again, a little overzealous in their duties. Now," he leaned forward, folding his hands on the desktop, "let me ask you something." Here it comes, James thought. "Why were you having coffee with someone who violently tried to break onto campus?"

"Let me answer your question with one of my own. Why was your T.A. trying to kill that guy in the middle of the street last night?"

Merrill sighed, "At the tolerance rally that man threatened harm to certain minority students on campus and even started shouting anti immigrant slogans. It seems he's in favor of a one-race nation. Scott told me they ran into him in Mountain View and remembering what kind of person he was they followed him to see what he was doing at night in that neighborhood." Merrill paused to make sure that James was getting all of this, "It seems you came into the middle of them trying to stop him from placing a pipe bomb at the boys and girls club."

"Ha!" The laugh burst out before James' brain could even process it. He knew for a fact that Rupert could care less about the ethnic makeup of the U.S. because if anyone could be said not to be from around here then he really wasn't from around here. And what was the deal with the pipe bomb. Why would anyone who could toss lightning around need to use a pipe bomb? "Look," James said, "If you're going to lie to me at least you could put some effort into it." James was seeing less and less of a chance to make it to his breakfast date in the morning.

"James," The professor's shadow extended toward James with a slight wave of his hand as he said, "why were you having coffee with this man?"

"He wanted to thank me for helping him."

"Helping him with what?" Merrill enunciated the words so as to make them clearer. Shadows around the room cast by the fluorescent lights bent and stretched toward James.

The words droned like giant bumble bees. Pressing into James mind. James wondered if the professor thought he was hard of hearing or just stupid, "Up off the ground," was all he could think to say.

"Now James, let's be clear about this. He's a criminal and I'm just trying to help you, so why don't you tell me what you two talked about in the café."

Oil slick shadows touched James' foot and he jerked backward, almost falling out of his chair. The hairs on his arms and neck stood up. Pushing his chair back as a tingle ran up his back he watched as all the shadows in the room seemed to snap back into place like overextended rubber bands. Shaking his head to clear the droning James took a deep breath and watched the professor stand up and come around his desk.

Looking concerned, the professor asked, "What's wrong James?" Again the shadows stretched out toward James.

James could feel the bees trying to press into his head again. Keeping an eye on the shadows he started to back toward the door.

"Where are you going James?" The professor's voice sounded honestly concerned.

Again the hairs rose on James arms and the same tingle ran up his back. James tried to look at every shadow at the same time while still watching professor Merrill, "What're you trying to do?"

The professor sighed and sat down on the edge of his desk. "You really did get yourself into something you don't understand didn't you James?" He looked down at his shoes and shook his head, "Look, if I wanted to hurt you I could've by now. In fact I could've just killed you out right, but I was trying to help you. I was trying to make it so everything went back to normal for you, but there's something about you that's fighting me."

"Well ya." James looked around the room again as he felt behind himself for the doorknob. "The shadows were," his brain deserted him and all he could do was wave his hand at the lamp stand in the corner.

The professor waved his hand at a chair, "Sit down James."

"No, I think I'll stay here thanks."

"The door's not going to open for you, James. You'll need help."

Well, thought James, isn't that just the ironic statement of the day. The only bright side was that this door wasn't invisible. He watched as the professor walked back around his desk and sat down again.

"James, you're going to need to make a decision."

Feeling behind himself James found the doorknob and tried to turn it.

The professor waved at the door, "You are standing at a door right now James, and the choice you make will influence everything that comes after it. I wasn't kidding about needing to see the bigger picture James. Things are happening right now and you can either help us or fight us."

"So I'm either with you or I'm against you? Is that it?"

"It's the way it has to be James. Things are moving too fast for there to be any other choices."

Yes, James thought, but what's the right choice? Who in this situation was in the right? Was Rupert right? He had done things, and those things made James believe what he was saying. On the other hand the professor hadn't killed him. Which under the circumstances was either not saying much or really saying a lot depending on how you looked at it. No, James was fairly sure the professor was doing something bad. There was no reason to attack someone like Scott had done with Rupert, and James just couldn't see Scott acting on his own in that situation especially when, by bringing James here, he had proven he was taking orders from the professor.

So, the question becomes, how to say no to the evil mastermind and still get away alive? His brain replied, keep talking and I'll try to figure something out. "I'm still a little confused about the helping me part. I was doing fine on my own in Wasilla and three of your goons shoved me into a car so you could have some kind of a late night mafia meeting with me in your office. Where is the helping part in that?"

"James..."

James continued on over the top of the professor's voice, "I was at the rally the other night too. I know Sam, he's a good kid. I still can't believe people actually threw things at him just because he spoke his mind."

"Spoke his mind?" Professor Merrill's voice actually cracked as he leaned toward James, his voice raising, "He was spewing hate and the students reacted like heroes to get him out of there."

James was struck by the instant shift in the professor's attitude, and he couldn't for the life of him picture Sam spewing hate at anyone. Sam didn't like spiders and James remembered he got kinda ticked off when they hid a big plastic tarantula in his sink. But even then he laughed really hard after he stopped screaming like a girl and running around the living room. "So the best way to get rid of hate is to hatefully throw things at someone?"

"They weren't hatefully throwing things," James was sure he saw movement again in the shadows around the professor, "and we are getting off topic here."

James, still tugging on the door said, "You are, without a doubt, the worst monster I've ever met. All you do is spout rhetoric and move some shadows around."

"So Rupert tried to convince you I was the monster." He laughed and his demeanor shifted back to the kind helpful professor, "Come now James, you've known me for years here at the university. If I was a monster then, as you say, I would be the worst monster ever."

Well, James thought, the making fun of him tact didn't work. "So your boys really stink at killing people. I mean they were stopped the other night because of a can of bear spray. Then the whole giving me a flat tire thing. I mean really, if you're going to try to kill someone at least have the decency to really try."

Merrill simply smiled at him, "It's unfortunate you got a flat tire, but that really is getting off topic."

This wasn't working at all James thought. Maybe tossing something at him out of right field could get a reaction, "He took me to see the door."

"Really," Merrill stared at him for a moment and the shadows started to gather around him. "How very interesting. What kind of a door."

This time James didn't hear buzzing. Something whispered and brushed at his ear, "There were people waiting for us when we got there."

"James, what door did he show you?"

Again James heard something whisper, almost like someone was trying to tell him something. He really wanted to tell Merrill everything he knew, but he was so irritated with all this that he clenched his jaw shut to keep the words inside. Something grabbed him. He tried to pull away and realized he couldn't move.

James was lifted from his feet and pulled toward the professor's desk. The professor's voice turned to a growl. "I'm through playing these games with you. Tell me what you know about the door."

Out of habit James raised his left eyebrow, "You realize, don't you, that this is a stupid plan."

"Really," with a wave of his hand Merrill forced James back into his seat.

If James could just keep him talking maybe his concentration would break and he could get out of this, "Getting people to tolerate each other isn't exactly going to bring the world to its knees."

"Oh, you'd be surprised." Merrill smirked at him, "Just look around the United States today. We've gotten to the point where we're taught as a society to tolerate even those that break the law. We're taught they must have a good reason for it. And people say it so much that even the criminals have come to believe it. If a criminal believes you have no right to tell him he's wrong, and you've been taught by society not to blame him for his actions then what kind of world are you going to end up with?"

James tried to move, thinking the short inane tirade might have caused the professor to lose focus, but nothing happened, "Wow, that is the long way around." He struggled a bit more. "Why not just start a war and be done with it."

"That's not my job. Now," he pressed down on James with the same invisible force that was holding him there, "where's the door?"

James could feel the air being forced out of his lungs. He hesitated for a moment thinking about holding out. He realized, however, that if Rupert was not the fighting kind and he could throw lightning around then they must have some really tough bad asses guarding the door on the other side. "You know where it is." He croaked the words out past the pressure on his chest. "You had people there waiting for us."

"Yes," Merrill shrugged, "yes I did. And I know it's somewhere in that area, but it would be a great sign of good faith for you to show me exactly where it is."

James didn't believe that but couldn't see a reason to hold back now. They obviously already knew where it was so telling them wouldn't change anything. "It's near Big Lake."

"That doesn't really help me much," The pressure eased up, "but it's a good start. Give me details."

James took a deep breath and wondered if this was how Rupert felt all the time, "Rupert led me to it. It's off some roads that don't have names out by Horse Shoe Lake."

"It's good that you're being cooperative. I would hate for something to happen to you."

"Yes," James smirked, "especially here in your office. You would have a lot of explaining to do when the work study kids come in to clean up."

Merrill nodded as if he'd actually been listening then walked over and opened the door. Leaning out into the hallway he called for Scott. Coming back into the room Merrill sat down and said, "Now then, you'll explain the route to Scott after which you will go with them to make sure you're not leading us on a wild goose chase."

Scott and his two friends came into the room and sat down in the available chairs. James proceeded to describe the route he had taken to get to the door. All the while trying to figure out what they really were going to do. They didn't need him to show them the way, so maybe they were just using this as a way of luring Rupert out into the open. Maybe it would be James as the bait on the end of a hook.

Merrill stood up, "Scott, I need to talk to you for a second. The rest of you can head out to the car."

James stood and was escorted out to the car. As he sat waiting he wondered what they could be talking about. All of this had gone too easily. This whole thing was ridiculous. He had to be missing something. This whole thing about tolerance didn't seem to sit right with him. Yes, he could see Rupert's point, and even the professor had admitted that if the world kept on the same course eventually things would fall apart, but that was such a slow way of taking the world into chaos.

So let me get this straight, he thought. Professor Merrill tried to influence my thoughts and when he couldn't do that he sends me off to show them where a door is even though they already know where it is.

Sounds about right to me.
Well, brain, since you are the brain, why?
Why what?
Oh man, are we ever in trouble with you in charge.
Look, I was there for the same stuff as you were so you tell me.
Okay. They use me as bate.
Right, then Rupert comes out to save you and they grab him.

Or most likely kill him.

Right again. Then they… Uhm… then they do what exactly.

Right. See that's the problem. What then?

The driver's door opened up, Scott got in and started the car. Well, James thought, he wasn't going to help them, but he needed time to think. He sat back and closed his eyes. It was after eleven now and he was really tired. He decided he would just let his eyes rest like this for a while then he would think seriously about what to do when they got to the door. Maybe he could run through it for help.

*   *   *

After Scott left Merrill's office the professor sat behind his desk and watched the car dive off. He knew James wasn't a threat, but it was possible he could become a threat. If others came through the door it was possible they could use James as a point of contact to move around in this world easier. Also, since James knew his name and where he could be found that would mean they could also find him, and he wasn't ready for a full-scale confrontation just yet.

The shadows in his office seemed to flicker like they were cast by candlelight. The movement caught his eye and he turned from the window to face his empty office. He had seen it happen many times but it always caused his scalp to tighten up and a shiver to go down his spine.

In the shadows eyes looked out on him. Two, three, ten, he could never tell how many eyes the thing had. They didn't glow red, or white. They were simply lighter spots in the shadows. There was no single shadow they came from. When they came they were in any shadow that he looked at. It was watching him from all around the room.

The voice that wasn't a voice entered his mind, "The boy is right. Your plan is taking too long."

The words seemed to scrape along the inside of Merrill's skull, and at the same time they were such a whisper he had to strain to hear them. "We have located the door."

"Yes," the voice sounded disgusted, "at least you did that."

Silence filled the room and the eyes watched him. The professor said, "My plan will work. James was right when he said he had no idea what was going on. You just have to be patient for a few days longer."

"Patience is not something I'm known for."

Merrill's mind raced over what it would do when it lost patience. He didn't care to think about it, "I told you two months, and things are going at pace."

"Maybe I need to find someone who is willing to take more direct action. Maybe I was wrong in teaching you the power."

"Everything's on schedule. We'll get rid of James, seal up the door, then we'll start the riots." He looked around the room and realized he was just looking at shadows. Normal shadows. Whether it was still there or not he wasn't sure, but at least with the eyes not looking at him he felt he could breathe.

Scott had his orders about the door and James. He would do what needed to be done. If there was one thing Scott was good at it was following orders. Now all he had to do was get things rolling for his grand finale. He knew Scott had prepared the anti-tolerance march. That would be the perfect kindling for the match he would throw tomorrow night.

He turned and looked out the window again. Anchorage Alaska, it was almost as far as you could go and still be in something that would be considered a city. It was on the edge of true wilderness, and yet it was also on the edge of modernized society. You could literally drive for thirty minutes and be in the middle of untouched wilderness where you had to worry about bears eating you, or you could take a walk downtown and see people sitting in coffee shops with their laptops wirelessly surfing the internet.

It was a city of beauty and ugliness. Everywhere you looked you saw soaring snow-capped mountains. They looked like frozen white capped waves. The tops reminded him of obsidian knives sharp enough to cut out a still beating heart. Moose wandered the city streets. He had seen a red fox running across the parking lot in front of his office. Even now when there were no leaves on the aspens, and no snow on the ground it was still beautiful.

Yet at the same time, as nature has its worms and maggots just below the surface, so too did this city. Trailer parks where people chose Hummer SUVs instead of heat in the winter. Mobile homes that had a satellite dish getting two hundred channels pulling down a wall and letting the twenty below zero weather into the baby's room. That wasn't it though, every city had its share of those things, and there were other cities that had many more problems than Anchorage, but here you were just far enough away from civilization that time would be needed to respond to any true problems.

After the natural disasters of the past few years in other places in the United States Anchorage had decided to take a look at its disaster response plan. What it came up with was a statement to the citizens of Anchorage that they would be expected to take care of themselves for up to nine days before expecting any help.

Trucks driving bottled water would have to come up the only road through Canada. It was a six-day drive from Seattle at the fastest. If boats came you would still have to drive the supplies to the docks, load them, sail them up, then unload them in possible bad conditions.

Take riots for example. How would you unload boats if all the workers were either taking part in the riots, or trapped because of them? No sensible person on that boat would get off in order to unload supplies he would most likely be mobbed for before he could get back on the boat. In severe riots trucks hauling goods and supplies would be stopped at the edge of the city by mounds of burning tires. Then they would be looted.

Now, most people in the lower forty-eight states would not picture Anchorage Alaska as a city primed to riot. For that matter most people in the lower forty-eight couldn't place Alaska on a map. Some even thought it was its own country. He couldn't count the number of times people had asked him if they needed to bring passports or exchange money to come to Alaska. If they did picture the population of Alaska they thought of Eskimos living in igloos. To be honest he had been shocked by the population when he moved to Anchorage.

It was one of the most diverse cities he had ever lived in, and it really had no right to be. It was cold and dark for most of the year, and when it was summer the sun never went down and it was still cold. This last summer it had been sixty degrees and cloudy most of the time. Why so many people from so many backgrounds and nationalities wanted to move here was, at first, a mystery to him.

Then he had gotten to know the entitlement attitude of Alaska. The attitude that said they deserved to have their cake and eat it too, along with having someone else's cake as well. Anchorage had no sales tax. On top of that Alaska had no income tax. On top of that they handed out free money in the form of a yearly paycheck just for living in Alaska. The lowest he had ever seen it was eight hundred dollars per person. Usually it was over one thousand per person.

Now that by itself answered the question about why so many people moved to Anchorage. People from warm climates such as Samoa, Laos, and Guatemala came to Anchorage for the free money and no taxes. It also was what made this city so ripe for the chaotic cherry picking.

After this no taxes and free money thing had settled in people thought they deserved it. When a new fire station needed to be built the people would rather die than institute a sales or income tax. When the question was posed to use some of the free money to pay for it a great cry went up from the population. They deserved no taxes, and they deserved free money. They were entitled to it. No politician could get elected if he ever mentioned instituting a tax, or using some of that free money.

The state could be going bankrupt, your house burning down because there were no fire men, and your daughter could be getting rapped because there were no police yet still they would vote against raising taxes or using their free money. This was exactly how he wanted it.

Diverse racial groups all feeling like they deserved something. Rich people angry at poor people because the property taxes on their huge houses paid for everything. Poor people angry at everyone because they were stuck living in a trailer park because property taxes were too high for them to afford a home. Gangs from strange places moved in because families wanted the free money. Diversity of all kinds clashing with each other because of this sense of entitlement, this sense that I deserve something, this corrupt idea of tolerance.

Eventually people would get so sick of society telling them to tolerate everything they would explode. He could hear the anti-tolerance march he had planned now. Simple slogans of "stand firm for your beliefs" and "wrong is wrong" would lead to shouts and thrown punches. That of course, would be broken up by the police, but what he planned for later would ignite the city. The chaos that would follow would feed the many-eyed shadow, and in turn it would feed him.

He grinned thinking about the gathering that took place on the lawn a few nights ago. It had all gone so well. He really hadn't expected anyone to stand up and challenge his views, but he was exceedingly glad someone had. It gave him a small view of what would happen after the march this week. Tempers had flared, a fight had broken out, and he could feel the chaos in the air. The many-eyed shadow had been right about the chaos. Once you knew what to look for it flowed around you like warm water. Feeling himself getting stronger as he pulled it in he hadn't been able to stop himself from smiling. It was all going so well.

Chapter Ten

Rupert's transport slipped swiftly between desert and city then back again. He didn't know how long he had been asleep and when he woke he looked out to see the edge of a city approaching. "Driver, what city is this?" Normally you wouldn't bother the driver of a transport. As with other things requiring the use of the power it took a great amount of concentration. Some drivers could answer a few questions while still holding the belief that the solid transport was flying to its final destination. Others not so much. His cousin had told him of a time when a driver had been asked a question and the transport just dropped out of the sky. He wasn't quite sure he believed the story because he would have heard the news if an entire transport had just dropped like a stone. He'd never thought much of his cousin anyway.

Without turning and in a flat voice the driver answered, "We're just on the outskirts of Gil Baleth."

Good, thought Rupert, not too much longer until they would be at the capitol. Then he was sure he could convince the council to send reinforcements in to help James. In the meantime it was nice to look out and see a familiar place. He could see the park where his family would go when visiting his aunt and uncle who used to live here. He didn't remember that glowing blue thing above the streets though.

As he wondered what it was he realized that it was getting closer. It sparkled and reflected the light. He vaguely thought he recognized it. He hadn't seen something like that since he took his mandatory self-defense class upon entering the order. Then he realized what it was, "Driver!" It had to be an accident, he thought, "there's an energy ball approaching us on the left." He glanced out the view port on the right and saw another one, "there's one on the right too." He felt like yelling but was too surprised. Why would anyone be shooting off energy balls in the middle of a city? The use of offensive energy in a city was strictly forbidden.

The transport shuddered and Rupert's stomach went into his throat as the driver dropped them under the converging glowing blue energy. Once Rupert had regained his composure he looked back out to realize they were skimming over the tops of houses. He would have asked the driver what was going on but these kinds of maneuvers in something as bulky as a transport required quite a bit of concentration.

Looking down on the wide streets he saw energy splashing against barriers causing sparks to jump to adjacent houses. Fires raged up and down the street. Some fires behind the barriers were being fought and put out. Others were just being allowed to burn. Fire would spread slowly among the mostly stone homes. His people had long ago learned to build without wood. It was a scarce commodity in the desert.

Even though they were past the heaviest of the fighting Rupert had been able to recognize the uniforms of the provincial military behind the barriers. He assumed they must be under attack by one of the outlying kingdoms, or by one of the nomad groups that insisted on living alone in the desert and worshiping their gods of sand and stone. However, as they banked away from the main city street he saw more pockets of provincial military and the people they were fighting looked to be dressed as civilians.

Looking closer he watched a person use a club to break into a neighborhood store. Farther down the street he saw three boys kicking a man lying on the street. He desperately wanted to ask the driver what was going on but at that moment he saw two more glowing blue balls rise from below and head toward them.

Rupert felt himself pushed back into the seat and watched through the view port as the last of the city fell away in a blur. Something had gone terribly wrong while he was away. He couldn't imagine what had happened in just a month. They had been at a time of almost unprecedented peace when he had stepped through the door. It was one of the things that kept him going in the other world was knowing he had a safe and secure world to return to.

Eventually they landed outside the capitol building and Rupert was escorted in. He waited impatiently outside the central chamber. The building was furnished with quite a lot of chairs so he easily had found a place to sit and wait, but he was fairly sure the seats had been designed as decoration and not with actual sitting in mind. Everything in the building was made of the sandy desert colored stone that was so highly prized by the wealthy. It was a throw back to the days that his people had lived in the very desert the stone came from. That, of course, had been over a thousand years ago, but fashion had no time limit.

The building was made of three domes. The central dome, being the largest and towering above the rest of the city, was the home to the ruling council. Beneath its stone arch it housed offices, meeting rooms, and the central chamber. The two smaller domes housed the other branches of government; the military, and religious departments. One would save or destroy your body and the other your soul.

The construction had taken over ten years. Most of the architects of the day had been employed here in the capitol. Even with their substantial powers of moving stone, and binding it together it still took a great while to get everything coordinated and everyone working together. Very few times did the power of belief collide so openly with itself than in the construction of this very building.

A person could only hold a single true belief in their mind at any one time. Every once in a while you would find a very talented person who could accomplish two things, but that was almost unheard of. A normal example that was used in schools to illustrate this point was to have someone try and think of a white rabbit hopping across a green field while at the same time counting by twelve's. At first people would say that was overdoing it, but then you realized that using the power of belief was an action. You had to see it in your mind doing what you wanted it to do, and seeing two different actions in your mind was a much more difficult thing than most people would think.

All of this led to the fact that the architect who lifted the massive stones couldn't be the same architect that fitted them together. Some things were simple to work together, such as lifting and fitting. Other things, such as getting the angle of the domes correct, was a different story. From one architect's position it looked as if the next block needed to go there, but from another's position it needed to go a few inches to the right. Eventually they had worked it out, but there were a few days where yelling was the least of the confrontations. The official record stated that it was a constructive problem and that all the parties had sat down and worked out a great solution. Unofficial stories talked about some of the massive stone blocks used to build the central dome had to be re-cut because they had been thrown back and forth by architects determined to crush their opposition.

The sandy colored stone had then been covered with tapestries that depicted the Empire's rise to prominence. There were scenes of victory in battle. Other scenes depicted the Great Flame blessing his people with the power of true belief. There were even some that were portraits of some of the great leaders of the Empire. Back when they had an emperor each one had a tapestry made of him. Now that the country was run by the council the practice had been done away with. Only some of the portraits were still hanging. Those of the founding emperors would not be taken down because they were considered religious and military leaders and not just Emperors.

The founding of the Empire had been a reaction to the lawlessness that had been a normal factor throughout the desert clans of the day. One particular clan had been able to gain predominance and amass a large number of followers. They had been the followers of the Great Flame. They believed the world had been born in light and fire, and that inside every person was a piece of that great fire. They had no name for the entity who had been at the beginning of all things he was only called the Great Flame. Some had speculated that the religion had sprung from an older desert worship of the sun, but that thinking had been crushed as heresy.

The main teaching of the followers of the Great Flame was one of moral order. They had no real laws. There were no do's and don'ts. They simply believed that everyone knew the difference between right and wrong, but some people chose not to do what was right. The official stance of the religion was that the only law was to follow the moral law. The truth of the matter was the leader, whoever he or she was at the time, usually was the one to define what the moral law would allow or not allow. In the early days things had been beautiful, if you could call conquering massive amounts of territory and uniting dozens of desert clans beautiful. Most, if not all, historians agreed the founding principles of the religion were sound. The first leaders and followers had done the right things. They had been good people. Their conquests had, more often than not, been bloodless.

The peoples of the desert tribes seemed ready for order and protection. They wanted stability in their lives, and most people agreed in principle that all people did know the difference between right and wrong. They even agreed the wrong doers should be punished. The troubles came when new leaders came to power who were either not there for the right reasons, or who when handed so much power did the wrong thing with it. Eventually one of them called himself the emperor and proclaimed officially that he had total control over the nation. No one seemed to mind so much because it was only stating what they all knew to be true anyway.

Eventually, however, one of the emperors took things too far. He built himself a pleasure palace. The people were horrified to learn what went on in there and a revolt had begun. The leading priests of the orders of the Great Flame had gathered together and led the rebellion to overthrow the emperor. That had been the birth of the council. Part of the council now sat in judgment in the central chamber. The other members of the council were scattered around the Empire doing whatever it was that leaders do.

Rupert wondered what it was they were judging. Not many trials came all the way to the council. There were still no official laws in the Empire. They had operated for the last three hundred years, since the founding of the first council, on the principle of the moral law. Everyone knew what was right and was obliged to do it. If you saw someone breaking the moral law it was your duty to either correct them yourself, or report it to the proper authorities.

At first this led to many people abusing their right to "correct" others, but after the excesses of the last few emperors the council would have none of this kind of behavior. They said firmly that misusing your privilege was itself against the moral law and would be punished as such. Lately things had gotten quite a bit more relaxed in the empire. No one was running to the military to report their next-door neighbor for putting their trash out too early. Some kids were even getting away with spitting in public. That made Rupert smile to himself and forget for a second that he had been sitting on a solid piece of stone for the better part of an hour. His grandmother would have turned his bottom red for a week if she had seen him spit in public.

Their society had seemed to achieve a delicate balance over the last three centuries. Misuse of the moral law was almost nonexistent, and breaking of the moral law was quite low. When society as a whole was given the task of policing its own this made a criminal think twice before breaking the moral law. It was also quite a deterrent to know that if you were caught the military got involved, and they were not lenient.

Watching two people leave the central chamber he wondered again what could be going on. Some trials took days. There were arguments over the defendant's intentions and whether a person's intentions had any bearing on the actual event. Other trials took only a few moments. As the two walked by he recognized one of them from his order. He couldn't remember the man's name, but he knew his face. Rupert remembered him taking notes for the official record when he had volunteered to go on this mission.

The head of their order had been insistent that an entire team should go through the door. "It is our duty as servants of the Flame to watch out for the less fortunate."

"But we don't know," the second in command of the military waved his hands, "what is on the other side. We don't know if they have seen the light, or even if they are servants of the darkness."

"Exactly why we need to send people through." He was emphatic but refused to rise from his seat. "We have a duty to see through what we started."

"We started nothing."

The abbot shook his head, "We opened the door and let that thing through."

"If I may remind you," The second in command now paced in front of his own seat, "we as a people did not open that door, and we as a people have more important things to think about. Like how to defend our own world rather than running off into the unknown to save a people who may not want to be saved."

"Just because a person does not see the danger doesn't mean we shouldn't save them from it, General. All the more, it means we should."

The general stopped in front of his chair and looked at the abbot, "We can not fight a war on two fronts. Already the outer kingdoms are on the edge of all out war with the Empire, and if someone opens that door…" he shuddered and everyone knew why. The memories of Winston's report from the world beyond the first door were fresh in their minds. "Devastation and evil the like of which we have never seen would come flooding through that door." He shook his head, "We can't leave the second door open when there might be even the slightest chance that something could come through it to harm us. Sending a team is simply out of the question."

"So what do you propose, General? Bury our head in the sand and pretend that nothing has happened? Pretend that we have no moral obligation to help those less fortunate than ourselves? Wait for them to ask for our help when they don't even know we exist?"

The General sighed, "I propose that we barricade both doors. Seal them off. We know, my good abbot, what the Flame says about helping others, but it is our first duty to help those in our world rather than rushing to the unknown of another." He stopped and looked around the room, "We speak of morals and obligations, but, to put it plainly, they are not us. They are not even of our world. They do not have our beliefs and our customs. They may worship the dark and hate the light of the Flame. I say that it is our moral obligation to help our own nation, and our own people. It is our moral obligation to help our neighbors, as the Flame says."

The abbot looked at the General with sadness in his eyes, "But who is your neighbor General? Is it only the person who lives in the home next to you? I say no. I say, as the Flame says, that your neighbor is anyone who needs your help. And if they do worship the darkness then they need help more than any."

Rupert remembered the arguments had gone on for days. Eventually the military had agreed to a limited mission. A type of scout would go through. A person who was trained to talk with people. A person who was able to make them understand what was happening.

After so many years of daydreaming about heroes Rupert put his name in for the mission. None of his friends had understood why, and he hadn't been able to explain. It wasn't until the morning of his last day on his own world that he'd even been able to admit it to himself. It was a desire for adventure. He wanted to be the hero. He wanted to come home to a parade. The great adventurer who had gone off to another world and saved them from this great menace all by himself. He remembered how people had greeted Winston. The look in their eyes was one of honor. They looked up to him. People came to him for advice simply because he had gone through the first door and made it back with these great tales. That was what Rupert wanted. Just without the life and death situations, and without the horrible monsters trying to kill him at every step.

In his mind he envisioned meeting with the leaders of great nations and convincing them of the peril that was knocking at their door, figuratively and literally. He saw himself speaking to great gatherings about the darkness and the Flame. He had even pictured them giving him a medal for saving them from this calamity.

He had wanted it so much. He was one year over fifty now. He had done nothing great with his life. He had negotiated a peace treaty between the Empire and one of the kingdoms to the south, but that was nothing but boring talk and paperwork. This would be an adventure. This time he would be able to claim the victory as his alone with no teams of negotiating advisors to help him.

He had gone blindly in and came screaming out. He sighed and shifted his weight on the stone bench. No one on the other side had listened to him. They would rather laugh at him than take him to their leader. And finally when someone did listen to him he'd possibly gotten him killed. He tightened his jaw. He had to get help and go back for James. Only the Flame knew what kind of trouble he was in right now.

Rupert realized he hadn't even had time to really explain things to him. He'd just given him brief examples that most likely had confused him. Against what Rupert had seen in the woods around the door James had no defense, and now that Rupert was gone there was no one who would believe him or help him.

The doors to the council chamber finally opened and a small group exited talking with each other. He stood and resisted the urge to rub life back into his rear end. Being a negotiator had caused him to learn how to sit for long periods of time, but no one found the benches outside the council's chambers to be comfortable.

Walking into the chamber he could hear secretaries and clerks opening files and shuffling papers. Rupert couldn't see most of the people until he had passed the outer ring of columns that supported the great central dome. Light flooded the room from dozens of windows set high above into the base of the dome itself.

Rupert walked down the long central path. The benches of the council members sat against the far curve of the wall. Rupert had counted one time just to calm his nerves as he went before the council and found that from the doors to standing before the council was one hundred and seventy eight paces. That still left him a good twenty paces away from the benches themselves. Looking up at the height of the dome itself made Rupert a little nauseous. He had been told by a friend that the letters in the words ringing the center of the dome were over six feet tall, and the mosaic of the Great Flame which was far above the seats of the council was well over twenty feet high.

Aside from the bright reds, oranges, and yellows on the mosaic of the Great Flame everything was done in the colors of the natural stone. The entire massive room reminded him of the shifting sands of the desert. He looked around at the sandy colored columns and followed them up to the sandy colored dome. Then his eyes followed the curve of the dome to the brightness of the Great Flame. The tiles that had been used to create the mosaic were polished and designed to reflect the light of the windows around the dome. It gave the impression, as you walked through the chamber, that the fire was actually flickering.

Finally, directly below the mosaic, sat the high council of the Empire of the Great Flame. Some called them the voice of the fire. Others called them the representatives of the Flame on earth. Rupert called them a bunch of crotchety old men, but only in his head. No one could ascend to the council until after their seventieth birthday. This meant they were wise and knew the moral law. This also meant none of them would aspire to naming himself a new Emperor, or so they hoped. All Rupert thought was it meant you had a group of tired cranky old men to deal with in a hot room. Everyone knew you didn't want to have the last audience of the day, but honestly even the youngest person wouldn't do well with sitting on a stone bench listening to a large number of complaints for hours on end in a room that could easily reach one hundred degrees.

Unfortunately he was the last to go before the council this day, but on the other hand he had seen there were only three cases to be heard by the council. He took a seat in the third row. It was close enough to hear and see everything, but just far enough away so as not to be called on for anything.

Rupert had been in this position enough to know where the supplicants before the council should stand, and he watched as a thin brown robbed monk stopped directly on top of a circular stone about the size of a man. When the building had been constructed they had designed it with certain acoustic principles. Rupert, as well as most people, had no idea how it worked, but if you stood on this stone everyone in the chamber could hear your every word.

One of the council members to the left was still talking with one of the clerks. Rupert had never been able to keep the names straight of the members of the council. Because of the age restriction most of them served only for two or three years, "Yes, yes," he was saying, "make sure the record clearly shows, again, that intent weighs just as heavily as action." Shaking his head as he came back to his seat, "I don't know how many times this council has to say that." Then he looked out at the monk standing before them, "Wouldn't you agree Winston?"

The monk nodded his head, "Of course council member. It is as the Flame says, 'that which burns in your heart will eventually burn in your actions.'"

"Yes, exactly," the council member shuffled through a mound of paperwork, "I just wish all those lawyers would remember that as well." He pulled out a sheet of paper and pushed the others aside, "This is the third time this week they filed papers to argue that the intent of a person shouldn't count." He looked down the line of council members, "Well, are we all ready?" After seeing nods of assent he looked back to Winston. "You are here to give a full account of the two anomalies referred to as the doors. Is that correct?"

Winston nodded, "Yes sir."

The speaking council member looked down at the papers before him, "You have already filed a report and given a statement to the military board I see."

"Yes," Winston looked around at the members present, "and I have already given a full account to this council as well."

Down the line of the council another voice spoke up, "Yes, and we understand that you may be a little confused about the matter, but the truth is that we need a thorough public record because of the recent military problems in the outlying regions."

Winston nodded, "I thought they might be connected."

"So do we." The council seemed to nod in unison.

"In that case," Winston looked around not only at the council but at everyone seated in the great hall, "I beg the court's permission to use the second sight."

Rupert looked around and saw the uneasy looks on faces. Even the council looked a little set back at the request. In the situation, and for what they were asking, it was perfectly reasonable, but still it was a little on edge. The art of second sight got into your head and put what Winston saw directly into you. What he smelled you would smell. It would be as real as if you had been there yourself. The only problem was that if a person resisted the art there could be damage. The power of belief was a strong one, but when it was contradicted by another equally strong belief there could be catastrophic consequences.

Finally the council came to a consensus. The central member rose and addressed the audience, "This will be allowed." He raised his hand to still a murmuring that had risen from those watching the proceedings, "For those of you who have been crying out to know the truth behind these events this is your ultimate chance, and for those of you who just happen to be here today you may leave if you feel uncomfortable with this turn of events." He paused, and watched half a dozen people rise and head for the exits. When the doors leading to the foyer had finally closed he seated himself and turned his gaze back to the waiting form of Winston, "You may begin."

Winston bowed his head and to Rupert it seemed as if he heard a door opening, but when he looked for it he was forced to shield his eyes.   They floated above a fire blasted and empty landscape like butterflies on gossamer wings. The landscape stretched away for hundreds of miles in all directions and burned with the colors of a glorious sunset. The flames on the distant horizon were jagged mesas thrusting their reds and oranges into the pale white sky.

Not many came to this lonely place. It was home only to twisted, water starved plants and a few animals that seemed to love the dusty holes they called home. The small group of delicate flying machines had no fear of inclement weather, or even of a stiff breeze. It hadn't rained in this place in over a century. The diaphanous flyers seemed out of place in this burning land.

From his position above and slightly behind the rest of the group Rupert could easily make out the white wings of the student's flyers as they contrasted sharply with the brilliant desert floor. It never failed to amaze him as he watched the frail machines glide through the blue white sky. They were basically thin cloth stretched over a skeleton of hollow wood. The students lay flat beneath the machines with their arms stretched over their heads grasping rods that controlled the pitch and yaw of the long wings. At their feet were pedals to control the small tail shaped rudder. The wings, by necessity, were long and narrow to catch the thin hot air.

The group cut diagonally across the face of a giant mesa. He watched over his shoulder as stunted trees and shrubs passed. It always amazed him how anything could live in such an alien land. Professors back at the university lectured on the existence of other worlds or even other universes. They talked endlessly about what form life would take on those other planets. Some suggested life must always take the same form, but looking around at this desolate place he wasn't sure.

As his feet touched down with a soft crunch on the pebble-strewn ground he began thinking about where would be the best place to set up camp for the night. The simple flying machines were not hard to take apart and put back together but they were awkward to carry uphill. With their long wings sticking up they could catch a breeze and blow you off the side of the mesa.

From off to his right Rupert could hear the professor in charge of the expedition, "Josh! Make sure no one buried themselves in the side of the mesa and get them started on breaking the gliders down!" He never even looked to see if the teaching assistant heard him. Rupert busied himself with breaking down the glider he had landed with, and somewhere in the back of his mind he realized it was not him doing any of this.

"Tony, what do you think you're doing?" He heard Josh's cavernous voice boom out. "That wing is not a toy, and if you keep poking Kate with it I am going to use your head to pound tent stakes."

"I didn't do it on purpose. The wind caught it and..."

"There is no wind genius. Why do you think the wing that you're using to annoy her is so stinkin' long? Now put it down and back away before you end up with no way to get home."

As Josh advanced on him it was an almost comical sight. Josh was about five and a half feet tall with shoulders about five and a half feet across. He was commonly referred to by staff and students alike as stump. Watching him back Tony down Rupert agreed that the nickname was a valid one. He had shaggy brown hair, brown eyes, and his legs and arms were as thick as tree limbs, but when it came to surviving out here in this wasteland there was no one better. When the Professor had put out the request for an assistant to help on these trips Josh had been one of the first to answer, and he was the only one who had ever been here before. He had come out with no wings, and no specialized camping gear like his students had. He had walked. Maybe that was why he acted a little strange sometimes.

On this trip there were three boys, and three girls: two geology students, two biology students, one archeology student, and as required by the university one priest.

"So, Winston, any sign of angels while we were flying in?"

Rupert looked up and realized the professor was speaking to him.

The reply came tumbling out of its own volition, "It's a good thing your parents are part of the order or I would think you were being sarcastic Thomas."

"Winston, why on earth would you think that?"

"I've been on three of these trips with you and each time I've seen both devils and angels. Which one are you going to be this time?"

The professor winced and placed his hand over his heart, "Ouch, you wound me. I didn't think priests were allowed to have a sense of humor."

Winston just looked at him, "Who said I was being funny."

The professor squatted down and started to help Winston with his glider, "I also ask you every time why you volunteer to come on these trips and you still haven't answered me."

Winston unhooked one of the wings and gave a half smile to the professor, "I have answered, and you just don't believe me. I'm looking for something that I might not be able to see, and as always I would appreciate it if you kept an eye out for it."

"Any less details and I would think the heat had gotten to you already, but I'm starting to believe you. Last time you wandered off on your own swinging a stick in front of you. How about I send Kris with you this time to make sure you don't fall off a cliff or something."

"Kris... Which one is he again Thomas?"

"He's the normal one. Except that he's an archeologist."

"Normal one? Oh, you mean the quiet kid over there?" They both looked off to the edge of the group and saw one of the boys sitting and waiting with his glider already packed. Every once in a while he took a sip of water from his canteen. "Yes, I suppose he does strike me as normal compared with some of the others."

Thomas surveyed his charges once more before deciding that they looked ready to move out. "Josh! Round 'em up!" His voice echoed back at him from the face of the mesa. It was a small lonely sound out here in this great expanse of heat and sand. Every time he wondered if it would get him this time. It waited very patiently for him to slip up. This wasteland had claimed better men than him and it had all the time in the world.

The five students and Josh gathered around Thomas at the base of the mesa. Each had their glider broken down and strapped to their back, separate bags with food and water strapped to their front and sides, and of course their goggles and a mandatory hat to keep the sun from turning their brains to mush. "We've gone over this for the last month so you all should know what to do but just to make sure," a groan came from every student as he continued, "what are you never supposed to do?"

One of the biologists answered in a flat monotone, "Never go off alone. Always have a partner."

The entire group repeated the phrase that had been pounded into their head for the last month, "Never go off alone. Always have a partner."

"Good," Thomas said, "now what about water?"

Kris, the archeologist, answered, "Drink at least two containers of water an hour during the day."

"Sir," the youngest girl of the group stuck her hand up as much as her three packs would let her, "I know we talked about it back at the school but I'm a little worried about where we are going to get that much water from. You didn't say anything about a river or a lake, and I didn't see one from the air."

"Winston," Thomas turned and looked at the priest, "would you like to take this one?"

"Well, you see, miss..." Winston smiled at her hoping she would refresh his memory of her name.

"Karen, Karen Lathrop." She tried to politely smile back but it was just too hot to move that much.

Winston nodded, "Well, you see Miss. Lathrop, the water comes from the source of all water. It is from where all things spring eternal, a well that never runs dry. If you would like to learn more about the source I will be around all this trip, and I am happy to answer any of your questions."

Thomas turned back to Karen, "As long as you consider that an answer to a question then you can ask him anything you want. As far as I know he waves his hand and we have water. It hasn't failed once in the last three years." He shook his head, "I'm glad to have Winston on this trip with us, and everyone should thank him for giving up his time to come out here with us. If you get injured or stuck or are just plain scared, call out for Winston and he'll be there in the blink of an eye. I saw him put a guy's arm back on once. Weirdest thing I've ever seen."

The mesa rose over one thousand feet above them and the climb to the top would take days. They would stop along the way and investigate whatever it was they had come here to investigate. Some would dig up wild flowers for transport back to the labs, and others would just dig to see what this monument of time was made of. The rest would be studying the very people who were around them. Thomas was doing a paper on the interaction of people in stressful environments. He wanted to see if his parents were right about people. They claimed everyone would see the light and turn to religion when in a stressful situation. Winston on the other hand wasn't writing any papers or doing any class work he was just a student of human nature. He wanted to know why people did what they did so he could better do what he did, which was lead them to the truth.

They stopped four times in the first hour of climbing just to drink and reapply sunblock. Every time they stopped the water bottles were full. After the first time they just accepted it and moved on. They had all seen little things like this all their lives. People pulled from wrecks with no marks, priests walking through walls, or candles lighting with no one doing anything. After the fourth stop Thomas brought the group together, "Once the sun goes below the horizon it will be safe enough to wander around on this level of the mesa. Drop your packs here and gather whatever tools you need for study." They all gave a huge sigh of relief as the heavy packs slid from their backs, "Kris, I'd like you to go with Winston, Karen with Tammi, Josh with Tony," that way he could keep the young fool out of trouble, "and I'll go with Kate." He turned toward her, "You said you wanted to try and get a sample of the wild flowers growing off the side of the cliff?"

Kate's eyes lit up, and she no longer looked as tired as she did a second ago, "Yes, sir."

"All right," Thomas started digging equipment from one of his packs, "get your climbing gear together. We'll have to descend from this level then climb back up."

Suddenly the world around Rupert blurred and started to spin. After a second he could see Winston's body off to his left and he seemed to be moving away from it. Then the blurring stopped and the world seemed to settle in place again. This time he was looking at Winston and the rest of the group. Not from Winston's eyes, but from someone else's.

His hand shot out and grabbed Tony by the arm, "Put your climbing gear back hot shot. We're not going climbing. You would just get in her way. She would end up cutting your line, and then I would have to go get your broken body and carry you all the way up to the top."

Tony glared at him, "But I'm a geologist and I need to study the stratifications of the mesa that are shown on the cliff face."

Josh used his thumb to point over his shoulder, "You mean like those ones right behind us?"

Tony waved at them, "Well, they're not exactly the same. There could be some minute differences that I may need to catalog." Rupert just stood there and stared through Josh's eyes, "Or you could at least give me some credit for trying to impress a pretty girl out here in the middle of nowhere."

Shaking his head Rupert realized that he was now seeing the world through the eyes of the assistant named Josh, and Josh answered, "Credit goes where credit is due, and endangering people's lives out here to impress a pretty girl gets no credit." He secured his few tools to his belt, shoved Tony toward what looked like a path that might have been used by a blind goat a few thousand years ago, and said, "I think we'll check out this lovely trail."

"Oh, joy," Tony rolled his eyes, "an exciting trail."

They walked for about an hour in what was the cooler part of the day. Neither spoke much for fear of using up all the fluids in their mouth then drying up and blowing away. They stopped at regular intervals so Tony could run basic tests on rock formations to look for specific minerals or sediments. Rupert watched through Josh's eyes as he took pictures of the trail in order to examine them closer back at the university. He wanted to know if it really was an ancient trail or if it was just a split in the sparse ground cover. If it was a trail maybe those who said this used to be an ocean with inhabited islands might be right.

Being inside the mind of another person was a strange and exhilarating experience. He knew why things were being done at the moment they happened, and at the same time it was quite disconcerting to speak without knowing what you were going to say. "Tony," he called for the geologist without looking up from walking along the trail, "have you found any evidence of water activity on the geologic formations?" Tony grunted something from behind him. Josh turned his head, "Tony..." His head hit the ground before his brain could process the fact that he had run into something. "Son of a motherless goat," he rubbed his head and started to roll over.

"Ha, oh man, don't make me laugh, my mouth is too dry." Tony covered his mouth and giggled behind his hand like a little girl,

"You really should watch out for the ground, it can trip you up something fierce." He sat down in the dirt of the trail, "I can't wait to tell them back at the camp that Josh tripped and bonked his little head."

"Tripped?" Josh lifted himself off the ground, "I ran into something right," he turned around and pointed into thin air, "there." He looked around and saw only air shimmering in the afternoon heat, some stunted shrubs, and an orange lizard. Slowly he looked around himself, "I swear by all I believe in that I ran into something."

"Right," Tony stood up and walked past Josh, "maybe it was a magical wall put there by little…"

Rupert felt Josh react and catch Tony before he hit the ground. Then he thought better of it, and dropped him, "Oops, you slipped." He looked down at him laying flat on his back in the dirt, "I'm sorry, did you trip on something? That ground can be mighty dangerous if you aren't paying attention."

Tony looked up at the clear blue sky and, laying flat on his back, he decided that there were times when sarcasm was just in bad taste. As soon as he got his breath back and his head stopped pounding he was going to kick Josh in the shins just for good measure.

"Quit laying there like you're dead. I did the same thing and it didn't hurt that much." Josh started walking forward with his hands out in front of him, "I don't know what it is but get up and help me find it."

Tony sat up, rubbed his head, shook it from side to side, decided that shaking hurt too much, and watched as Josh went into what looked like a mime routine. His palms flattened out in mid air and he started sliding them away from each other over the invisible surface until he seemed to reach the edges and his fingers wrapped around it. "Is it a wall?" Tony stood up and stared as hard as he could thinking he could see it if he just tried hard enough.

"If it's a wall, it's a very small one." Rupert ran his hands along the edges as they traced an invisible arc above his head by about a foot. He slid them back down until his left hand hit something at about waist height. "Tony, come here and feel this."

Tony grunted and said, "If it's all the same to you I think I'll stay back here a ways."

"It's not going to kill you. Just come here, I want you to feel this. I think it's a door knob."

"Right, and if we open it the good spirits my mom's always talking about will come out and give me a lollipop."

Rupert felt the familiar grain of the wooden door while Josh let his hand rest on it and turned to look at Tony, "Oh, but I bet if Kate were here you'd be all over this." He reached out with his right hand, grabbed Tony's belt, and pulled him closer, "Now just put out your hand and tell me what it feels like."

Tony closed his eyes and slowly reached out. When his fingers touched the door he jumped and opened his eyes.

Josh just stared at him, "Well, you're still alive. Think you could try a little farther this way?"

Again it occurred to Tony that there were just certain times that sarcasm really wasn't needed and he would make sure to tell Josh just that once they got back to the university. He reluctantly slid his hand over to where Josh was holding what he said was a doorknob. "It feels like…" his forehead scrunched up, "It feels like the door knob to my grandma's place."

Rupert looked up through the eyes of Josh at the evening sky and realized they didn't have much time left before they would be standing in the darkness trying to see something that wasn't there. Then something occurred to him. "Didn't Winston say to tell him if we found anything odd?"

"Oh, I don't think this qualifies as odd." Tony said with a dry look, "I mean it's only an invisible door in the middle of an inhumanly hot desert thousands of miles from any form of civilization. I'm surprised you haven't tried to talk me into opening it yet."

"That's not a bad idea, and if something evil lives in there maybe it'll eat you and you'll stop talking for long enough for me to think. Now what did Winston say about if we found something that we needed to tell him about?"

Tony shrugged, "He said to call him. I think he can do that whole monk out of thin air thing like the medic monks do back home."

"You're probably right." Rupert recognized the constellations as Josh lifted his eyes to the quickly appearing stars and called, "Winston, we found something!"

Again Rupert saw the world grow blurry and tilt. His perspective spun one hundred and eighty degrees until it settled again in who he presumed must be Winston. He felt himself speak, "Really, what is it?" Both Josh and Tony almost fell off the cliff face as they jumped back at the sound of his voice. "Come now, calm down. It isn't as if you've never seen a monk do that before." Winston walked up to them out of the now pitch black night, stopped, and stared at their hands resting in mid air. "It feels like a door?"

Surprised Josh said, "Ya, how did you know?"

"I've been looking for this since I first became a monk. It took me years to realize this desert is where it must be. The ancient scriptures tell of us coming to this world from another by passing through a door that was held open by those who came before." He walked up to them and extended his hands toward the door. "The scriptures talk of our people fleeing some great conflict, being saved by the Great Flame, and led to this place of refuge through the door." His hands traced the frame of the door while Josh and Tony stepped back and watched him. "I believe," Winston continued, "that this door leads to the realm of the Great Flame and his glorious kingdom." He found the doorknob and with a triumphant laugh he turned it and pulled.

Light flooded through the widening crack in the sky and lit up the desert night like the sun reflecting off a drawn sword, and then the sound hit them and threw them to the ground. A scream of hatred flew from a thousand tongues and was answered by the trumpet calls of a thousand soldiers. What they saw before them through the open door was like watching the sky bleed as twisted beings of dark and blood threw themselves onto the swords and spears of giants made of fire and light. The land beyond was one of desolation and ruin. The smoking remains of buildings were highlighted by the blinding light of massed ranks of soldiers fighting to hold the tide of darkness at bay.

One turned and looked at them with eyes flashing lightning, a look of horror on his shining face, "Close it!" His scream sounded like giant waves pounding a cliff, "Close it or all is lost!" A shaft of darkness pierced his head from behind and he fell in a flash of light smothered by darkness. From inside of that darkness eyes looked up at them and charged the door.

Winston was the first on his feet and he hit the door with all of his strength trying to force it closed before the darkness could make it through. "Help me!" He yelled back over his shoulder to Josh and Tony. Both reacted instinctively and threw their shoulders against the door they couldn't see. As it slammed shut something slightly darker than the night around them squeezed through and flew into the night.

Rupert found himself staring up at the dome of the great hall straining to see the shadow against the stars that weren't there anymore. He blinked and looked around at the assembled audience to see them doing the same. All except one. He could hear sobbing coming from somewhere in the back along with a voice calling for a medic. Out of the corner of his eye Rupert saw Winston run down the aisle. He watched him kneel then vanish.

"Well," Rupert turned as the council member spoke, "normally I would have stopped our witness from leaving, but I don't think he had anything to add after that. Let's take a moment to ask the Great Flame's healing touch to be with the gentleman that collapsed." The council member paused for a moment then continued, "The art of second sight can be a trying experience for the best of minds." He wiped a bead of sweat from his forehead, "Now to the next order of business." He passed a piece of paper down the line of council members to the guard at the end of the row.

Taking it the guard called out, "Rupert Mundovi you have been summoned to speak before the council of the Great Flame."

Rupert stood and made his way to the same circular stone Winston had just left in such a hurry. He straightened his clothes wishing he had taken time to clean up rather than coming straight here.

The council member looked up at him from the pile of paperwork in front of him, "You are here to give your report about what you saw and encountered through the second door, is that correct?"

"Yes, council member," Rupert paused. His formal report would take quite a while and he wanted a few things answered first, "But first I would like to know about the rioting in the city of Gil Baleth."

"Yes," the council members looked at each other for a moment, "well, you see Cleric Mundovi we can not answer that at this time. It's an event that is currently being investigated by the council."

Rupert looked at them a little oddly and shifted his feet. He felt like pressing the matter. You couldn't just ignore the fact that an entire city was on the verge of burning itself to the ground. On the other hand he didn't have the rank or the personality to question the high council. If they said they had it under control then he would leave it at that.

"Do you have any other questions, Cleric Mundovi?"

Rupert wasn't quite sure but it sounded like the council member was being sarcastic. The second sight brought on by Winston had been rough, and maybe they were all just a little tired. "I do have a request that goes along with my official report, council member."

He could almost hear a collective sigh come from the council, "Yes, and what would that be?"

"The world that I came from needs additional help. I would request that at least one platoon of the provincial military be sent through to aid those I made contact with."

"That is out of the question." The council member shifted himself on his seat, "Now if we may continue with your actual report."

Rupert was stunned. They had denied his request without even a second thought. "But sir, they are in desperate need of our help. I left people back there so I could come here and get help for them."

"It is not up for discussion Cleric Mundovi. We are unable, at this time, to send anything else through the second door."

Rupert could feel his lungs closing on him, "So you are saying we're just going to abandon them?"

"They are not our concern, Cleric."

Rupert could feel his voice raising, "But it's our fault that they're in that situation."

The old council member looked calmly at him, "And how is that Cleric?"

Rupert wanted to pace but couldn't move from the circular stone set into the floor, "The darkness came through from our world. It was here because we opened the first door and let it through."

Farther left another council member spoke up, "How did they react to you Mundovi?"

Confused, Rupert looked at the council member, "What do you mean sir?"

The council member sighed, "When you came to them in that world how did they react to you? Did they greet you as a savior? Did they thank you for your information and your efforts? How did they react to you?"

Rupert gave a little shrug, "Well, it took me a while to find anyone that would listen to me sir."

"And when you did?"

Rupert hesitated. His breathing came shallow and he realized what they were getting at, and if he answered he knew what conclusion they would come to. So instead he did what he had been taught to do as a negotiator. Answer a question with a question, "Is it our stance to help only those who welcome us with open arms? If they were ready and waiting for us to help they wouldn't need our help. It is those that are the most in the darkness that need our help the greatest."

The council member cocked his head a little to the left, "It is difficult to help another when your own house is burning down around you."

Rupert stopped and thought of the riots. They must be too concerned with the riots. They don't want to weaken their forces when they may need them for whatever was causing the disturbance. "But sir," Rupert tried to slow his breathing and take deeper breaths, "Your metaphor is flawed," he paused and thought to himself that he had never spoken to a council member like this before, "the empire is huge. We are the largest nation in this world. Surely we can spare a handful of soldiers to help those who truly need help."

"There are many who truly need help here at home."

"But it is my responsibility sir. They are in danger because I told them about it." Rupert paused, unable to continue. He realized that he was getting too agitated and that it was causing his lungs to close down even more. He looked up to see some of the council members discussing amongst themselves and others looking at him in concern. When he had gotten his breathing under control enough he continued, "I was attacked on the way back to the door with a companion from the other world. Our attackers used the power against us. They were untrained and sloppy about it but they still had the use of it. I don't believe there were many of them, and I think with a small force we could eliminate them for good."

"Your sentiments are noble Cleric, but the population has become weary with war."

Rupert was confused. There had been no fighting when he had left. Even if they were not at peace with all their neighbors they weren't at open war with any of them either. "Who did we go to war with, council member?"

The head of the council looked down the row at the others and waited until he saw a nod of acquiescence from each. "It was decided to attack this problem of the doors on both fronts after you left. The door that you went through was closed behind you so we had no access to that world unless you returned, but it was decided that the second door held the smaller of the two dangers in any case.

"The details Winston gave led us to believe that the greater threat came from the first door. He had spoken of survivors in that world. People that had nothing in a world laid waste by tyranny and evil. Your own abbot convinced us it was our moral responsibility to help them."

He paused and a different council member said, "Moral responsibility can only hold public opinion for so long."

Rupert looked confused, "What do you mean? Are you saying that we invaded the other world?"

"Yes," they all seemed to nod in unison, "we had no quarrel here at home to watch over so we threw everything at them."

The second council member continued, "In our arrogance we thought our great armies would be greeted with cheers and adulation."

"But," the high council member continued, "the fighting was horrendous. We lost thousands in a matter of days, and as my esteemed colleague stated, moral responsibility holds only so long before public opinion turns."

Rupert was shocked, "Are you telling me that the leaders of a nation run on the moral law bowed to public opinion rather than to what was morally correct?"

The one high council member who had not yet spoken all but glared at him, "No, Cleric Mundovi. It is still up to debate whether sending the invasion into that Flame forsaken place was our moral obligation in the first place, but we did not bow to public opinion."

Rupert was a little surprised to hear his own voice say, "And thus we have riots in our streets."

"Yes," the leader of the high council sounded suddenly weary. He looked up at the windows high above and watched the light stream through them for a moment. "We sit here in our hallowed halls and talk about right and wrong. We judge people based on whether we think their intentions were right or wrong."

"Sir," Rupert interrupted, "you know as well as I that there are things which are right and there are things which are wrong. You can not be doubting the very foundations of our nation, of our faith."

He smiled slightly, "No, Rupert, I do not doubt that there is a very definite line between right and wrong. Even if our words do not show it all the time our very actions toward each other speak to the fact that we know the difference. The problem comes because we are only human." A muttering of agreement came from the rest of the council. "As much as the population and the news like to call us the voice of the Flame, we are not. We are humans. We sit here in judgment over this nation and to the best of our ability we try to discern what are the right choices and what are the wrong choices, and we have never deliberately taken the wrong choice."

Rupert cocked his head a little to the right wondering if he had heard correctly, "But that does mean that wrong choices have been made."

Another of the council members spoke, "Of course they have. Don't be naive Mundovi. We're not omniscient, we're not all seeing. We are old men who can barely walk down the hall by ourselves." He looked down the row of council members, "If I may speak for all of us for a moment." He waited for a nod from his fellow members. "At the beginning of this incident we didn't see any conflicts between right and wrong. The discovery of the doors was an interesting fact for the academics to explore. The fact that something had come through the first door was also simply something for the military to take care of.

"When groups started calling for an expedition through the first door we, again, thought nothing of it. An expedition had no impact on the question of right or wrong. Scientific fact has no right or wrong, it is merely information, and that is what we thought would be gathered in this trip. Views of another world, interactions with other cultures, we believed that it would be the same as if a new continent had been discovered across the sea. Of course contingencies had been set up just in case they turned out to be hostile, but we believed that because the only way to open the door was on our side there was nothing to fear. Then Winston returned."

A shiver went down Rupert's spine at the memory of that first brief account given by Winston. It was in this very hall. Winston's voice had rang out with more conviction than Rupert had believed he would ever have, "This is the most direct confrontation between good and evil that has ever been fought." He thumped the staff he had been leaning on into the stone of the floor for emphasis, "The things which have ravaged that world want nothing more than to consume and destroy. The people that are left huddle in fear in dark places. Some are used as we would use cattle. Others still fight even though their whole world has been destroyed."

Rupert could only imagine what Winston's journey through that place had been like. He was sure it had been told to the high council, but not when the gallery was full of spectators.

The leader of the high council pointed to where Rupert was now standing, "All the questions of right and wrong started with Winston standing right where you now stand Cleric. If he was to be believed then we had a real battle on our hands. We had a clear-cut case of right and wrong. We were the good and they were the evil. He talked of people being rounded up and beaten. He talked of whole groups of people being killed outright because they stood in opposition.

"Voices were raised saying that we had a responsibility to help them. We were the stronger and we had to help those who were weaker." He paused and looked at Rupert for a second, "If I recall that was the argument you and your Abbot used to get permission for you to go through the second door."

"Yes sir," Rupert prepared himself for an attack, "and it was the right thing to do."

"No doubt," the council member nodded, "no doubt." He looked around for a second as if at a loss for words, "Which is the right choice Cleric Mundovi? Should we have not gone and saw to the needs of our own people and nation while ignoring the obvious needs of others? Yet when we went to help the others the needs of our own were not met. We could not do both. What was the right and what was the wrong?"

Rupert wondered if he really should answer the question. When he saw that they were all looking at him he realized that it wasn't just a rhetorical question. He breathed in slowly then out and thought what he would have done in their situation. "I don't know sir."

"That is not an acceptable answer, Cleric. A decision has to be made. You can not look weak or vacillating. If you are leading the most powerful nation in the world you must be decisive. You must either seal up the door and tend to your own people while ignoring the plight of others, or you must go through the door with all the power at your disposal and for a while ignore the plight of your own people."

"Couldn't a small force go through the door and try to help while the rest stay here and look after the country?"

"It's not a question of how many go where. It is a question of money. Do we spend the nation's money on guns or on butter? If we send soldiers through the door then we have made a commitment to the soldiers to support them until their job is done. In that case we do not have the money to fix a town's road system at the same time because that money is going to feed and arm the soldiers. If you try to do both you end up with a bad road and dead soldiers."

"So are you saying, sir, there is no right or wrong answer in this case?"

"No, Cleric, I," he again looked at his colleagues, "we are not. What I am saying is that we don't know what it is."

For a moment Rupert was stunned. The purveyors of justice in his world had just admitted to not knowing the right answer. These were the people that told everyone else what was right and what was wrong and they didn't know it themselves. What did that mean for him? What did they mean for his nation?

"Do you know which is the right choice, Cleric? Because if you do, we would love to hear it so that we could take your advice to heart and do something about it."

Rupert thought for sure they must be missing something. He thought that right and wrong were as clear as day and night. He looked down at the stone floor. Worn smooth by hundreds of years of feet walking over it. He could see the minor distinctions between the stones. Lighter sand colors faded into darker tones. He looked up at the symbol of the Great Flame over the heads of the council. Maybe, he thought, inspiration would come and he would know. The light from the windows made the flames of the mural dance and flicker. Yellows and reds mixed in the light of the sun. Finally he looked back at the council. "Where do we go from here then?"

"You have to understand something, Cleric. We are not infallible. We do believe there is a right choice and a wrong choice, and we hope we made the right one." This time it was the council member's turn to look up at the mural of the Great Flame. He had to turn in his seat to look at it properly. "I wish the Great Flame had come down and told us what the best course of action was, but that didn't happen." He turned back to Rupert, "And to the best of my knowledge has never happened. So we had to make what we believed was the right choice. We make mistakes. Sometimes we admit them, sometimes our pride gets in the way and we insist that it was the right choice when it wasn't. What we ask be remembered is that we are only human."

"But a greater responsibility rests on your shoulders. If I make a bad decision, dinner is ruined. If you make a bad decision thousands of people could die." Rupert heard his own voice echo off the walls of the great hall and couldn't believe he had said that to the high council.

"Yes, and we do not make our decisions lightly. Weeks of discussion went into this decision. Deciding to let you go through the second door alone was in itself not an easy decision, but to be honest with you it was just one life. The decision to send our army to the aid of another world was a much larger one and we believed we had thought it out. We believed we had the people's support. We believed they wanted to help others as much as we did. Now it seems they would rather see other people die so their road can get fixed.

"We made a decision. Whether it was the right one or not remains to be seen." He reached out and shuffled the papers in front of him then looked up again, "There is a right or wrong answer," he shook his head a little, "I just wish I knew which was which." He looked to his right and his left, "I hope I did not overstep my bounds by speaking my mind," murmurs came from the other members showing that what he had said was fine, "Good. Now back to the business at hand."

"Actually sir," Rupert interrupted, "I think that my business does relate to what may be happening here."

"Really?" He sounded tired, "How so, Cleric?"

"I had a chance to witness first hand the entity that escaped through the second door in action, and I believe it does relate to the riots here at home."

"Please," now a little curiosity had come into his voice, "continue."

"The creature was trying to create conflict in that world. It was setting up two groups to oppose each other. One group was preaching absolute tolerance while the other was preaching solidarity and in some cases intolerance of certain topics." Rupert stopped and thought to himself for a second.

"What is your point Cleric?"

"The entity convinces people they're doing the right thing even if that thing is opposed to someone else. He then raises their level of anger somehow so that a simple thing like having a bumpy road is something worth fighting over."

"So you think one of them has gotten into our world and is influencing events?"

One of the other council members spoke up, "That might make sense. Do you remember the school incident last week?" He looked down at the leader of the council, "It seemed such a simple matter and turned into a full riot with teenagers burning cars and destroying half a neighborhood."

"Well, Cleric Mundovi, it seems you have just been promoted."

Rupert looked confused, "What are you talking about?"

"You are the only one that has seen these things in action aside from Winston, and his interaction with them was on a completely different scale. You will be assigned to a military group and you will see if your hypothesis is correct."

"No, I can't."

"What?"

"Respectfully sir, I can't do that."

A silence seemed to descend on the great hall, "And why not Cleric?"

"I have to get back to help James."

"And who is this James?"

Rupert tried taking two deep breaths to steady himself. He had never dreamed he would be telling the leader of the high council no about anything. "James helped me. He believed me, I think. And because of me he is in great danger from the entity that is in his world. I believe, no, I know that I need to go and help him." Before they could say anything he continued, "It's the same choice you had to make before. Either help those here or help someone you've never met in a world you've never been to, but I have been there and it was because of my actions that he's in jeopardy." His breathing was coming shallow and quick now, "I just ask for a short time. I believe the situation over there can be remedied quickly. I know where the entity is, and I think it's too weak to challenge a trained monk directly." Again he had to pause to breathe. It rasped like wood over very fine sandpaper, "All I ask is for a little time, and there are monks who would be much better at tracking down something here. Please," a hint of desperation crept into his voice, "let me finish what I started."

Chapter Eleven

"So, is he still out?"

"Ya, I think so."

"Good, it'll make things easier when we get to the mine."

The sound of voices drifted into James' dreams causing him to turn his head. After sleeping for nearly forty-five minutes in the back seat of a car his neck had taken on the shape of a Christmas candy cane, and when he tried to turn his head the candy cane felt like it was breaking. His initial reaction made him want to massage his neck then take a day off to go see a chiropractor, but something inside of him convinced him to lay still.

He had always watched movies and TV with a certain amount of irritation. No matter how smart or rational the character was they always did something obviously stupid. He figured that it was just a device used by the writers to create or build tension in the story line. I mean really how interesting is a character that always does the right thing? So instead of staying in groups they would split up and the monster would kill them. Instead of staying put where it was safe they decided that they should walk through the dark with nothing but a baseball bat.

Now it was his turn and he decided that pretending like he was still asleep was a better idea than announcing to the bad guys that he was wide awake and listening.

"So when we have to get him out of the car how is this going to work?"

"Try to keep your voice down, we don't want to wake him up."

The conversation was quieter this time, "So how are we going to handle this?"

"Easy, we tell him we're there, we all get out of the car, Bobby whacks him over the head with the bat, and we toss him into the mine."

At the statement of, "whack him over the head" James' brain went into overdrive, come on man! Do they really need to hit me with a bat? I mean what did I ever do to them?

Stupid, stupid...

What? I really don't think now is the time to be calling names, if you know what I mean.

The main character always makes one stupid mistake, and I really did it.

Did what?

Well, think about it. Why do they need me anymore since I gave them the directions to the door?

So your beat up car is found in a parking lot in Wasilla and your body is never seen again.

Do you think Katie'll cry?

Hello? I think I'll cry if you don't do something fast.

What? You're the brain. You think of something.

Fine, fine. But first I need to know where we are.

Right.

James slowly opened his eyes trying not to move anything that would alert them that he was awake. As he tried to look out the window without turning his head he wondered to himself if everybody talked to themselves or if he really was a little bit strange. How else would you figure out a problem if you couldn't talk it out with someone?

He realized that he couldn't see anything in the darkness out his back seat window. He needed to be able to see out the front where the headlights were shining. Hoping they wouldn't notice he lifted his head slowly until he heard a crack echo through the entire car. He cringed at the sound of it, but at the same time realized that his neck felt much better. He had to do something quick so he reached up and rubbed his neck and said, "Oy, I must have been out for a while. How much further is it?"

Scott, who was driving, looked back at him, "Not far now. Maybe five or ten minutes."

"Great," he looked out the window to try and get his bearings, "this has been a long night you know." Flashing through the headlights he saw a road sign just before they crossed over a bridge. It read Little Susitna River. Flexing his neck to the left he felt it pop. Where was the Little Susitna River? It was nowhere near the door. Especially not five to ten minutes from it. He needed to put all the things together. They had said something about tossing him in a mine, and they had just crossed the Little Susitna. Hatchers Pass, they were headed up Hatchers Pass. If he remembered his geography correctly, that was about thirty miles northeast of the little lake that the door was next to.

Okay, okay, don't panic, he thought. Don't panic. What was that from? It was on the cover of some book, and now wasn't the time to try and remember which one. What should he do?

It's easy.

Right easy. So what is it smarty-pants?

You know what, for the moment I'm going to pretend I didn't hear that because we have bigger issues at stake here than your ego.

You are my ego. Now spit it out.

It's dark right?

Wow you are smart. Dark? At night? In Alaska? Good job Sherlock.

Oh my gosh. You're a jerk. I don't know what Katie sees in you.

Hopefully she sees more of me. Now what's the plan?

We jump.

Right.

Sarcasm is not needed right now thank you very much.

Right.

Listen, sarcastic pants you've been up the pass before. It gets all crazy with the hairpin curves right?

Right. I mean, ya, you're right.

Darn skippy I am. Now in the dark, and with the tight curves they'll have to slow down to a crawl.

And then I jump.

He looked at the door to see what was up with the locks. He was riding in an old Ford Taurus and luck of luck it had manual locks. All he would have to do was pull the handle and jump. At the speed they would be going he most likely wouldn't even fall. He could hit the ground running. If he remembered the area right the scrub brush would be at least waist high in places and he should be able to keep away from them for long enough to hide out until morning. Then he could head to the lodge and call for help.

He smiled to himself a little smugly. He wasn't going to be one of those stupid characters and get himself stuck in something. Then he saw it. As the car angled up the pass he realized the one flaw in his plan. Even though it hadn't snowed in town yet it was much higher here, and there was snow everywhere. He could see the headlights reflect off the hard crusty surface of the snow and he knew what it would feel like to try and run through that. Because it hadn't snowed in a while, and because the temperature had been fluctuating between freezing and just above freezing, the top of the snow was a crusty shell.

When he had first experienced it he had thought of that topping you put on ice cream. The magic shell stuff. It came out a liquid then hardened into a shell the moment it hit the ice cream. It tasted great, and what he was looking at out the window was not going to taste great no matter how hard he tried to pretend. There were points where you could walk or even run on top of the snow because of the crust, but then you would hit a thin point and break through. One leg would be on top and the other would be four feet down with crusty snow poking you in all the wrong places.

If it had been fresh snow he wouldn't have minded. It would move aside like fine powder, but this stuff would be like breaking through glass with every step. It meant that to get a good run he would need a road, and they had a car. Those worked much better on roads than he did. He needed to delay them. Figure out something else. Maybe there was a side road he could make it down, or maybe he could convince them that he wasn't a threat.

Might as well try, he thought. What's the worst that could happen? I could be hit over the head with a baseball bat and thrown down a mineshaft. Right, let's try not to think about that, "So where are we really going?"

"What do you mean?"

"Well, you see, there's this stuff called snow outside." He stopped himself. Getting sarcastic with a group of guys who planned to kill you on their time off was not the smartest thing. "It's just that there is no snow around the door."

"We decided to take a short cut so that we could get you home quicker."

"Look," James leaned forward in his seat, put his right hand on the back of the seat in front of him and tried to face Scott in the driver's seat, "Let's cut the B.S. we both know this isn't the way to the door." He looked around at the other two in the car. They wouldn't make eye contact with him. "We know each other. We have the same friends. You know that I'm not a bad guy, and I know that you're not bad guys. So how bout you just let me out on the road? It'll take me a long time to make it back to anywhere and we'll call it even."

Scott kept his eyes on the road, "Sorry James."

"Why are you doing this?" James was starting to get desperate. If they suspected what he was thinking about doing they may not wait till they got to wherever it was they were going.

"I don't have a choice."

"That's just stupid," again he wondered about his choice of words, "Of course you have a choice. I haven't done anything to you. I'm not a threat to anyone."

"Look," Scott looked back over his shoulder at James, "It's nothing personal."

"What's that supposed to mean?" James felt like hitting him in the face right then, "Of course it's personal. How could it be anything but personal?"

The guy sitting in the back seat with him grabbed him by the arm and pulled him back into his seat, "How bout you just calm down and I'm sure everything will work out just fine."

"Just fine for who?" James mumbled while glancing out the window at the small community of tourist shops that was going by. The white washed fronts almost glowed in the dark giving the whole setting an eerie children of the corn feeling. He sighed and felt his hope slipping away as he watched the snow grow deeper on the side of the road. Finally he looked into the rear view mirror and saw Scott looking back at him, "You said you didn't have a choice, but you do. It's obvious what choices you have, Scott." There were coming to the tight hairpin turns that he had been thinking of using as his way out, "You can make the right choice and let me go, or you can make the wrong choice and do something that you'll regret for the rest of your life."

"You know," Scott reached up and adjusted the rearview mirror, "I guess I don't see it that way." He looked at his compatriots and continued, "The way I see it is that we get the power to change the world by making you go away. You've seen what the professor can do, and we're going to be able to do the same thing. So the right choice is me doing what I need to do, and the wrong choice is me going against the professor and getting killed."

Well, James thought, that's my cue to find a way out of here. He tried acting calm while searching out the window for a spot in the snow that he could make it through quickly. He saw a road sign up ahead. It was a dark color and impossible to read, but it brought up a memory of the only time he had been over the pass.

It had been a lush rainforest at that time. It had been raining in the area for almost two weeks and the entire area had turned an amazing array of greens. He had chuckled to himself on the way up to Hatchers Pass thinking that if a person had worn these different shades of green together it would be insane, but in nature it looked great.

His friends all told him they were going to take a trip up Hatchers Pass and he had really wondered about their idea of fun. It was summer time and he really didn't know if he should waste one of his days off from work driving up a road and then back down again. But he was assured that they would have a great time. They were going to be doing something called geocaching. He had heard of it but never had the money to buy a handheld GPS unit. Finally they had talked him into going mainly because he wanted to meet one of the girls that was going along, and he had a thing for gadgets.

The whole point of geocaching was that someone had hidden something somewhere and you had to find it. They would usually put something like an old army ammo can under a bush and put a notebook in it. Once you found it you would record when you found it and the names of the people in your group in the notebook. Some of them had little trinkets that you could take out of the ammo can as long as you had something to put into the ammo can. The hiding spot would be posted on the internet with latitude and longitude coordinates, that way you could use your GPS unit to find it.

They were looking for two different ones that had been hidden somewhere on Hatcher Pass. The first had been near an old mine. The entire area was riddled with old mines. Most of them had warning signs to stay away because there was danger of falling in or getting caught in a cave in, because of the instability of the old mine, but there was one safe one called the Archangel mine. If his memory served there was a dirt road going to it.

Rick had told him that in the wintertime they kept the road fairly clear so that people could get into the area for recreational use. Things like snowmobile riding and sledding were done in the area around the mine. He said it was actually nicer to use the road in the winter because most of the potholes had been filled in by snow and it wasn't as bumpy. Another thing was that you definitely needed studded tires or chains and four-wheel drive.

If he could get out of the car at that intersection there wouldn't be any snow to slow him down, and he would have a clear path to get away. Even if they were able to back up and head down the road after him they would be sliding all over the place, and hopefully by that time he would be far enough away that even if they got out of the car he would still be able to find a place to hide.

"You know you're wrong Scott." James needed to distract them from his movements. He glanced to his right and saw what he expected. The lock on the door was just above the handle, and all he had to do was push it to unlock it. He needed just a few seconds where they weren't aware of what he was doing.

Scott looked at James in the rear view mirror again, "Face it James, there's no such thing as wrong. I'm doing what's best for me, and you should have done the same and kept your nose out of this."

"Well," James hoped that this would work, "tell that to the moose." He nodded toward the road ahead and pushed the lock at the same time. Without looking he slid his hand down and pulled the handle. Scott and his other two captors were squinting into the darkness at the side of the road as he pushed the door open and leapt from the car.

His feet tangled with each other and he fell hard onto the frozen dirt at the side of the road. His moose ploy had taken a second or two longer than he had hoped and he was past the road to the Archangel mine by a good twenty yards. Putting his hands out in front of him reflexively he felt the frozen dirt and rocks bite into his palms. Hearing yelling behind him he realized that he couldn't take the time to get his bearings as much as he would have liked so he simply pushed himself up and started running back toward the intersection.

He lost his footing again as he tried to make the ninety degree turn onto the dirt side road. He couldn't see any ice but his feet seemed to have found it easily enough. Again his hands were raked across the sharp frozen pieces of earth beneath him. A part of his mind hoped that he cold would keep his hands from bleeding too much until he could find a way to wrap them up. He knew in that part of his mind that wasn't dealing with the immediate problem of having to get up and run that cold would constrict his veins and arteries in his hands to slow down the bleeding. At the same time another part of his brain, the part that was concerned with running from a group of killers, told him that it really wasn't important if his hands bled a little right now because he needed to get up and run.

He made the conscious decision to slow down just a little so that he was sure of his footing rather than just trying to run as fast as possible and falling every twenty yards. He really wanted to look back over his shoulder and see what was happening behind him, but he didn't want to waste the time. He figured it would be better if he spent his time getting away rather than looking back. Again that little disinterested part of his brain started talking about how that was really a great life lesson if he would just take the time to think about it. It was a great example of how people waste their energy looking back when they should be putting it to better use by moving forward.

Lovely, James thought, just lovely. My brain picks now to go on an existential trip down life's highways. How about I take your advice brain, he yelled at his own head, and spend my energy on moving forward! At that moment, as he picked his way up the frozen dirt road, he noticed a darker line against the night sky. He had only a moment to wonder what it was as he came up on it before his now very interested brain started yelling something about a crossbar. He had a brief flash in his memory of looking out the passenger side window of his friend's truck at a crossbar that must block off the road during non access times. In that moment all he could think was, oops.

Because he had slowed down he was able to put out his hands and absorb most of the blow with his arms rather than hitting the bar with his belly button. His already double minded brain decided at the same time that it was very painful to ram his already torn up hands into a very cold metal pole while also wondering if he was bleeding enough for his hands to freeze to it like a kindergartener's tongue to a flagpole.

Quickly pulling his hands away from the pole he lowered himself down and scooted under it. As he stood back up he decided now was the best time to take a quick look and see how the bad guys were doing. They were down hill from him and silhouetted against the starry sky. Seeing one of them fall he couldn't help but laugh to himself as he turned and started to run up the road again. He tried to figure the distance they were behind him as he carefully jogged up the hill. He wasn't that great with judging distance anyway but he figured they must have been a good twenty to thirty seconds back.

His amusement at seeing one of them fall was doubled when he heard a loud umpf from behind him followed by a string of curse words. Without looking back this time he figured they too had found the crossbar. Hopefully that would extend his lead by a few more seconds. Enough to find a place to hide until the sun came up and he could head down to the shops on the road below. The only problem would be if they weren't open at this time of the year. Then he would have to trek all the way to the top of the pass and find the lodge. The next closest thing was about a fifteen-minute drive back down the pass toward Palmer.

The mountain rising in front of him meant he was harder to see because there was no sky to contrast with. On the other hand he was trying to run uphill, and he didn't know how long he could keep it up. The adrenaline boost he had gotten when he first jumped from the car was starting to wear off and he was breathing hard not to mention his temperature problem. His hands and head were freezing while his torso was drenched in sweat.

Down in the Anchorage bowl it was in the thirties and forties for the daytime temperature, but up here in the mountains it was well below freezing even when the sun did finally make an appearance. He took stock of what he had as he jogged up the winding dirt road. He was still wearing his down coat. If he remembered correctly it was good down to negative something so he wouldn't freeze to death, but when he stopped moving the sweat might freeze to his skin giving him hypothermia and killing him. He had no hat so his head might get too cold overnight again giving him hypothermia and killing him. He was wearing denim jeans and hiking boots. The denim would be no help at all. It already felt like it was freezing into a solid sheet of cardboard on his legs. His boots on the other hand were a definite bonus. He hadn't noticed what the other guys were wearing, after all he was a guy and he wasn't in the habit of checking out other guys shoes, but he was fairly sure that they wouldn't be wearing hiking boots. That should give him an advantage on this kind of terrain. At least my feet won't get hypothermia and die, and if sarcasm could keep a person warm I should survive the night he thought.

Turning a corner to the left he realized that his eyes had adjusted enough to see that the road was going to get steeper in a few yards. The cold air was already hard to breathe and his legs were burning. He really wanted to walk for just a little bit so that he could get his breath back.

Hearing his lungs pull in each freezing breath reminded him of Rupert. This must be what his whole life is like he thought. It must be really irritating to never take a normal breath. It must also be irritating to be chased by goons up a mountain in sub freezing weather. He really wanted to blame Rupert for what was happening, but he just couldn't do it. He knew that he had made the choice to go with him. He knew he had made the choice initially to help him when he had seen him in the middle of Mountain View getting attacked. Now that he thought about it he realized he had come full circle with the guys who had chased down Rupert now chasing him.

As the road grew steeper it also angled more along the side of the mountain. It was enough to give him a view of the road below without having to slow down. He could see two of them slipping and using their hands, and he realized that he had been right about the hiking boots. The other one was out in front, and he assumed it must be Scott. He couldn't tell from here but he knew Scott was in good shape. He was on the university's hockey team and was most likely having a much easier time of running up a mountain in the cold than James.

One good thing so far was that no one was throwing fireballs at him. Thinking of Rupert had reminded him of that whole incident. He realized he didn't know the man very well, and what he did know had been very strange, but he hoped that he had made it out of there in one piece. He really did seem like a nice guy, and it seemed the things he had been talking about were true. All things considered, even though it was good no one was throwing fireballs at him, it sure would have made things warmer and that wouldn't be all bad.

His momentary distraction by his thoughts was broken by a cramp in his side. He really couldn't keep this up much longer. He was going to have to slow to a walk or find someplace to stop soon. Maybe he could hide and wait for them to catch up then clobber them over the head with a big stick. That would work if there was only one, he thought, maybe even two, but with three he just couldn't see himself being able to get the job done fast enough. Besides that was a movie trick and those never work in the real world. It was like breaking a wine bottle over someone's head. Had any real person ever felt a wine bottle? Those things would break your head before the bottle broke. What would most likely happen would be that he would hit Scott over the head with a big stick and all it would do would be to tick him off so that they killed him slowly rather than quickly. No, his best bet would be to just avoid them until they went away. He didn't remember them being any better dressed for the cold than he was so hopefully he could outlast them.

Speaking of outlasting them, this mountain was killing him. Every year around the fourth of July the city of Seward Alaska held a race called the Mountain Marathon. They ran up a big hill then back down. There were great shots in the newspaper every year of some poor guy or girl or both running then tumbling down the hill. He thought they were insane; completely, certifiably, insane. He was fairly sure that sometime he had said that the only way you would ever see him running up a hill was if he was chased by wild man eating animals. He guessed he would have to add power hungry killers to that list.

All of this thinking and reminiscing about newspaper articles and talking with friends about man-eating animals was great but he was still cramping and trying to find a place to hide. In his peripheral vision he saw something move. His recent thoughts about wild animals made him jump and then slip. He caught himself with his right hand before he started to literally roll back down the road.

He felt hands grab his shoulders and someone pulling him up. His mind told him it couldn't be any of the three who were after him; they were too far behind, but at the same time no one else was out here in the cold and darkness.

"I'm so sorry I startled you, but it's so hard to see that I really wasn't sure anyone was there at all."

James looked over at a man that had come out of nowhere. All James could tell was that he was black, and he was wearing dark clothing, "I, uh, it's fine," he realized that he was losing precious seconds of lead time, "I'm just in a hurry is all."

"I hate to bother you," James couldn't see any expression on the man's face in the dark, but he sounded panicked, "but my grandson has gotten stuck in an old mine shaft over there and I really need help getting him out."

The tone of the man's voice was so urgent that even in the dark James was sure he could almost see tears in his eyes. His heart went out to him but his brain yelled that he needed to keep running. He looked over his shoulder and down the winding dirt road. He could see winter dead brush poking up through the hard crust of snow, but no people. He looked harder and still couldn't make them out against the star lit background.

"Please," the man's voice brought James back from his search, "I know this is strange, and I know it's in the middle of the night, but there's no one else around and I can't get him on my own."

James wanted to disagree with him and tell him that there actually were other people around, and if he didn't get moving right now those other people were, ironically, going to stick him in a mine shaft. He wanted to help the man but he didn't have a choice. He was just going to have to tell him to head to the lodge and get help.

Almost as if the man had read his mind he turned and looked up the hill, "I was heading toward the lodge but these old legs aren't what they used to be and I'm worried about my grandson in the cold. If he's stuck down there for too long I don't know what might happen."

James wanted to scream at the man that it really was a matter of life or death here, but it was his own life and possible death. And what was an old man and his grandson doing at the top of Hatchers Pass, in the middle of winter, and at night to top it off?

"Sir," James was getting desperate, "I really don't have a choice. I really need to get going." In these circumstances James was sure he was being more than patient. He'd already lost about a minute of lead-time.

"My wife, God rest her soul," James hated to do it but he turned and was about to start jogging up the hill again, "would have said that we always have a choice to do the right thing even if we don't like it."

Hearing his own words thrown back at him James stopped in his tracks. His back was to the man and he could see the big dipper just over the ridge ahead of him. "But it's not the same."

"What was that?"

James shook his head. He didn't realize he'd said anything out loud, but it didn't change the thought. He turned back to the man. "Fine," he said through clenched teeth, "Where's he at."

"Thank you so very much." He pointed off behind him toward a trail of packed down snow that James never would have noticed as he was running. "He's just up this way a spell."

James followed the old man as they left the dirt road and started walking single file over the beaten down snow. To his left and right James could see an almost unbroken expanse of white. Here and there the brush was tall enough to break through the top layer of frozen crust. In some places there were even trees, but they were few and far between. The black of the old man's coat stood out against the white of the snow and James realized his dark red coat would be doing the same. He'd gone from hard to see against the dark background of the dirt road to sticking out like a red cartoon thumb against the reflective white of the snow.

Every step they took crunched and crackled over the frozen snow like they were walking through one of those proverbial glass houses where people had been throwing stones. Wincing with every step his hope of using this trail for escape dimmed. He had been trying to convince himself this unused side trail, which didn't even look like a trail, would turn out to be his salvation because they would run right by it. Now it was looking like he was backing himself into an area with one way in and one way out. Maybe the old man would help him if he explained his situation. On the other hand in the time he had left he didn't think it would be possible to explain his situation. He wasn't even sure he understood his situation. All he really knew was some guys from his university were trying to kill him on the orders of a crazed professor who could do magic, or at least something that passed for magic.

That actually sounded close to normal. Where it got weird was when he tried to think about why they were doing what they were doing. On that point he had no ideas. It was getting so frustrating not to know what was going on. On the one hand he knew who was involved and kind of what they could do. On the other hand he had no clue why they were doing anything and as such he had no idea how to either stop them from doing it, or convince them he wasn't a threat to them.

The man in front of him looked back over his shoulder, "Again, thank you so much for coming with me. I know you said you're in a hurry, and I hope I can make it up to you." James saw him reach into the left pocket of his coat and pull something out. His first thought was, wouldn't it be just perfect if he was up here hiding from the law and now he's going to kill me. Instead James watched as the old man held something out to him, "I noticed that for whatever crazy reason you're not wearing a good stocking cap. I bring along extras of everything because I can still hear my wife telling me you never know when you're going to need it. So here you go." With a kind of detached amusement James realized that the man was offering him a black knit stocking cap. At least he wouldn't die with a cold head he thought. "I know this doesn't repay you for taking your time to help a crazy old man and his grandson, but I hope it helps."

"Yes, actually," James took the offered hat and gratefully tugged it onto his head and down over his frozen ears. "In my rush I forgot to grab one, and it helps quite a lot." He decided the best course of action would be to not tell the man anything unless it was absolutely necessary. There was no reason to scare him. He was under enough stress with his grandson being in trouble. That thought made him remember his whole conversation with Rupert in his Geo on the way out to see the now infamous door. Rupert's indecision over what exactly to tell him echoed in his own mind now. Would it be better just to tell the man everything so if he wanted to run away he could, or was it better to just not let him worry about it until he really needed to?

"So, you're probably wondering what an old gentleman like myself is doing out here with his grandson on a night like this, am I right?"

"Well," James really wished the man would keep his voice to a whisper, "yes, actually, I was a little interested in that." Sound would carry in this cold air like it was a cell phone call for anybody to pick up.

They had to stop talking for a few seconds to navigate their way through a section of the trail that wound between some scrub brush and large rocks. Seeing the moon reflect off some of the rocks reminded James he really did need to pay attention to where he was stepping. He didn't want to escape from his killers just to die because he slipped on some rocks and rolled down the hill. The disconnected part of his mind came back to play trivia for a second and with a chuckle said they could name the movie <u>The American That Went up a Hill and Died Falling Down a Mountain</u>. Maybe they could get Hugh Grant to play his part in it.

"Well, you see," they were back to crunching their way along a fairly straight trail, "my grandson's been reading these adventure books, and he wanted to know what it was like to do some of those things. Together we researched how to build a snow cave. The first one we built was during the day and it was closer to home. This time we decided we would stay in it for one night. Normally there would be enough snow by this time to build one in our own backyard, but instead we had to come out here for it."

James listened to the old man's story with one ear and tried to listen for sounds of pursuit with the other. James glanced back down the path anytime he was sure enough of his footing that he could take a few steps without looking at his feet. Since they had turned onto this trail he had lost track of the three following him, and for whatever reason he couldn't hear a thing beyond the crunching of his feet and the drone of the old man's voice.

"His Mama wanted us to just set up a tent in the backyard, but when my grandson realized he was going to have a chance to sleep out here like it was a real adventure there was no talking him out of it." Looking up from his feet James realized he could just make out a light up ahead. "If there was anything that boy got from his grandma it would be his stubbornness." The old man stopped in front of James, "I just need to get my breath back here for a second." James realized in all the commotion the cramp in his side had gone away and his breath was almost back to normal. He was also very happy to notice he had feeling in the tips of his ears again. "You can see our camp light just up ahead."

During their brief break James looked as hard as he could down the hill toward where he thought the car would be. Maybe they had gone back to the car to get flashlights or guns or something. Trying as hard as he could James still couldn't make out anything to suggest where his former captors were.

Hearing the crunching of footsteps James looked back over and saw the old man was walking along the trail again. James realized the trail had flattened out and he didn't need to watch his feet as much anymore. Without the constant fear of falling James decided that it would be a grand idea to put his hands in his coat pockets. They were, at that moment, the most beautiful little pockets in the history of, well, pockets. They were lined with polar fleece and filled with real imitation goose down. He tried flexing his fingers while they were in the lovely pockets to get the blood flowing through them again, but that just made them hurt. He remembered watching a survival show on TV where the host had said the best way to get the blood flow back was to spin your arms at your sides like a pinwheel. It would force the blood out to the extremities and stop any possible frostbite from setting in. James considered doing that for just long enough to picture himself being thrown off balance by the spinning motion and slipping on some hidden rock. He would then repeat the final scene from the movie his brain had been making, <u>The American That Went up a Hill and Died Falling Down a Mountain</u>.

He thought about blowing on his hands to warm them up faster but vaguely remembered reading something about the moisture from your breath freezing and causing more problems, so instead he just hoped that the old man had a heater at his camp. If he was going to die tonight he would like it if he was a bit warmer. At that thought his brain started to laugh and talk to him as he slowly trod his way forward.

If you're going to die then I'm leaving.

Oh, and where would you go? You wouldn't have any legs.

I'd think of something. I am, after all, your brain.

How about we save the mental issues for later. I'm a little busy right now.

Yes, yes, I can see that. Very busy putting one foot in front of the other. It takes a lot of brainpower to do that, you know.

Thank you, sarcasm is not needed right now.

Ah, but what sarcasm may come once we have shuffled off this mortal coil?

Great, now I'm misquoting Shakespeare to myself.

"So," the voice from in front of him brought him out of his own thoughts, "I told you my story. Why are you in such a hurry to get up here at this hour of the night?"

James looked at him for a moment, "Well," he could see the light of the old man's camp just around a patch of scrub brush, "I'm not so much in a hurry to get to something as I am to get away from someone."

They came around the brush and James was greeted with the sight of two canvas camp chairs next to a campfire. He was so happy to see anything that put out heat that he walked right past the old man and squatted down as close to the warm orange glow of the fire as possible. Stretching out his hands toward the heat he remembered a time when a snowmobile he had been riding sunk into a creek that was hidden beneath the snow. He and his brother had stood knee deep in sub freezing water pulling on the runners while his girlfriend had worked the throttle on the machine. When they'd finally gotten out he was sure he was going to lose his feet, and he was also sure his brother was never going to let him forget it. To this day he distinctly remembered watching steam rise from his feet as he propped them up next to the fireplace in the lodge. It had been slightly disturbing seeing how close his feet were to the fire and realizing that he couldn't feel the heat.

That was almost how it was now. It took a few long moments before he could feel the heat from the campfire on his fingers. Once he had a bit of life back in them he turned to the old man, "So which direction is your grandson? We'll need to get him back to the fire as quickly as possible."

The old man sat down in one of the camp chairs and crossed his feet on a rock next to the fire. "Well, to be honest with you, I don't have a grandson."

James slowly looked over at him. Finally his brain joined with his body in a unanimous vote to get out of there as quickly as possible. A second later, however, the thought occurred to him that if the old man had wanted to do something to him, why wait till they were here? All James could think to say was, "I'm a little confused."

"Understandably so." The old man smiled at him, "I get the impression you've been a little confused for a while now." He paused, took off his gloves, and extended his hands toward the crackling fire. "Why were you in such a hurry to get up a mountain in the middle of the night James?"

Multiple trains of thought decided to try and use the same tracks in his mind right then, and after the inevitable derailment and loss of life James decided he'd had enough weirdness for one night. "Look, sir, I don't mean to be rude but could you just tell me what is going on? You know my name, you lead me out here for a reason that doesn't exist, and I'm really tired of not knowing what's going on."

The old man looked at him for a moment then burst out laughing. James was sure he had stepped off the edge of the world and was now somewhere else. It was all starting to get a little surreal with the firelight jumping in oranges and reds across the face of an elderly black man who was laughing himself sick. Running, James decided, was out of the question. He was too tired to run anymore. His only other options were to try and walk away or to just sit there until the old man stopped laughing and hope he didn't end up dead by the hand of some deranged mountain man.

After what seemed an eternity the old man stopped laughing. He wiped a tear from his left eye then turned to James, "I'm really sorry about that. It's just that in my line of work you never have anybody who just says it like it is." He sighed and smiled at James, "Everyone's always trying to be so elusive. They dance around the subject never really wanting any real answers. They just want enough information to come to their own conclusions, which are almost always wrong. I mean look at history. It's just littered with people taking a little bit of information then making their own conclusions. Whole religions have been started because someone only wanted to hear part of the truth.

But not you James," he leaned back in his camp chair, "no sir, you want to get right to the heart of it."

"Who are you?"

"Well, still in a hurry I see." The old man pushed himself up out of the chair and walked over to a stack of logs. He grabbed a couple, came back, squatted down and arranged them on the fire, "Don't want it to go out. It's a tad bit chilly out here if you haven't noticed." Standing back up he pointed back down the mountain, "You don't need to worry about your friends finding you up here. The trail we took can't be found by normal people." He turned back and smiled at James again, "You're safe here for the moment."

Normally James would have had dozens of questions competing to get out of his head, but after all that had happened tonight his question creation center seemed to have decided it was done for the foreseeable future. A little sign was placed on the door saying that all future inquiries should be routed directly to the mouth. So all James could do was to look at the old man and say again, "Who are you?"

The old man remained standing, "Why did you come with me James?" He reached down, picked up a long stick, and started to poke at the fire with it, "You were being chased by people who wanted to kill you. You were almost out of energy running up a mountain in the cold." He looked up from the fire at James, "Why did you come with me?"

"I," His shoulders slumped. He really was out of energy. The cold, the long night, the constant stress of the strangeness of the situation, all of it had just sapped the energy out of him. "I don't know."

"Yes you do. Just think about it."

James looked up at the old man and watched the firelight dance in his dark eyes. "You said something back there on the road. It made me think of something I had said not too long before that."

"That's not much of an answer."

"You needed help. It was the right thing to do."

"But what if by helping me you had been caught?"

"Then I would have been caught. I don't know." James scooted his chair closer to the fire so that he could feel the heat on his face. "I didn't really think that far ahead I guess. I was tired." He looked over at the old man again, "I answered your question but you didn't answer mine."

"No, I didn't." The old man continued to poke at the fire. Finally he looked up, then pointed with the burning end of the stick back down the mountain, "Why didn't they help you?"

James sighed. Again people were asking him questions and not giving him any straight answers. He was just about done with answering questions. "I don't know. Go ask them. And while you're at it, bring back a mug of hot chocolate would you. Oh, and some biscuits. I haven't had anything to eat since that cup of coffee at Barnes and Noble."

Without looking up James heard the old man laugh again, "Fair enough. Here you go James."

When he looked up he was only mildly surprised to see the old man holding in his left hand a tin camping plate covered in steaming golden brown biscuits and in his right hand a blue metal mug with what James could only assume was hot coco. He shook his head and mumbled to himself, "I don't know where I am Todo, but it sure ain't Kansas." He took the plate and cup from the old man. Setting the plate down on his lap he could feel the heat from it seeping through his frozen jeans.

"You'll have to give the drink a second to cool down or you'll burn your tongue."

"Ya, sure, thanks." Of course, James thought, because no one who is being chased by killers and then gets handed a magic plate of biscuits wants to burn their tongue because that would be crazy.

The old man waited while James ate two of the biscuits. "You are, all things considered, amazingly patient."

James looked up from his meal, "What other choice do I have?"

"Oh, you've always got other choices."

"Like what?" James looked around, "I guess I could start screaming because you just made biscuits and a cup of coco appear out of thin air, but I'm hungry and screaming isn't going to help that."

"That doesn't mean it's not a choice." He chuckled, "I have seen grown men faint when something like that happens, and after all you've been through tonight I wouldn't be surprised if you had just gotten up and walked away."

"Well, it's been fairly obvious, so far, which people are trying to kill me and which are trying to help me, and you haven't tried to kill me." He paused for a second and looked down at the biscuits, "Unless you poisoned the food."

"In any case I haven't answered your question yet have I?"

"No," James said, "You haven't."

"Well, I'm sorry to say I can't really tell you who I am."

"Of course you can't." James shook his head at the world, "Because that would be too easy wouldn't it."

"It's nothing like that. I just don't really have a name. At least not one you would recognize. I'm just a messenger."

"Any messenger that can make food appear," James said around a mouth full of biscuit, "Is not just a messenger."

"Well, thank you." He smiled at James over the fire, "That's very kind of you."

"So you're a messenger. Are you supposed to give me a message?"

The old man walked back over to his chair and sat down, "That's what I was trying to get to before you remembered you had a stomach."

"Oh, right." James took a slow drink from the mug, "What were you saying again?"

The old man started poking at the fire with his stick again, "Why did you help me when you didn't even know me, but those three down there, who know you, didn't help you?"

James looked into the fire, "Different situations I guess." He thought about it for a second, "Right before I jumped out of the car one of them said something to the effect that it would be bad for him to help me. And I believe him. If he'd helped me he could've ended up dead."

"But there was a good possibility that by helping me you would have ended up dead."

James nodded, "I guess we're just two different people."

"The point is," at this the old man lifted his stick into the air and started waving it around over the fire, "you both had choices to make. Essentially the same choice. He chose one thing, and you chose the other." James looked over and saw the word choices written in smoke hanging over the fire. The old man looked from the word hanging over the fire to James, "What do you believe James?"

"Look," he was at the end of his rope for all of this mumbo jumbo, "I just want to know what's going on here. I mean, I do thank you for the food and for getting me away from those three goons, but really, what is going on around here."

The old man sighed, reached up with the stick and poked at the smoke, "Why would I have just asked you about what you believe right after I talked with you about the choices that you and Scott made?"

Again James wasn't really surprised that the old man knew the exact name of the person chasing him. "Because people make choices depending on what they believe." He felt like he was being lectured by one of his professors.

"That's what you would think isn't it? But the problem here is that people don't believe in anything. I put you through a test James. I wanted to see if you were worth saving. I had been given a message for you but it was contingent on what you did."

"Did I pass?" James wasn't really sure if he cared or not.

"You had to make a choice, almost the same choice Scott had to make. If you'd turned me down and kept running, in essence you would have been no better than the people you were trying to get away from. So, yes, you passed. If you hadn't come they would have caught up to you, and you would be at the bottom of an old mine shaft right now." He looked over at James, "The choices that we make are important James. They define who we are. Do we make the right choices? And believe me there are right and wrong choices."

"But the choices that people make do depend on what they believe. I can't really fault Scott for making the choice that he did because he believes something different than I do."

"No, he doesn't. When you really get down to it, the people that believe anything believe the same thing, and the rest don't believe anything at all. You can fault Scott for making the choice he did. It wasn't just this one choice, it was a whole series of choices that brought him to the place where he had to kill you just to stay alive. He might say he has no choice now, but he did. He made dozens of choices to get to this point, and most of them were wrong. If you were to ask him, in a moment of brutal honesty, he would even tell you they were wrong.

"That's the problem with the world we live in today James. You don't fault people for making bad choices, but really whose fault is it if it's not theirs? No one made those choices for them. No one got inside their head and forced their arms to move. People say they believe different things and so you should respect their different choices, but those are just words. Their actions say things completely differently. On one day they say that there is no such thing as right and wrong, but on the next day when they come to call in a favor you owe them they show there is a right and a wrong. It's wrong for you not to live up to your promises and follow through with the favor. If they actually lived what they said then you should be able to blow off the favor and do what you want and they couldn't get angry with you because you believe it's fine to ignore repaying favors. The truth of the matter is, however, that they know the difference between right and wrong, they just want an excuse to get out of it themselves when it comes their turn to repay a favor."

The old man had been sitting and talking quietly while poking at the fire the whole time. Now he turned and looked at James. James could see this time that it wasn't a reflection of the fire in his eyes. There really were flames dancing in his pupils. Even in his numb state this caused his heart to jump and he almost stood up. The old man spoke quietly, "Belief James. It all comes down to belief." He held out his left hand and a white light began to shine in his palm. The light grew till it was the size of a tennis ball then split. The two lights began to spin in a circle above his hand. It was like a juggler, a very strange juggler. "This world is losing its beliefs. And when belief is gone then the people are hollow shells waiting to be filled up with something. People want to believe in things. They need to have something to hold onto when the night gets dark, or when a loved one dies." The lights continued to spin, forming a brilliant white circle in the air. "The end result of many things happening in the world today is the loss of belief. Tolerate everything and believe in nothing. Allow those who make the wrong choices to go free because they're just different than you. There is no such thing as right or wrong, it is all a matter of perspective. At the end you raise a generation who believes in nothing."

Within the circle of light there was only darkness. A darkness so deep James knew if he looked at it too long he would be lost in it and never find his way home. The old man's voice came through the darkness in a soft almost hypnotic way, "If a person is empty then anything can come along and fill them up. They wish to be passionate about something, anything. And when someone comes along and offers them that passion they take it. They hunger for it. Since they've been raised thinking there's no difference between right and wrong they don't care what it is they're passionate about as long as they feel something. As long as something fills that emptiness inside of them." The swirling white light turned a dark red and James could almost see something move in the darkness. "This is where he comes in. He whispers in your ear. Convinces you the passion can be yours, the world can be yours. All you have to do is open the door and believe. Believe and the floodgates will open. The emptiness inside you will be filled. You will be happy." Suddenly the circle of red light collapsed in on itself with a brief flash and deep boom that James could feel in his chest.

He found himself looking into the eyes of the old man. After the deep soul wrenching darkness of the circle he found a certain comfort now in the strange fire flickering in his dark brown eyes. "But where does he come from?" James whispered.

The old man sighed, "Where do I come from?" He held up his hands in a show of submission, "I know that is not much of an answer, but for now it's all I can give you. There are many things out there you don't need to know."

Frustrated James almost shouted, "Then what do I need to know?"

"It isn't what you know James. It is what you believe." He took his stick in both hands and broke it in half. Tossing half of it to James he said, "Do you believe you made the right choice in helping Rupert?"

"Yes."

"Good. Do you believe you made the right choice in helping me even when you knew your life was in danger?"

James felt his frustration melting away as he realized that yes he believed he had made the right choices. "Yes, I believe I did the right thing."

"Then you are not a hollow man James." The fire in the old man's eyes seemed to grow. Its light illuminated the dark world they were sitting in. The snow around them sparkled like a million tiny diamonds, and the world grew warmer. "Look at the stick in your hand." James looked down and saw a plain pine branch slightly burnt at one end, broken at the other. "Now look at mine." Again James looked over to see the other half of a plain pine branch. "When you believe, two things can happen. The darkness inside of you can move and can help you do things, or the darkness can be burned away by the fire of true belief. Look in my eyes James and see the fire."

At first it hurt to look into those strange burning eyes, but then he realized he'd been wanting to look into that fire for so long. He remembered all those times camping with his family when he would just sit and stare into the campfire. He would watch it dance and play over the logs. It fascinated him like nothing else ever had. He thought of stories of arsonists that said they had started the fires just so they could watch the flames. They would start bigger and bigger ones because they wanted to see the flames, they wanted to feel it. James wanted to feel it.

"James," James took a breath, it seemed like it was the first one he had ever taken, "picture the fire in your mind. Hold it there. Feel its warmth. Now picture that fire on the end of the stick in your hand."

James felt a door open in his mind. Behind that door a fire burned. He looked down at the pine stick in his hand and one end of it was burning. All he could do was stare at it. Everything was changing. He could feel it. The world was different somehow. The cold was gone from the air. The darkness was lighter. He'd opened the door, believed, and it was done. Looking up at the old man he said, "Is that all there is?"

"Oh no, not by a long shot. You see," the old man raised his right hand straight out with the palm up and a bright orange ball of flame sprang to life over it, "belief is a conduit." The orange ball grew to be the size of a basketball. "By itself belief can do nothing. It is nothing in and of itself. What belief does on a regular day to day basis is influence the choices of the believer. If you say you believe in something and yet you make choices that go against that then you don't really believe do you?" He looked over at the ball of fire in his hand, "We are drawn to the fire. The light drives away the fears of the darkness. The heat warms us and protects us. Belief can do the same thing, but again it is only a conduit, a pathway. It's like a light switch. By itself the switch does nothing. By itself the wires and the light bulb do nothing, but add power and you have light." The ball of fire started to stretch and lengthen, "Belief can cause things to happen. Prayers are answered, monks survive in below freezing temperatures, and people survive life-ending diseases." The fire started to curl around the old man, "The choices of those who believe change the world. They either make it a better place or a worse place. In either case they believe and that belief gives them access to power. A light switch is neither good nor evil. The wires that connect it are neither good nor evil. How they are put to use is the question." The flame had wrapped itself around the old man's body like a burning orange anaconda, "There are really only two choices. You can open the door and let the darkness fill the empty void and do whatever you want, or whatever it wants. Or you can open the door and be filled with the flame and drive the darkness away."

Watching in a kind of hypnotic fascination James heard himself saying what any good college student would say, "But the world is more complicated than that. There are always more than just two choices."

"That is why you have been confused for so long James. If a teacher were to see a student add two plus two and come out with five would it be all right for that teacher to say the student made the wrong choice?"

James couldn't keep his eyes off the dancing reds and yellows of the twisting flames, "Yes, but life is more complicated than two plus two."

"And calculus is more complicated as well but there is still a right answer and a wrong answer. Just because it is more complicated doesn't mean that any answer will do. It just means the right answer and the wrong answer will be harder to see." The flames began twisting slowly around the old man's fingers, "This is where your belief comes in. It influences your decisions, your choices. You cannot separate a person from their belief. Even those that say they believe in nothing still believe in that. They hold onto the belief that nothing is there tighter than most people believe the sun will come up in the morning, and they make their choices based on the belief that nothing is watching, nothing is there." The fire became brighter and James had to hold up a hand to shield his eyes. The old man's voice seemed to float out of the light, "But when you don't have the light of the fire all you can see is darkness, and the only conclusion you can come to without losing your sanity is that nothing is in the darkness. Because if you acknowledge there are things in the darkness," James heard something and looked away from the light, "then you have to acknowledge anything could be out there and all the choices you have made could be wrong."

Out beyond the light James could see Scott and the two others walking down the road. He knew they were far off but could see the details on their faces. He could see the darkness surrounding them, and in that darkness he saw something familiar. It moved with them, and looked over them with dozens of eyes. It was part of each of them yet slightly separate. Behind him, from inside the light he heard the old man say, "They've made their choices. They cannot deny that. They have opened the door of their soul to the darkness."

James turned back to the old man who was wreathed in light and fire. This time James did not cover his eyes but looked directly into the light, "Why? Why would they choose that?"

"Unfortunately, for many reasons. Each of them has his own reason. One of them was brought up believing there was nothing out there so whatever you can grab in this life is all there is, and when he was offered power he took it. For another he didn't want his choices brought into the light so he decided to stay in the darkness and deny those choices were wrong. The other was hurt by someone who claimed to walk in the light and he turned his back on anything that had to do with the light believing it was a lie."

James took a step toward the old man, "But what am I supposed to do?" He was growing frustrated again. The light show was all well and good, and it was one of the coolest things James could ever remember seeing, but it didn't alleviate his confusion at all. "I still don't understand why I'm here, or what I'm supposed to do."

A small string of flame extended itself from the light and touched James on the shoulder, "You are here because of the choices you made. Those choices proved you believed in the light. I was sent to show you the truth. You have come close to the voice in the darkness and had no way to protect yourself." The thin string wrapped itself around James' arm, "You have a choice to make James, and with that choice comes responsibility. With that responsibility comes power." In his mind James saw the simple pine stick in his hand as it burst into flames. He remembered twin bolts of blue white lightning leaping from Rupert's hands. He saw an unknown attacker pull up a tree and throw it at him. That was what the old man meant by power. James looked down to see the thin string of flame had wrapped all around him. He felt warmth. He looked up but couldn't see the old man through the light.

A voice drifted to him through the warmth and light, "Your belief shapes your choices, and your choices can change the world."

James finally thought he understood. He closed his eyes and sighed, breathing in the warmth of the fire. It wrapped around him and he could feel his mind drifting. His last thought before sleep overtook him was that his father would be proud of him for making the right choices.

Chapter Twelve

The sky was becoming cloudy and blocking out the starlight on this dark Alaskan morning. Don Chon looked at his watch and realized he had twenty minutes until his eight thirty class. It still felt a little weird to be going to classes in the morning and it was still dark as midnight. He always got the feeling that some wild animal could come charging out of the darkness and drag him off and no one would notice. There had been reports around the campus of a bear that was trying to get into the dorms. The campus security had been posting warnings not to leave anything out with any kind of strong smell. Everything from cheerios to toothpaste was to be put away so it wouldn't cause an incident with the bear.

Looking into the darkness of the pines and aspens along his route to class he tried to picture what he would do if the bear came out and decided it liked the smell of his deodorant. That made him wonder, was deodorant on the list of things they weren't supposed to leave out? Could the bear smell his deodorant? Had he doomed himself to a horrible death because he wanted to smell good and impress Sharon in calculus class this morning? Which scenario would he rather live through, being mauled by a bear or smelling like body odor while sitting next to the girl he thought could be the one? That was a tough choice.

"Don?"

When people say they almost jumped out of their skin they're usually just using it as a figure of speech, but in this case Don was certain he almost left his own skin standing there so it could be a distraction to the bear he was sure had just come up behind him. Part of his mind tried to reason with him that a bear, no matter how well trained, would not be saying his name. Once that part of his mind had convinced the rest of his body that everything was alright Don put his skin back on and turned around to see who'd tried to give him a heart attack. "Professor Merrill," Don covered his heart, "you scared me."

The professor smiled, "I apologize, what with the bear wandering around the campus and all I should have tried harder to let you know I was coming up behind you."

"It's all right. I've just been a little on edge lately."

"Have they figured out who sent the letters yet?"

Don shrugged, "No, and I doubt they will. All they've told me was they weren't actually mailed."

"Ah, so someone placed them there."

"Ya," Don shrugged, "and of course there aren't cameras or anything in the mail room."

"No, I suppose there aren't."

"Well," Don sighed, "I made a choice and I have to live with it."

The professor motioned for Don to walk with him, and they started off down the tree-lined path that led to the back of the professor's building. The thin white branches of the winter dead aspens seemed to reach out to them as they passed. The dead hungering for a brief warm touch of the living. Out of the corner of his eye Don thought he saw something move between the trees and stopped. Looking hard and listening for the sound of a bear he missed the ripple of darkness as it moved on toward the building.

The professor touched him on the shoulder, "You thought you heard something?"

"I guess it was nothing."

"So," the professor again directed Don down the path toward his office, "how're your parents taking all this?"

Don looked over at the professor and sighed, "My Dad doesn't seem to mind all that much. I think he figures that whatever I want to do with my life is fine as long as I don't end up in prison. My Mom on the other hand is taking it like I decided to become a stripper in Las Vegas."

"Really?" The professor stopped and opened the door for Don, "What's so bad about what you're doing?"

Don shook his head and frowned as he went through the door. He had been up to the professor's office so many times in the last few weeks it was almost second nature now. "She thinks, to put it more politely than she did, that I've gone over to the dark side."

"Really?" the professor said again.

"Ya, she yelled at me for leading the parade the other day. She feels that I've thrown out my Catholic heritage and chosen to side with the devil."

The professor gave him a slight smile, "So I guess that would make me the devil?"

"Oh yes," Don opened the door at the top of the stairs that led out into the professor's hallway, "she's convinced you've somehow brainwashed me."

"Well, try not to be angry with her. She just wants to protect her only son."

"I know." They paused as the professor unlocked the door to his office. "I just wish she could see that what I am doing is right. I tried to explain to her that it isn't that I'm condoning the actions of certain people, I'm just trying to make sure those people are treated decently."

"Ah," said the professor as he maneuvered around the chairs and stood behind his desk, "the old adage of love the sinner but hate the sin?"

"Exactly," Don dropped himself into one of the closer chairs, "but saying it and doing it are two different things. I'm fairly sure my Mom can't differentiate between the sinner and the sin." Don shivered as a breeze blew through the professor's open window. The door behind him slammed shut with the change in pressure in the room. Don glanced over his shoulder and thought he saw something move in the darkness between the bookshelves. He pointed to the spot and said, "I think you may have shrews living in your office."

"Oh we have lots of problems in this old building." Don turned back to the professor in time to see him raise his hands.

The professor stood behind his desk and said to the darkness between the bookshelves, "Now what do you think would be the best way to leave him?" Don could faintly hear whispers, but it was like a mosquito buzzing at his ear and he couldn't quite make out what it was saying. He was starting to think this was all some kind of a joke when a thick black smoke started filling the room and blocking out the lights.

The dimmer the lights became the clearer he could hear the buzzing voice. "Bind him then wake him. He needs to look into the eyes of his death. I need to feed on his fear."

The professor looked down at Don as he came around his desk. He thought he should feel some type of pity or remorse for this, but it was really the most reasonable thing. He needed something terrible to get the sheep here at the university bleating. They needed to be angry enough to riot in the streets and this was the first step. Don was a well-liked student who'd stood up for people's rights. They all knew after the tolerance march he had been getting anonymous hate mail. They all knew that his mother had all but disowned him on the basis of her religious belief. This would be the icing on the cake, or the straw that broke the camel's back, on any other figure of speech that would finally start his endgame into action. By the time he was done the students would be in a frenzy. He could see it now; streets would be barricaded with burning tires, people would be beaten with tire irons and baseball bats, and none of them would admit they'd started it. Which, of course, would make the other side even more incensed. The end result would be chaos. This city on the edge of the wilderness, the farthest from help, would burn, and it would be only the beginning.

He leaned over Don and slapped him until he woke up. It really wasn't necessary, he could have simply spoken and the sleep he had put over him would have been lifted, but it felt better to hit something. He had spent so much time thinking about things that he missed being able to use his hands. It felt good to physically take part in his own plan.

"Now then," the professor could feel the buzz of hunger float through his mind, "shall we begin?" He looked into his victims brown eyes and tried his best to make it look like a hate crime. He was glad no one else was in the building this morning. It was so much nicer when he could hear the screams.

Chapter Thirteen

Katie took her time finishing her cereal. To her left a half dozen round tables were packed with other students. Some had textbooks open and were flipping frantically from page to page while others laughed and talked over their morning meal before heading off to classes. The university was the place to see every type of person imaginable. You could see people from every continent on the planet except, she corrected herself, for Antarctica. She hadn't seen any penguins in the dining hall. Not yet at least. This was university life and you never knew when someone would pull a prank that would end up with penguins marching their way through the dining hall. Once they had all woken up to salmon poking their heads out of the drink machines. Thank goodness there was ice in there, she thought, or that could have ended up smelling horrible.

She chuckled to herself remembering doing a double take as she walked by the orange juice machine to make a waffle. It wasn't every day you had a salmon staring at you from the top of the juice machine. But it was university life and you just let some things roll off your back, so after she looked at it for a second she decided it would be nice to have that waffle. Especially when she noticed they had put out strawberries and whip cream that morning.

Looking around the room again she noticed two of her girl friends at a table to her right and waved. They gave her the universal unspoken look that asked where her date was. She returned the universal gesture that said she didn't know. She had talked with only one of them the night before about her date with James and how excited she was about it all. Katie had told her friend that she was supposed to meet him here for breakfast. The fact that it looked like every single girl at the table knew about the situation wasn't strange in the least. Word travels fast on campus. As much as they were all there to get a degree of some kind and learn something, relationships were almost equally as important. In fact sometimes they were more important. They jokingly referred to some girls as being there to get their Mrs. degree. It just seemed like they were only there so they could end up married. Katie didn't disagree that this was most likely the best place to find a guy. It was amazing. You had four years to try out every kind of guy until you found the right one. If you couldn't find one here then you would have a terrible time finding one after you graduated. Here none of the "outside" rules applied. Things like not dating where you worked didn't apply because class wasn't a job, and if you did work with the person the job was just temporary because you were going to school. Some of her friends from back home had chosen their universities based on the percentage of guys to girls. One of her guy friends from high school had chosen a university where the population was regularly five girls to one guy. Now that would be tough for a girl. Good for her guy friend though.

The dining hall doors opened and a group of foreign exchange students walked in. She knew a couple of them. They were friends with Don. The guys had short cropped hair that they would spike up in the back, but leave a long strand of hair to pull down on either side of their face. The effect reminded her of Japanese animation she'd seen on the cartoon network. She guessed that was where the style had started, or it could be the other way around. The girls kept their hair straight and long. When it wasn't pulled up in a bun or ponytail. Their black hair seemed to shimmer as they walked. You could almost see your reflection in it. Katie only had a class with one of the girls. When Yuko let her hair down it easily came to her waist. Katie, who's hair was just below her shoulder line, thought hair down to your waist would be a pain to deal with. Just washing it would take forever, and talk about going through shampoo like crazy. Yuko said she couldn't cut it because it would bring bad luck, and if she left it long it was good luck to bring a good man into her life. Again, Katie thought, relationships defined most of what they did here at the university.

Yuko was brilliant. She was here to study marine biology, and was a good friend of Don's. Katie was fairly sure Don had a crush on her, but Katie didn't really feel like she knew him well enough to ask about it. She didn't really get to know him until she had volunteered for the tolerance march they had put on. He was a great leader, and very passionate about what he thought was right. She hadn't really had any time away from preparing for the march to get to know him. They didn't have any classes together, and other than the meetings for the march they didn't really see each other. It was surprising, really. This campus wasn't all that big, and she felt like she knew most of the people here, but knowing people and actually being friends with them were two completely different things. She was fairly sure she could call Don her friend now. They had been through a lot together. He'd even come over to her room a few nights ago to talk about the hate mail he'd been getting. He tried not to let on but it really scared him. She told him, and she believed it, that as long as he stayed on campus and around people he should be fine.

Finishing her cereal she looked around again. Even before they were dating James had never been late. It was one of the things

Katie liked about him. If he said he was going to be there then he was there on time. Most of the time he was even early. Usually that was a good thing, except for the time her roommate had been running around the house in her underwear and James showed up five minutes early. That had been hilarious. She could still remember the look on his face as her roommate stood frozen in the middle of the kitchen in nothing but her bra and a pair of boxer shorts. They were matching red with little white flowers, and James had nodded his head and said calmly, "Red really brings out the color of your eyes Jenny." Then he had turned and walked back into the living room and sat down just in time to watch Jenny run through and into her room.

Walking across the dining hall she checked out the windows one last time to make sure he wasn't running up to the outside doors before she put her dishes in the cleaning area. She sighed deeply and wondered what could have happened. She knew he'd intended to drive to Barnes and Noble last night, but that shouldn't have been a problem. His little doughnut tire should've been able to make it there and back, and even if it didn't he would have called her last night. She shook her head and walked out into the dark Alaskan morning.

Not having a class for another hour she wasn't quite sure what to do with herself. Deciding that she would head over to James' dorm room and see if anyone was there she started walking down the shortcut trail that led through the trees. She was trying to decide if she should be angry or worried when she was distracted by blue and red flashing lights at the end of the trail. The lack of snow and the fact that all the underbrush had died off for the winter gave Katie a good view through the thin aspens and arctic pine. The flashing lights cast alternate shadows across the trail making Katie's view ahead blur then snap into focus with each step.

As she moved closer she could make out people in uniforms rolling out yellow caution tape. For a brief second her curiosity was peaked. It was like an episode of CSI or Law and Order. She wondered what had happened, and the first thing that came to mind was that the bear had finally gotten someone. At that thought her heart started to race. Her mind screamed at her that this was the way to James' dorm room and he had never been late for breakfast before. Without another thought she started to run.

The flashing lights made her stumble over roots that had pushed up through the trail. Catching herself on an aspen she saw the lights illuminate a body. It was swept by red then blue and Katie's mind couldn't make sense of what she was seeing. She had come prepared to see a body on the ground mauled by a bear, but this was something completely different. It was something out of a nightmare.

It hung lifelessly tied to an aspen. The ropes were wrapped around the torso keeping the body upright as if it were standing, or leaning against the tree. Katie's legs moved of their own accord, propelling her closer to the flashing lights, and the drooping head of the body tied to the tree. It was like he was looking for something on the ground, and his arms dangled as if he was reaching for whatever it was he had lost. It looked like if they took the ropes off he would simply bend over and pick something up and walk away.

Finally Katie made it to the edge of the trees and stopped. Her mind said that it couldn't be James, but at the same time she had to know. She couldn't see his face from here, and something was wrong with his hair. Part of her wanted to walk over into the macabre scene and lift up the head to look into his eyes. Would she see his bright blue eyes looking back at her? Another part of her didn't want to know. It wanted to run and hide, to pretend that whatever this was she had never seen it. Wasn't that possible? No one had seen her yet. She could just leave, and never know. But she had to know if it was him. She had to know what had happened to him. Was he coming to see her, and because of that he'd walked into something he shouldn't have?

All the while she looked at him and something didn't seem right. The red and blue lights played with her vision so she couldn't be sure if what she was seeing was right, but it looked like parts of his hair were gone. And other things looked like they were the wrong color. She walked closer to get a better look and was startled when a hand clasped her right shoulder and pulled her back.

"Miss."

Katie looked over at the officer as if she were in a dream. She started trying to figure out what this person was doing here looking at her.

"Miss, I'm going to have to ask you to step back please."

"What?" She looked from the officer to the body still hanging there. Still reaching for that something on the ground.

"Miss, are you all right?"

The words swam slowly into her mind. Was she all right? What did that mean? She looked back at the officer and realized the world was getting smaller. It was like turning off her grandfather's old TV set. It all went to a single white dot in the middle. Then to black.

A cool breeze fanned her face. For a moment she thought she was waking up in her dorm room with the window open. She had a brief memory of red and blue lights washing over a nightmare in a dark forest. She blinked her eyes open and looked up at a dark sky framed with the dead arms and fingers of leafless aspens. Her breathing quickened and her heart sped up. She sat up and her head started spinning. The world filled with little sparkling white lights.

"Whoa there," hands pulled on her shoulders, "you need to lay back down before you fall down." She agreed with the hands and allowed them to guide her back down until she was looking again at the dark sky.

She looked over at where the voice had come from. Lights framed the dark figure from behind making it impossible to see the face. Eyes seemed to glow white out of the darkness and look down at her. Fear washed over her as those glowing eyes seemed to look into her. She felt as if they would devour her if she looked away. A wash of white headlights followed by the low rumble of a diesel engine snapped her away from thoughts of nightmares. Now where the glowing eyes had been a face was illuminated by the headlights of the truck just pulling up.

Professor Merrill smiled down at her, "I was walking by when you fainted. I told the officer I knew you and would stay with you until you woke up."

"What," she sat up a little and waited until the white lights stopped dancing through her vision, "what happened?"

"Well, it seems you saw something that caused you to go into shock."

"Saw something?" The memory flashed back in a frame by frame slideshow in her mind. The red and blue lights flashing through the trees, the body hanging, ropes tied around it, arms reaching for the ground. She felt like she was drowning. The air around her was too thick.

"All right," hands again pulled her back so that she was looking up at the blank dark sky, "let's try not to faint again."

She lay there staring up at the starless sky gulping in air like a salmon on a river bank. Finally when the world had righted itself and the ground didn't feel like it was spinning she turned her head and looked at the professor, "Who," she didn't know if she could get the rest of the question out.

He looked down at her sadness in his eyes, "I was told by the officer in charge that it was a student named Don Chon."

Katie simply stared at the professor. The words rolled inside her head and wouldn't come to rest so that she could get a good look at them. "Don?"

"Yes, Katie." The professor sighed and looked over her toward where she could hear other people talking, "It seems those letters he was getting turned into something real."

"Don." The name sunk in and the words stopped rolling. It wasn't James. She was glad the professor was looking away right then because she couldn't help but smile. It wasn't James. Then it hit her. It was Don tied to that tree. He had come over so many times that week telling her how scared he was of those letters. Telling her he was thinking of just going home for the rest of the semester. She remembered her own words. Telling him people liked to hide behind anonymous letters, and people like that would never have the courage to actually do anything. She'd convinced him the best place for him was here. Convincing him that if he left they had won. So he stayed. Now he was, what? What was he? "Professor?"

He looked back down at her, "Yes?"

"Is he all right?"

"Don?" He slowly shook his head, "No, Katie. He's not all right. He's," the professor paused and cleared his throat as if the words were sticking, "he's dead Katie."

"Dead?" Her mind told her that couldn't be right. Don couldn't be dead. People didn't just die. College students didn't just die. She looked at the professor, "What," she took a deep breath, "what happened?"

"I'm not going to go into details." He put a hand on her shoulder, "Do you think you can stand up?"

She took a few breaths and waited to make sure the world was where it was supposed to be then said, "Ya, I think so." The professor stood up beside her and extended his hand. Taking it he pulled her slowly up until she was standing. The world moved a little and she put out her hand and grabbed a tree to steady herself.

After waiting a few seconds the professor asked, "Everything all right?"

"Ya." Katie looked around. She wasn't quite sure where she was. Leafless trees surrounded her on three sides and cars filled in the fourth side. She looked around hoping not to see what she now knew was Don, and yet in some way also hoping that she would see him.

The professor put one hand on her shoulder and the other on the small of her back, "Let's walk." He gently guided her away from the cars and the noise. He looked over at her, "You doing okay?"

She had been watching the ground as it slid beneath her feet. It seemed that if she stopped moving her legs the ground would just keep moving. She looked over at the professor, "I think so."

They came out of the trees into an open expanse of grass. To her left the Chugach Mountains were starting to glow with the imminent rise of the sun. The sharp peaks were dulled by the white blanket of snow. It was as if someone had tossed cotton over razor blades. They looked deceptively soft but every now and then a sharp crag would jut up and try to cut open the sky. They said these were some of the youngest mountains in North America. None of their edges had been worn off by time or weather. It was as if God had just carved them yesterday and the world was fresh and new.

Everything seemed unreal to Katie as she was guided along the pathway toward one of the buildings ahead of her. Students were walking by talking. The sun was coming up like normal. The sun shouldn't come up when someone dies, Katie thought. The people should stop walking around. Didn't they know what had happened?

The professor opened the door in front of her and held it while she walked in. He guided her up the wide carpeted steps to the second floor. As she turned into the hall of the second floor she felt something on her cheek and tried to brush it off. Her finger came away wet. She stood in the hallway and looked at her finger. She hadn't realized that she was crying. She didn't remember thinking about crying, and shouldn't a person have to think about crying?

The professor gently guided her by the arm down the hall and into his office. Once in he shut the door behind them and motioned for her to sit down. She sat there and looked around the office wondering how she had gotten there. She remembered the woods and the mountains, but she didn't remember opening any doors or thinking about where to go next. She felt empty, hollow, waiting for something, some feeling to fill the space. She looked across the desk at the professor, "Why?"

He shook his head and Katie was almost sure she'd seen a tear at the corner of his eye. "There's never a good reason for something like this." He looked down at his feet and shook his head again. "The officer told me a note was found attached to..." he looked up at Katie, "Well, anyway, a note was left."

A quiet voice whispered in her mind of rage and revenge, and something started to burn inside of her. Don had been one of the nicest people she'd ever known. All he'd ever wanted was for people to look beyond themselves. He'd talked about not being self-centered, and to the best of any human ability he'd practiced what he preached. If you'd asked him for the shirt off his back he would have given it to you, even if he'd never met you before. He seemed to believe that nothing in this world was really his anyway so what did it matter if he kept it or gave it away. How anyone could do something to a person like that Katie just didn't understand. "What did it say?"

The professor looked her in the eyes for a few seconds trying to decide what to tell her, "Are you sure you want to know?"

"It's going to come out on the news by the end of the day anyway." Katie replied.

"Yes, it probably is." The professor sighed and looked around as if it would be easier to talk about if he wasn't looking directly at her. "You know, don't you, what religious affiliation Don was raised under?"

"Yes," Katie replied, "he was Catholic."

"Well," the professor paused, "I don't know if what was written had anything to do with his being Catholic but I can't be sure one way or the other." He paused again. It seemed to Katie he was having a hard time getting the words out and she waited thinking he just needed time to compose his thoughts. "Anyway," he finally said, "the officer told me the note said he would burn in the pit with the gays he loved so much."

Katie gasped. Her hands gripped the armrests of the chair until her knuckles turned white. The whispering grew louder in her mind and began to fill up the empty spaces inside of her. She knew it had been a hate crime, and she knew the letters he'd been getting had referred to hell and things about his stance toward homosexuals, but she hadn't been ready for something like that. Not really. You can think about it all you like, but until it happens you don't really understand it.

"I'm" the professor coughed to clear his throat, "I'm not exactly sure it was said like that. The officer didn't read it to me, he just told me what was on it."

The room darkened and the whispers turned to shouts in her mind. The picture of Don hanging on the tree flashed across the darkness of her mind. A door inside of her opened and the voices flooded in. She couldn't concentrate on anything else as she listened to the voices say what should happen to people that committed crimes like this. She had never been one to hate, but she had never had a good reason to hate someone before this. The voices whispered to her of revenge and how the police would do nothing. She could see a person sitting in a comfortable jail cell getting three meals a day and watching cable television while Don hung from a tree beaten and lifeless. That was no punishment, the voices whispered in her ear. There was no justice in that comfortable jail cell. At that moment she wanted to hit something. She wanted to find the person who had done this and smash their face in. At the same time a feeling of helplessness washed over her. What could she really do? Nothing.

The professor cleared his throat and Katie looked up at him, "You know," he looked over her shoulder at something and seemed to nod, "I was wanting to talk with you about something anyway, and this seems like as good a time as any."

This was not a good time for anything Katie thought. She didn't want to talk about her grades or her paper. The world needed to stop and she wanted to get off. What could be important to talk about now?

"It's time we took action Katie." The professor stood up and reached for a book on the top shelf next to him. He pulled down the book and flipped it open to a sheet of paper that was in the middle of it. "I've been thinking about this for a while, but now I finally have a good reason." He sat back down and looked across the desk at her, "Going on marches to convince people to be more tolerant isn't enough, and this attack on Don proves that. People aren't going to change their minds unless they have a reason to." He handed her the paper across the fake glass expanse of his desk. For a moment Katie thought she saw another pair of eyes reflected in the glass as she took the paper, but when she looked again nothing was there. As she took it the professor said, "Remember what you said in your own paper Katie. It's not a question of right or wrong. It's a question of what is best for the people, and what is best for our community."

She looked down at it. She had never really believed in anything before. Nothing had ever seemed right enough, or good enough, but now she believed in something, she believed in this and it streamed in through that open door and filled her.

Chapter Fourteen

James walked down the hall of his high school knowing he was going to be late for class, but not quite knowing which class he was supposed to be going to. He didn't quite remember this hallway being here, or was it just that it was here but not quite in the same place? He knew he needed to hurry or his teacher would be mad. On the other hand he couldn't quite picture who the teacher was that would be mad. If only he could remember what class he was going to then it would all be sorted out.

He turned the corner at the end of the hall and saw an older black gentleman mopping the red shag carpeted hallway. The old man looked up at him and smiled. James was sure the man said something but he couldn't quite hear it. As James came closer he noticed the old man wasn't mopping; he was actually holding a door open. Then James remembered. He was supposed to be going into the auditorium for a special assembly. That must have been why he couldn't remember what class to go to because it wasn't a normal class.

He walked into the auditorium. The walls were a deep blue and lights glowed from so high overhead that he couldn't make out exactly where they were coming from. He thought he should have found it odd that there were only two rows of seats but he was sure this was his high school so that must be right. He scooted himself down the aisle and took a seat in the middle of the second row. He realized he must have known the other students, but he couldn't quite remember their names so he decided to just sit and wait for the assembly to start.

James wasn't quite sure how long he waited. It didn't seem that long, but at the same time he wasn't really sure how much time had passed. Finally behind him he heard someone shuffling around and turned to see the old man setting up a projector. It reminded him of the one his parents had down in the storage room in the basement. His dad had been talking about taking the reels in to someone and getting them transferred onto thumb drives. He remembered watching black and white cartoons on a white sheet in the basement. The characters never talked as they flickered across his mother's best white linens.

Finally he saw the old man finish threading the filmstrip through the old machine and he turned back around to see that a screen had lowered down from the ceiling. Sitting back he counted down with the giant black and white numbers now flickering on the white screen. Once the number one was wiped away by a swirling line a door appeared on the screen. It opened and a handsome gentleman stepped through wearing a suit and tie and what James thought of as a fedora on his head. He took off the fedora and set it on a hat rack that had appeared on the screen. Turning to the audience he unbuttoned the single button on his suit coat and put his hands in his pockets. Opening his mouth to talk James was not surprised to see words appear at the bottom of the screen rather than sound.

Greetings. The screen said. I understand you may be confused by everything that's happened in the last twenty-four hours, but you have to admit it's more interesting than going to your art history class this morning. James nodded in agreement. He could sleep through his art history class and still get an A. We all would like to thank you, first off, for joining the cause. The man walked over and sat down in a dark, easy chair. Now that you have, in a sense, agreed to join up with the good guys there are some ground rules. He leaned forward and looked at James. For the first time James noticed that it wasn't all in black and white. When the man leaned forward James had noticed his eyes for the first time. In the center of each pupil a small fire burned. James didn't know how he'd missed it before. The red of the flames stood out in stark contrast to the black and white of the rest.

First, sliding over next to the man a little cartoon character held up his index finger, what makes us different from them is that we must always treat others as more important than ourselves. Another little cartoon character came out and the man smiled as the first character proceeded to help the second over a cartoon brick wall that had now appeared. I know that sounds a little trite and cliché but that is the right thing to do. The two characters had made it over the wall and were now smiling out at the audience. James at once found it comforting and a little creepy. Second, you must realize the power that has been given to you is a great responsibility. James thought of Spiderman and wondered if the man in the film had gotten permission to use that idea from Marvel Comics. If ever you use it for your own gain, or in a way that we deem to be unfit there will be repercussions. The two cartoon characters glared out at the audience and cracked their knuckles. No sound was heard but below them in large black letters was written the words Crack! Crack! Again James was struck by the fact that if it hadn't been so creepy he might have laughed.

Finally, and this isn't a guideline it's just a helpful reminder, if you don't believe that what you want to do is possible then it won't happen. At this he stood and walked back toward the door. He buttoned his coat and reached for his hat. Turning to the audience he spun his hat on one finger and said, Good luck James. With that he popped his hat back onto his head. Opening the door he revealed a world of bright blues and greens. Before it closed James was sure he saw the man turn into a pillar of fire, but then the door closed and the screen went blank.

James looked around and saw the other students were getting up and leaving the auditorium so he decided it must be time to get back to class. He squeezed his way out from the two rows of seats and started heading toward the door. Before he got there the old man who'd been running the projector grabbed his arm and stopped him. James was about to ask him what he wanted when the old man reached up and covered James' eyes. James reached up to push his hand away and realized there was nothing there.

Opening his eyes James found himself looking up at what he could only assume was the inside of a tent. As he tried to sit up he realized he was wrapped in something and looked down to find himself zipped up in a blue down filled sleeping bag. His confusion only mounted when he looked around the tent and couldn't remember a thing about how he'd gotten there.

With the strange dream still fresh in his mind he unzipped the sleeping bag and looked down to find himself wearing long johns and a long sleeve thermal shirt he was sure he didn't own. He tried to decide if he was still in a dream or if he was awake. Normally in his dreams things seemed normal but weren't, like his high school that wasn't really his high school. This on the other hand just seemed strange. He knew it wasn't his tent, and he knew he didn't remember getting into a sleeping bag. On the other hand it was a really nice sleeping bag. He reached down and squeezed the bag to feel how much down was in it. If he wasn't dreaming he wondered if he could get away with keeping the sleeping bag, and as he looked around again he decided that the tent wouldn't be too bad either. Would it really be stealing if he didn't know who it belong to in the first place? Glancing around he didn't see anyone else's things in the tent. It was big enough to hold two people. Not like when the description of a tent says that it holds two people but they actually mean two hobbits that really like each other. This tent could actually hold two normal sized people. His brother had gotten a two-man tent for them to use when they had been going through Colorado. He was glad he was comfortable with his brother because in that case two man had meant only if you were under five foot four and willing to stack yourselves in the tent like wood.

He looked around the tent until he found the rest of his clothes rolled up below his feet. It really concerned him that he couldn't remember taking his clothes off and zipping himself into a sleeping bag. Normally he would have stopped and tried to figure out what had happened but he realized it was really cold outside of the down bag and decided that getting his clothes on was a more important priority. The tent, while being quite nice, was not all that tall and didn't afford much room to stand and get dressed, so after struggling to put his pants on while laying down James pulled his sweatshirt on over the thermal undershirt and then grabbed his down jacket. Looking around he found the black stocking cap that the old man had given him, and inside of it was a matching pair of black thermal mittens. He pulled the cap on and stuffed his now very cold hands into the mittens.

Now, looking very much like a red a black marshmallow, he decided he was warm enough to sit and figure out what had happened. He'd read enough books in the last year of college to be aware of how people usually reacted to these situations. Normally it would be described as memories swirling around, or pictures in their minds being jumbled up. So to avoid either of these situations he decided to start with what he knew for sure. He knew for sure that three college students had driven him up Hatcher's pass with the intent of killing him and leaving him in an abandoned mine. He knew for sure that he had jumped out of the car and ran up a dirt road toward Archangel mine. Then there was the old man who had stopped him on the road and asked for help with a grandson that didn't actually exist.

Without being able to help it the pictures in his mind started to get jumbled up. There was a mental picture of the old man on fire and floating off the ground and there was also the picture of the old man threading a reel of film in a bizarre shag covered auditorium. James shook his head and realized that shaking your head doesn't actually do anything. It wasn't like you actually had pictures in your head, and if you did what use would shaking them up do? There were metaphors and similes about shaking loose the cobwebs or shaking off the dust, and he was sure he knew some people that had cobwebs in their head, but in this situation it didn't really help.

What he needed to do was sort out one set of memories from the other. He was fairly sure that one was a dream while the other was real. The question was which was which? It was ridiculous, he thought, that a person wouldn't be able to tell reality from dreams, but in this situation he decided to give himself the benefit of the doubt. He'd seen people throwing around fire and lightning like it was a football, and an old guy had been juggling fire that ended up looking like a snake. In those sorts of situations you kinda had to just sit back and give your mind the chance to set itself straight.

Now, he was fairly sure the whole incident with the auditorium was a dream so that meant all the other stuff had to be real. He looked around the tent and was still sure that even if the on fire burning snake old man was real that still didn't explain the tent and the sleeping bag. Thinking hard he tried to get to the last real thing he remembered. He remembered setting a stick on fire with his mind, and that had been cool. He thought for a second about trying it again, but not knowing where he was made him pause before lighting his immediate surroundings on fire. Other than that he only remembered a bright light then the dream about the auditorium. Of course there had been a lot of mumbo jumbo about belief and choices tossed in there, but that didn't explain how he ended up in a tent.

Sighing he decided it was just going to be what it was going to be. It was time to get out of the tent and decide what to do from there. As he reached for the zipper he was struck by the fact that he could see the zipper. It was light out. That meant the sun was up, which didn't happen until close to eleven in the morning. Well, he had been tired so he guessed it was a good thing to get a good night's sleep. Even if he had dreamed about creepy guys in black and white with crazy little cartoon characters. Again he decided that moving on would be better than trying to figure out the exact details of the craziness from the night before.

Unzipping the door to the tent he wasn't quite sure what to expect so when he was greeted with an abandoned campsite all he could really do was shrug. It was at least the last place he remembered being. That was as good as could be expected. He walked over to the fire pit and saw there was new wood stacked inside the ring of rocks. Looking around for matches or a lighter he wasn't really surprised to see there was nothing but the tent and two camp chairs. Turning back to the fire pit he decided now would be a good time to light something on fire. He grinned to himself as he walked toward the neatly stacked wood and thought about all the times as a kid he had wished he could do something like this. A brief flash of doubt sparkled for a moment in the back of his mind, but he was so determined to do this he didn't even recognize it as doubt. He stared at the wood and remembered the night before. He could see the fire crackling in his mind, and it was warm and inviting. A week ago he never would have believed this was possible, but he had seen it done, and sometimes seeing is believing. He pictured fire crackling on the logs in the circle of rocks and watched in childish glee as they burst into flame. Deciding that if there ever was a time to do a victory dance it was now he started hopping around the fire and waving his arms.

He looked down at an unburnt log in the circle and watched with glee as it too burst into flames. Looking at another he couldn't help but laugh out loud as the flames crawled out of his mind and licked their way up the surface of the log. It was insane but it was the coolest insane he had ever seen. He wanted to call his brother and say, dude guess what I can do? But of course no one would actually believe him. That was good and bad. On the one hand he didn't want to be picked up by the government and studied at some secret area fifty one location. They might try to dissect him to find out how it worked and that sounded uncomfortable. On the other hand what use was it to be able to do something amazingly cool and have no one know about it? He guessed it was like Batman in that you had to choose the people you told very carefully. Of course superheroes always seemed to tell their girlfriends about their powers then break up with them in the sequel and realize now there was a girl running around out there who didn't like them but knew all their secrets. Now that he thought about it, that was really true of just about any relationship. You confided in the person and then inevitably something happened and you broke up. Then there was someone running around out there that knew all your deepest secrets and didn't really have your best interests at heart.

So on the whole he decided this had been a fairly good morning. He had gotten a good night's sleep, minus the crazy dream, and had woken up with crazy mind powers. Sitting down in a camp chair and warming himself by the blazing fire he wondered if there were other things he could do. He extended his right hand toward the fire and pictured one of the burning logs rising from the ground. As it did he was struck by the fact that, all joking aside, he would need to be really careful with this stuff. It was like the crazy black and white guy in his dream had said about responsibility and not using it inappropriately. He let the log drop back into the fire with a shudder as he pictured the weird cartoon characters from his dream hunting him down because he smacked some poor homeless guy with a magical stick. Not that he would ever do that. He looked around warily to see if he was being watched.

He thought about trying to make biscuits and a cup of coco appear like the old man had but decided he wouldn't push his luck. It was one thing making a log float in the air a little, but it was another all together to make an entire meal appear. He was worried if he got it a little bit wrong he would end up poisoning himself with hot cocoa made out of who knows what. So instead he just warmed himself for a moment longer at the fire and tried to decide what to do next.

It really wasn't a question of should he do anything, it was more a question of how to do something. He was stuck at the top of Hatchers Pass over sixty miles away from anything that might be going on. From the sense of urgency that had been projected by Scott and the professor he assumed something was going to happen fairly soon, but how was he supposed to get anywhere. Maybe he could fly. He looked up and spotted what he thought was an eagle far off on the horizon and decided that while that might be something to try later on he wasn't so sure about just jumping off a mountain and hoping it worked the first time. Instead he decided to walk down the pass a little and see if he could find a phone to use. Hopefully by that time he could think up a likely enough story to convince one of his friends to come and get him. He doubted any of them would have heard anything different about him by this morning. He wouldn't put it past the professor and his goons to spread lies about him, but they really hadn't had enough time yet, and maybe Scott was too scared to tell the prof he had let James get away. That could work in his favor. The bad guys always failed because they never wanted to admit they made a mistake. Good guys always were willing to admit their mistakes. James chuckled to himself as he got up and thought, ya right. Even the good guys had to be convinced to admit being stupid sometimes.

Glancing at the fire he grinned again as it went out with a poof of gray smoke. You couldn't be too careful about forest fires up here. He would feel terrible if he were the cause of Hatchers Pass going up in smoke. He smiled at the fact that he was being a good person and decided to ignore the fact that since it was surrounded with snow nothing was likely to catch on fire anyway. But that was beside the point he decided as he pulled his cap down farther over his ears. You should be a good person even when no one was watching and even when nothing may happen. Why? Because he could start things on fire with his mind he thought to himself with a self-satisfied smile. He knew, of course, as he walked back down the trail his reason for being good was not a real reason. Looking around at the clear white blue sky and the snow capped mountains running in waves back into the distance he knew in a way his reason was valid. Being good did bring its own rewards. His life was happier when he did the right thing. People were more willing to help him and were more willing to give him the benefit of the doubt when he eventually messed up. It seemed to him that when he did the right thing, even when no one was looking, someone still found out, and good things seemed to follow. People always used the cliché that doing the right thing was a reward unto itself, but in all reality there were so many rewards that came from just being good he couldn't understand why people choose to be jerks.

Tucking his hands into his pockets he tried to think about what the old man had said about why Scott and his buddies had chosen to be the way they were. If you truly believe something then yes it did affect the choices you made in life. If they did believe there was nothing but this world, which his being able to light fires with his mind had convinced him otherwise, then why would you want to waste your time helping people instead of yourself? Because, he thought, even if this was all you got, your life would still be better if you were just a good person.

James stopped and took a deep breath of the freezing air. He was happy for the moment just to be alive. After everything that had happened since saving Rupert on Mountain View he was delighted to find he was actually doing just fine. Nothing was broken. He remembered being hit with a tree and shook his head wondering how many people could say that? He didn't even think he had any cuts, scratches, or bruises to show for all he had been through. Again he thought it was all a blessing and a curse. He kind of wished he had gotten a good scar out of all of it so he could show Katie and have something to brag about. She had seemed very impressed with his story about fighting the guys off with the can of bear spray. Come to think of it, he hadn't really looked at where the tree had hit him. He just remembered that Rupert had done something to fix it and had forgotten about it since then. Looking down at his jacket he decided it was a wee bit too cold to be lifting up his down filled jacket to see if he had a good scar. That could wait for warmer times and places.

His stomach grumbled and told him that standing here was not getting them any closer to a meal. James looked down at his stomach and thought it really wasn't in any position to complain. He wasn't going to starve and everything was still attached and in seemingly good working order. But still he decided he should stop lollygagging around and try to make it back down to the main road.

When he finally made it to the dirt road he'd been running up the night before he realized he hadn't given any thought to what he would do if Scott and his two friends were sitting here waiting for him. He could always set them on fire, he thought, but that wouldn't be very nice. Setting someone on fire seemed a little bit like a last resort kind of thing to do. Maybe he could just push them like he had lifted up the log. He pictured himself standing in the middle of the road with his hands stretched out in front of him. Scott and the other two, whatever their names were, would be dangling in mid air begging and pleading with him to put them down. Realizing he was grinning again he decided if they were waiting for him that was what he would do. Maybe he would even try to pick up their car. That would be awesome.

The air around him felt like it should shatter as he moved through it. It was the perfect Alaskan winter morning. The air was a frozen blue white and the mountains looked crisp beneath their blankets. The absolute clarity of the morning sky made him think of the dream from the night before. Nothing about it had seemed clear. He hadn't known where he was going, or what was happening. The only clear thing about it was the fact that he could still remember it, and that was odd. He wasn't the kind of person that could remember his dreams for more than a few minutes after he woke up. He remembered having dreams and every once in a while something would happen during the day and trigger a foggy memory of a dream, but on average he couldn't tell you what dreams had come while he slept. The fact he could remember every detail about this one kind of freaked him out. It was like growing used to being blind then having a moment of absolute clarity for five minutes and not knowing why. In this case, however, he did know why.

It was all amazingly strange if you looked at it on its own, but it all fit together perfectly if you looked at it as a whole. That and you had to believe. He had the feeling if he told anyone about this situation, even if he left nothing out, they would think he was crazy. But since he had actually experienced it he knew it was real, and he believed. He remembered Rupert asking him on that first drive when he was taking him back to Eagle River if he believed in anything. To be honest with himself he hadn't really believed. At least he didn't think so, but it seemed there had been the beginning of something. His parents had taught him to make certain choices, and that had led him to have a certain view of the world. He'd constantly read books, and comics about the good guys defeating the bad guys, and he'd wanted to be one of the good guys. He'd been ready to believe. Everything seemed to have been leading up to this moment, and now he believed.

As James rounded a bend in the trail and still couldn't see the main road leading through the pass he was slightly amazed at how far he had run the night before. He wondered if it really had only been one night. What if he had slept for years? No, that would be ridiculous. There would be no reason for that. Of course he would be hard pressed to give a good reason for most of anything that had happened to him over the last day. Finally up ahead he sighted the paved road. He had never been up this way during the winter and had no idea if any of the shops up here were even open. Now that he thought about it they probably weren't. They were most likely open just during the tourist season and closed down around September. That would be just great. If he remembered correctly it was miles to the next place. He faintly remembered a shop that sold ice cream on the way up to the pass, and there were a few houses and some scattered shops before or after that. Being a college student with a very limited budget he really didn't drive around very much.

Getting to the road he looked around and was slightly disappointed that he didn't see Scott's car. He'd really been looking forward to hanging them upside down in the air. Starting out he had thought it would be good to just hold them up there, but somewhere along the dirt road his mental picture had changed to them being upside down. Isn't that what all the superheroes in the comic books did was hold people upside down until they confessed or told you what you wanted to know? The only problem was he really didn't have any information he wanted from them. He just wanted to hang them upside down. Oh, and he wanted to pick up the car.

James tried out a maniacal laugh just to make sure he had it down. You could never be sure when you would need to give a maniacal laugh while throwing a car around, and if he was going to be some super powered whatever then he might run into those kinds of situations. After the insanity and confusion of the night before it felt good to finally feel like he could handle the situation. Laughing at it, and turning the whole thing into a kind of farce helped him deal with the surrealness of it all.

On the one hand he really did think it was cool that he could do things he thought only happened in the movies, but on the other hand if he really thought about it he was worried. He felt like he had made a deal with someone, and he really didn't know what the terms and conditions of the contract were. He had kind of agreed to it sight unseen. In a way he wished Rupert were there so he could ask him about it. He wasn't quite sure but he did think Rupert could explain the whole thing. Thinking about it all made him remember the dream. Why hadn't he been able to ask any questions? In the dream he hadn't thought about it because it was a movie and you couldn't ask questions to a movie and expect answers, but it had been a dream and anything was possible in dreams. Why hadn't they, whoever they were, just sat down with him in the dream and said hello, do you have any questions?

A noise from his left snapped James out of his thoughts and made him look up the hill. Someone was standing about two hundred yards up the slope. James stood there and stared wondering who would be up in the middle of a snow field at this time of the morning. After thinking that, James decided he really had no place to say anything, and also he really didn't know what time in the morning it was. Beyond that he was only slightly sure it was still morning. This thought caused him to glance at the position of the sun. It didn't help him at all. He had never been one for knowing his east from his west. He knew the sun came up in the east, but since he hadn't seen the sun come up he had no clue as to what direction he was facing. And the fact that in the winter it didn't really come up in the east. Stupid tilted world he thought. He was sure there was a perfectly good reason for the world being tilted but it made telling directions up here by the Arctic Circle a real pain.

Trying to decide what to do about the person he'd spotted he realized he had two good reasons to stand around and wait for them. If they were bad guys looking for him then he really did have a chance to try out his new abilities, or powers, but saying powers sounded too melodramatic. It made him feel like putting his hands on his hips and waiting for theme music to break out. The other good reason was that if the person wasn't a bad guy looking for him then they might be willing to give him a ride. In the grand scheme of things that would be better than getting to throw around a few minor bad guys. Although, he thought, he could take the bad guys car after tossing them around. That idea kind of bummed him out for a second because he really had his heart set on tossing their car at them after he put them down. But he did need to be practical about it. No reason to waste a perfectly good car.

After waiting for he didn't know how long, James decided whoever had left him the tent and sleeping bag should have left him a watch as well. When he had been walking the cold really hadn't bothered him. His nose had been getting a little chilly but that had been about it. Now, however, he was just standing around turning into a popsicle. Maybe he could find some wood and set it on fire. There really was no reason to have crazy powers if you couldn't even keep yourself from freezing to death.

Just as he decided to start looking for some wood to combust he noticed the figure was coming down the hill crosswise to his left. Good, he thought, until he realized it meant he had to walk back up the hill the way he had already come. New very cool mental powers aside, all this walking was getting to be a pain in the butt. As he began heading back up the hill he realized he was amazingly sore from his run last night. It wasn't like he had time to stop and stretch out before heading up the mountain in the dark. Now each step up the hill sent little spikes of pain through the backs of his legs. Maybe if he just stood in the middle of the road the person would stop and pick him up, and maybe it would be his luck they would be going to the other side of the pass and not even come by him. The fact that he hadn't seen any cars or other people caused him to decide to keep going. This might be his best chance to save himself a walk of miles upon miles.

Trying to keep the person in sight, he realized they were going past the dirt road he had come down. Realizing he would have to go up even farther than he had come down he let out a sigh and kept walking. The euphoria of the morning had definitely worn off.

The road bent around to the right after the intersection with the dirt road and as James rounded the corner he saw a car parked in a turn off up ahead. He looked up the hill and realized the person was headed directly down the hill now. James felt like sitting down on the ground and waiting but knew if he did his denim jeans would soak up the moisture on the ground like a sponge, so instead he settled for leaning against the car.

His wait was a short one as he realized that the person was coming down on snowshoes and moving quite fast over the crusty layer of white. He could tell the person had spotted him because he slowed down and started walking rather than running down the hill. James decided it would be better if he walked over to the person with his hands out so he didn't look like he was trying to mug them or steal their car.

"Hello!" He called out when the person was about twenty yards up the hill, "I was wondering if you could help me!" James couldn't tell much about the person because of the heavy winter gear they were wearing. The down jacket, black snow pants, and especially the thick ski mask made it impossible to tell anything about them. James stood at the most likely spot for the person to come off the snow and onto the road, "I'm a little bit stuck out here and was wondering if you could give me a lift?"

A muffled voice came out from under the black ski mask, "Sure, sure. Just give me a second to get my snowshoes off."

The oddness of asking for a ride from a perfect stranger wearing a ski mask made James think of all the banks in Anchorage that had signs in their doors during the winter telling patrons to please remove all ski masks when entering the bank. The first time he had seen that he'd laughed; now he understood. Watching as the person reached down and flipped the buckles that undid the bindings on the snowshoes James wondered what he would tell the person when he was asked why he was stuck up here. Well, you see, he would say, there was this old man with flames. On the other hand maybe a lie would be better. That thought made him wonder. If he was in the position he was in because he made the right choices even when they were difficult then wasn't it the wrong choice to lie to someone? It would make the situation easier for him, but wasn't that the fallacy of the whole thing was that people were making choices that were right for them rather than making choices that were simply right? Maybe he could just say he would rather not say why he was stuck up here, but thank you so much for the ride and could he pay for gas? In fact maybe he could do the whole magically appearing gas trick like Rupert had done.

James put out a hand to help steady the person as he stepped out of the snowshoe bindings. "It sure is a beautiful day for some snowshoeing." He hoped he didn't seem like some crazy guy.

"It really is." The muffled voice replied, "You really have to take advantage of the sunlight while you have it each day."

James smiled, "Isn't that the truth. I'm in classes usually when the sun is out and it can get a little depressing when the only time you get to be outside is when its dark."

The person reached down and picked up the snowshoes. He fiddled around with them until he could carry them with one hand then reached up and pulled off the ski mask. He turned and smiled at James, "It's good to see you James. A little strange to run into you up here, but whatever."

When the ski mask had come off James felt his heart stop. So many things lately had been too coincidental. It was almost like someone had been setting the whole thing up. Here he was by himself at the top of a pass covered with snow and he ran into the one person he's almost sure would help him no matter what the situation. "Hi, Sam. I would shake your hand but they're both full."

Sam set his snowshoes down on top of the car, unzipped a pocket, and pulled out his keys. "So," Sam looked over at James as he opened the trunk of his Toyota, "any reason that you're stuck up here or did you just decide to go for a really long walk?"

"Well," James paused and tried to decide what to say, "I can't really say, but I have gotten a good walk out of it."

Sam smiled, and after shutting the trunk he walked around to the passenger side of the car to unlock the door, "Fair enough." He paused as he lifted the door handle and looked over his shoulder at James, "You know if there's anything wrong..." He let the statement hang in the air unfinished.

James knew. Sam was one of those old-fashioned white hat kinds of guys. He would help you simply because you needed help. It didn't matter who you were, or even if you had been rotten to him in the past. All James could do was nod at him and try to slow his mind down for a second. He climbed into the car wondering if he should tell Sam about everything that had happened. Sam would help. Heck, he might even believe him.

Sam climbed in and started the car. A blast of cold air assaulted James from the vents. Out of the corner of his eye he saw Sam visibly jump before shutting off the fan. "Sorry bout that." He blew into his now ungloved hands to try and warm them up before placing them on the ice-cold steering wheel. As he pulled out of the small parking area he glanced over at James, "So, do you just need a ride back to the campus or what?"

"Well," James paused again, still debating with himself, "it's a little complicated. I think my car is in Wasilla if it hasn't been towed by now, but if you're just headed back to the school then that's fine too."

"Wasilla?" Sam looked over at James with a question in his eyes then did a three point turn in the middle of the road. "I guess it would be easier to go the other way if I'm going to drop you off in Wasilla."

James had met a lot of people in his life who had something against letting people help them. There was this belief among a lot of Americans that charity was a bad word. If you offered to pay for dinner they would fight you for it even if they were flat broke. If you offered to give them a ride they would decline, or in most cases they would just put up a good show of declining and let you convince them. James on the other hand had a sense of what goes around comes around, or what some people in the world would call karma. He figured that if he helped people then he should let them help him. If it was out of their way he would make sure to repay them in kind by doing something that was out of his way. The chance to repay them may not come the very next day, but it would come eventually. So sitting here in this car he really had no arguments against letting Sam take him to his car. It would be very helpful, and Sam didn't seem to mind, so why not. Some people would say he was taking advantage of the situation or taking advantage of Sam's good nature, but he would say what it really meant was some time in the future Sam would be able to take advantage of his nature by asking for repayment. Not that a person like Sam would ever ask for repayment, but the idea was the same.

"So," Sam broke the silence, "I hear you went on a date with Katie."

James smiled. That was university life for you. Relationship information went around like a wildfire through dry grass. "Ya, we went out to Thunderbird Falls."

"Very nice. How was the weather?"

"Tad bit cold," James shrugged, "but what do you expect this time of year?"

"Normally," Sam said, "we expect snow."

"That actually would have made the time better. The snow would have made the setting, shall we say, more romantic."

Sam laughed and turned the car onto the dirt road section of the pass that would take them to the Wasilla side of the mountains. "I bet a bunch of leafless dead trees and frozen bare ground made for a very romantic setting."

James smiled, "Well, you gotta work with what you have."

Silence fell in the car and James couldn't help but think about what Rupert had told him. How Sam had stood up at the gathering and been attacked for what he said. Maybe that was why he wasn't in any hurry to get back to campus. On the other hand it happened a few days ago and things like that tended to blow over fairly quickly on campus. James wanted to ask him to see if what Rupert had told him was true or if Rupert had just seen it differently than what actually happened, but he didn't really know how to broach the subject.

James decided, with everything that had been happening, he really couldn't be sure of how much time he had for things. Who knows, he thought, a giant flaming bat might fall from the sky and try to kill me in a few minutes, so the direct approach might be the best. "So, Sam." He paused, not knowing exactly what to say.

"Yah?" Sam glanced over at him.

"I heard from someone a kinda crazy story about the big tolerance gathering the other night." Sam didn't say anything so he continued, "I guess I was wondering if I could hear from you what happened so that I would know if what I was told was true or not."

This time Sam didn't look over at him, "And what did you hear?"

"Something that really disturbed me actually. I was told you got up and spoke a little bit and people started throwing things at you." Again silence from Sam was all that greeted his statement. "Did they actually throw things at you?"

"Mostly empty water bottles."

"Son of a…" James had been wanting to think Rupert had just been mistaken about the whole situation, or even was making it all up to somehow get James to help him. "I'm sorry man."

"You don't have anything to apologize for. You weren't there."

"No I wasn't but that doesn't change the fact that someone needs to apologize to you."

Sam smiled, "And why does someone need to apologize?"

"Because what they did was wrong."

"Oh, but they would say what I did was wrong and they were right in getting rid of me."

By the tone of his voice James could tell Sam had been holding in a lot about the situation. "Look, Sam, I can't tell you why I'm up here looking for a ride to my car that's not within miles of here, but I can tell you that in the last twenty four hours I've had a lot of conversations about the nature of right and wrong."

"Really? And what did you learn from all of that?" His voice dripped with sarcasm, and Sam wasn't normally a sarcastic type of guy. That in itself worried James.

"I know there is a right and a wrong." James thought back to all the conversations he had over the last day and even the ones in dreams the night before. All of it pointed to the fact that there really was a right and a wrong, but now that he thought about it no one had really explained to him how you were supposed to tell the difference. The old man had told him he had done a good job of doing the right thing even when it wasn't in his best interests, but that didn't really tell him anything about the nature of it all. All that really told him was his parents had raised him well.

This time Sam did look over at him, "Well, knowing there is a right and a wrong is one hundred percent better than most of the people who were there the other night." He looked back at the dirt road they were driving over, "What I don't understand is how they try to have it both ways. On the one hand they try to say there's no such thing as right or wrong, they call it all situational. But when they've been wronged they're quick to point out they're in the right and you're in the wrong. It's like they want to be able to choose when to apply the rules, and if they don't like them at some point then they refuse to apply them to that situation. I say if you're going to say some things are right or wrong then you should have to admit there really is such a thing and not walk around all the time saying, well, it really depends on the situation. Bull pucky, pardon my French, if it's wrong for someone to steal from you or lie to you then it's wrong for anyone to do it any time." Silence descended over the car like a blanket. After a few moments James realized he was focusing on the sound of the tires going over the rocks in the road. He wasn't sure why, but he was waiting for Sam to say something else.

Finally Sam sighed, "I've been wanting to say that for a while now." He looked out the driver's side window at a river far below them in a gorge, "You're not going to throw something at me now are you?"

James couldn't help himself and he laughed, "No, Sam, I'm not going to throw anything at you. For one thing you're giving me a ride to my car and I don't want to be pushed out here in the middle of nowhere. For another thing I think you're right." Thinking back James realized that only a day before he had said he really wasn't sure what he believed in, if he believed in anything. Now he knew he believed in something, the situations he had been through had dictated that he come to believe in at least what was happening to him. One of those things he was sure of now was there really was a right decision or action and a wrong one. He might not always know which was which, but at least he admitted it was there. That was a good question actually, "Sam?"

"Ya."

"How do you tell the difference?"

Sam didn't answer for a second as he concentrated on avoiding a pothole in the dirt road that could have swallowed a brontosaurus much less a Toyota Camry. After they were back on the straight and narrow Sam shrugged and said, "People just know. Look around the world and you'll see the markings of it everywhere. People have to convince themselves to do the wrong thing, they have to work themselves up to it, or be mentally deranged. They make excuses when they do the wrong thing, even if it's just to themselves. They try to justify it and explain it away. If they can't do that then they try to hide it or wait till no one's looking. Have you ever seen a thief walk into a store without a mask, without a gun, and pick up something, walk up to the counter, tell the person he's going to take whatever it is without paying for it then just walk out? No, they hide it. Even little kids who really don't know much of anything try to hide when they steal a lollipop. On the other hand people just know that doing the right thing is the right thing. No one tries to make excuses when they help someone who tripped. No one tries to hide the fact they donated blood to the Red Cross. The man who defends his family from attack is praised by his neighbors.

"People who don't believe would say it's a cultural thing and each culture has a different standard of right and wrong, but that's just not true. The same reasoning about hiding things applies to every culture. Just look at their religions. Buddhism wants you to set aside your own selfish desires and help others, Islam wants you to be a servant and one of their principle statements is that you must help the poor, Daoism and Confucianism call for respecting your family and your elders and putting the welfare of the people as more important than your own, and one of Christianities main tenants is to love your neighbor as yourself. Now how did all of those groups, in all different cultures come to the same conclusion about right and wrong?"

"It's built in." James said it out loud without meaning to.

"Right." Sam said, "It's almost like someone put a fire in humanity, and when you do the right thing the light of that fire shines out and people see it and smile. They like you better, and they want to be around you more. Just like people are drawn to a campfire."

James' memory snapped back to the old man with the flames burning in his eyes then to a dream where the only color had been the same flames burning in the eyes of a black and white gentleman seated on a black and white chair.

The passenger side window suddenly exploded and tiny shards of broken glass flew across the right side of James' face. Sam swerved the car thinking that something had hit them but not knowing what it was. A loud cracking noise was followed by a sharp pain in James' right leg. He looked down to see blood starting to seep from the side of his jeans. Pressing his hand to the spot he looked out the now shattered window and tried to make sense of what had just happened.

Sam saw them first. "What the…" he pointed with his right hand and tried to keep control of the car as it slid on the dirt road with his left. James looked where he pointed and saw Scott standing at the side of the road rifle raised and pressed to his shoulder. Both James and Sam ducked just before they heard a thwack and the driver's side window exploded out from the car.

"Go! Go!" Was all James could think to yell, and somewhere in the back of his mind he was thinking that saying that was really cliché and most likely unnecessary.

Sam floored the gas pedal and they both felt the tires slip and spin on the cold dirt road. They were saved from another bullet by the very fact that the road was frozen. The gravel had been turned into a solid mass by the biting cold and gave the car much better grip than it would have normally. After what James thought must have been exactly a second and a half of spinning the tires caught and the Camry shot out like a rabbit from the chase.

Almost losing control of the car as they sped around a corner Sam yelled something unintelligible and James looked up from his bleeding leg to see a car parked across the road with two guys standing on the other side of it. It effectively blocked the road. To the left the ground dropped off to a river over a hundred yards below and to the right the hill shot up steep enough that going that way would flip the car. James had read once in a survival handbook that if you want to get through something like this what you need to do is aim your car at either the back or front quarter of the car blocking your way. Try not to hit it too fast because you don't want to deploy the airbags, but you have to be going fast enough to push the car in an arc. They recommended about twenty miles an hour as the appropriate speed. In this case they should aim for the trunk of the car to their right so as to possibly push the other car down the slope, and not accidentally push themselves down into the river. The problem with all this was that it really didn't come to James quick enough to explain it all to Sam, and Sam wasn't really the kind of person to read survival handbooks that would have ways to get through situations like this so he had no idea what to do. In his mind he had two choices. Either hit the car in front of them dead center, which would damage his car badly and deploy the airbags without getting them any farther down the road, or stop the car and deal with the situation from there. Slamming on the breaks the car slid to a halt about ten yards from the makeshift roadblock.

Coming around the trunk of the car the two others each raised a handgun and pointed it at the car. James looked over to see Sam raise his hands in the universal symbol of surrender. He could see in Sam's eyes the question of what was happening, and James wondered if he should have told him why he was stranded up here after all. He couldn't think what good that would have done. Knowing all the facts is a good thing, but it won't stop bullets you don't know are coming.

"Get out of the car!" The assailant on the left yelled.

Sam dutifully opened the door and started to get out. James hesitated then thought that whatever was going to happen they would need to get the roadblock out of the way anyway so there wasn't much use in staying in the car. Keeping his right hand pressed to his leg he used his left to open the door. As he swung his leg out he finally had to come to grips with the fact that being shot really hurts. The pain flooded up his leg and caused his whole right side to twitch. In all of his imaginings and daydreams from earlier that morning he never thought he might have to deal with the bad guys after being shot in the leg. He knew how to start a fire, and he knew how to pick up a log, but he had no idea how to stop his leg from bleeding. Actually just stopping it from hurting would be great.

James swung his other leg out of the car and then used the door to pull himself to a standing position. "What's wrong?" A voice from in front of him called, "Did you hurt yourself James?"

The sarcasm wasn't lost on him and as he looked up he wondered if he would be able to concentrate on doing anything with this pain constantly throbbing through his mind. "So," James decided that he needed to buy some time until his leg stopped throbbing or, as the other part of his mind said, until he bled to death, "how'd you guys know I would be coming down this direction? Or did you set up something on the other side too?"

A voice from behind him answered, "It wasn't hard to figure out which way you'd go." James turned around to see Scott walking toward them with the rifle now hanging over his shoulder by a strap. "You needed to get your car, and when we saw Sam was the only one up here, amazing coincidence since we were trying to find him anyway, we figured he would be willing to take you to it."

James realized that as strange as it was they were falling into the classic bad guy trap. They were so sure of themselves they were telling him all about their plans and how everything was working. When he saw this in the movies he always thought it was a joke because no one would do that, but now he realized bad guys in general weren't that smart. "So you waited out here for me all night?"

"No." Scott said, "After you pulled your little disappearing act we headed back to the campus figuring the prof wouldn't know the difference." James heard muttering from the other two after this statement and watched with relief as Scott lined himself up nicely beside the other two. He hadn't been sure what he would do if Scott had stayed behind him. He couldn't focus on two directions in his mind at the same time, especially since he was starting to feel a little lightheaded.

"He figured it out, didn't he? Probably not too happy with you letting me get away was he?" James would have laughed to get under their skin but he just didn't have the energy to laugh. Maybe some heroes could laugh in the face of a bullet wound but he didn't see how, unless they were insane.

"No he wasn't." James heard one of the others mutter something about darkness and eyes but couldn't make sense of any of it. "Now, Sam, what are you doing with this fugitive?"

James realized Sam hadn't said a word the entire time, but was glad their eyes were off him for the moment. He needed to think of what to do. Now that he was faced with the situation he wasn't so sure he could do much at all. He looked over at Sam and wondered if he would come up with something brilliant.

Sam looked at the three who were pointing guns at him, "He needed a ride."

"Sure he did." Scott nodded as if that was exactly what he had expected to hear. "Well, it saves us the time of finding you somewhere else."

"And why were you looking for me, Scott?" Sam emphasized the fact that he knew Scott's name. Hoping the familiarity would breed a little bit of sympathy. It didn't.

"We need to kill you Sam." Scott took his rifle off his shoulder and worked the lever action, "It's nothing personal. You just happen to be the right person in the right place for us."

"What?" Sam's voice cracked, "Why do you need to kill me? This is ridiculous?"

"No, actually it's quite brilliant." Scott looked into the open bolt on the rifle then blew into it to remove any dirt that may have gotten into it, "You see you'll be the counterpoint to Don's murder. Together they'll help spark the chaos that will begin the new order of things."

"Don's murder?" Sam had no idea what was going on, all he knew was that Scott was putting a shell into the rifle in preparation for shooting him.

All the while James' mind was whirling. He figured he could pick them up but they had guns and you didn't need to be on the ground to fire a gun. He even thought for a moment about setting them on fire, but he just couldn't bring himself to do it. He wasn't really paying attention to the conversation until he heard Scott say something about killing Sam, and then he said something about Don being murdered. He looked up from thinking and saw Sam staring right at him. Looking from Sam to their captors he realized Scott was getting ready to do something very bad.

What would Rupert do? The first thing James thought of was the wheezing sound Rupert made when he tried to breathe. Then he thought of lightning shooting from Rupert's hands in the darkness of an Alaskan forest. Maybe, just maybe... If it didn't work at least it might distract them for long enough that he could think of something else.

Raising his arms James formed a picture in his mind of blue white lightning crackling around his open hands. He didn't look down at his hands but kept his eyes focused on the three in front of him. They were all staring at Sam as Scott raised the rifle to his shoulder.

The pain from his leg thundered in his mind in time to the mental image of the crackling lighting on his hands. He pictured it building up stronger and stronger until he could feel it wanting to leap away. Just then the one closest to James decided to look over and make sure he wasn't trying to slip away. As his eyes grew wide from the site before him James could see blue white light reflected in his attackers pupils. In that moment all doubt was swept away. He believed. He believed he could do something that before he would have said was impossible. He believed there was a power out there greater than himself and it was helping him for some crazy reason. Never before had he truly believed in anything, but now his mind was clear and the belief swept the pain away. In that moment he let the lightning go. With a clap of thunder it flew from his hands. Splitting into multiple branches as James willed it in his mind to hit each of the three in front of him, it threw them backwards off their feet and slammed them into the car behind them.

Silence and the smell of ozone hung in the air. Even though he was the one who had done it James was a little shocked it had actually worked. He also realized Sam was saying something and when he turned to him he was again shocked by what was coming out of Sam's mouth. It wasn't so much the language that shocked him, he had heard it many times before, it was the fact that Sam was saying it. He had been under a certain, obviously mistaken, belief that Sam didn't know those kinds of words. He was also grammatically amazed by the fact that one word had been used as a noun, verb, and adjective all in the same sentence. Finally Sam calmed down and just stared at James as if he was waiting for James to explain everything that had just happened. Thinking there would be time enough for that latter James decided it would be in their best interest to check on the three lying on the ground in front of them.

They hadn't been thrown very far in the event. Mainly because the car behind them stopped them from going more than a dozen feet backwards. As James started to walk toward them he was forcibly reminded that his leg had been shot. Bending over to look at the wounded area he realized it was decidedly unfair for the ground to move out from under him like that at a time like this. Reaching out his left hand he stopped himself from bashing his head into the ground as he fell, but still managed to end up lying there looking up at the beautiful blue Alaskan sky. He watched as little white lights danced in front of his eyes, and hoped he wouldn't pass out. The last time that had happened Rupert had been there to patch him up. This time all he had was Sam, and while you never knew if someone had any secret superpowers he wasn't going to plan his schedule around it.

The pretty white lights were replaced soon enough by Sam's face looking down at him. James gave him a rather dumb smile and said, "I've been shot and was wondering if you had anything to fix that?"

The exasperated look on Sam's face was immediately replaced by one of worry, "Are you serious?"

James nodded then decided not to do that again because the world and his insides decided to move in two different directions when he did. He closed his eyes and said, "My leg. On the side."

A few more words that James didn't think Sam knew came through the darkness of his closed eyes and then he could hear feet moving over the gravel road. This was followed by the sound of something opening on a car. James really thought it would help if he could see what was going on, but at the same time the world moved so much less if he kept his eyes closed. Finally after what seemed like at least five minutes of nothing happening he heard feet moving back over toward him. As he heard them continue past him he almost used one of those words he had heard Sam use a few moments ago. Sam's voice floated to him from over his head, "I think they're dead." Then the feet came back over to James. "Where did you say you were shot?" Without opening his eyes James pointed to the spot on his right leg where he was trying to keep pressure with his right hand. He could feel the sticky wetness of the blood cooling and starting to freeze between his hand and his jeans. "All right. You're going to need to move your hand so that I can get a good look at the wound." Slowly lifting his hand James could feel the denim pull away with it. A moment later he felt Sam pull at his jeans and could feel the cold of something metal against his leg. "I'm just cutting a bigger hole around it so I can get at it and patch it up." James had this odd vision in his head of a medic in the Army leaning over some poor grunt. He was immeasurably glad Sam knew what he was doing. Even if he didn't know what he was doing James was glad he was at least acting like he knew what he was doing.

After a few more seconds James felt something wet pour over his leg and felt a sharp sting prickle up his leg and cause his eyes to try and retreat back into his head. Thinking he was glad that at least he could still feel his leg he smelled the odd tang of alcohol. The small voice in the back of his head popped off with, I wonder if we get any of that? The curiosity of smelling alcohol overrode James' need to keep his eyes shut and he finally decided he really needed to see why Sam, of all people, would have alcohol. Slowly opening his eyes he took a few seconds to look up at the few clouds that floated across the sky. His mind was quick to tell him the little one to the left looked like a pirate ship. That's great, he thought. Finally he decided to move his entire head rather than just his eyes to see what was being done to his leg. This process caused the universe to rotate a good eighty degrees directly under him. After this wonderful event James was able to see that Sam had taken out some gauze from a bright red backpack and also had gotten out a roll of something looking like white tape or what you would wrap a fashionable mummy in. Looking around as much as he could without moving his head again James saw a strange assortment of things around the red backpack. There were things that looked like pumps and other things that looked like metal rods that you would use to beat away nasty smallish rodents with. Finally he saw what he had been looking for, a clear plastic bottle that was obviously marked vodka. Without meaning to, he found himself laughing out loud.

Looking up at him as if he was wondering if James had been shot in the head as well Sam said, "I didn't think being shot in the leg would be funny, or are you just hallucinating?"

"No, sorry. I just didn't expect to see a bottle of vodka."

Sam looked over at the bottle and actually blushed for a second, "It's the best stuff for cleaning out wounds and it's actually cheaper than buying a thing of rubbing alcohol in the same size." He went back to looking at the gauze in his hands and mumbled, "I don't drink the stuff. It tastes nasty."

He was learning all sorts of new stuff about Sam today, James thought. He decided to close his eyes again as Sam pressed the gauze onto the bullet wound. Pain shot up his leg as he felt Sam wrap the tape around his leg and tighten it down. He clenched his teeth together to keep from yelping and tried to concentrate on the fact that Sam was helping him and not hurting him on purpose. Even with this thought at the front of his mind he had to concentrate to keep himself from hitting Sam as hard as he could. Finally the pain subsided and he heard Sam say, "That's as good as I can get it out here. You're going to need to go to a doctor and have it taken care of. It looked like there were other pieces of things along with the bullet that went in with it, and you'll need to get them removed before they get infected."

James nodded slightly as he opened his eyes. This time he saw Sam leaning over him with his hand outstretched. Reaching up, James was very glad it had been Sam that was out here with him. He didn't know what he would have done if he had been on his own. After getting up and putting most of his weight on his left leg James reached over and put his hand on Sam's shoulder, "I know this is all kinds of crazy, but I really want to thank you for helping me."

Sam shook his head and gave a half smile, "My car has been shot up. I was almost killed, and I think I saw you shoot lightning out your hands. The jury is still out on whether or not I'm happy about this whole situation. I'm sure you have a great explanation for all of this though don't you."

James tried to give his best smile and said, "Of course I do." He leaned back against the car and waited for Sam to gather up his homemade first aid kit, "I'm not quite sure you'll believe me, but I do have an explanation. I had no idea they would be looking for you, and I really didn't want to get you involved in anything so I figured if I just let you drop me off at my car I could get everything straightened out without you getting mixed up in it."

"Well," Sam tossed the red backpack into the trunk of the car, "here I am mixed up in it." He looked over at James, "Now what?"

"Well," James thought for a moment, "I guess that depends on how attached to your car you are right now."

They both looked over Sam's shot up Camry and started to laugh. The tension of the last few moments was forgotten and the odd fact that they were standing there looking at bullet holes seemed so absurd. James looked down at the door that he was leaning on and said, "I don't know about you but I really don't feel like driving all the way back to Wasilla with both windows missing."

"Not just missing," Sam said as he came around to James' side of the car, "shot out."

"Yes, that's maybe not an important fact right now, but a very interesting one."

They both stared at the car for a moment and then Sam walked around the passenger side door that James was leaning on and squatted down. James leaned through the shot out window and watched as Sam put the pinky finger of his left hand through a hole approximately leg high on the door. "Well, that would explain that, wouldn't it." Looking up at James he said, "On one condition."

"What on one condition?" James thought he knew what was going to be said but he just wanted to make it clear so nothing was taken for granted.

"I'll take their car and get you back to yours on one condition."

"And what would that be?"

"I want to know what's going on and what just happened."

James thought about it and realized what must have been going through Rupert's mind when James had demanded to know exactly what was going on. He knew there would be some questions he wouldn't be able to answer. Like why they were looking for Sam in the first place. He understood why they were looking for him, but the whole thing with Don and Sam was beyond him. Nothing had been said about it when he was in talking with the professor, but he supposed not all bad guys fell into the same trap of giving up their plans simply to hear themselves talk. It seemed the professor had left quite a lot out when he was trying to convince James to go with Scott. It was understandable from a bad guy's point of view, but James really wished someone would fill him in on why everything had been happening.

Finally James decided Sam had the right to know as much as he could tell him simply because they had tried to kill him, and maybe would try again if they found out it hadn't worked the first time. "All right. You take me to my car, which I hope I can actually drive with a bullet in my leg, and I'll answer as much as I actually know."

Sam nodded and stood up, "Are you sure you wouldn't rather have me take you to a hospital?"

James thought about it for a second and closing his eyes he believed the bleeding had stopped and the wound had closed. When he opened his eyes again he knew beyond the shadow of a doubt it really was closed. He wasn't sure how good of a job he had done and the fact remained there was still a bullet in his leg, but at least it wasn't bleeding any more and it wouldn't get infected as quickly. Completely beside the point it was cool to think about the fact that he had a bullet in him, and in all reality it wasn't really in anyplace life threatening. It wasn't, he thought, like it was lodged up against an artery or anything. He looked over at Sam, "No, I have things that need to be done first. Like figuring out why they killed Don."

James then looked over at the three dead bodies. They were almost sitting up as if they had just decided to rest for a second and fell asleep leaning up against their car. At least they looked that way until you noticed the charred black hole in the middle of each of them. He realized you couldn't see all the way through but it was close enough to make his stomach start to take a field trip up toward his mouth.

Sam saw James' face turn a little more pale than it had been and turned to see what he was looking at. He sighed and nodded then looked back at James who was still staring at the dead bodies. "All right then," he took James by the arm and wrapped it around his shoulders, "let's not look at the three dead guys for too long okay?"

"Right." James looked at the ground as Sam helped him limp his way over to the other car and leaned against it facing away from what he had done to the three former university students.

After Sam, thankfully, found the keys to the car in the ignition and didn't have to search their pockets they headed down the pass once again. On the way James tried to get Sam to understand what exactly had been happening over the last few days. He decided it would be best to start with his very first meeting with Rupert on that dark city street and go from there. By the time they reached his car Sam was almost as confused as James was, the only difference was that Rupert had done some really cool tricks to convince James and all James had was one moment of insanity with lightning shooting from his hands. Thankfully that seemed to be enough to convince Sam, at least for the time being.

Again Sam found himself squatting beside a car and looking at something that he didn't think he would ever see. He looked from the burn marks on James' Geo Metro up to James, "So what're you going to do now?"

"I," James licked his lips, "I hadn't really thought that far in advance."

"Do you know what they're planning to do?"

James sighed, "I know exactly what I told you."

"That doesn't help much."

"No, it really doesn't."

They stood there for a moment and just stared at each other. James wanted to laugh out loud at the whole situation but decided not to because Sam didn't seem like the kind to find getting shot at all that funny.

Chapter Fifteen

The last time he had stepped through this door he had come just like a pig to the sausage maker, but this time he would be prepared. At first, in his mind, Rupert had been planning to say it had been like a lamb to the slaughter but somewhere in there it got turned into a pig and sausage. He wasn't quite sure why he thought of himself more as a pig rather than as a nice white lamb. He looked down at himself and thought, oh right that's why. He shrugged and waited for the guards around the door to say it was okay for him to pass through. He had come to accept his physical image a long time ago, and his choice to enter one of the orders had taken care of the fact that girls never wanted to date him. Now they couldn't. It didn't really solve the fact that he still wished someone had found him attractive at some time, but that was an issue for later.

He cracked his neck from side to side then cracked his knuckles. None of it was done because he needed to, it was all done because that's what he thought you did when you were getting ready to enter a fight. And as far as he could tell this would be a fight. It also helped him feel not so intimidated around the guards. Even though they were all only five or six inches taller than him just the fact that they all looked like they could break a tree in half with one hand kind of lent itself to the intimidation factor. That was their job, however, to look big and intimidating and he thought they were doing a marvelous job of it. Really, what kind of guards would they be if they all looked like him, he thought? The sneaky kind. They would lure you into a false sense of security then when you struck they would all go into asthmatic shock and scare you to death.

This line of thinking was not helping him and he decided he just needed to get though the door and start doing something rather than just standing here thinking about how unqualified for this he was. He had argued vehemently to the council for them to let him go back through the door, and when they had agreed he had been initially very excited. Now, however, he was starting to have misgivings.

Finally after what seemed like an eternity, or at least an hour, the guards told him he was cleared to go through. They let him know that this time they would be keeping the door open so if he needed help they would be able to assist him. He thanked them and stepped up to the hole in the sky that was the door to James' world. The military had built around the door to protect it from the Flame knew what. Rupert couldn't think of anyone that would be out in the middle of a desert with enough firepower to take out the guards. Then it occurred to him that maybe the building wasn't there to protect the door but to protect the guards. Why would anyone want to stand out in this kind of heat guarding something that was invisible? Well, maybe the military was nicer than he had thought at first.

"Are you waiting for something sir?"

Rupert looked at the over muscled guard standing to his right, "No, no I'm just," he had to think of something quickly so that it didn't look like was getting nervous about stepping through that door again, "I'm just deciding on which way to go once I get through. You know, picturing the lay of the land in my mind so I know where I want to head. I figured I would rather be standing here and thinking about it than standing where I could possibly be attacked and thinking about it."

"Very good sir."

Darn right, Rupert thought. It actually was a good idea too, and he started trying to picture the other side in his mind so that he would know what to do if something happened when he stepped through. He finally decided there weren't many options. There was one trail straight ahead, and a lake directly behind. To each side the brush was passable because the leaves had all fallen off and some of the underbrush had died back for the winter, but it was, as he recalled, very scratchy and irritating to run through. Finally he decided the best course of action was to protect himself as he headed up the trail as quickly as possible. He closed his eyes for a moment and imagined the air hardening around him. When his shield was complete he turned, looked at the guard, nodded goodbye, and stepped through the door into another world.

The shock of the cold bit into him through the shield and stole his breath away for a moment. It was like jumping into a lake. He looked around and changed that mental picture into a lake with floating chunks of ice. After taking a painfully cold breath he made the chunks of ice much bigger. He closed his mouth when the air felt like it would crack his teeth and tried breathing through his nose. Instantly he encountered a sensation he was certain he had never had before in his life. The hairs in his nose froze solid and the boogers turned into tiny ice picks that were trying to poke holes in the walls of his nose.

He had known it would be cold and had tried to prepare himself for it, but coming directly from the desert with temperatures somewhere around that of the sun to this was a little difficult. Taking his backpack off he knelt down and started rummaging through it pulling out anything that would make him warmer. With all his careful planning and thinking about what he would do if someone was waiting for him on the other side, his first concern was what to do about the cold. He wasn't trained to be a soldier and to first check the immediate area then to find somewhere concealed to dig through his pack. Instead as soon as the cold hit him he knelt down in the most open and obvious place without even looking to see if anyone was standing on the trail in front of him. Because of this he completely missed the trio of figures that darted off the trail and into the woods.

Tommy tried to stay hidden behind the thin trunks of the aspens while at the same time keeping an eye on the person who had just come through the door. His orders had been to seal the door shut, and if that wasn't possible then to make sure no one coming through it survived. He didn't like taking orders from the professor. The man was so arrogant that half the time Tommy just wanted to punch him in his overeducated face, but he understood something the others didn't. The orders weren't coming from their precious professor Oren Merrill. Tommy had noticed the darkness that hung around the professor, and he had even commented on it to Scott, but Scott seemed to think it was just the image of the professor's power. Tommy wanted to laugh in his face. This wasn't some movie. People didn't have things like that. It was almost like Scott and the others expected the professor to have his own theme music as he walked into the room. Tommy could almost hear them all humming the music for Darth Vader anytime Merrill walked toward them. He was also very sure that Merrill loved the fact that they thought of him like that. No one else noticed the eyes in the darkness. No one else thought to look into the darkness when it gathered around the puffed up professor. They were all so ignorantly concentrating on Merrill himself they failed to notice the truth. Oren Merrill was merely a puppet. This had been proven true when the darkness spoke to him. Merrill had called them all together in one of the lecture halls to make sure everyone knew their part in this upcoming melodrama. Scott was given the lead role because he had proven he would do whatever the professor told him to do, while Tommy was sent out here in the cold because he was the only one who doubted the infallibility of the great Oren Merrill. When the professor had been handing out assignments and explaining the details to those who couldn't quite grasp the situation Tommy had been looking for the eyes. Finally he found them. It was almost as if the darkness had pooled like old oil in one corner of the room where the light didn't quite reach. It was more than just a shadow and as Tommy looked deeper into it he saw it looking back at him. He had smiled to himself and stared directly into those eyes wanting to prove he wasn't afraid. That was the first time he heard the voice. The whispers told him of power and the chaos that could be his. It whispered to him about the lies of religion, and he nodded remembering the hate spewing sign wavers outside the clinic as he walked in with his girlfriend. It whispered about the flexibility of truth, right and wrong and he was reminded of Jean Val Jean stealing a loaf of bread to feed his family. By the time he left that room he had opened a door and a hole inside him that he had never wanted to admit was there had been filled. If you had looked into his eyes that night you would have seen yourself reflected back in an oily sheen.

Very few of Merrill's followers had been taught how to bend reality. Even fewer of them had been able to do it. Even though Scott said he could do amazing things Tommy was sure he had never been able to even lift a pencil with his mind. Scott just couldn't bring himself to believe it was possible. Tommy could tell every time Scott tried he let that little doubting voice in the back of his mind tell him what he was trying wasn't possible. Tommy on the other hand could do more than any of the others combined. The great professor had never deemed to show Tommy how it was done, but the eyes had spoken to him out of the darkness and Tommy knew the truth. Out in the woods on a moonless night the eyes had surrounded him and guided his hands and his mind. By the end of that night nothing seemed impossible to him.

Now watching the odd figure that emerged from the door he was struck by the realization that he could snuff out this man's life in any number of ways. It wasn't what he had expected, and it definitely wasn't what the darkness had expected. This looked as much like a soldier as a pig looked like a sheep Tommy thought. This chubby older man must be hiding something. Who in their right mind would stop in the middle of the clearing and just kneel there waiting to get blasted into oblivion. He must be a decoy to flush them out into the open Tommy thought. Most likely if they attacked now dozens of soldiers would appear from nowhere and turn Tommy and the others into dust. So he decided to wait. The man had to do something, and there was only one way out of this area. Once he was out of the trees it was all open muskeg. Tommy and his guys could stay in the tree line and open fire while the stranger would be out in the open with no protection.

Tommy looked at the open door and remembered trying to close it. The guys with him had just wanted to walk up to it and push it closed, but Tommy had been told the truth by the darkness. There was a whole other world through there, and there would be people guarding the door. Even if they weren't guarding it from this side they would be there on the other side. If they just walked up and tried to close it someone would stop them and then the other side would know Tommy was there.

Tommy had sent someone to try and lightly push it closed, hoping that those on the other side would think it was the wind or a tree branch that had fallen against the door. He had made sure the guy he sent came at the door from the right side so the door itself would shield him from being seen. He remembered watching as the door started to swing shut and just before it closed all the way something stopped it. Then the proof came as he saw through his binoculars a very heavily muscled man push the door back open and stick his head through to see if anything was there.

He knew beyond a shadow of a doubt they weren't going to be able to get the door shut without a fight, and they weren't prepared for the kind of fight that it looked like those on the other side could bring. Amazing things could be done with this new found power of his, but he was unwilling to take a risk against an unknown opponent. Did they have the power as well? How many of them were there? The man that had poked his head through the door had been wearing a very immaculate uniform and that said only one thing to Tommy: he was part of a large organization. With all of the newfound power he had Tommy didn't think he could face an entire army.

Knowing there were people waiting on the other side of the door, and that this man crouching out in the open could possibly be a trap he decided to wait and see what would happen. His patience was rewarded in a matter of moments. The man who had come through the door stood up, straightened his pack, and started down the trail. Tommy motioned for his men to fall back into their prearranged positions. Now all he had to do was decide whether he wanted this person alive for questioning or if he should just kill him. That decision wasn't really up to him though so as he slid through the trees he looked into the darkness that clung to the underside of leafless bushes and finally found what he was looking for. As soon as he saw it he knew every shadow around him had eyes that were looking out at him, looking into him. The soft voice whispered to him and he nodded. He would do as the darkness said.

Rupert felt a little better after putting on almost everything in his pack, but he could still feel the bite of the cold through his clothes. It stung his eyes and his every breath hurt. He just wasn't used to such cold temperatures. He remembered it being cold when he had left, but after living in this world for a month he had gotten a little bit used to it. Now coming straight from the desert heat this was ridiculous. After a few steps he remembered he was in hostile territory and chided himself on mentally letting his guard down. He wasn't too hard on himself though because he had kept his shield up so even if someone had been waiting for him he would have been ready. Now, though, he needed to start being on the lookout for anything strange or out of place.

Keeping his shield up he started looking into the trees as he walked along the path. The fact that the sun was up gave him a certain sense of security. The light would surely reveal anything strange in the woods. On the other hand, he thought, would he know if something were out of place here? He was from another world and any number of things could be out of place here and he wouldn't know it. He would just think they were normal here. So what should he be looking for? At that thought he started to get worried that he had missed something, and began looking over his shoulder every few steps.

Finally he emerged from the tree lined trail and onto the dirt road he and James had just been on. It seemed like that whole fight had just happened. He remembered the firelight flickering through the thin trees and the look on James face as things exploded around him. Rupert turned left onto the dirt road and shook his head. He prayed to the great flame that James was all right. Prayed he had been able to escape from whoever was after them that night. Rupert was almost sure it was that professor he had run into. He knew without a doubt the professor had dealings with the other side, but he wasn't sure if the two things had been connected. If they weren't connected then they were dealing with more than one problem over here. In that case he desperately hoped this was all connected. It would make everything so much easier. He could just get to the university, confront the professor, and be done with this.

To his right there was an empty expanse of muskeg that rolled out for over a mile like a great green expanse of shag carpet. It was deceiving in the fact that it looked flat. In reality there were dips and rolls in it that could hide a person easily, especially if you weren't looking for them. Because of this Rupert had his entire attention focused on the tree line to his left. Once he had passed them by a few steps he couldn't have seen the two figures that rose up out of the seemingly flat terrain. They raised their hands as if preparing to direct an orchestra and unleashed two identical balls of fire directly at Rupert's back.

The tiny hairs on the back of his neck stood up and he turned his head just before the two balls of flame impacted his shield. The simultaneous impact was enough to toss him from his feet. He landed with a solid thud that knocked what little breath he had out of his lungs. Gasping for breath and trying to roll onto his knees he forced his mind to remain focused on his shield. He was out in the open and wouldn't be able to put up a counter attack until he could breathe again. On top of that he had no idea if he could strike back and keep his shield up at the same time. He had never practiced it, and wasn't sure if it was even possible. He had always been told that a very well trained person could do two things at once if they were similar, but this was not a good time to try something new.

Just as he was getting to his knees another blow knocked him back onto his right side. Without taking the time to really think about it Rupert extended the shield in his mind out away from his body. In his mind he formed a bubble around himself large enough to stand up in. He knew the power was there, and he knew the great Flame was on his side. He knew beyond a shadow of a doubt that nothing except the great Flame himself could get through his shield, and his belief became reality.

Taking a few dozen shallow breaths to try and steady his nerves he looked around for his attackers. Two of them were advancing on him from out on the muskeg. It was like they had appeared from thin air. He was sure he had looked out there and seen nothing. Glancing back at the trees he saw another figure coming out onto the road. That meant he had two behind him and one in front of him. Standing up he watched three fireballs splash against his shield like miniature fireworks. He was very happy to see it was holding up just like he had imagined, but then he realized he couldn't just stand here forever he had to think of some way out of this. If he lowered his shield he would only be able to strike back in one direction or the other, which would give the other side a chance to hit him from behind. He thought of just running with the shield up around him, but that wouldn't get him very far. Mainly because he couldn't run very far, and when he was too tired to run anymore he might lose focus and the shield would go down.

This time blue sparks danced across the surface of the shield as his attackers tried something new. Thinking about this fight Rupert realized again how inadequate he was for this task. He wasn't a soldier. He wasn't trained to fight three people at the same time. The more he thought about it the more he came to the conclusion he wasn't the person for this job. Maybe, he thought, he could make it back to the door with his shield up and the soldiers would come through and help him. The mental image of the looks they would give him caused him to pause. He remembered the doubts that had been expressed by the military leaders when he had said he was going back through. They had only allowed him to proceed because he had the blessing of the council. He wasn't a soldier they had said with their eyes. He was fat and wheezed when he walked too fast. The soldiers at the gate had looked at him like it must all be a big joke.

Watching the lightning dance across his shield he decided he wasn't going to run. He wouldn't give them the satisfaction of being right. There had been too many times in his life he had done just that. Those times hadn't really mattered, but this time someone's life could be at stake and it was because of him. He just had to think of it differently. At that he felt the ground beneath him start to crack. He looked down and realized again they were trying something different. Looking up at them he realized they were smart little buggers. If they couldn't get through the shield then why not go under it. He had to do something fast before they figured out a way to really get at him.

That thought reminded him of a negotiation he had been part of. It was his first time being the lead negotiator. People had tried to give him the strange advice that it was like a battle and he would have to come at it like a fight. He remembered looking across the table at the opposition's negotiator and realizing he wasn't a soldier. He couldn't come at it like a war, or a fight. He was exactly what the soldiers thought he was. He was fat, and he liked it. He did wheeze when he walked too fast, but he still got to where he was going and that was all that mattered. This was just a negotiation and he was good at that. He stopped thinking about it like a fight and started thinking about it like an argument. Each side presented their points and the other side had to counter them.

They had him surrounded and he needed a way to knock them all out at once. He needed something that could touch them all at the same time without compromising his position. He watched as the two that were together whispered to each other and he realized they were trying to come up with something as well. The rasp of his breathing was getting in the way of his thinking. Normally he didn't even notice it, but inside this bubble it seemed to reverberate off the shield and amplify itself. That was when it hit him. He was breathing. They were breathing. Air was everywhere. It didn't have to take time to reach them, because it was already there. But what could he do? Did he want to just knock them out, or did they deserve to die?

Shaking his head he decided this was no time for a moral dilemma. He would do what was necessary and if they died then he would deal with how he felt about that later. He closed his eyes to shut out the world around him and thought about what could be done with air. Different facts about air started tumbling through his mind. You could bring the air together and make it solid, or you could thin it out and make it harder to breathe. You could push people around with it or pull them toward you with it. It was made up of different things and you could separate them out and use them for different purposes. His eyes snapped open and he had it. When he was younger a man from one of the universities had come to his school and done a show to try and get young kids excited about research and science. Most kids just wanted to learn to be soldiers at that age. One of the things he had done to get their attention was fill up a balloon and make it explode. All you had to do was separate out the right parts of the air and then add a spark. Of course he didn't tell them which parts of the air because every kid in the room would have gone home and promptly blown up his house trying to do the same thing, but Rupert had learned what the parts were when he went to university.

Closing his eyes Rupert pictured the area around him and in his mind he separated out one part of the air from the other. In his mind's eye he could see around him the air breaking down into its composite parts, and when it was ready he added the spark.

The ground seemed to roll and pitch beneath his feet and he could feel an immense heat on his face. He put all his will power into maintaining the shield around him, but he hadn't thought to drown out the noise. The shield protected him from the blast and the shockwave, but not the noise. The initial boom after the spark had partially deafened him and the concussion from the explosion had knocked the air from him again.

Shaking his head in a desperate attempt to regain his hearing he pushed himself up off his knees and forced himself into a standing position. His whole body ached as if he had just been run over. He tried to think of anything back on his world that would be large enough to cause this much pain and he came up blank. He stuck his finger in his ear hoping he could pull the ache out that way and realized two things. First he realized that if a house fell on you it would feel about the same, just without as much noise, and second he realized there was something wet in his ear. In a slight daze He pulled his finger away and looked at it only to be shocked to see that it was red. He wondered for a moment how that had happened then it all seemed to hit him at once. He looked around for the first time and saw what he had done. The blood on his finger was the smallest damage that had been done. Try as hard as he could, he wasn't able to see the three men who had attacked him, but then again there really wasn't anything to be seen around him for at least fifty yards.

His attack had carved a perfect circle around his shield. Trees were either gone all together or burning in little pieces scattered amongst the rubble of dirt and rock that had been thrown around. If he had been able to hear anything he would have looked up at the sound of pieces of tree and dirt hitting the top of his shield. Now he knew why the man from the university so long ago hadn't been willing to explain the details of the experiment to a bunch of eleven year olds. He could just picture houses exploding all over town.

While sitting down and pulling a container of water from his pack there was no way he could have noticed the movement in what was left of the tree line over fifty yards away. Tommy was pushing tree branches and other various bits and pieces off himself. He was astonished by what he had just witnessed. Being reluctant to put himself in danger for professor Merrill he had hung back and watched as the others had attacked the lone figure. He wasn't quite sure what was going to happen when they attacked so he hadn't been too surprised when their initial attack didn't accomplish anything more than knocking the man over. Half expecting other people to appear from somewhere he had continued to hold back until he could assess the situation. All the darkness had said to him was that this man needed to die. They had no need to question him about anything, so Tommy had separated out his three men and set them up to attack from both directions at the same time.

It had amused him to watch the three try to figure out how to get through the man's shield, and at the same time Tommy was trying to figure out how the shield was created. It would come in handy if he knew how to do the same thing. Watching as they hurled first fire then lightning at the shield he shook his head. They were so uncreative. All they could think to do was exactly what they had been taught to do by Merrill. Tommy tried out a theory of his by moving the ground around a little bit underneath the man and he was rewarded by noticing that the shield didn't extend that far. All he had to do was think of a way of getting something under there, or doing something with the ground itself. What he needed was a better vantage point so he could see down into the shield and focus on the ground beneath the man's feet.

Turning away from the action he found a small rise in the ground about twenty yards away that would give him a better view of the area between the trees. Getting up there he noticed the air was getting a little bit foggy around the four men on the road. Thinking it must just be the sun evaporating off some of the moisture from the morning dew he neglected to notice the faint odd smell in the air. He had just started getting a good idea on turning the ground beneath the man's feet into spikes when the world exploded.

He was thrown backwards by the concussion and the heat in the air singed the hair on his head. For moments that seemed like eternity he couldn't breathe and bits of tree, dirt, and rock rained down on him like a bizarre snowfall. Finally he had been able to breathe enough and move enough to start digging himself out from under the random detritus that had half covered him. He was bleeding from multiple cuts and the only sound in the world was the pulse of his blood as it thundered in his head. Looking out on the devastation he saw, amazingly, the man standing almost calmly in the middle of a ring of carnage. He was standing in a perfectly clean bubble surrounded by burning chunks of trees and torn up earth.

Tommy shook his head and knew he was in no shape to try and kill this man. Anyone that could do what had just been done wasn't someone Tommy was willing to attack on his own while injured, especially since he no longer had surprise on his side. Clumsily rummaging through his pockets he pulled out his cell phone and flipped it open. He was slightly surprised to see it was still working. Pressing speed dial number five he held the phone to his ear and waited to hear it ring. After a few seconds he came to the conclusion that he couldn't hear anything and simply looked at the phone to see that it claimed to be connected. Having no idea whether he had actually gotten through or had just ended up on voicemail he started talking. "They're all dead." His voice came out as a rasp and he tried again louder, "Someone came through the door. We tried to stop him, but he killed all my men." He paused to take a breath. Not knowing if someone was actually listening or if they were trying to talk to him he continued, "If you want them dealt with, Merrill, you come and do it yourself."

Flipping the phone closed he staggered off in the direction of his car at the end of the dirt road. He thought about asking the darkness for help, but knew that would be useless. It helped no one but itself, and that was what he needed to do now.

Chapter Sixteen

The frozen blue of the sky contrasted sharply with the thoughts running through James' head as he drove his beat up little Geo back down the Glenn Highway and toward Anchorage. He had parted ways with Sam for the simple reason that they had two cars and only two people. Sam had tried to talk him into leaving the Geo there, or even leaving the stolen, or borrowed, car there and sticking together, but James thought it would be better if they had a backup in case something happened. When Sam asked him what could possibly happen James gave him a look that said don't you remember the last few hours, and Sam had let the matter drop. That, however, wasn't what was bothering him. Don was dead. They had come after Sam to kill him, and it all seemed to be wrapped up in whatever James had gotten involved in.

It just kept repeating through his head that Don was dead. He honestly couldn't think of a single person that would want to actually kill Don. He remembered he'd been getting some hate mail lately but James was sure it would just blow over. As he watched the leafless bone white aspens and the dark green of the pines slide by, he knew Don's death had nothing to do with the tolerance march, or maybe it did. Hadn't Rupert said Merrill was involved in that? But why would Merrill kill one of his own little soldiers? Did they have a falling out? Had Don realized something was wrong with the whole setup so the professor got rid of him? It didn't make sense. If they were trying to destabilize the world by pushing this idea that no action, no matter how depraved, was wrong then why would he kill off one of the students that was leading the charge toward moral ambiguity?

Passing the North Birchwood exit he couldn't get the idea out of his head that the whole plan, as far as James could see it, was simply ridiculous. Humankind didn't need any supernatural help to send us sliding down the path toward moral ambiguity; we were doing that all on our own. How could that be the plan to take over the world? On the other hand James had to admit bad guys never really had a great plan. They always thought they were so clever but their plans always ended up being something silly like using lime jell-o to hypnotize all the children in the world. All the while the hero thought it was something diabolical only to laugh himself silly at the realization that it all had to do with lime jell-o. James seriously hoped it would be something like that, but now that people were getting killed he knew there must be more than he was seeing.

Heading through Eagle River he looked over to the right where a construction crew was hard at work finishing up something before the world completely froze and was covered in a blanket of snow. He did a double take at the banner hanging from the building they were finishing. He craned his neck and risked hitting a few cars to see if he could catch a glimpse of it again. There between the flag pole and a partially empty office building he saw it again, a snow white banner and at the top of it a flame stitched out in reds and oranges, at the bottom a group of people looking up to the flame with hands raised.

James wasn't big on signs or believing in things like that but when something hits you in the face you probably should check it out. He knew a lot of different religions used the imagery of the flame to represent something or other, but this being here right now was almost too much of a coincidence. He'd already passed the exit so he took the next one and circled back around toward the banner and the construction site. He stopped and waited to turn left at a red light and watched out the passenger window as men worked on an expansion to a local Wal-Mart. It made him think of ants and how they all seemed to work together for the greater good. He doubted anyone would call expanding a Wal-Mart part of the greater good, except maybe the stockholders. After he turned he went past the police station on the right and the fire station on the left. He slowed down with the rest of the traffic to watch a display that took his breath away.

In the parking lot of the fire station someone was tossing out large chunks of meat, and winter starved bald eagles were crowding around to get bits and pieces of it. Everywhere he looked eagles were hopping, swooping, and circling. If there was any space left by the great birds it was filled by the deep black of ravens. None of them were pecking at each other; none were fighting. They seemed to have an unwritten set of rules for their society. They knew when it was appropriate to take a piece of meat left over by another bird, and they knew when it wasn't appropriate. The ravens knew they could take the smaller pieces without causing any fights, and as such they would hop right by larger pieces leaving them for the eagles.

James almost rear-ended a truck because he was watching a massive bald eagle slowly float by his driver's side window. Looking over his shoulder as he slowed down at the next stoplight he wondered about the whole set up. Why was it, he wondered, that birds and other animals knew there was a certain way things were supposed to work, but humans tried their best to convince themselves that there wasn't? Animals seemed to take it for granted that there was an order, and things would work better if you followed that order. People on the other hand, at least lately, seemed bound and determined to convince themselves that there was no such thing so they wouldn't feel guilty doing whatever they wanted to.

Maybe that was it, he thought to himself as he watched people waiting in line at a local tire shop to get their studded tires put on before the snow flew. Maybe it all came down to people trying to avoid feeling guilty. I'll tolerate you, at least in principle, so that I can tell you that you have to tolerate me. That way I don't feel guilty for my actions. Convince enough people there is no order and they'll let you get away with murder because who's willing to tell you otherwise. If they tell you that you're wrong then they have to admit at sometime they might also be wrong, and no one wants that.

That was all well and philosophically good, James thought as he looked for the road to the banner, but it still got him no closer to figuring out why anyone would want to kill Don and Sam. In this day and age it just didn't seem like someone's modus operandi to kill people over a philosophical difference.

James realized after a second that he wouldn't need to turn down any roads to get to the construction site because it was directly in front of him. As far as things go it was a fairly good-sized construction project. He could tell it was meant to be an add-on to an existing church, but it was slightly humorous in the fact that the add-on was at least as big, if not bigger, than the original church. From the stick frame of it he couldn't tell what it was going to be eventually, but he assumed it would be some gymnasium area, or multipurpose room. He couldn't really think of any other reason unless they were starting a school.

James shook his head when he realized he was mentally babbling to himself because he really didn't know what to do now. He'd pulled up to the site and was staring up at the banner. From the highway it'd looked white but from up close he could tell it had seen better days. It was a little dingy and obviously rained on, but the form of it could still be easily picked out. At the base of it were five figures. They were all black and stood out well against the semi white of the background. Their hands were raised and their featureless faces were turned upwards. They looked like shadows, but with no solid form attached, and above them was the flame. This close he could tell it was merely layered cloth. Orange and yellow mixed with red to give it the illusion of depth and movement. It was well done for its size. The impression from the highway had been one of a flickering flame descending on a group of worshipers. Here, however, it was simply stitched pieces of cloth.

James sighed to himself and wondered if he was starting to go loony. He couldn't blame himself, he thought, after all he had been through. It would be perfectly understandable to go a little loony after the events of the last few days, and it might even be good for him. Trying to stay absolutely sane in these conditions would drive anyone mad.

He was just about to put his car into reverse when he noticed a man in a hard hat walking toward his car. Not wanting to seem rude or strange he rolled down his window and waited for the man to get there.

The man nodded his head, "Good after noon."

James looked at the clock on his dash and realized that it really was after noon. He smiled up at the man who he assumed was the foreman, "Good after noon."

The man's orange hardhat bobbed as he nodded a hello, "Is there something I can help you with?"

He said it in a nice enough way but James understood the underlying implication. He had worked a little bit of construction himself and there was always the worry of people trying to walk off with your tools while you weren't looking. James hadn't really thought about asking anything but he didn't want for the man to think he was a weirdo so he needed a reason to be there, "Actually there is something you can help me with." He pointed up at the banner, "I saw that from the highway and was curious what it meant."

"Huh," the man turned and looked up at the banner as it flapped in the little breeze that had picked up, "Well," he scratched his cheek, "I can't say I really know what it means." He looked over at James a little sheepishly, "I've been working on this for a few months now and it's been up there as long as the walls have been there to hold it, but I guess I never really thought about it."

This time it was James' turn to say, "Huh." He was about to say thanks and go through the normal ritual of saying goodbye in the right way to get himself out of an awkward situation when the man spoke up.

"I guess," he looked back up at the banner, "It has something to do with power from heaven coming down on those followers there."

"Power?" James' curiosity was peaked.

"Well you know what I mean."

James smiled politely and thought to himself that a flame and power from heaven meant something totally different to him today than yesterday, and he wasn't about to start into it with this guy right now. On the other hand he was still a little curious, and he needed a good way to get out of the conversation so he could move on without seeming weird. "Actually I don't really know what you mean. Could they fly?"

"Well no, no. Nothing like that. I think," he took off his hardhat and rubbed his head, "if I remember my Sunday schooling right it was just stuff like speaking other people's language and raising people from the dead."

James blinked. He had been zoning out a little bit and looking over the man's shoulder. He was almost sure that he had seen one of the figures on the banner move and look at him. "I'm sorry," James looked over at the man then back to the banner, "did you say raise people from the dead?"

"Well," again the man seemed a little unsure of himself, "ya, I think so. I'm pretty sure I remember some stories about them being able to bring people back."

This time James was sure he had seen it. One of the figures at the bottom of the banner turned its head and looked at him with white cloth eyes and winked. James looked back at the man and smiled his best smile, "You know what? I think I'll have to come by on Sunday and sit through a service." He nodded and started rolling up his window, "You have a nice day."

"You too." Came the expected reply and James didn't even hear it as he shifted his car into reverse and pulled out of the parking lot and headed back toward Anchorage.

His mind was racing with strange possibilities as he got back onto the highway. On any other given day he would have thought the idea was crazy. Any other day he would have thought seeing cloth men on a banner wink at him was crazy, but not today. He smiled at himself. Today was the day to be a little loony, and that loon inside him was starting to form a plan. Maybe, just maybe he could finally get some answers. The only problem would be figuring out where the man was that he wanted to talk to. Even that shouldn't be too hard, he thought. Not on a day like today when everything seemed to be just crazy enough for it all to work.

Chapter Seventeen

It was an odd sensation being frightened. It was something he hadn't felt in quite a while. The power he had gained through his association with the darkness had given him a certain amount of assurance. He felt he could do things no one else could so why should he be afraid of them. He had, of course, been afraid the first time he'd encountered the darkness. Any sane person would have been afraid, even most insane people would have been.

He had been so angry, and yet felt so impotent. They had simply refused to argue with him. He was right and they simply refused to stand and fight. Those religious, dogmatic, freaks of human nature. Once they were backed into a corner that they couldn't logically get themselves out of they reverted back to the tried and true method of claiming faith or belief then refused to argue the point further. They knew they were tearing the world apart by refusing to let go of their outdated ideas of moral absolutism. Each faith brought their own absolutes to the table and since none would back down, again on the basis of faith and belief, the only course of action was to say the others were going to hell, or sheol, or gehana, or whatever they called it in their language.

They all claimed to be tolerant of each other, and yet in the same breath they also claimed they were the only way to find truth or get to heaven or whatever they called the upward direction in their religion. He tried and tried to get them to see the light of true tolerance. The fact they were all right in their own way, and they all had the right to do what they wanted to. He didn't believe in any of their doctrines, but that wasn't the point. The point was that no one single ideal was any more valid than the others. They, of course, couldn't see that. They, of course, stuck to their belief that one of them had to be right therefore the rest had to be wrong, and none of them were willing to admit they might be the wrong ones.

The meeting had ended in chaos. Groups were shouting at each other and accusing each other of trying to kill off certain parts of the population. The word terrorist was flung around like candy falling from a piñata. Sometime after the shouting started and before he had stormed out of the conference room was when he had started hearing the voice. At first he just accepted it as his own mind looking for an outlet for the things he wanted to say to these holier than thou religious bigots, but after a while he realized it was whispering things he had never thought before. Its silky voice seemed to flow over his mind soothing his raging nerves. It pointed out the power that could come from a chaotic situation like this. The fact that his interests could best be served by guiding the chaos and not fighting it. They were, after all, going to fight anyway. Why not make sure the group which he wanted actually won. It even suggested the only way to make sure that happened was to make sure there was chaos to work with in the first place.

Eventually he had simply gotten up and walked out in the evening sunlight. It was the middle of summer and the sun wouldn't be going down until after eleven. He wandered the pathways of the campus until he came to a spot the sunlight didn't touch. All around him the sun would continue to burn for hours yet, but here in the shade of the school library he felt he could find some measure of solace. It was there he first saw the eyes looking out from the darkness. It was there he realized the truth. In chaos there was true power, and he wanted that power to be his. He had agreed to do whatever it would take, and he had watched as the eyes came closer and closer. They burned into his mind and scoured his soul. Then he had been afraid. Looking back on it now he realized how dangerous a thing it was to make a deal with chaos. By their very nature you could never know if they would keep their end of the bargain, but he had been desperate.

Once again he was desperate, and once again he was scared. Professor Orin Merrill knew he was the victim of the oldest fear known to mankind. He was afraid of the unknown. The message he had received from Tommy was, to say the least, disturbing. He had always been wary of Tommy. He couldn't control him like he could with Scott. At first he had thought of just getting rid of him but he had become too useful. Scott was controllable and strong enough to get most things done, but they both knew that if it came down to a fight Tommy would brush Scott aside like a fly. Because of that very fact Merrill had decided it was better to keep him around for as long as it was useful, and lately it had been very useful to have someone that wasn't worried about getting his hands a little dirty.

He was involved with the two seemingly unrelated homicides that had started the unrest in the Mountain View community, the burning of the gay couples home by supposed religious fanatics, and the retaliation against the religious community by supposed groups of gay rights activists. That had been only some of the work Tommy had been good at. Nothing seemed to faze him. That was one of the things that irritated Merrill, because not even he seemed to faze Tommy. His sense of irritation had grown and so had Tommy's semi traitorous statements in front of the others. Once they had located the door he thought it would be a great idea to send Tommy out there in the cold to watch it. That would cement his position as the one in charge, and Tommy's position as simply a lackey. A very strong lackey, but still simply a lackey.

The professor liked having lackeys. He even liked saying the word lackey. It made him feel somehow like a pirate captain about to kick some little sniveling brat off the side of the ship into shark infested waters. They needed more of that in the world lately. There were too many sniveling brats that were being allowed to hang around. Too much tolerance for his taste. This made him smile. He knew the truth of the matter, but it was so useful to pretend that he sided with one or the other. It didn't really matter which side he picked, as long as people around him knew which side it was. He had decided at the beginning of this plan that he would stick with what he'd already been talking about so no one suspected him of anything. There would be less explaining to do if he didn't change positions. Besides this was where the world was right now. Tolerance was dripping like blood off the bitten tongue of humanity. The argument had been changed. It was no longer an argument of good versus evil, or even right versus wrong. Now it was an argument of tolerance versus intolerance, and he liked that. You could be on either side and still convince yourself you were a good person and the others were the bad people.

As he turned to head down Horseshoe Lake Road he saw a man walking toward him along the opposite side. He thought he recognized him and slowed down to get a better look. They made eye contact through his driver's side window and he saw the look of shock spread across the man's face. At the same time he realized where he had seen him before. It had been after the outdoor meeting. The man had said he was looking for Sam. It was him.

The lightning left a smoldering hole in the pavement and Rupert cursed to himself about lack of practice and not being able to aim. He gathered his thoughts and started pulling in the energy to fire another blast when he saw the door of the car swing open and a stream of fire lanced out at him. He barely had enough time to switch his thinking from the bolt of lightning he was about to throw to hardening the air in front of him. Just before the flames started licking his face he erected the wall and watched the red and orange dance across the now solid wall of air before his eyes.

Almost instantly Rupert's breathing turned loud and shallow. He needed space to regain his breath. In his mind he formed the wall of air into a semi circle and pushed outwards. The raging flames fled and eventually he even saw the car pushed sideways off the road until it was pressed against a stand of leafless birch trees. For a moment he thought he had literally gained some breathing room and then the ground underneath his feet exploded sending his feet to where his head had been only moments before. He landed somewhat upside down on his left shoulder. His head twisted and he continued over until his face was in the dirt of the roadside ditch. As if asthma wasn't bad enough now his breath had been totally knocked out of him and he was face down gasping in piles of frozen dirt. He knew somewhere in his mind that he needed to get up and defend himself, but he couldn't. It wasn't a question of mind over matter. It wasn't a question at all. He couldn't breathe. He got his hands under himself and started to push up when he felt a great weight press him down into the sharp shards of the frozen ground.

"So," the voice hovered above him, "I was right about you." The pressure increased slightly making it even harder for him to regain his breath. "They all said I had nothing to worry about, but I knew you were a threat. You wouldn't have shown up at the gathering and tried to find Sam because of some innocent coincidence."

Concentrating more than he ever remembered doing in his life Rupert formed the belief in his mind that his lungs were fine and he could breathe as well as any man going for a normal afternoon stroll. At first nothing happened because he couldn't let go of the nagging life long doubt in the back of his mind that his lungs just weren't any good, but eventually that was overridden by the undeniable fact that the power never failed. The flame had said that with true faith a man could move a mountain, and Rupert had seen it happen. What was a little air in his lungs compared to that? He believed, and he could breathe. True pure belief has power. Even a mad man who believes his tulips talk to him has a certainty that breeds power. The house cat that protects her young from a bear believes she can win, and she does because her belief gives her power. Enough power to change her own world for that moment. For Rupert it was enough that he could breathe. Now all he needed was a little bit of time to come up with a plan.

"Tommy must not be as tough as I thought he was if you took all his guys out."

That's right, Rupert thought to himself, keep talking. Give me enough time to figure out what to do.

"So," the weight lifted from Rupert and he was lifted into the air and dropped on his back, then the weight pressed down on him again, "I just want to get a look at the man who took out my tough guys." Rupert could feel the weight press on him, but he knew it would do nothing to his breathing, and it didn't. He recognized the professor leaning over him, "Tell me little man, did you come alone?" Rupert didn't answer. He acted as if he couldn't breathe, and found that it was easy for him. He had, after all, spent most of his life looking like he couldn't breathe. "I doubt you came alone. Just look at you." The professor shook his head and Rupert realized he was feeling a little bit angry. Why were people always looking down on him because he was a little bit pudgy? "Come to think of it, I doubt you were the one who got rid of Tommy." At that the professor looked up and started scanning the tree line at the side of the road. He whispered more to himself than to Rupert, "You must be a decoy."

  Rupert smiled at this. That's right, he thought, I'm not alone. The thought gave him a grand idea. Seconds later noises that sounded a lot like footsteps sounded out from the trees. The professor took his attention completely away from Rupert and crouching made his way toward the sounds. Rupert closed his eyes and imagined three soldiers of the empire walking through the woods parallel to the road. He could see them clearly in his mind's eye. They were decked out in their formal gear and carrying the thick clubs of rank that marked the front line soldiers. He believed they were walking through the woods looking for him, and at that very moment he heard the professor gasp as he caught sight of them between the trees. Rupert opened his eyes and saw the professor's back was towards him. As quietly as possible he raised himself up onto his hands then pushed himself into a sitting position. His first thought was to knock the professor on the back of the head with a fist of air, but he needed to question the man. His two confrontations with him had proven that the professor wasn't what Rupert was looking for. He did, however, believe the professor had contact with the thing. Because of that he needed to question him. In order to act, though, he would need to release the idea of the three soldiers. He couldn't hold the two ideas in his head at the same time so he would need to strike quickly.

  Merrill had just decided that the better part of valor in this case would be to leave the scene as quickly as possible then come back later with Scott and his guys. He was smart enough to know he might not win a three on one contest. Before he could turn to head back to his car a movement caught his eye and he realized that the soldiers he had been watching were gone. Turning to see what the first man was doing he was struck by a thin bright blue ball of energy and he fell shaking to the ground. This time it was his turn to look up and see someone leaning over him as he tried to move. Whatever had struck him had at least temporarily immobilized him.

Rupert looked down at him and went into his negotiator mode, "You're in contact with a wanted creature from through the door. You will tell me where the creature can be found and I will consider letting you stay on this world. If you do not cooperate I will be forced to take you back to my world and turn you over to the inquisitors for questioning." He realized, after saying it, that it really wasn't negotiating if you simply demanded something. He waited for a reply and then realized something else. The shock he had given to the man had rendered him unable to speak. Well, he could be patient. He was getting quite cold, and it was possible someone would drive by and stop to see what was going on. The thought made him wonder if anyone was coming right now. Standing he looked down the road. Seeing nothing he turned back toward the professor. He was warmly greeted by a bright red flash of light and wave of heat that knocked him backward and off his feet again. A still small voice in the back of his head quipped sarcastically that he really would do better at this if he could just stay on his feet. Ignoring it he lashed out with a wave of flame. Hearing a yelp of pain he used the moment to scramble back onto his feet and looked around.

Seeing a huge rock flying at him he realized someone should invent a permanent shield so he didn't have to keep putting one up. This time he decided that he would rather use the time that it took for the rock to fly through the air to fire back and simply avoid the slow moving object. Dodging to his left he crystallized the cold air around him and sent frozen darts flying in the general direction of his opponent. In the brief respite gained while the professor was avoiding being stuck with a few dozen flying icicles he came to the conclusion that he still needed to get information out of this whole encounter. Simply surviving wouldn't be good enough. "There's nothing you could hope to gain from all this you know." He shouted across the road.

"What?" The professor called back, "Are you going to offer me more than he did, because I really don't think you can."

Rupert made sure his shield was up and not only covered the area around him but under and over himself as well, "And what did he offer you that made you think he would ever keep his word?"

An invisible force slammed into Rupert's shield rocking him back onto his heels for a moment before the answer came, "He offered me nothing. What he did was show me how to take it for myself."

"He's using you professor. He could care less about you."

"Oh, you think I don't know that? Of course he doesn't care about me, but he needs me."

"So you're content to be a tool? He'll use you up and throw you away."

The professor stepped out onto the road, "You have no idea what you're even talking about do you?" Rupert took the chance now that he could see him clearly to send a swarm of tiny balls of flame flying at him and watched in irritation as the professor brushed them aside with a wave of his hand. The professor shook his head, "You really are here alone aren't you?" He looked around deliberately then back at Rupert, "We've made enough noise out here to wake the dead and no one else has shown up so I guess that settles that little question doesn't it?"

Seeing they were at a kind of stalemate Rupert walked close enough that he wouldn't have to keep yelling, "You think I don't know what I'm talking about and yet here you are thinking you can control that thing?"

The professor raised a fist into the air, "I've looked into its eyes and seen that it's week. I can become stronger than it ever was."

"And in the process be damned for all eternity."

"Eternity? Do you even know what you're talking about? I've seen it. I've looked into the darkness and seen that there's no eternity. There's only what you can get here and now."

Rupert shook his head, "Of course that's what you saw when you looked into the pit, because that's what it wants you to believe. That is what the darkness believes. If it ever for a moment believed there would come a reckoning for its actions and let doubt creep into its being it would be undone. That type of evil, by its very nature, refuses to believe there are consequences for its actions. That's what makes it evil. That's what makes it powerful."

"No, what makes it powerful is the fact that it has seen the truth and realized there are no consequences. There is only now. If you get caught, that only means you're a fool, not that you're somehow evil."

Again the ground under Rupert shook, but this time he was ready for that type of attack and easily pushed it down, "It feeds off your belief in it and grows stronger by the very fact that you're acting the way you are."

"I'm growing stronger, and soon I'll no longer need its whispering voice and prying eyes to show me anything. Soon I'll be the master and it will be destroyed."

Rupert's eyes opened wide in a mix of wonder and recognition, "So, I'll be the first of my people to see where demons come from. We had always thought they existed before us, but now…"

"Demons, ha. Again with those outdated religious ideas. There are no demons, no angels, no gods, only man."

"Maybe you're right on that first count." Rupert shrugged, "Maybe we are the demons, but you are sorely mistaken if you think there is no God." Rupert looked up at where the setting sun was painting the clouds in hues of flame and burning gold. "He watches us even now. Looking down over the many worlds along the path, and even now you have a choice."

"Religious drivel. The foundational blocks of the world's greatest hypocrisies. That's what religion is. It's good for one thing only: to stir up the masses and convince them to do whatever you want. Religion is the ultimate game of us versus them, and if you play both sides right you come out a winner no matter what. Speaking of which, I have a date to keep with a new saint in Eagle River. It's been fun but you'll have to die now." With that he raised his hands like a mad orchestra maestro and the ground around Rupert lifted like twin tsunamis. With a clap of his hands the ground engulfed his little shield and crashed down like thunder. The professor pounded the little lump that was left with the largest trees he could find until it was perfectly flat, then he got into his car, started it up, drove back onto the road, and sped away.

Chapter Eighteen

This isn't going to work.
And why not?
You don't even know if this is the right place.
Well, it stands to reason they would have taken him to the nearest place.
That is without a doubt one of the silliest sayings ever.
What?
It stands to reason. Nothing stands to reason. If anything it might trip over reason while it's on its way to steal someone's hubcaps, but nothing actually stands to reason.
Quiet down for a second I actually need to concentrate for this to work.

James smiled politely and walked up to the reception desk. He was concentrating as hard as he possibly could and hoped the other part of his mind wasn't right about the whole situation.

It had taken him the better part of an hour to figure out where bodies were taken to be autopsied. He thought it would be a little bit more obvious, but no one actually hung a sign outside the building saying they were cutting up dead bodies inside. At first he thought it would be easy to look it up in the phone book, but then realized he really didn't know what to look up. There wasn't a section in the yellow pages for dealing with dead bodies, and he thought that if there were they wouldn't be the kind of people he'd want to talk with anyway. He tried looking up the coroner's office but couldn't find anything like that in the phone book. After a while he really started getting frustrated. In the TV shows and movies they never really showed where the stuff actually took place. They just made sure to light it well so that it looked creepy but scientific at the same time. Half way through that line of reasoning he decided that TV shows probably didn't show where it was because they weren't at a real coroner's office. They were most likely on the back lot of some studio or shooting in a local train station that happened to look cool in blue light.

Finally he decided to ask a cop. He was a little unsure about the whole idea, and the not so small nagging voice in his head constantly reminded him that if the officer started asking why he was looking for a dead body he would need some really good answers that had nothing to do with shooting lightning out of his hands. Fortunately, like most American kids, James had done his fair share of lying when he was a kid so he really didn't feel out of his element here.

On top of that he was proud of the fact he had starred in a few plays in high school. In its own way acting simply was being a professional liar. The best course of action, he decided, was to stay as close to the truth as possible, so when asked he told the truth. He was looking for Don.

The officer knew what James was talking about. It seemed word of the campus murder had gotten around pretty fast, and he was more than willing to let James know where the autopsy was being done. On the other hand he had to remind James that only family was allowed in to see the body at this time. James nodded knowingly and simply said he just needed to know where to drop off some flowers.

It had all seemed so simple then. Just head down to Tudor Road and find the Police headquarters. He had driven past it dozens of times, but for some reason he hadn't thought it would be where they would do stuff like that. He had figured it would be in a hospital. Pulling into the parking lot was where he started having doubts about his plan. It wasn't like he was going to give up, because it was really the only plan he had, but he was just a little worried about the execution of it all. Even then just thinking about the word execution as he walked into this place gave him goosebumps.

"Good evening." James smiled at the clerk behind the desk. In his mind he fixed the image that he, James, was supposed to be here, and that not only was he supposed to be here but he was also someone you didn't question. "I'm here to see the murder victim from the university. Which direction would it be?"

The clerk blinked a few times and shook his head slightly as if things were a little bit foggy in the space between his brain and his eyes, "It's," he blinked again, "It's to your right."

"Thank you." James said and walked away as if he owned the place.

There, now that wasn't so hard.

Right.

Don't get sarcastic with me. Just admit that it worked.

Well, to be honest with you, that's not the part I was worried about.

Oh really, and what would you be worried about?

That.

James had pushed through a swinging door and was staring at the partly dissected remains of Don laid out on a shiny metal table. He was glad the coroner's back was to him because in that moment his concentration cracked and he was simply James staring at a dead friend. Then the coroner turned to see who had come in and James quickly had to pull himself together. He realized it was much easier right now if he didn't look at Don, but the simple fact that the coroner was wearing a blood spattered plastic facemask didn't help a whole lot.

"And what are you doing in here?"

The coroner pointed at James with something that looked disturbingly like a medieval torture device. He could almost picture it being used by some inquisitor while the poor person swore she wasn't a witch. Oddly enough that image actually helped him pull his mind away from the morbid scene around him. All he could really think of was a blond woman with a carrot tied to her face, and some dirty peasant in the crowd saying that she turned him into a newt. The last thing that rang through his mind was, "I got better." James focused, believed he was supposed to be here, and that he should be obeyed. "I'm here to take a look at the victim."

"Oh." The coroner put down the odd device, picked up a cloth, and wiped the blood from his mask.

"I actually need to be alone in here." James' voice was insistent and the coroner didn't even look back over at him as he took off his mask.

"Well, I could use a cup of coffee anyway."

James watched him leave with the slight thought that things were going rather well then turned back to the body of Don and changed his mind.

Now what smarty pants?

I have to try.

It's not going to work.

As long as you keep saying that then no it's not going to.

James forced the doubts not only to the back of his mind but completely out of his mind. He remembered the feeling when he saw the old man covered in living flame, and knew that anything was possible, even this.

Walking over to a rolling stool James pulled it up next to the metal table that held Don's earthly remains. Sitting down he tried to keep his eyes on Don's face. It was untouched. Below that was another matter.

"So," his voice sounded strange as it emptied out into the silence.

"Don't quite know what to say, do ya?"

James watched, unsurprised, as Don pushed himself up into a sitting position, "Not really." He gestured around at the obvious surroundings, "I guess I could apologize for your situation."

"No," Don looked around, "you have nothing to apologize for. It is what it is."

"Well how bout all the normal stuff about how you were too young, and it wasn't your time."

"That doesn't work either." Don shrugged and James tried to keep his eyes away from the strange movements of human parts that you never really thought about. "Time is time and I seem to have run out of it." He looked James directly in the eyes, "What did you need to talk about?"

Finding himself slightly fascinated by the milkyness of Don's eyes James couldn't think of what he wanted to ask. Don lifted his right hand and waved it in front of James face, "Hello? Dead guy here."

"Sorry," James shook his head to clear out the morbid thoughts that were building, "it's just…"

"I know, I know." Don smirked, "I mean, really, how many times do you get to talk to dead people?"

James frowned a little and tilted his head to the right. His mother had commented that he must have picked up the expression from his dog who would do the exact same thing when it was confused. "You don't seem surprised at all to be in here and talking to me."

"Eh," Don shrugged his shoulders, "my capacity for strangeness has been maxed out just by the very fact that I'm dead. On top of that, what am I supposed to do, scream? You wouldn't believe the things I've seen recently. This little episode right now is actually a nice little break."

"Really," James leaned forward, "What did you see?"

"Well, that really depends."

"What'd you mean?"

"There are some things I can't tell you."

"About?"

Don paused and looked around the room. "Well, about death, and the stuff that happens afterward."

"What, did you see a bright light or something?"

"Ha!" Don reflexively put his hands on his stomach when he laughed then stopped and looked down at them, "Well," he moved his hands and looked into himself where the coroner had been pulling various things out for examination, "that's something you don't see everyday."

James took a deep breath and looked around the room until his stomach had stopped trying to crawl up his throat and jump out his mouth. "So," he looked back over at Don and decided to definitely not look down at what Don was doing with his hands, "you can't tell me what happens after you die?"

Don looked back up at him, "Right."

"Are you alive now?"

A look of sarcastic confusion crossed Don's face as he looked from James to his own internal organs that were still laying in a tray off to the side. "What do you think?"

"I," James paused, "well, I thought I could bring you back with," he waved his hands around in a small imitation of someone doing a magic trick, "you know with all the stuff I can do now."

Don shook his head, "One thing I can tell you is that once you're gone you're gone for good."

James frowned a little, "So, did someone stop you on your way back here and say, 'hey there's this guy who's going to call you back from the dead and we want all this to be a nice big surprise so don't tell him anything about the piñatas or the roller derby, okay?'"

Don nodded at him, "Something like that, sure."

James blinked a few times and wondered if Don was joking or what. Finally he just shrugged, "So is it alright if I ask you about what happened to put you in this sad state of affairs?"

"Certainly, and to be honest with you I can't wait to tell you what happened."

James nodded, now things were going to get somewhere. Finally he felt like he could get some answers. "Well, let me start by saying that I ran into Scott and a couple other guys and they hinted at the fact that you had been killed. So, my first question is who killed you?"

Don nodded, "That's an easy one. Professor Oren Merrill lured me into his office and, well, the rest is complicated."

Hearing the professor's name, James stood up and started pacing around the room, "I knew it." He turned back to Don, "I knew he was doing something, and I knew it had something to do with weird powers."

"Look who's talking about weird powers Mr. I bring people back from the dead to ask them questions."

James smiled at this bit of irony, "Very true, but what I haven't been able to figure out is why." He looked hard at Don and didn't even register the literal holes in his late friend, "Why did he kill you Don? I thought you were one of his favorites. You helped lead that march he was so proud of, and you stood up for his idiotic ideas of tolerance."

Don sighed, and James realized how strange it was to hear someone sigh when you knew their lungs were in a metal pan on the table behind you, "I thought I was one of his favorites too, and yes I did all the things you said. I almost lost my family because of the stance I took." He looked up at James, "I still believe that hating people isn't going to solve anything," James nodded at this, "but at the same time I did find out a little late that the professor was playing both ends against the middle. He talked me into coming with him up to his office before the rest of the building was open and honestly it was the perfect movie bad guy setup. The only difference was that he told me all his evil plans after he killed me, whereas in the movies they tell you then try to kill you and of course the hero always gets away." He looked James up and down, "So I guess you're the hero and I'm just the extra going on the away mission who everybody knows is going to die."

"Well," James paused, "you know you didn't actually answer the question right?"

"Oh, right." Don nodded, "He killed me because he needed to get a certain section of the population worked up. You see, even though we marched for tolerance we're really intolerant people at the core. If you do anything we see as being intolerant we'll tear you apart like wild dogs. People like me think so much that we're in the right that we aren't willing to admit we might be falling into the same trap as those we're preaching against. He figured that since I was so well liked amongst that crowd my death, excuse me I mean my murder, would be a good catalyst to get them going."

"Well that was an amazingly honest answer."

"Not too much of a reason to lie or candy coat anything. I am dead after all."

"I take it you didn't die in a very nice fashion."

"Oh, no, not at all. On the other hand if your going to be murdered then mine was a fine murder. He wrote all kinds of anti tolerance stuff and tied me up buck naked to a tree in the middle of campus. I must say I did look a little Christ like."

"An Asian Christ. Interesting thought."

"Hey, you gotta take what you can from the situation. I mean that was it for me. Except for the stuff I can't tell you about."

James nodded, "Ya, thanks for that."

Don smiled back, "He, no problem. Don't worry about it. Everybody finds this stuff out eventually."

James started pacing around the room again, "So he killed you to get a bunch of students riled up, and he tried to kill Sam today."

"Really?" Don started to move like he was going to stand up then decided it would be better if he remained sitting.

James had his back turned but answered, "Ya, I was with him when Scott and the others showed up to kill him on the professor's orders."

"What happened?"

James shrugged as he turned around, "I shot lightning out of my hands and killed them."

Don only raised one eyebrow, "Right. Lightning. Why not? It's not like anything else strange has happened today."

James laughed, "Exactly my feeling." He went back over to the stool and sat down, "So are there any details that might help me know what's going on or what he's going to do next?"

Don nodded, "You can imagine my surprise when he started doing crazy magic things, and then killing me, but I could still hear what he was saying and I even had my eyes open for most of the time to see what was going on."

"And?"

"He's following the orders of something else."

"Who?"

"That's why I said some Thing else, not someone else. The darkness around him seemed to have a shape and all I could really see were the eyes. Lots and lots of eyes." Don's dead body shivered and he looked around at the dark corners of the room, "They seemed to be talking to each other but I could only hear what the professor was saying. Half the time he was talking to me as if I was supposed to respond. In a really weird way it was like being at the dentist and they try to have a conversation with you when you have that sucker thing in your mouth. The darkness around him wasn't frightening to me anymore because I was dead, but I knew there was something deeply wrong with it, something my mom would have called evil, and I guess looking back with what I know now there really are evil things in this world. The professor was talking about how the city was at a breaking point and a few good pokes here and there could bring the whole thing down into chaos." He looked up at James, "I realized I was only part of a bigger plan when he started going off about different people and how they would cause the same reaction my murder caused. He seemed to think it all would come together if some big new church was set on fire."

James raised his left eyebrow, "What would setting a church on fire have to do with any of this?"

"Look, I only know what he told my corpse as he tied me to a tree. He said the church would serve as a symbol for certain groups to rally around, and for other groups to rail against. He went on and on about how religion was great as a catalyst." Don paused and shrugged his shoulders, "I guess I never noticed how melodramatic he was until I was dead. All his ideas seemed great when I first heard them. It wasn't until he was telling me both sides of the story that I realized most of it was just manipulative junk." He looked up at James, "He sees himself as some sort of savior. He thinks bringing the city into a state of utter chaos will give him the power to make everything over again in his image."

"Break a few eggs for an omelet sort of thing?"

Don nodded, "He talked about how you have to destroy the old ways before you can set up better ways. He really started sounding crazy toward the end. And of course my view on it all was a little skewed since he was hanging my dead body up for everyone to see."

"Ya," James nodded, "I might think someone was a little crazy too if they were doing that to me." They both smiled at this little bit of humor in an otherwise non humorous situation. "Do you think it'll work?"

"Well, like you, he does have some kind of weird powers, and I have seen people get pretty riled up about silly things so if it were about something serious it might just work."

"I was told people like the professor and the thing you saw with him feed off the chaos events like this create. He might have been totally serious when he said he'd become strong enough from these events to really do something."

Don frowned, "I guess I just have one question after all this."

"What would that be?"

"Why here? Why Anchorage Alaska? I mean," he gestured to a small window in the far wall, "we're in the middle of nowhere compared to other areas, and if you want chaos why not just go to downtown Baghdad or Jerusalem?"

"Well," James stopped and considered how much he should really tell Don about what had happened to him over the last few days, and what he knew about the doors. Looking over at Don he decided that if he could trust anyone to not tell his secrets to another living soul then it would be a dead guy. "It happened here because this is where the door is. This is far from the eyes of anyone who could stop it. It's here because we're on the edge of nowhere. A few riots here wouldn't make the evening news in most places. A little chaos to feed their power would be completely unnoticed, and once they're strong enough then off to bigger and better places. I have a feeling," James stood up and walked over to the window to watch the last of the sun sink beneath the mountains, "if they aren't stopped here it'll be even more difficult to stop them from pulling the whole world down."

"Man," James turned to see Don laying back down on the table, "if I weren't already dead I'd say you're being a little melodramatic yourself, but under the circumstances," he winked a milky white eye at James.

"Hey," James had the feeling Don wouldn't be there for much longer, "What church did you say he was going to?"

All he caught was a whisper from Don, "Something to do with a saint."

Behind him a door opened and James jumped. "So, did you find what you were looking for?"

Turning slowly so he could gather his composure James nodded to the coroner, "Yes, I think I did."

Chapter Nineteen

Rupert thanked the man and waved several times as he watched the truck drive away. On the ride in from the valley the man had gone over all the ways something called duct tape was actually holding the truck together. On the one hand this had caused some concern in Rupert's mind because it sounded like it was a temporary fastener of some kind, but on the other hand at least the man knew where each piece was.

Walking toward the parsonage he'd been staying in the last time he was here he continually had to stop to remove a piece of dirt from random locations. His plan had worked almost as well as could be expected. It was just the fact that he hadn't thought it out completely which really got him in the end. He knew the professor would do something and he would have to play dead to make it through the encounter, but when the ground rose up around him and his feet dropped out from under him there was a moment of worry. His belief, however, had been stronger than the moment of panic and he knew he'd be fine. While sitting and waiting in that small bubble under the ground he'd tried to decide what to do next. He didn't know his way around that well and he knew he would need help in finding the right location. He'd thought momentarily about trying to find James again but knew of no way to contact him or even where to begin looking. He decided instead to turn to the only other person who'd helped him on his first trip.

After what he considered a sufficient amount of time sitting in what he came to think of as his early grave he decided the professor must be gone, at least he hoped that was the case. It really had nothing to do with timing, or if he'd heard a car drive away, what it had to do with was the fact that it was getting very stuffy and hot in his small hole in the ground. He hadn't considered the fact he might need a hole to let air in if he had to be down here much longer, and what air was in there with him was getting a little bit old.

Now as he walked across the parking area he was continually finding new places the dirt had gotten to on his way out of his hiding place. He had gotten it in his hair, up his nose, and in other places he really didn't want to think about.

He paused for a moment to take in the sunset. If anything in this other world could remind him of home it was the sunsets. Behind him in the near velvet of new night the mountains looked like waves frozen in place ready to crash down on him in the blink of an eye, but in front of him the sun was giving off those desert colors that reminded him of home. In layers of color the clouds seemed to be burning like the sands around his hometown. Reds faded to oranges then blended to what looked like freshly polished gold. The sky burned and Rupert knew beyond a shadow of a doubt that even here the great flame watched over the faithful. This, he believed, was the true image the mural in the great hall was trying to replicate. It helped him realize that, even though he was physically alone, he was never without help in his time of need. Turning back toward his goal he hoped the cleric here would be able to help him.

*   *   *

James knew where he was going. He knew what was going to be there. What he didn't know was what he was going to do about it. He had to stop the professor, but what did that look like? The professor had killed people, and was planning on killing more people so he could do what exactly? James waited for his brain to chime in with something, anything that could help him figure this whole situation out, but nothing came. He needed someone to talk to. His conversation with Don had been informative, and very surreal, but it hadn't really helped. He'd learned where he needed to go. He'd learned why the professor was doing what he was doing. That last one was nice to finally figure out. All this time, and all these weird things that were happening finally had a purpose. What he hadn't learned was what he was supposed to do about it. It was all well and good to say he was supposed to stop the bad guy from doing bad things, but really what did that mean?

Adjusting his rearview mirror James gave the guy nod, which signifies everything from hello to so what are you going to do today, to his brother who was now sitting in the passenger seat.

His brother looked around, nodded a few times at the scenery going by the little Geo, then turned to James, "You don't seem surprised to see me here so I'm going to assume you know what in the world just happened."

"Sorry bout surprising you like that but I really needed someone to talk to."

His brother just stared at him, "Right. Aside from the fact that we both have cell phones and you could have just called me. You do realize I was just sitting in my living room and now I'm in your car don't you?"

"Ya, about that."

"Yes," his brother said, "why don't you tell me how I went from watching MacGyver to sitting in your car in Alaska?"

James bit his upper lip for a second, "Is there any way I could explain that later? I really need your advice on a situation here."

"You," his brother paused, "I just," he gestured around the car, "Do you have any idea?" James nodded to him and tried to look as sorry as possible about the whole situation. Finally his brother sighed, "Look little brother I'm going to expect a very detailed explanation about all of this because, well, for obvious reasons."

James nodded vigorously, "Of course. I'll tell you everything. I just don't have time to go through it right now." He looked out the window at the setting sun and knew if the professor was going to do something he wasn't going to wait too much longer after the sun had set.

"All right." His brother shook his head, "What's this situation that you need advice about? If it has something to do with a girl I'm going to hit you, hard."

"No, nothing like that." James shook his head. "I, well, I'm going to need you to just take some things on faith for right now. It's not that I'm trying to leave anything out, I just don't have time to fill in all the details."

"Right." His brother looked around, "Where are we anyway?"

"Just outside of Anchorage. Eagle River is up ahead."

He shook his head, "So, what's this all about?"

James sat there for a moment trying to think of what to say. There was so much he wanted to tell his brother. They hadn't always been friends, but that was the way of brothers. Eventually they had come to respect each other for the things they had done, and then they had come to like each other for who they were. James looked over at his brother and saw a little bit of himself looking back. The same eyes, the same hair color. The only real differences weren't in physical features but in where they had ended up. His brother was married, and she must be worried sick about what had happened to her husband right then. Just a week ago James had talked with them on the phone and they were telling him all about how they were trying to get pregnant. He'd insisted they leave out the details and just tell him the names they were thinking of.

If he told his brother what was happening then he would insist on coming with him and helping. That was how family worked. They might not have always gotten along but when it came down to it you could always depend on each other. James knew if he let his brother come along he would be risking his life, and now that he thought about it he just couldn't bring himself to do that. Don had already died at the hands of this maniac, and Sam almost did as well. Come to think of it, if there hadn't been some miraculous intervention he, himself, would have ended up at the bottom of a mine shaft with no way out and no one the wiser.

"Actually," James looked over at his brother, "you helped me a lot just by being here." He smiled, "I swear I'll tell you what this is all about sometime, but right now it was nice just knowing you're there."

"Look, you can't just drag me up here with who knows what going on and expect..." He was gone. There was no proof. No popping sound or flash of light marked his passage back to his couch and his episode of MacGyver. He was just gone.

James knew there would be a lot of explaining to do in a few hours, but for now he had the answer he was looking for. The thing that irritated him the most was how cliché it was. Movies, books, television shows, even comic books ended the same way, and with the same decision being made by the hero. On the one hand James really liked referring to himself as the hero. On the other hand this wasn't a comic book or movie and the hero had a good chance of ending up dead. This wasn't the worst idea after his conversation with Don. At least he knew there was something more. He had always held his good American belief that there was a heaven for good people and a hell for bad people. Most people would say it was a religious idea, but it really had become part of the American dream to believe in a reward. That was the whole idea here right? Pull yourself up by your bootstraps and earn your way into heaven. That still didn't stop James from realizing that death, while not necessarily final, could still be quite painful.

So now he found himself riding on his white steed, metaphorically speaking, into the sunset. He looked around and realized the sun was actually setting off to his left, but that wasn't really the point was it. He was going to be the hero and he had decided what to do. Somehow he needed to stop the professor. His conversation with his brother had settled that in his mind. He wanted to know his brother and sister in law could raise their child in a safe and sane world. He might not be able to fix a lot, but he could at least make sure this would not affect them. He could make sure their baby would grow up in a world without strange evil black things coming through invisible doors and trying to kill people.

Okay so you're going to stop the evil professor and his killer mist.

Right.
What does that look like exactly?
Uhm. Well.

Were you picturing something like tying him up and calling the police?

Sure. That would work.

And what would you tell them?

Well, he's obviously going to do something bad at the church and blame it on someone else. So if I can catch him doing it then I can call the police.

Right. So aside from the fact that he has powers, how did you plan on doing this?

I don't know. Do you happen to have the blueprints to the church out there, or do you know exactly where he's going to be so I can sneak up on him?

No, and that's my point.

What's your point? You're starting to irritate me.

Right, and what exactly are you going to do about that?

Look, just get to the point about your point, or whatever.

And you say I don't make a lot of sense.

Hey!

Right. Anyway, just make sure you don't go rushing into a dark room backwards. I have a little bit of a stake in the outcome of this too.

Right, I know.

He saw the lights of the church as he took the exit into downtown Eagle River. The sunlight was fading and it reminded him of one of the pieces in his mom's Christmas village. There was no snow yet, but his mom never could get the snow to work right around the little village either. He came up the exit ramp and followed it to the left across the overpass. To his right he saw the new construction he had stopped at earlier that day. The banner with the flame on it hung limp. The church he was headed to was up to his left. He wasn't exactly sure this was the place but it fit the scenario Don had laid out.

It was a new Catholic church. The design was as old as Notre Dame and was laid out in the shape of a great cross. This however was no stone and marble giant. This was a modern church that was designed to compliment the surroundings. It was earth toned and blended into the fading twilight background perfectly. A few lights had come on in the parking lot, but you could tell nothing was going on inside. James smiled at this. At least there would be no one else to worry about.

Turning off his headlights, and his engine James allowed his car to coast to a stop at the bottom of the driveway leading up to the church. For a brief moment spy movie music played through his head and he thought this might not be so tough. He didn't think the professor would have more henchmen. Pausing at that thought he realized he really hadn't thought that part through. If there were five guys there what would he do? He stood for a moment and looked up at the church. There was no turning back now, but he did need to do some recon first.

Circling up and to the right of the driveway he got himself into a position to look out over the parking lot and directly at the main doors. Making two circles with his hands he held them up to his face as if he were holding a pair of binoculars. Belief is an amazing thing. It keeps people alive long after they should have died. It brings families back together, and even helped humanity land on the moon. In this case it gave him a pair of binoculars where none really were. Strange as that was, it got worse when James realized they were out of focus. Twisting his left hand a little the image of the church parking lot snapped into focus and James distinctly saw only one car in the parking lot. He didn't recognize it, and he couldn't bring himself to believe the professor would drive his own car to the scene of a crime and park it right in the open. On the other hand there were no cameras James could make out, and no one else was around to see anything so what difference did it really make. Scanning the rest of the area around the church he came to the conclusion that no one else was around, and the only thing even visible was the car. It didn't even look like there were any good hiding spots for goons to jump out of.

Bringing his hands down James flicked his right hand out away from him and heard a slight metallic clink as the binoculars that didn't exist landed on a rock. Chuckling to himself over the weirdness of that whole situation he stood up and brushed himself off. Shivering a little as the cold night descended he pulled out the stocking cap the old man had given him and pulled it on. Walking onto the pavement of the church parking lot James tried remembering every book, movie, or comic he had ever read where people had super powers. If they could do it then so could he, and he might need some good ideas about what to do in the next few moments. At first he thought about flying in, but the door was at ground level so that was a little silly. Then he thought about being invisible, but that really worried him. Could he get everything back to normal after being invisible, and would he actually get everything to be invisible in the first place? It would be a little silly to be spotted because you forgot to believe that your sneakers were invisible.

Again the spy movie music started playing through his head and he was trying to decide if he should look for another way in, or if he should just go in as quietly as possible through the front door. The single car in the parking lot sat darkly to his right and he glanced at it just long enough to see there was no one in it. Pausing to get his mental bearings and decide what his next move should be he was understandably startled when a voice came from behind him.

"Please don't move." Now he could hear feet scuffling on the pavement behind him.

James' feet landed after jumping a little and he said, "Okay, what would you like me to do?"

"What're you doing here?"

James was again startled when he realized it was a girl's voice, "You seem very polite for a robber."

"I said," the polite tone dropped quickly, "what are you doing here?"

James decided to chance it and turn around. He had survived one gunshot wound today, and as long as she didn't shoot him in the head he should be fine, well not really fine, but still livable. He turned to his right slowly with his hands a little raised showing he was holding nothing. The light from the closest streetlight cast a strange orange glow over the whole scene. Shadows stretched out and multiplied into darker and lighter versions of themselves. The nearest reflected dully from the muzzle of the gun being pointed at his chest. "I'm here because I was told something bad was going to happen."

The girl stepped close to him and shoved the gun at him, "Who told you anything about this?"

James gasped and stepped backward as the light fell across her face, "Katie? What are you doing here?"

"What?" She sounded confused and the gun lowered from its menacing position. "Who are you?"

James stepped sideways into the light and took his stocking cap off, "It's me."

Her eyes widened and the look of confusion was replaced by a mixture of shock and joy, "James." She ran over to him and threw her arms around him hugging him as tightly as possible. Looking up at him she asked again, but with a much different tone, "What are you doing here?"

"I told you," he looked down at her and concern started creeping into his mind, "I heard something bad was going to happen and I came to stop it."

She pushed away from him, "What do you mean exactly?"

"I was told someone was going to try and burn down the church."

She looked slightly away from him, "Who told you that?"

"It's a long story." He stepped back from her and looked her over. In all their time together no one ever could have convinced him he would see her pointing a gun at him. "Why're you here Katie?"

She sighed, "Did you know Don was murdered?"

"Ya, and I know who did it."

Her eyes flared wide, "Did they catch them? Those Catholic good for nothing..."

"No, Kate, they didn't catch them, and why would you say they were Catholic?"

Again she looked slightly confused, "Didn't you read the note that was on his body?"

James thought about his conversation with Don and decided this wouldn't be the best time to tell her about how he learned who the killer was, "No. I didn't know there was a note."

She clenched her teeth and literally stomped off a few paces, "If you'd read it you would know James. It was, it was, horrible."

He thought he saw tears in her eyes, "Is that why you're here?"

She gestured around with the gun and for a moment looked a little bit guilty, "Kinda."

"Is anyone else here with you?" he said.

She nodded, "Professor Merrill came with me."

James clinched his teeth, "Let me guess, this was all his idea?"

"Yes," she said slowly.

"Katie," he paused, not knowing quite how to continue, "Merrill is the one who killed Don."

"What?" She stepped back involuntarily and bumped into the car.

"He's been using people Katie. His whole speech about tolerance is a big lie to cover up what he's actually doing."

"And what's he doing James?" She said through clenched teeth.

James held out his hands, "He's playing people against each other to start riots. He killed Don and tried to kill Sam and myself today."

She had to strain to hear James as the voices started whispering in her mind telling her James was trying to protect the people who did those horrible things to Don. She shook her head a little, "So he wanted to kill you and Sam?"

"Yes, Katie can't you see? He was playing one end against the other."

She thought for a moment that he was making sense but the voices kept reminding her of what had happened to Don. They wouldn't let her think straight. "Why are you here James?"

She heard him as if through a long tunnel, "I'm here to stop Merrill, Katie."

"I can't let you do that James. What he's doing is necessary."

"What he's doing is wrong."

The voices snapped at her and she snapped at James, "Wrong? Who are you to judge what's right or wrong James? Who is anybody?" Her voice started to raise, "That's why they killed Don, James, because he was wrong. They said what he was doing was wrong so they butchered him." She started to scream simply so she could hear herself over the voices in her head, "Is that what you're going to do James? Are you going to kill the professor because you think he's wrong?"

James stood rooted to the spot in stunned silence. Something wasn't right. Katie never acted like this. "Katie, sweetheart, I liked Don…"

"You have no idea do you? You don't know what he went through. All the hate mail and the threats he got. The professor was right. People that say there's a right or wrong are just stupid bigots trying to further their own ends. We do what we have to James, to teach the world it won't be tolerated anymore."

James took a small step toward her holding out his hand, "You're not making sense Katie." He wanted to tell her to keep it down because Merrill was sure to hear this noise and know something was going on.

"Since you seem to know the difference James," she cocked her head off to the right and used the gun to point at him, "what exactly is the difference between right and wrong."

"Katie," he tried speaking softly to calm her down, "you can't preach tolerance then attack people who disagree with you. Simply by the fact that you're attacking them you're saying you're right and they're wrong. You're setting up your own standards."

She simply repeated what the voices in her head were saying, "And what's so bad about that?"

James sighed, he didn't want to have some existential philosophical conversation with her right now. He had to stop Merrill, which meant he needed to end this conversation. It also meant he needed it to end with her not having a gun pointed at him. "If everyone keeps their own standard of right or wrong the world will devolve into chaos, and in that chaos evil wins."

Her voice came out layered with the buzzing of dozens of flies, "There's no such thing as evil James."

"I have to go Katie." He shook his head, "Something's wrong and I really need to find Merrill."

"You can't go." The voices in Katie's head told her to shoot him, but something else in her mind screamed not to. As long as she could keep him there the voices didn't have a reason to shoot him.

"I have to Katie. Merrill's going to do something here that will make things bad for a lot of people, maybe even the whole world." He realized in the back part of his brain this was all sounding a bit melodramatic, "Please Katie," he took a step toward her and reached out his right hand, "Please just give me the gun."

She slid along the car to get away from him and thought that if she could get him to chase her then everything would be fine. They would be away from here and no one would get hurt. She looked over her shoulder for a place to run and out of the corner of her eye she saw movement.

James lunged forward not believing she would ever shoot him and was surprised by the sound as the gun went off. Instinctively he pushed back against it with his mind, and Katie screamed. He watched her slide down the car toward the pavement, and he seemed to watch himself in slow motion as he jumped forward and caught her. He didn't know exactly what had happened but his momentary confusion was swept away by the dark red blood that started pumping from Katie's neck.

"No, no, no, no," James pushed his hand onto her neck and tried to focus on what to do, but his concentration shattered as her eyes flickered open.

"James?"

Her voice was so quiet he wasn't sure he'd heard anything, "Katie, baby, don't worry I'll get you out of this. Everything'll be fine." He tried to focus again. He knew if he could just get the image of her being okay in his head then everything would be fine.

"The voices are gone." She smiled and closed her eyes.

"Voices? Katie," he held the wound closed with one hand and shook her a little with the other, "Katie you can't go yet. We haven't done the stuff," he shook her again, "you know all the stuff together." He closed his eyes and felt the warmth of his tears against his winter frozen cheeks. Finally the picture of her whole and unharmed formed in his mind. She was unbroken, perfect, uninjured. All would be right with the world. Opening his eyes he removed his hand from where the wound had been and saw there was only unbroken skin. He smiled and shook her a little thinking she must just be unconscious. When she didn't open her eyes he leaned close and realized he couldn't feel or hear her breathing. "Katie," He clenched his teeth and shook her a little bit harder, "Wake up baby."

Still she didn't move. Tears streaked down his face as he felt for a pulse and couldn't find one. He closed his eyes and knew she was alive. He believed it more than anything he had ever believed before. More than he believed he was going to draw his next breath, more than he believed his own heart would beat. She was alive.

He opened his eyes and looked at her. She looked like she would open her eyes at any moment, say something slightly sarcastic, and everything would be fine. He let his head fall forward and his eyes closed. Twice today he had tried to bring those he cared for back from wherever it was they had gone, and both times he had failed. Don had told him death was final. He looked up at the Catholic Church and wiped his tears away with the back of his hand. Death would be final for someone else tonight as well.

Standing he felt flames begin to lick at his feet. In his mind all doubt was washed away in the fire of anger. His enemy had done this. He knew from the moment he saw her with that gun something was wrong. The voices had stopped, she said. James clenched his fists and felt the blue white of electricity dance over his knuckles. He had wondered how this would end. Now he knew.

Walking toward the closed door he could feel the heat behind him as the car burst into flames. His footprints darkened the sidewalk and steamed as he lifted his right hand. With a wave of force the double doors flew from their hinges and slid across the entryway. His eyes were consumed with the fire that burned from inside him. He let the heat reach out and lick the walls as he entered the church.

"Merrill." His voice caused the walls to crack and windows to shatter.

The doors to the sanctuary slammed shut in front of him, and he knew without a doubt that they would open at his touch. He placed the palms of his hands on them and for a brief moment he remembered another door. All this had started with an open door. Maybe it was fitting that it was an open door. Merrill had left a door open in his soul and let the darkness in. Katie had allowed anger to open a door into her mind and the voices had started whispering to her. Now here he stood with a door closed in front of him. He smiled slightly at the dramatic irony then with a scream the fire leapt from his hands and the doors turned to ash.

Through the dust and smoke he saw a man standing at the end of the isle. He watched the man raise his hands and dark things flew from his fingers. James brushed them aside but wasn't surprised to hear little whispers in his mind. They whispered to him of how right it was to kill this man. They told him revenge was what this man deserved for what he had done to Katie. James nodded in agreement with the voices and stepped into the sanctuary itself. The man in front of him raised his hands again, and again James heard the voices telling him to kill. It would be so easy to pull the building down on top of them both.

Closing his eyes James pictured once again the old man by the campfire. He could see the ropes of flame wrapping around him and the red orange light dancing in his eyes. He remembered him saying it wasn't always that you believed, sometimes what was more important was what you believed in.

James let the fire consume him. He let it burn in his mind until it was white hot, and in the light of that fire he saw the voices. There were no more dark places in his mind they could hide. No more corners, or dusty rooms. It all burned, and the voices fled from the light.

Opening his eyes he pushed everything away from himself. The pews piled up against the walls and the pillars cracked and bent away from him. Each step he took forward cracked the marble of the floor and when he raised his right hand the roof shattered like spring ice.

Raising his two hands in front of himself Merrill tried to erect a barrier. This was madness, he thought. How did James come to learn the secrets? Where had he come from? Looking around the room he called out for the darkness to save him, but the more he looked the more he realized there was no darkness here. Here there was nothing but light and heat.

James looked to the sky and watched as the clouds gathered directly above. He wondered momentarily whether it was right to kill Merrill. Was what this man had done bad enough to warrant death, and was it his place to act as judge, jury, and executioner? Then a voice somewhere in the back of his mind said, why?

Why what? James asked as he watched the sparks dance across the clouds.

Why are you going to kill him?
Does it matter?
Oh yes, it matters.
Because he deserves it.

The action is the same no matter what James. It's your intent that will be judged here. What is your intent?

He killed Katie. He killed Don. He would kill my brother and my unborn nephew if he needed to.

So is this all because you're angry with him, or is it because he deserves it?

James lowered his eyes from the gathering storm and looked at Merrill. "You will tell the truth." Merrill hissed at him like a cornered alley cat. "Why did you do this?"

"I don't have to answer to you, boy." Merrill spit the words as if he could use them as weapons.

Leaving behind a trail of blue white fire James lowered his hand and walked toward Merrill. "Yes, you do."

Merrill looked into James eyes and saw only fire. It seemed to wrap around him. It pushed its way into his head, and for the first time ever he saw his actions laid out before him. He saw how they had affected those around him, and he saw how his words had inspired chaos and evil.

"Answer me Oren Merrill. Why did you do this?"

Merrill hunched down as if a great weight was being laid on his back, "For power." His head snapped up and he looked again at James, "How dare you judge me. I did the same thing they all do. I used my words to gain power. I used my actions to gain power. Fear brings power. Chaos brings power." Waving around at the church he continued, "Religion is just fear and lies to gain power for those in charge. Politics are the same. If you are going to judge me for these things then you must judge the whole world. Tomorrow this town will be in flames. With me dead or alive, what I have done will show you." He pointed out the window, "They don't trust each other. They don't care about each other. All they want is the same, power."

James sighed. His mind had been right for once. He was going to kill Merrill because he was angry, and that wasn't good enough. Anyone could kill someone out of anger, but now that he had heard what Merrill had to say he knew what he had to do. He turned his back on him and walked out of the sanctuary. Behind him he felt the rush of air as the massive bolt of lightning slammed into the spot Merrill stood. He hadn't killed him because he was angry with him.

Across the bridge at the parsonage of the Catholic priest Rupert jumped as he saw the massive bolt of lightning flash across the sky. He knew instantly it wasn't natural. He could feel the lingering power of belief in the air just as the priest could smell the ozone from the strike. Rushing out they both jumped into the priest's car and sped toward the church. Pulling into the parking lot they saw the church burning and the roof falling in. Rupert could only sit dumbfounded wondering what had taken place to cause such a display of power. He shrieked and hit his head on the small car's roof when someone tapped on the window of the car. He couldn't believe his eyes as he watched James motion for him to roll down the window.

"Hey," James leaned on the car, "I'm exhausted, you think I could get a ride home?"

Chapter Twenty

The nights were long here. The blessed cold wrapped around him. The little heat was dimming as he slid away from the blazing church. It had all been so easy, and so much fun.

He had worried at first. That man's rage had harnessed his belief into a whirlwind of power. He thought he'd been clever to have the girl there to meet him. He thought that would change everything, throw the man's mind into doubt and chaos. It had been so easy to confuse the girl, but it seemed the man's mind had been hardened. When she died the world seemed to crack around them. The darkness had seen this before, but it was long ago and on another world. He didn't think anyone here had the ability to warp reality so completely.

In the end, however, the outcome didn't matter. It never had. If Merrill died that was fine. If he lived he would just have to kill him eventually. He could find others. He knew of one waiting for him now.

Some plans failed, that was the way of things. He had expected this one to fail sooner than it had. That it took the bending of reality to bring this farce to an end was a testament to how ripe this world was for the picking. If one unknown professor could cause even this much damage, think of what could be done with simply a little more time.

There was a little worry. The memory of the fire bothered him. He'd tried to slip into the man's mind. He'd tried to influence him like he had with so many others. Then the fire came. For a moment he feared he would be undone, but the man focused on Merrill. Thinking all this had been done by Merrill he focused his rage in the wrong direction. So while they argued he simply left. He knew the way of things would bring the man hunting after him once he figured out the truth.

He heard voices up ahead. A pool of light spread from a back door. A man stumbled drunkenly onto dead grass. From inside a woman yelled. Eyes glittered out from between bone white trees and the darkness smiled. Time would bring him more. He whispered to the drunken man and watched. This would be a fun distraction, and really who would notice two more dead?

Epilogue

James heard on the news the next day that three community leaders had been murdered that night. Each one was designed to look like the other group had done it. Gang wars were declared, and ethnic lines were drawn. By the time the sun came up people knew to stay inside. If they had to go out they knew what neighborhoods to stay away from, or what grocery stores to avoid.

At a Shell gas station on Mountain View Drive a man with a red baseball cap pulled a gun on a man with a blue baseball cap. On Richmond Avenue a Samoan man started an argument with a Laotian woman and soon the street was filled with both their families. In front of a grocery store on the corner of Muldoon a teen in a car with his friends saw a guy who had insulted him at school over a month ago and decided now was the time.

An elderly gentleman walked out of the Shell gas station reading his newspaper and wandered in between the red and the blue baseball caps. He paused, looked at them both, and shook his head in disgust. Folding his newspaper under his arm he started talking with them.

A single mother of three walked into the middle of Richmond Avenue and asked if anyone could loan her money for milk. The arguing stopped and three people she had never met offered to drive her down to the local store. She asked them why they were arguing when they all knew each other, and they all counted on each other just to make it through the week. She turned first to one and reminded him how she had helped him pass his driving test, and she turned to the other and reminded her how her kids always played with his at the park down the street. After she drove away they stood in the street and couldn't remember what they had been arguing about.

The teen in his car revved the engine and waited for his high school enemy to step into the parking lot. A little to his left he saw movement and looked over to see his little sister waving to him. A wave of guilt washed over him and he pictured the look on his sister's face as she realized her big brother wasn't what she believed him to be.

A few fistfights broke out that day. The cops answered calls and found there was no one to arrest. The city didn't explode. The people knew each other. New leaders stepped forward. A student from UAA led an impromptu memorial march for those lost in that strange night, and although it wasn't perfect the day ended.

Printed in the USA
CPSIA information can be obtained
at www.ICGtesting.com
LVHW091128151123
763926LV00005B/220